I0655415

Vendetta

Nights of Shadow

Lianne Miller

Copyright © 2015 by Lianne Miller

All rights reserved. No part of this publication may be reproduced, distributed or transmitted in any form or by any means, including photocopying, recording, or other electronic or mechanical methods, without the prior written permission of the publisher, except in the case of brief quotations embodied in critical reviews and certain other noncommercial uses permitted by copyright law. For permission requests, email the publisher, with "Permissions Coordinator" in the subject line, at the address below.

Lianne Miller
publisher@liannemiller.com
Saco, Montana
www.liannemiller.com

Publisher's Note: This is a work of fiction. Names, characters, places, and incidents are a product of the author's imagination. Locales and public names are sometimes used for atmospheric purposes. Any resemblance to actual people, living or dead, or to businesses, companies, events, or institutions, is completely coincidental.

Editor: Christina M. Frey, Page Two Editing
Cover Design: Steven Novak, Illustrator

Vendetta–Nights of Shadow (Book Two)/ Lianne Miller — 1st ed.
ISBN 978-0-9963768-3-9
ISBN 0996376836

TABLE OF CONTENTS

Dedication

Regardless of the path, destiny is unavoidable, while fate merely provides the challenges and choices we face during our journey in this life.

I dedicate this story to those who meet fate with courage and love with perseverance, while embracing their journey by accepting every test or challenge that brings them another step closer to their destiny.

In memoriam ...

To a man who completed his journey and met his destiny. He was witty, funny, charming, fiercely loyal, strong, brave, a bit crazy and wild, and a true patriot. His character and personality were but one influence for the development and creation of Matt Wolfe.

Rest in peace, Mike "Dirty Devil" Zorn (9/12/2014). You are now free to color with your crayons on the walls in the corner as you wish. You are missed by the many lives you touched, and this author is proud to have known you and called you friend.

Confirmation

The commotion in the corner of the tavern draws her scrutiny. Nine people, talking and arguing, are sitting there without drinks. Most would never pick up on such an obvious tell, but even in the dim light the petite woman can see what they are. There is a preternatural quality to their appearance—the aged but ageless glint in their eyes, the flawless skin, the graceful movements too fast for the human eye to see. These vampires are the best among their kind, and she smiles at their ignorance of her; she's been stalking them undetected for weeks.

The tall, dark-haired man seated among them glares coldly around the room. "I think we'd best take this elsewhere. We're attracting too much attention here."

His gruff voice fails to quiet their noise. "Enough!" He slams his hand on the table, and they fall silent. "I said, it's time to go."

Nine pairs of angry eyes sweep the room. Without another word the group rises and leaves the tavern.

I hope they don't go far, or this will be another long night of getting nowhere. The petite woman pulls her long black hair into a ponytail and cautiously steps out of the tavern after them. Keeping to the shadows, she trails them to a warehouse near the docks and slips inside. The sound of their voices guides her to the back of the building, where she crouches between the rows of crates to listen. She smiles in relief as their argument continues.

A man is speaking. "I'm telling you, his mind is gone. It was as if he didn't know us, couldn't see us. I don't think he knows himself. We never got one intelligent response from him."

"Maria says he's so far gone that even Master has stopped tormenting him," a woman says, sounding concerned. "I don't know what anyone can do."

Another woman adds, "Maria claims Elizabetta drove him to this madness."

The first man confirms it. "I'm not happy with her, but I don't blame her. We all know who is ultimately responsible for this."

Elizabetta. Maria. Master. The petite woman tenses, fighting the urge to look over the crate at them. Now she needs confirmation of where their loyalties lie. The man paying for her services has offered a handsome bonus if she can report this detail.

A third woman impatiently asks, "What did Elizabetta do to him?"

"The rumor is that she threw a tantrum about everything she believes he's done to her."

"I don't care what she did," the first man bellows. "If

Master has done this to them, what's to stop him from targeting one of us next?"

A third man's words are cautious, measured. "What are you suggesting?"

A ripple of excitement courses through the petite woman in the shadows. *Bonus time?*

"I don't know if it's possible to undo the damage to Dmitri. There may be a chance to restore Elizabetta's memories, if Maria doesn't ally against us." He pauses. Silence engulfs the warehouse for a long minute. "It may be time to consider righting a wrong."

The warehouse falls silent for several long seconds and then erupts into heated argument.

Smiling, the petite woman slips out of the warehouse and starts running.

Confirmation.

CHAPTER 1: DMITRI

The Void

"Dmitri, please come back ..." The voice is speaking again. It is one of two voices he hears, and he's not sure he knows either, but this one is hauntingly familiar and pulls him away from the darkness. The other voice, the one he hears the most, he assumes is his inner one; his outer voice disappeared, and he hasn't found it here within the shadows.

The void is coming to take me.

Someone has found him in the darkness and is lifting him to his feet, compelling him to move. He doesn't want to leave, but his body rarely listens to his mind anymore.

The void is taking me.

The next few moments flicker images from the world outside. The lovely woman with long, dark hair is here again. She's talking, but no sound comes out. *Do I know her?* He feels as if he should. Sometimes he wishes he could stay ...

The void is my companion, my friend.

A tangle of memories, dreams, and reality melt into the sensation of a woman's arm curled around his side and her breath at his back. Dmitri realizes they are lying on a bed. He should know this touch.

Then he remembers it is hers.

Elizabetta.

Suddenly the pain is excruciating. Walls, heavy, thick black walls, are rising up, moving in, and surrounding him, and he welcomes their embrace. Another set of black walls comes forth, layering upon the first. Then another, and the pain is less—more walls, too many layers to count, too many to care. There is no pain. There is nothing.

I am safe.

Millennia pass for Dmitri, and every few hundred years the black walls crumble, revealing a world beyond the secrets of the darkness where he lives. Fragmented memories suggest there used to be others here on the outside, but they are no longer there when he leaves the void. There's only one left; he's forgotten who she is and can't understand why she remains. He finds her breathtaking ... heartbreaking. New walls build, and the darkness wraps its arms around him again.

CHAPTER 2: ELIZA

Impulsive Decision

I can't wait to get out of here. Nine o'clock can't come soon enough. It's daylight, but instead of sleeping, Eliza Ross hurriedly packs her suitcases. She'll be leaving the Belyakov castle in Novgorod, Russia, in less than eight hours for her next set of nights off—and she won't be returning anytime soon. The coven has been here nearly four months, and their master, Shashenka Belyakov, has finally announced the inner lair's move to the estate in Venice. Eliza's nights off overlap the relocation, and she plans to spend time with her friend Matt Wolfe in Waiheke, New Zealand, before she joins the others in Venice. A month has passed since she last saw him. She's anxious for an update on the latest developments in their plans, and she's almost desperate to learn the results of his search for Elizabetta Rossellini.

When she steps into the bathroom to pack her toiletries, she notices that Dmitri Markov's meager possessions are still arranged in two neat rows in the bottom drawer. She was horrified when Shashenka first forced them into the adjoining rooms that share this bathroom, and in some ways it was worse than even their master could have imagined; in her attempt to protect Dmitri, she destroyed his mind. Eliza glances at the bathroom door that leads to his room, unsure if he's even capable of packing to leave.

A tremulous sigh escapes as she leans against the counter and stares at the floor. Every night she lives with the reminder of what she did to him. Six weeks ago, in front of others in the great hall and to the utter delight of Shashenka, she eviscerated Dmitri's mind when her planned tirade spiraled out of control. She only meant to push him away, to protect him—not to devastate him. Afterward she found him curled up on the floor of his room, wounded by his attempted suicide and completely gone out of his mind. She tried to help him that night, but he was too lost within himself to even notice her presence—and he has remained unresponsive to her efforts since. If anything, his condition is worse now. He's seldom even seen, and those rare sightings are of a man more lost within himself than the secrets hidden behind the walls of this old castle.

You've destroyed a man. Way to go, Eliza. She has no idea where he hides during daylight hours, but he hasn't slept in his room for the last two weeks. Others have seen him in the halls just before sunrise, though they don't know where he goes when dawn breaks. Dmitri doesn't speak to anyone anymore.

It rips her heart out, knowing she's done this to him.

Quietly she turns the handle and pulls the door open to peer inside his room. It is empty—the condition of the unmade bed and position of the suitcases stowed beneath the frame haven't changed since Eliza last checked. He hasn't packed at all. *Would Shashenka leave him behind?* The thought panics her, and she rushes out of his bedroom to Sally Davis's room down the hall.

The short-haired blonde looks sleepy when she finally opens the door. "Eliza?"

Breathless, she brushes past Sally. "Do you know where Dmitri is?"

"I thought he was in his room."

"He's not." She glances at the door and lowers her voice. "Do you know if Master is bringing him with us to Venice?"

Sally's brows pull together, her eyes narrowing. "I don't know ... I never even thought about ..."

Can't she see ... doesn't anybody care what happens to him? Eliza races out the door, down the hall to the great room, and into the corridor leading to Maria D'Arcy's quarters. Her fists beating on the door echo the aching pain that pulses in her heart. She doesn't think Dmitri's capable of taking care of himself anymore, and she has a sick feeling that he's going to be left behind.

When the witch finally opens the door, she scowls. Eliza sees in her eyes the reminder of the witch's threat to kill her, and she flinches in spite of her resolve not to react. Since the night of Dmitri's breakdown, Maria's been cold toward her. "What do you want?"

Meeting Maria's smoldering gaze, Eliza draws a ragged

breath. "I need to talk to you about Dmitri."

"Why?"

"I need to know if he's going with the inner lair to Venice." She swallows against the lump forming in her throat. "He's not in his room. He's not packed at—"

"Why should it matter to you?" Maria's scornful tone mirrors her stiff posture.

"Maria, please." Tears well in her eyes. "I-I'm afraid he may ... what will become of him if we leave him here?"

Maria motions her to a chair and closes the door. "You haven't answered my question." Her jaw flexes and she looks away.

Eliza folds and unfolds her hands in her lap before answering in a hushed whisper. "I'm ... it ... I ruined him. I'm afraid of what may happen if we abandon him."

The witch's sharp eyes study her for a minute, and Eliza resists the urge to shrink from the scrutiny. "Shashenka intends to leave Dmitri here. He's functioning less every day. He may even be put out of the coven if he doesn't improve while we're in Venice."

"No, he can't!" Eliza's eyes grow wide with panic. "We can't do that to him!"

"What difference does it make to you?" Her voice rises and drips with unspoken accusations. "You're the one who regretted ever laying eyes on him."

I don't need a reminder of that horrific night. Words fail to reach her suddenly parched mouth, and Maria continues, disgust coating every word. "I think leaving him behind is kinder than continually subjecting him to you."

"No! God, Maria, no." Tears roll down her cheeks. "I

never meant to hurt him." Then a wild thought surfaces, and she clamps her hand around Maria's wrist. *There has to be a way.* "You have influence with Master. Get him to change his mind."

A sudden spark lights the witch's green eyes. Reaching across the space between them, she grabs Eliza's chin and waits until their gazes lock. "Why should I do that?"

Eliza's mind races for an answer. Maria's history with Shashenka creates a familiar and uncomfortable dilemma: say too little and risk failure or too much and expose her plans to overthrow Shashenka. Her standing with the Druzhinas and Maria is already on shaky ground because of Dmitri's condition; pushing for this may bring her into their good graces. A bleak thought twists her stomach. *Dmitri is the key I need, or I've doomed us both.* She doesn't know where he fits in, but the instinct is too compelling for her to ignore. Taking the risk is the lesser of two bad choices; there's no way she can leave Dmitri behind.

Eliza splits a fine line and reveals a sliver of truth. "When I hurt him, I was trying to protect him from Master. I knew Master was using me to torment him, and I only meant to make it stop. After what I did ... he's so lost now. I can't leave him like that."

A pained smile barely pulls at the corner of Maria's mouth. "I see."

Eliza waits for a sign that Maria will help, but the long silence seems to indicate the witch won't intervene. Her gaze drops to the floor. She's already standing to leave when the other woman says, "I will make sure Dmitri is brought to Venice for you."

"Thank you, Maria." Eliza crosses the room and starts to open the door, but turns back. Although she's been in the Belyakov coven for months, she still doesn't trust any of them—the witch included. They turned her into a vampire, hunted her down when she escaped, and forced her to work as a concubine in the inner lair. Even when they were on friendlier terms, Maria was there at every step to ensure Eliza's integration into the coven.

"Do you know where he is right now? I'm leaving soon and would like to help him pack before I go." She must ensure that Dmitri makes it to Venice—regardless of the witch's promises.

Maria's scowl reappears. "He hides in the last cell on the dungeon's second sub-level. You'll probably find him there."

The dungeon? Stunned, Eliza stares for a moment before she bolts for the gloomy staircase that leads to the lower levels. In the more than three months she's been at Novgorod, she's never ventured into the more sinister parts of the castle. After her brief time in a cell at Big Sky, Montana, she had no desire to see what horrors might lurk beneath this ancient fortress.

This dungeon, she finds, is worse—far worse—than Big Sky's. The narrow passageways are dark and musty. The putrid stench of decaying flesh, bodily waste, and old blood fills the stale air. She places a hand over her mouth and nose, her steps faltering as she swallows hard against the constriction in her throat. There is no logical reason for anyone to willingly be in this place. *What is Dmitri do-*

ing down here? Why?

Iron bars seal the torture rooms, while the individual cells have heavy wooden doors; it's well known that Shashenka enjoys depriving prisoners of light. The further she goes down the hall, the less light there is, and a sick feeling twists and rises inside her—as if she's been held prisoner here before. She knows she hasn't, but her skin is crawling, and she shudders and almost turns back. *If Dmitri is in one of these cells, there is no way I am leaving him down here alone.*

The door to the last room is shut. "Dmitri?" There's no response. The hair prickles on the back of Eliza's neck. Her hand trembles as she reaches for the latch, fearing that whoever is on the other side may not be him after all.

It's so dark inside that she doesn't see anything or anyone at first. Then a slight motion in the shadows draws her attention. She steps through the doorway and calls out in a soft, nonthreatening tone. "Dmitri, is that you?"

There is no answer. She inhales a shallow breath and confirms his scent among the horrid odors that permeate this dungeon. "Dmitri?" She crosses the tiny room in small, careful steps, stopping when the toe of her shoe bumps into a body. *This is awful, atrocious.* She reaches down, and her fingers trace his body until she finds his hand and pulls him into a sitting position. Dmitri hasn't made a sound—she can barely see his eyes looking questioningly at her.

"Please come with me." Eliza tugs on his wrist, urging him to stand. "I need you to come with me."

When he remains sitting, she moves behind him, slips

her hands under his arms, and lifts him to his feet. He refuses to take a step. She lets out a heavy breath, and drap-
ing his arm over her shoulder, wraps her arm around his
waist. At least he doesn't resist as she walks him forward
into the hall. She glances up and sees his dark eyes, almost
feral, watching her. Confusion, uncertainty, and pain etch
his face. Guilt and humiliation flood her; the unbearable
weight of consequence forces her to look away. *I have to
fix this, even if it takes me a hundred years to make it
right.* Silence hangs as stagnant as the air between them.
Dmitri doesn't speak to anyone anymore, and Eliza can't
find a single word buried in the layers of her shame.

They reach Dmitri's room; Eliza seats him on the edge
of the bed and searches the dresser for pajama bottoms.
"You need to go shower." He continues sitting there,
blinking as if he doesn't understand her words any more
than he recognizes the pajamas she places in his hands.
She drags him into the bathroom, repeats the command to
shower, and closes the door, waiting on the other side until
she hears the water running. *I am not leaving him here.*
She doesn't quite trust Maria, and she certainly won't give
that despicable goblin king the chance to throw Dmitri out
of the coven. With a sigh she grabs his suitcases from under the bed and packs his clothes.

When Dmitri walks back into the bedroom, her heart
squeezes in pain at the sight of him. Water drips from his
shaggy hair onto his face and shoulders, droplets rolling
down his scarred chest. There are so many scars—a testament to the years of torture he has endured at Shashenka's
hands.

A vampire must be all but drained of their blood and on the verge of death to develop permanent scars; otherwise their quick healing abilities fully restore wounded flesh. Her self-loathing gives way to anger, and a snarl erupts from deep inside her. *Shashenka. That vile, evil son of a bitch is going to pay for this.*

Dmitri grimaces and his dark eyes blink rapidly, possibly reacting to her growl. Eliza takes a deep breath—she doesn't want to frighten him—and tries a reassuring smile. Nothing. He flinches when she steps forward and takes his hand. *No man should ever be this broken, especially not him.*

"You are going with me. I'm not going to let you out of my sight again."

His only response is an unfocused blink as she leads him to the bed and tucks the bedding around him. Gently her fingers brush his long, damp bangs away from his face. "You need to sleep now. I'll get everything packed—we're leaving tonight."

Dmitri stares at the ceiling as she finishes packing his clothes and other possessions, but she notices that his gaze follows her when she steps into the bathroom to collect his toiletries. She wonders if he actually sees her or if the movement captures his attention without his registering who or what is in motion. Eliza double-checks to make sure she's not missed anything, then stacks his suitcases near the door.

She isn't sure what to do next. She's afraid to leave him alone for the day. When Dmitri curls onto his side and his body trembles with silent, broken sobs, it nearly rips her heart out. *I've wronged you so horribly, and somehow I will make it right by you. I promise you will be whole again. I will make sure no one ever hurts you again.* The need to calm him overwhelms her. She sits next to Dmitri on the bed, encouraging him to roll onto his stomach, but hesitates before laying her palms on his shoulders. She doesn't know if the scarring causes him pain.

Dmitri relaxes when she begins massaging his neck and shoulders. A song comes to her lips, one that is often in her memory-dreams. The melody is poignant yet carries notes that sound hopeful and full of unspoken promises. For her it epitomizes two hearts speaking as one, a pledge made between souls that binds them for eternity. Eliza smiles at her romantic notions of the piece; she has no idea what the song really represents, only that she finds comfort in it. She can only hope it has a similar effect on him.

When Dmitri finally closes his eyes, she lies next to him and watches him for hours, unable to sleep herself.

At twilight Eliza asks Sally to watch Dmitri while she goes to see Maria. *I am not leaving without him.* She can't expose her intention to take him with her, and somehow that witch is going to help get Dmitri out of this castle tonight. Her tone is defiant as she bluntly informs Maria of her plans. "I need you to get him to the airport. The flight leaves at nine." She'll take Dmitri to New Zealand and bring him to Venice when their holiday is over.

Maria coughs to cover what Eliza suspects is a laugh. "You're awfully sure of yourself, aren't you? I haven't even spoken with Shashenka yet about Dmitri going to Venice."

"No, but you will, and I won't give Master the chance to leave him behind. Dmitri. Is. Going. With. Me."

Maria's shoulders shake with laughter. "So it seems. This should be good." She pauses. "Dangerous but good."

Eliza gapes; she expected resistance, even argument, but not this reaction, and the witch's demeanor is unnerving. She suddenly feels less confident. "Will you keep an eye on him this evening and make sure he's at the airport by eight thirty?"

"I'll make sure he's there. Is he packed?"

"He's ready to go—his suitcases are in his room."

Eliza thanks her and is about to walk away when Maria grabs her arm. "Eliza?"

Her gaze darts from the hand on her arm to the sudden, intense look in the witch's eyes.

"Find that which is lost ... mend the fatal wound."

What is she talking about?

Maria lets her go and strides across to the wardrobe. An ominous tone shadows what she says next, and a chill runs down Eliza's spine. "There is only one correct path— all others lead to ruin. Choose wisely, Eliza." Then she retrieves a dress and smiles again, looking back over her shoulder. "Now, if you'll excuse me, it appears that I have a special assignment to tend to this evening."

She tries to decipher Maria's strange comment as she prepares for the remaining few hours at Novgorod. Eliza avoids both the witch and Dmitri, yet her tension rockets to fight or flight levels whenever he's out of her sight for more than a few minutes. *Paranoid much? Get a grip and stop panicking.* The decision to bring Dmitri with her to New Zealand was impulsive and without forethought to risk or consequence. She's already taking a leap of faith that Maria's participation in her scheme will prevent Shashenka's wrath. Doubtless the vile monster won't bother to account for Dmitri's whereabouts until after the inner lair's arrival in Venice, but he won't be happy when he finds out how Dmitri got there. *This is either the stupidest thing I've ever done, or it's brilliant. I hope I don't regret it later.*

Dmitri is settled in the cabin of the jet when Eliza arrives at the airport later that evening. The witch apparently gave him a sleeping potion to prevent him from wandering off—he's unconscious and sprawled on the three-seat couch—and Eliza's hands tangle in her hair as she huffs in frustration. *So help me, if this doesn't wear off soon I'm going to lose it.* She sighs. It is a long flight from Novgorod to Auckland, but she has no idea where he's retreated to within his mind or how long it will take to draw him out—or if that is even possible. She may need every minute they have together.

They are a few hours into the flight when Dmitri wakes. His eyelids open and blink several times as he peers around the cabin. Eliza watches the cascade of fear, uncertainty, and confusion surge in his eyes and wash over him as he gulps and half chokes on a breath. He doesn't seem to notice her, but she smiles and reaches for his hand.

"It's okay. You're on a plane—we're alone and on our

way to Waiheke for a holiday."

Dmitri's gaze shifts toward her, but he just stares, tilting his head to the side as if he doesn't understand.

"You need a holiday. We need to get you back on your feet."

He still doesn't respond. His eyelashes bat at his long bangs, and she expects him to raise a hand to sweep them back. When he doesn't, Eliza realizes it's a motion she hasn't seen him do in over a month—not since before she destroyed him. Dmitri flinches when she reaches to brush his bangs aside. *Jeez, he's like a kicked pup expecting his next beating. What have I done to him?*

She tries to hold eye contact as her fingers settle on his forehead and gently stroke his hair from his eyes. The deer-in-the-headlights look he's giving her leaves her speechless. Her hand trails down until her palm cups the side of his face. He doesn't react. She tries apologizing again and takes his hand in hers, but the blank, unseeing expression returns.

Not knowing what else to say, she looks down at the hand loosely clasped in hers. His fingers barely curl—she knows that if she lets go, his arm will fall to his lap. Using her free hand she closes his fingers tighter and squeezes, but the hoped-for response doesn't come; Dmitri shows no sign that the contact even registered. Nothing. For hours she attempts to get him to show a voluntary reaction to touch, even resorting to begging him to do something, anything—he stares blankly. There's no emotion or movement from him except an occasional blink, and she's no longer confident that it's possible to fix the mess she made of him.

It's ripping her to pieces.

Hours later she settles him down to sleep and watches him until her own eyelids grow heavy and close. More disappointment greets her when she wakes and sees Dmitri sitting up, staring, looking through her. Eliza walks away as her tears well up. *God, how do I reach him? I need him to forgive me for what I've done to him.*

When they arrive after sunset at the Belyakov mansion in Waiheke, the locals' warm greetings melt into concern as they realize Dmitri is unresponsive. Eliza simplifies his condition—he doesn't feel well. *I think they got that memo.* The awkwardness of the situation and the way some of the locals react toward Dmitri remind her of what she saw from the Druzhinas. *If they find out I did this to him, they're going to hate me too.* She tries to blunt their curiosity by turning the subject to the beauty of the home and island, and to her relief it deflects any further questions about him.

Waiheke reminds her of the other lesser-used Belyakov estates. Unlike the homes in Prague, Novgorod, and Venice, these smaller, more private compounds rarely house the inner lair, and when they do it is merely for a short vacation before Shashenka moves on to one of the others.

This sprawling white two-story structure appears modest from the outside, but its beauty is in its design and the view from within the compound. The U-shaped layout encloses a private courtyard with outdoor tables, a swimming pool, and a garden. The exterior walls facing the courtyard are mostly floor-to-ceiling windows with several exits leading to the patios and pool. The glass walls have the same shuttering system she remembers from the estate in Arecibo. Doubtless this home has seen the same depraved horrors, too.

The interior, Eliza finds, is tastefully decorated in shades of blue, white, and natural earth tones accented with medium and dark shades of wood. Her eyes sweep the rooms and halls as they pass. The atmosphere is calming and warm—a good retreat for Dmitri's condition. *This will work. He's going to get better.*

A local, Matilda, shows them to a bedroom on the second floor. *A single room?* Matilda prattles on, addressing them as if they were a couple, and Eliza doesn't correct her assumption—it may be preferable to Dmitri being out of her sight. The last thing she needs is for him to wander off and end up in the ocean, swept away on the tides. She shudders at the thought.

After Matilda leaves, Eliza coaxes Dmitri into the bathroom and busies herself laying out his towel and soaps, trying to ignore that he's staring at nothing again. A few seconds of silence is all she can stand. *Maybe if I just leave him here, something will click, and he'll get it.* She goes back to the bedroom to finish unpacking their suitcases, but her eyes keep shifting toward the bathroom door. Still no sound. Her attempt to keep busy doesn't quell the voice inside telling her this isn't going to work. Each minute that falls off the clock ticks louder than the one before it; the water has yet to turn on, and there is no sound of movement. *What have I got myself into with him? What if he's too broken?*

She knocks on the bathroom door. When there is no

reply she opens it to find Dmitri standing in front of the shower—where she left him—fully clothed, staring at nothing again. An exasperated sigh escapes her. "Dmitri, you need to undress." Nothing. "Please ... get in the shower." When he still doesn't move or react, she realizes that she'll have to remove his clothes herself. With great reservation she does so, but seeing Dmitri naked only adds to his vulnerability and deepens her embarrassment and shame. *Don't have a lucid moment now—the humiliation of this will kill me.*

She tries to keep her gaze averted, but the overlapping scars on Dmitri's back, hips, and legs hold her eyes hostage. Until now she never knew just how many scars his tortured body bears—far more than any one person should have in a hundred lifetimes. Remarkably, there are none on his face. *Why did Shashenka leave that part of him untouched?*

A blush creeps across her cheeks as she realizes that her study of his body isn't getting him bathed. She places a hand on the small of Dmitri's back and guides him into the shower stall. He startles when the spray from the showerhead hits him. When he seems past the shock, Eliza places a bar of soap in his hand and directs him to wash. It's a small relief when his hands move to lather the soap over himself.

How do I fix this? What can I do to help him? Eliza closes the shower door and watches the blurry figure of his body through the frosted glass. Deep breathing releases some of the tension from her shoulders; at least she didn't have to bathe him.

Several moments after he stops moving, she reaches in to shut the water off and hands him a towel. He's slightly more alert and even begins drying his body, but becomes motionless again after a few moments. Once more she must help him dress; his vacant, unseeing eyes confirm he's lost within his mind again.

Afterward she sets him in a chair with a book and leaves him to read, stare, do nothing, while she goes to shower. Still, she's afraid to leave him alone too long and hurries through her normal routines. She's grateful to see Dmitri is still in the chair when she's done, though the book is on the floor and he is once more staring at something she doubts his eyes even see.

Eliza glances at the clock on the bedside table and realizes it's time to head back to the mainland—she's supposed to meet Matt at his hotel in Auckland. Her gaze shifts to Dmitri. *What am I supposed to do with him? I really didn't think this trip through.* Bringing him complicates matters, but letting him wander unattended may be a worse decision. She doesn't know the locals well and is reluctant to leave him behind at the estate.

Hauling Dmitri to his feet, she tows him along to meet the local, Richard, who will take them to Auckland and bring them back to the estate in the morning. The short helicopter flight isn't enough to distract her from the bigger problem; she has no idea how she's going to explain this to Matt. *He's going to freak.*

CHAPTER 3: ELIZA

Unraveling Mysteries

Eliza is in a quandary as she drives away from the congested traffic of the airport. In some ways Dmitri's presence here feels like a colossal mistake, but it's impossible to ignore her instinct that he needs to be here. Looking at the empty shell of a vampire sitting in the passenger seat—not blinking or moving, unaware of all around him—increases her uncertainty. Before arriving in Waiheke she believed that once they left Novgorod he'd snap out of it and return to normal. *Sell rainbows and lollipops much?* Given the way Dmitri functions, or rather doesn't function, she's come to one conclusion: he shouldn't be left alone. *He should be in an asylum. Freaking miracle worker I'm not ... evidently.*

Bringing Dmitri to Auckland poses several problems. Aside from the obvious displeasure Matt will show, there is no way to know how aware Dmitri really is. Reality seems to be something he barely dabbles in, but it's the moments

when he does that leave Eliza unsure how much he com-
prehends or retains—or what he may reveal to others. He's
an unknown risk, and that truth unsettles her. The irony
isn't lost on her that for months she pushed Dmitri away
to protect him and hide her plans. Now, because of his
condition—which she caused—and her impulsive decision
to bring him to Waiheke, she is dropping Dmitri right into
the middle of her campaign against the goblin king. Unless
Matt can figure out how to proceed with Dmitri present,
they may not accomplish much during their time in New
Zealand.

Regardless of what happens this week, Eliza and Matt
will need to increase their contact. Progress is too slow
and makes her time in the inner lair interminable. The
longer it takes them to put this revolt together, the more
likely that Shashenka will discover what they're plotting.
In the months since she was taken by the Belyakov coven,
Eliza has gained some of the goblin king's trust and
earned a slight amount of freedom. She expects the privi-
leges to continue when she arrives in Venice—perhaps it
will present a way for her and Matt to increase their contact and further their plans.

Eliza and Dmitri arrive at the luxury hotel at Mission
Bay in Auckland and wait in the lobby for Matt to come
down from his room. When he steps off the elevator, a
smile breaks across Eliza's face—the sight of him always
warms her cold heart. But Matt's dimpled grin fades when
he sees Dmitri, and she notices his posture tense.

"No flipping way. What the hell is he doing here?"

Yep, not happy. "It's a long story. Let's go to your room

and I'll explain."

When he keeps glaring at Dmitri, Eliza punches him in the arm. "By the way, it's good to see you too."

Matt rolls his eyes and wraps her into a hug. "It's always good to see you, baby vamp."

To her relief he keeps their kiss brief and friendly, not intimate. While their friendship is solid, the moments when Matt pushes for an exclusive relationship creates uncomfortable tension between them. In that regard Dmitri has been like a ghost standing between them from day one—something she can't explain or even fully understand herself, although she has tried. Matt's dislike for Dmitri is reasonable; Dmitri turned, stalked, and hunted Eliza until she was firmly enslaved as a concubine in Shashenka's inner lair. *I should hate Dmitri too, for what he's done to me, but I can't.*

Matt grabs her hand and growls at Dmitri to follow them. They take only a few steps before Eliza realizes Dmitri is still sitting in his chair, unresponsive and staring at the floor. She turns back, grabs him by the arms, and forces him to stand.

Matt gives Dmitri a hard look. "He's kind of creeping me out. What's wrong with him?"

Everything. "Long story." Eliza sighs, apology written across her face. It's no surprise that Matt is demanding an explanation, but admitting how monstrous she is deepens her shame. A part of her fears he will change his mind about their friendship once he learns she's just as evil as other vampires.

They take the elevator to the top floor in silence, and

Matt unlocks the door to his suite. Dmitri's gaze remains on the floor as Eliza seats him on a sofa; he doesn't even blink at the change in position.

"Okay, now. Tell me, what is he doing here and what the hell is wrong with him?" Eliza winces—the disapproval and anger on his face leave her wishing she could crawl under the carpet and avoid this conversation.

Better still, she'd give anything to go back and undo that night in Novgorod. *Yeah, well, I can't, so I'd better get this over with.* She begins by reminding Matt of their last meeting in London, and her earlier admission of the way she'd hurt Dmitri.

"Well ..." She blows out a breath. "This is the aftermath. The goblin king was going to leave him in Novgorod, possibly throw him out of the coven, and I couldn't bear the thought of that happening—not after what I did. Dmitri is not capable of taking care of himself anymore. Since I'm not going back to Novgorod, I had to bring him with me to make sure he gets to Venice."

Matt walks over to Dmitri and snaps his fingers in front of his face. Nothing—no reaction. He lets out a low whistle. "Is he always like this?"

Embarrassed, Eliza says, "Yes, mostly." She can't maintain eye contact with Matt as she explains that Dmitri barely functions, doesn't talk, and is so lost inside his mind that she doesn't know how to reach him. No one else can, either.

"Remind me not to get on your bad side." Matt's smile is sympathetic. "You know a hundred clichés are coming to mind. The cookie has crumbled. The wheel is spinning, but the hamster—"

"Matt, don't." A nervous laugh escapes her. Desperate to do something, anything, she moves to sit next to Dmitri and sweeps the hair from his eyes. A heavy sigh carries the weight of her guilt. "I don't know what to do. Even our witch—the one who saved you—can't do anything to help him."

Concern creases his forehead. "So what are we supposed to do with him? I mean, can we trust him not to hear anything we talk about?" She's unsure how to answer; a small part of her hoped that seeing Matt would provoke some reaction from Dmitri. The first time the two men met was almost six months ago, during the battle that wiped out Josh Cleary's pack—her werewolf family—in McAllister, Montana. Each man wanted to keep her away from the other, and fought until Eliza stepped in to save Matt's life. Their last meeting wasn't much better; when Matt found her in Novgorod, the two men exchanged heated words laced with unspoken threats. Eliza is painfully aware of their hatred—she has had to contend with it for months.

Matt clears his throat—he's still waiting for an answer. She sighs again. "Very little seems to penetrate his thoughts, but if you ask him to do something ... sometimes he will do what you ask."

Matt frowns as he peers into Dmitri's eyes. "Can we leave him alone in a room or stand him in a corner somewhere?"

"He's not a potted plant, Matt." She's more afraid he may wander off. "Before I left Novgorod, I found him in a cell in the dungeon. If I lose track of him here, I wouldn't know where to start looking."

They agree to put Dmitri in the bedroom and leave him there staring blankly out the window. When Matt takes Eliza's hand and leads her back to the table in the other room, Eliza wraps her arms around his neck and gives him a quick kiss. Oddly, Matt doesn't try to make more of the affection. *Has Dmitri's presence upset him that much?*

"I wanted to go out before you head back in the morning, but something tells me those plans are on hold."

Disappointment rounds out each syllable—it makes her feel even guiltier. Eliza doesn't trust herself to reply. The tension is stifling. An awkward silence follows, and her gaze moves toward the manila folders banded together on the table. *Perfect distraction.* "Search results?"

He grimaces. "Yeah, we'll go over those in a bit." Matt seems indecisive on where to begin, and she wonders if it's Dmitri's presence or the content of the folders that's bothering him.

She pulls his attention back to business and asks for an update on the mergers and acquisitions report. The tension dissipates slightly as he explains that four of the Belyakov businesses are ripe for a takeover—the only way they can ensure one of his lackeys doesn't rise up and take his place. Shashenka has entrusted these businesses to questionable managers who will be at the top of the list to retain or neutralize when Eliza and Matt get ready to take the goblin king down. Matt is sending people to meet with Belyakov's other business partners to probe whether there's support for ending Shashenka's control. They'll close the vile monster's illegal ventures afterward.

In the meantime Matt's surveillance of the Druzhinas and personal guards has increased; several werewolves and two vampires are now tracking their movements and activities. The information will further Eliza's attempts to sway the Druzhina to their side. Then Matt announces another vampire has direct access to the Belyakov coven from within the inner lair: Stephanie Reynolds, one of the courtesans Eliza doesn't know as well. Stephanie's duties as a concubine keep her outside the estate most of the time; in fact, Matt gained Stephanie's assistance through one of the outside vampires watching the Belyakov estate in Prague.

This latest revelation stuns Eliza, and she's not sure what to make of it. Questions explode from her lips—hope and trepidation spar for her attention. *This seems too good to be true, but if it is ...* "You're certain she won't turn on us?"

"Stephanie's hatred of Shashenka and most of his cronies runs deep. She has some unusual alliances—like you, she's befriended a few werewolves."

"Is that how you recruited her to our effort?" She smiles, recalling when she first met Matt in Yellowstone. *Vampires and werewolves—mortal enemies. Ha! Like that stopped us from becoming friends.*

"Yes." Matt grins broadly. "Her best wolf friend is a guy named Vincente Falco—she'll put you in contact with him when you reach Venice. His pack is watching the villa there. We are gaining allies willing to move against the Belyakov coven when the time comes."

Matt rifles through a stack of papers on the table and slides a photo toward her. "The vamp she spends the most time with is, in fact, no fan of Shashenka Belyakov, although he does a considerable amount of business with him. Janek Novak. He'd like to see the devil vamp destroyed—he's providing critical information to aid in our takedown of the Belyakov empire. Janek gives Stephanie cover to carry out some of our search and surveillance missions."

Go, Stephanie! Shashenka's cruel treatment of the courtesans may yet be his undoing; it raises her hope of success.

Using Janek as cover, Matt says, Stephanie is working as the main go-between with a rogue vampire named Teresina De Luca. Teresina is spying on the Druzhinas and reporting unusual activity among them. Already she's discovered that they gather more frequently than usual and often reroute for clandestine meetings before they resume their standard duties for the coven.

Eliza's mind races to sort and file these new developments, and she almost misses what Matt says next. "I think we may be able to put most of the Druzhinas on our side eventually. Teresina reports growing discontent among them, especially after what happened to your friend Dmitri." He grimaces, glancing at the closed bedroom door.

"Are we really that close to co-opting the Druzhina?" Eliza has seen them in action; they are highly skilled and deadly fighters. She'd much rather have their support than fight them, but she's afraid she's already sabotaged that chance. "After Dmitri's breakdown they weren't very friendly to me."

"It's because of Dmitri that they're tipping in our favor, regardless of their feelings for you."

Ouch. The surliness in his tone feels like an accusation. Eliza doesn't understand what is behind Matt's mood, but she's beginning to suspect it is more than just Dmitri being in the other room. Matt either ignores or doesn't see her reaction and goes on to claim that Teresina has managed to eavesdrop on three of the secret Druzhina meetings. "They are bickering over whether it may be time to take Shashenka down."

Oh God, this is huge—a huge freaking break for us. "Has Teresina said whether the Druzhinas are meeting as a group?" She wonders whether the rogue vampire's skills are that highly developed, or if the Druzhinas have become careless. *Could it be a trap?*

"Two of the meetings were held with the entire Druzhina present. Teresina described their conversation as heated and their debate as intense." Matt looks over his notes. "Four—Vladimir, Anna, Katherine, and Kees—are pushing to end that goblin king of yours."

Matt outlines the positions of the remaining five. Alexander and Sofia form the strongest opposition. *Shock face. Why am I not surprised?* The other three—Stephan, Victoria, and Justin—are leaning toward Vladimir's group but have yet to commit. Matt speculates that the biggest hurdle may be their fear of Shashenka. Still, this is a pivotal change, and Eliza knows it.

Matt reaches for the bound folders. Unbundling them,

he turns one over and sets it aside. "The fact that Teresina is a rogue, available to the highest bidder, makes her an asset and a liability. She doesn't belong to any coven—her work ranges from odd jobs to mercenary missions. We'll have to keep the money pot sweet enough that she'll stay with us until this is over."

What if she sells us out? "Are you sure it's good to use her, then? I mean, is the risk worth it?"

Matt shrugs. "I plan to work with her directly as she continues stalking the Druzhinas. The fewer go-betweens there are, the better I can keep an eye on her, and the faster I can move on the information we gain."

Matt grabs the stack of folders and places them in front of Eliza, announcing that they have new information on the history of Belyakov's coven. This time Eliza bristles at his nervous glance toward the bedroom door; he seems unsettled, almost spooked. *Why is he acting so weird? He can't possibly see Dmitri as a threat.* She wants to ask him why he's on edge, but she's afraid to hear the answer. Matt clears his throat. With a shrug Eliza says, "Sorry, I zoned out there a moment."

He shakes his head and repeats what she missed. Twice in Belyakov's reign, he tells her, members of the coven have tried ousting him. The first attempt, over eight hundred years ago, was led by Shashenka's brother, Ivan. The man failed miserably and met a gruesome death at his brother's hands. Then slightly more than five hundred years ago, two members of the Druzhina organized a small rebellion.

Matt glances again at the folder lying face down, a little

away from the others. Then he looks at the bedroom door again and opens and closes his mouth twice. Eliza can see he's struggling to find the right words. *This has something to do with Dmitri, but why would that bother him?*

He takes a few deep breaths before he begins. "Your friend"—he nods in Dmitri's direction—"was one of those Druzhinas."

"You're flipping kidding me, right?" Eliza's eyes pop wide. The man she has come to know isn't capable of such bravery, let alone acting as a leader of anything.

"Dmitri Markov has been, or was, a Druzhina for over six hundred years." Matt gulps and sips his glass of water. There's a slight tremble in his hand. He takes another deep breath and says, "Dmitri had a mate, and together they led the rebellion. Your devil vamp found out what they were up to—he sent a mole to infiltrate their group and brought them all down before they could act."

Her stomach roils. She knows Shashenka well enough to understand his penchant for evil. *Dmitri's scars ... five hundred years ... a leader. Tortured.* A spark of truth settles among her fragmented thoughts—this is about revenge.

"Their comrades were executed, but Dmitri and his mate were spared—at least initially. This is where it gets murky, and we're still looking for details."

"What do you mean?"

"We know Shashenka imprisoned and tortured Dmitri for decades, and that when he let him out Dmitri returned part-time to his duties as a Druzhina."

Eliza follows Matt's gaze to the lone folder. *Do I even*

want to know what's in it?

"The unknown mystery is what happened to his mate—she is rumored to be dead. Some reports say Shashenka murdered her five centuries ago."

Is that why he stalked me? "Do you think I remind him of her?"

His lips purse, and he studies her face for an endless minute before he slowly reaches for the lone folder and picks it up. It's slightly thinner than the other folders—icy fear races through her. Matt turns the file over in his hands and stares at it for a half minute before sliding it in front of her. "It's one of two possibilities."

CHAPTER 4: DMITRI

Holiday

Dmitri opens his eyes, expecting to see the blackness of the void, but the beautiful woman is in front of him again. *Who is she?* His eyes shift past her as he tries to understand where they are—it is familiar—but she takes his hand, and the thought falls away. Her mouth is moving. He only hears a single word: "holiday." Then he feels gentle fingers brush hair from his face, and she presses her palm against his cheek.

Her touch is—

A disembodied voice shouts, "Elizabetta." The black walls spring into place, wrapping and molding themselves around him. Dmitri tries to hold on to her image—her deep-brown eyes, long hair, slender figure—but the darkness seeps in and washes over it until it is gone.

There is nothing here. I am safe.

Hands reach through the walls, pull at him, take him somewhere other than here, and he's trying to understand, but darkness pries at the hands and the arms connected to them until all is gone once more. Then a stream of water erodes the walls, and Dmitri realizes that he's in a shower, holding a bar of soap in his hands. The water feels good as the warm droplets run over his cold skin. Somehow he lathers the soap, washing his limbs and parts of his body that he's almost forgotten exist. The sensation seems foreign to him; he is still marveling at the simple act when the void claims him again.

The awareness that he's holding something hard nudges him back from nothingness. Puzzled, he looks at the object—it's a book. He sees words printed on the page, but he cannot read them. Then those hands, her hands, are back, and he stumbles as she leads him somewhere he cannot see.

I should know her hands. I should know ... her name. In this moment, only her touch matters to him.

The now-familiar voice wails like a banshee. "Elizabetta!"

Elizabetta ... yes, I ...

The darkness rapidly rebuilds, layer upon layer, until he's encased in its oppressive weight and he loses hope that the light will ever find him again. Without it, he knows he'll wither and die.

From the depths of overwhelming despair, Dmitri feels the woman's palms tenderly cup the sides of his face. Her eyes are pleading, pulling him, forcing him to look deeply into the hauntingly familiar dark-brown pools. An ache grows in his chest, but whatever it is floats out of reach as he sinks once more into the blackness.

CHAPTER 5: ELIZA
Elizabetta Rossellini

Eliza reads the name on the tab of the folder: "Elizabetta Rossellini." She touches the words, her fingers trembling as she remembers the way Maria spat that name at her the night Eliza shredded what was left of Dmitri's mind.

That name has become an obsession; a spectral entity permeating all aspects of her life. Trying to find information on someone who disappeared over five hundred years ago has been an incredible challenge, but if there is a connection to Eliza, solving the mystery of Elizabetta Rossellini's identity may be crucial to their plans going forward. For months she's speculated why she was turned, and when. She must know who she is before she can act on the information they've gathered on the Druzhinas, Shashenka's goons, and the witch.

Am I ready for this? Do I really want to know? The truth may be inside this folder, and it's chilling to be this close to it. She looks up at Matt. Something is obviously bothering him—he's nervous, fidgety, even uptight. As her fingers move to open the manila file, his hand suddenly covers hers.

"You may need time to process this—there's a lot to take in." His attempt at a smile fails, adding another knot in her already writhing stomach. "I'll go in and sit with your friend ... I'm sure we'll have a lively conversation."

Her voice breaks with trepidation. "What's wrong? Is there something in here that ..." She can't finish the thought. She wants to know who she really is, but Matt's behavior fills her with dread.

"I don't know ... but we'll figure it out."

Matt stands and leaves the room without looking back. Several minutes march silently by as Eliza stares at the name on the tab.

Did I leap to conclusions, make wrong assumptions? Am I so desperate that I'm clinging to another lie? What if I'm not her?

What if I am?

Yet her bones seem to resonate with truth, and her mind races to fill the gaps. Dmitri's mate—vanished five hundred years ago but never confirmed dead. Elizabetta Rossellini—a mystery vampire wrapped in an enigma. Eliza Ross—her name, a name that by coincidence or accident resembles the name that's come to haunt her. Shashen-ka—devil vampire, destroyer of lives. Matt—spooked, uncomfortable, and evasive. Dmitri—shattered and ruined. All are connected somehow—she knows it—but she's leapt to so many conclusions that she's no longer certain about anything. *I'm like a freaking frog jumping around. I need to stick with the facts or I'm going to end up dead.*

Breaths shallow and fast, Eliza opens the folder with shaking hands, shoving against the fear that this puzzle piece may permanently alter her life. Her eyes clench shut for a long minute. When she opens them, she keeps them unfocused as the blurred writing on the page comes into view. Eliza is astonished with herself—she's lost her courage to face the truth. With each new ragged breath she draws, the page's contents sharpen into discernible words: "Elizabetta Rossellini." Turning the cover page aside, Eliza reads the synopsis:

Elizabetta Rossellini

Date of Birth: 1400–1425, Padua, Italy

Father: Benito Rossellini

Mother: Giuseppina Consiglio

Siblings: Sergio, Dante (brothers); Paoli, Melita, Bernicah (sisters)

Family Bloodline Status: Ceased 1501

Date Turned: 1423–1448, Venice, Italy

Mate: Dmitri Markov, married 1423–1448 to 1514–?

Occupation: Druzhina; specialized skills assassin, tracker, warrior, historical researcher;

Belyakov Revolt leader (1513)

Ceased Existence Date: Unknown

Last Known Location: Novgorod, Russia, 1514

Genealogy standards applied to dates of this report.

So Elizabetta was Dmitri's mate.

The report claims that for decades Dmitri and Elizabetta lived and worked together as one of the most feared, respected, and proficient teams within the Druzhina. Elizabetta's research expertise was a critical asset to the coven and enabled Shashenka to orchestrate human uprisings against governments that went against his wishes or harmed his interests. For decades he manipulated warring factions, later influencing the French and the Turks against the Italians during the Habsburg-Valois Wars.

Shashenka used the cover of that war to murder his rivals, and scores of human lives were lost—collateral damage to him, but Elizabetta Rossellini's remaining relatives were among those targeted and killed. It was rumored that these deaths were deliberate. Elizabetta had not completely cut ties with her human family's descendants, something Shashenka saw as a grave risk in a Europe inundated with folklore about succubi, incubi, werewolves, witches, and fae. As long as human men hunted the creatures deemed by their churches to be evil, Shashenka wouldn't allow Elizabetta's human connections to lead the hunters to his coven. He sent a group of Druzhinnikis to take care of the perceived problem.

Elizabetta was enraged when she discovered that he had ended her family bloodline. In retaliation, she and Dmitri planned and led the revolt, which ultimately failed. Their compatriots were put to death. Dmitri suffered decades of torture. But Elizabetta simply disappeared or ceased to exist—whether executed, imprisoned, or escaped and in hiding since, no one seems to know. The only point of agreement is that slightly more than five hundred years ago, Elizabetta Rossellini's whereabouts became unknown. Now Eliza understands why Matt said her theory was one of two possibilities. If she simply looks like Elizabetta, it's rational that Dmitri—after years of torture—mistook her as a reincarnation of his lost mate. It would explain the profound pain in his eyes and his maniacal stalking of her this past year.

If she is Elizabetta, she could be over six hundred years old—and five centuries of her life are missing.

I can't even fathom that length of time. Eliza is certain that Shashenka, the Druzhinas, Maria, and Dmitri know the truth, but she doubts any of them will ever reveal it. Her mind flashes back to Big Sky, when Dmitri admitted that he turned her but wouldn't say when or where. *Is it possible he turned me that long ago?*

Her brow furrows and she looks toward the bedroom door. *If Elizabetta was alive, wouldn't Dmitri have gone looking for her?* She thinks about the broken shell of a vampire sitting in the other room, and her blood boils, overcoming her shame.

Her chair topples over as she rises from the table and barges into the bedroom, where Matt is flipping through channels on the television. He pauses and looks up at her from the bed. "Eliza?" His eyes fill with questions, but she shakes her head as she approaches Dmitri near the window.

I have to fix him. He has to tell me the truth. Matt mutes the television—she can feel his eyes following her. Eliza moves in front of Dmitri and scrutinizes his empty expression. "Dmitri, please hear and see me." Her pleading turns to a shout. "I need you to tell me the truth."

There's no reaction. She takes his hands. "Please talk to me. Tell me who I am."

Matt rises from the bed, walks over, and places his hands on her shoulders. "I think his mind is too far gone. I've never seen anything like this, and I'm beginning to think he'll never be right in the head again. He's a few fries short of a Happy Meal."

Choking back tears, Eliza ignores the attempt at humor and looks over her shoulder at her friend. "I can't accept that, not when I pushed him over the edge. He knows who I am—he knows the truth. It's all my fault ..."

Sympathy lights Matt's hazel eyes as he motions toward Dmitri. "I cannot imagine enduring what he's been put through for centuries, and I'm surprised it took this long to demolish his mind. You may have been the last straw, but there's only one monster responsible for this."

Eliza shakes her head—platitudes aren't going to re-solve the problem. She guides Dmitri to a chair and urges him to sit. Kneeling before him, she desperately searches his eyes—there isn't one spark of recognition or aware-ness. Her shoulders slump in defeat. "Is there anyone that can help him?"

Matt moves alongside her and looks down at her. "This is the first I've ever heard of a vampire going bonkers—didn't think it was even possible. I doubt we'll find vamp shrinks with ads in the Yellow Pages. I'll be amazed if there is anyone out there dealing with this type of prob-lem."

Slowly Eliza reaches up and cups Dmitri's face in her

hands, forcing him to look at her. "Please, please come back. I need you to tell me who I am."

A slight quiver in his bottom lip appears as his eyes seem to search hers, but before she can hope, his blank, unseeing expression returns.

Damn it. She grinds her teeth and turns to Matt. Doubtless he's already considered this more thoroughly than she has—he's had more time to absorb the information about Elizabetta. "I agree with you—there are two possibilities. Which do you think it is?"

Matt shrugs, stuffing his hands into the front pockets of his jeans. "I've been asking that since the damn report arrived. I'd like to think it's a case of mistaken identity, that you have a similar name and maybe look like her."

"But?" Eliza watches his chest rise and fall, and she wonders what he's battling with or if she even wants to know.

Then their gaze locks. "If you are Elizabetta ..." He swallows and inhales sharply. "If you are her, then it means you're married ... to him." His tone carries a hint of resignation tinged with pain.

Matt's words are a punch to the gut. She read the file, but her mind latched onto the incomprehensible dates and the length of time between then and now. Her eyes narrow, a subtle shift rippling through her as she looks back at Dmitri. *He's so beat down and undone. Is the mate bond really that strong, or is it because he can love that deeply? Is it because I'm his ...* She can't even think the word— can't even imagine.

Her gaze drifts between the two men before freezing on

Dmitri's empty eyes. "Oh crap, this can't be ... can't be real, not happening." The palm of her hand presses circles to her forehead. *This is ridiculous! How can it even be possible?* Thoughts scatter as she tries to sift through the implications of what this means for her, Matt, Dmitri, and their future ahead.

What if it's true?

"It would also mean that you're not a baby vamp," Matt whispers.

Her eyes dart toward Matt's face. His sad expression conveys what he doesn't say—there never was a chance for the two of them. Her tone is sharper than she intends as she says, "I'll always be your baby vamp, your friend. None of this, whichever it is, will change that between us."

A faint smile tugs at the corners of his mouth, and she understands that he's always hoped for more.

The implication is a sledgehammer blow that mangles her future. Eliza thought she knew its possibilities, but what lies ahead is unrecognizable. This impacts everything: making a choice between Matt or Dmitri and even deciding how to proceed against Shashenka. If Dmitri simply mistook her as his mate, then she will have to deal with his false attachment to her—if he ever returns to normal. Eliza refuses to stand in the shadow of Elizabetta's ghost, and she has to accept that he may never see her any other way. Under those circumstances she'd need distance from him after they destroy Shashenka and she gains her freedom. A relationship with Matt could provide that distance. *But what about how wrong that feels?*

If Dmitri accepts that he's confused her with his mate,

then in fairness to both him and Matt she could take time to decide which man is best for her. But if Dmitri is her mate, her husband—a terrifying, yet not totally unpleasant thought—the bond between them will remain until they cease to exist. There is no other way to break a mate bond.

This is nuts. I'm not that old. "I don't understand why, if I'm her, I wouldn't have memories of living beyond twenty-three years ago."

Matt paces over by the window. "I haven't talked to anyone about this yet, and I've been trying to get it right in my head because ..." He doesn't need to finish the thought; Eliza knows what he's leaving unsaid.

"When we were in Yellowstone, you told me you've heard of vamps wiping human minds and altering their memories. Do you think it's possible ..."

The silence echoes the hurt in Matt's eyes. It's all the answer she needs.

Eliza rises to her feet and takes Matt's hands, trying to convey reassurance that their friendship is still strong. "I have to know the truth. If I'm not her ... then maybe Dmitri ..." It's her turn to leave a thought unfinished; it feels wrong to say that she wants him out of her life, but she may have no choice. "If they took my memories, wiped my mind, I need to know if it can be undone. I need to know who I am. I want my life back!"

Matt nods in apparent understanding and they head back to the living room, leaving Dmitri sitting stone-still on the chair in the bedroom. *Fate ... that cruel, fickle, heartless megabitch! What am I supposed to do with this mess?* Eliza barely listens as Matt places a few calls. He orders a search of any records or legends about vampires that have gone insane, but there is little else they can do; it will take days, if not weeks, to find answers to Dmitri's predicament.

Dwelling on the issue isn't a solution either, and they refocus on the new information Matt gained since their last meeting. Without express agreement, Eliza and Matt substitute Dmitri and Elizabetta's names with "the Markovs" as they speculate what went wrong with the failed rebellion. There are not enough details to determine whether they are repeating the Markovs' mistakes or if now they are in a better position to succeed. Regardless, failure is unacceptable for Eliza, and she's more determined than ever to end Shashenka Belyakov—if for no other reason than to make him pay for what he's done to Dmitri.

When it's time to return to the estate, the unresolved mystery of Elizabetta Rossellini Markov creates an awkward parting. Eliza tries to reassure Matt that nothing has changed between them, but deep within she knows that the truth that once resonated has now cemented inside her despite the doubts that still nag at her. She forces a warm smile to her lips and tells Matt to rest well—she and Dmitri will be back after sunset. She doesn't miss the strange look he gives Dmitri, but this time she chooses to ignore it.

CHAPTER 6: ELIZA

Who am I

Eliza is still picking apart the issue when she and Dmitri reach their room at the mansion. It will take time to study the search results more closely. She must start grounding herself in facts—assumptions will only create chaos and confusion, especially if the truth is something other than what she believed. *I still can't wrap my head around the idea that Dmitri may be—* Her snort cuts off the thought as she looks over at him.

He's standing in the middle of the room where she left him. *Will you ever snap out of it and tell me what I need to know?* Her sighs echo across the room. The answers won't come tonight, and she knows it. Instead she directs him to put on his pajama pants and goes to the bathroom to change into her nightgown. When she returns a few minutes later he's sitting on the edge of the bed, his gaze riveted to the floor. *Do you even see the ground beneath your feet? Do you see anything at all?* She pinches the bridge of her nose and squeezes her eyes shut. Somehow she has to reach him.

She encourages him to stand while she turns back the bedding for him, then settles him on the mattress. Dmitri lies facing her; his eyes are vacant. Eliza hesitates a moment before she pulls back the covers on the other side of the bed and lies next to him, staring up at the ceiling. *Dmitri Markov. Elizabetta Rossellini. Husband and wife— mates. Me ... am I Elizabetta?* The possibility that Dmitri is her husband does not give her a moment's peace. *Is that why it's never felt awkward to be near him?*

Eliza scoots next to him, trying not to feel self-conscious. Being this close to Dmitri could give him the wrong idea if he has another return to his surroundings. But it's impossible for her to deny the need to be near him, and she reaches out to touch him. Dmitri flinches when her hand settles on his side. Is it her touch that startles him or the shred of a memory from the abuse he's suffered at their master's hands? Slowly she forms her body to Dmitri's long, lean frame—her knees tuck behind his and her hand moves up to his chest as her arm wraps tighter around him. She places her nose against his spine and inhales deeply.

Why does this calm me so much? Does it comfort him at all? His scent soothes her troubled mind. "I don't know if you can hear or understand me, but I need you to come back. Please." Eliza presses a light, lingering kiss between his shoulder blades. "If ... if you're my husband, I need to know. I wish I knew how to reach you." *God, I wish he'd talk to me—squeeze my hand, move, do something.*

Hours gobble minutes as they lie together, and it's late in the afternoon when Eliza finally falls asleep. The familiar sensation of being watched rouses her at twilight— Dmitri is standing at the foot of the bed, staring at her. *Talk about coming full circle.* For once he's not looking through her, but the distant, confused glaze is still in his eyes. As she gets off the bed she whispers, "Good evening."

Of course he doesn't respond. He never did, not even before he lost his mind.

Eliza takes advantage of his semi-aware state and moves him to the bathroom. While Dmitri showers she spends a few minutes reviewing the files; they have a couple of hours before meeting Matt again. Their new allies seem promising. Stephanie, it appears, has a tendency to stay closer to the Belyakov estates in Venice and Prague— doubtless because of their proximity to Vincente and Janek. When Eliza arrives at the Venice estate, she will need to further her rapport with Stephanie and arrange to meet her friends.

Teresina De Luca also lives in Venice but apparently spends a good deal of time traveling around the world. Eliza hopes to meet with the rogue vampire as soon as her duties at the inner lair allow. She's keen to hear more on the Druzhinas' debate to overthrow Shashenka. A hollow laugh accompanies a stray thought: she is the last one the Druzhinas will ever talk to about their plans.

When Dmitri finishes showering, Eliza closes the files and seats him in a chair to stare out the window while she showers and dresses. He's still sitting there when she returns; it's both a welcome sight and an increasing aggravation for her. For a moment she wonders if this is her penance for destroying a good man.

Again she tugs him along to see Matt, first holding on to Dmitri's hand, but when he stumbles she slips an arm around his waist to steady him. Although he's likely unaware, she feels self-conscious in light of what she's learned about Elizabetta. This time when they arrive at the hotel, they don't stuff Dmitri in a corner or leave him in another room. Dmitri just sits there—detached, unmoving, unblinking—and it is disconcerting at first, but Eliza and Matt soon grow used to his quiet presence. As far as Eliza is concerned, he's too far gone to care about their plotting, and even if he weren't, he'd probably join their crusade against Shashenka.

Eliza leans against Matt as they review the upcoming tasks outlined on the screen of his laptop. Eliza will first seek out Stephanie and attempt to speak with the four Druzhinas most inclined to help them. Depending on the level of freedom she's given in Venice, Eliza will meet Vincente's pack, gauge their interest, and learn their numbers. Since there is little new information on Maria, they agree that Eliza should be wary of exposing too much to the witch.

If possible, her next meeting with Matt will be far from a Belyakov estate—she feels spied on by the locals and knows they report her activity to Shashenka. Wherever she and Matt meet, she will also have to decide whether to leave Dmitri at the Belyakov villa in Venice or to bring him along again. *Montana, the Caribbean, Paris, or somewhere in the East?*

"Nothing personal, but I hope you can leave him there. He's a bit of a wet towel." Matt looks sheepish. "I mean, it's one thing to have a third wheel for sightseeing, but in his present state it's difficult to imagine going anywhere."

Eliza sighs. "I really don't know what to do with him. If your search ... somehow we need to break him out of this ..." Frustrated, she waves indecisively as her voice trails off.

Matt's tone turns serious and a muscle flexes in his jaw. "How is this supposed to work for you? You spent months pushing him away to convince Shashenka that you can't stand the guy, and now you're like, oh, don't mind him—he's my shadow."

She's already considered the problem. At the inner lair, she'll have Sally and perhaps Stephanie help watch him; Maria may also be an option, regardless of whether Eliza can trust her, since the witch seems to care about Dmitri at least. "I'll keep my contact with him to a minimum, or at any rate away from prying eyes and ears."

Reaching across the table, she sweeps Dmitri's bangs off his face again, trying to ignore the way Matt tenses. "My biggest concern is taking him to Italy from here, then sneaking him back out for our next meeting. I left Novgorod in such a hurry that I didn't give serious thought to how Shashenka will react when we show up in Venice together."

Matt looks away, but even in profile she can see his hurt and disappointment. After another long minute he reaches into a briefcase and pulls out a cell phone. "I want to give you this."

"Mind reader—I needed a phone."

He manages a brief smile and tells her about the phone and its features and services. Matt insists on paying the bill for the account and ignores Eliza's arguments against it. "Look ... my number is already in the phone."

She's about to object again, but he turns the phone around to show her the contact list. There's one entry—Mattie Wolverton—with an unknown woman's photo displayed with the number. Eliza laughs as Matt says, "Figured you could say it's some gal you met. Just make sure not to save any incriminating messages from me." He pulls a tablet of notes from his briefcase; it's a list of current cell phone numbers for those she plans to co-opt or kill. "May as well put your new phone to use, baby vamp."

Eliza smiles; it's only the second time he's called her by his favorite nickname since they arrived in New Zealand. *Maybe I won't lose him and we'll be okay.* She takes the phone out of her pocket and enters Sally and Maria's numbers into her contacts. She'll need one of them to help sneak Dmitri into the villa after their arrival in Venice.

With only a few hours left until sunrise, Eliza and Matt decide to relax with mindless entertainment—but their newfound knowledge and Dmitri's presence hamper their normal movie-watching routine. Matt keeps a respectful distance from Eliza on the couch; their new awkwardness seems to leave him as uncertain as Eliza is about how much familiarity to share.

Eliza and Matt take a break from their planning and meet at Cactus Bay after nightfall the next evening. The secluded location is near the Belyakov estate, and though Matt must rent a boat to get there, Eliza and Dmitri can access it directly. Belyakov's land borders the cove with another private owner's, and only those two properties have access to the beach. *At least it's a place I can take Dmitri and not worry about what people think.*

The three walk along the beach, holding hands—Eliza in between the two men—except that Dmitri doesn't really hold on to hers, and she knows his hand would fall away if she let it go. It's a relief to see something spark in Dmitri's eyes when they decide to go for a swim. Without assistance or prompting from them, he's quick to float or go into a front crawl stroke. There's only one catch—there's no pattern or direction to his swimming, and it quickly becomes a game of retrieval as Eliza and Matt take turns going after Dmitri whenever he starts to swim away.

Somehow it evolves into a competition. They allow Dmitri to swim out a good distance and then race after him while dunking or splashing each other in an attempt to catch him. The winner is whoever reaches him first, and the loser must tow him back to shore. She and Matt haven't laughed this much together in months, but still Eliza can't escape her concern over Dmitri's condition; in some measure it drags on her heart like an anchor caught on the ocean floor.

They spend the last three nights enjoying the nightlife in Auckland, with Dmitri along as a seemingly oblivious third wheel. By now they've grown used to Dmitri's silence and his often frozen presence. Any reservations Matt held seem to have dissipated, and he doesn't hesitate to guide Dmitri along by grasping his elbow. He even calls Dmitri "buddy" in a friendly, caring tone. Eliza marvels at the sight; it's in stark contrast to when they tried to kill each other in Montana.

While Dmitri still appears unaware of almost everything around him, Eliza notices one minor improvement— he listens when told to do something. It allows her to leave him seated at a table while she and Matt dance at a pub on their final night in New Zealand. But even then she barely takes her eyes off Dmitri; she's still afraid he'll wander off and get lost.

At the end of the night Eliza and Matt say good-bye with too many unanswered questions hanging between them. The sadness in Matt's eyes provides the punctuation mark to their awkward reunion. Eliza tries not to think about it—until more is known, she can't do anything to change it—and instead focuses on Dmitri as she settles him into bed at the mansion. *I'm running out of time ... I wish he could tell me how to help him.* Although he still doesn't respond, she repeats the routine of the past few nights until she falls asleep.

When she wakes before sunset she's surprised to find Dmitri showered, dressed, and actually turning pages in a book. It's the first autonomous action she's seen in him other than swimming, and while he doesn't seem to notice her, at least it's not his chronic blank stare.

Progress? Now? Doesn't that just figure. To her astonishment, Dmitri silently gathers and packs his own clothes and toiletries as she packs her suitcase. Eliza holds her breath and waits for him to say something, but his gaze remains elsewhere and he never utters a sound. A fleeting wish for more nights alone drifts away as she determines to make the most of their remaining time together; it's a long trip to Italy, and her hope grows that he's turned a corner, that her efforts weren't meaningless after all.

Richard takes them to the airport, where Belyakov's jet is waiting to fly them to Venice. He and the other locals were friendly; instinct tells her that they wouldn't mourn Shashenka's demise. But then his parting comment stuns her. "It was nice seeing you both on holiday again. Perhaps Mr. Markov will feel better next time you come."

Again? Eliza stumbles through a response. "Uh, um, yes ... I'm sure we'll look forward to our next holiday here."

"You're still one lucky bloke, mate." Richard pats Dmitri's back and walks away.

Eliza watches him climb into the helicopter and prepare for takeoff. This is her first trip to Waiheke. Isn't it? *Was that an attempt to acknowledge the truth of my past?* The impact of his statement hits hard, and she starts to run after him, but the helicopter is already in the air. She screams after it, "Am I Elizabetta Markov?"

She looks at Dmitri and wonders if he will tell her the truth someday.

CHAPTER 7: DMITRI

Adrift

Suddenly the voice—her voice, that beautiful, soft voice—sounds anguished, and he hears her say, "Please, please, Dmitri, come back to me. I need you to tell me who I am."

He wants to ease her pain—he must hold back the weight of the black walls. He must find her name. A familiar voice whispers it from inside the void, and a memory cuts through him like a thousand razor blades. *Elizabetta ... moyata svyetlina ... amore.* Her pain crashes into his, and he tries to say something, anything, but his tongue strangles the words before they reach his lips.

Dmitri notices a tremble—his chin quivers. He tries to move his arms, wills them to rise, to reach for her, but the black walls slam back into place. He's powerless to stop them. The weight of their layers threatens to suffocate him as they bury him in the darkness.

Through the emptiness of the void he feels an arm wrap

around his side. Soft lips move against his back, and a gentle breath feels like feathers and silk against his skin. *The void is perfect with her arms to hold me.* It seems right, so familiar, but somehow he knows it is wrong. His body is raw from the sensations coursing through him. His mind can't process the overload to his system, and the black walls squeeze tighter around him.

He is floating, he thinks. A bobbing, rocking motion—yes water embraces his body. Dmitri can't understand why he is in the water, but he enjoys swimming and welcomes the chance to do so now. It soothes him—it always has. That lovely woman is here again too, with him in the water. She stops his arm midstroke and rolls him onto his back as her arm wraps around his chest. He revels in the feeling of being here with her, wherever here is. Then the sensation of her hands fades—she's gone again. *Why?* Dmitri ponders her strange appearances and disappearances, but his mind stops thinking when his arms begin to move almost on their own, making long, powerful arcs as his legs propel him forward through the gentle waves. *It has been so long ...* He can't recall the last time he went swimming.

The water is gone. The black walls have returned. Resentment and longing writhe inside him; it's the isolation of this place and his need for something ... for what? Dmitri wishes to swim again in the darkness with her. *Where is she?*

The silence around him is oppressive. Slowly he realizes there is nothing in the void—not even, to a large degree, himself. *Where am I?* He has no memories of what happened to the world he once knew, or how long he's been here. Within the vast darkness time ceases to exist. *Why am I here?* It's hard to think in the pitch black of the void, but he makes the effort. Dmitri wants to leave, needs to leave, but he doesn't know how to get out. He pushes against the wall.

I wish ... I want to be with her.

He shoves the wall again; it doesn't move. *Does she know how to tear them down from the outside?* Now Dmitri realizes that the black walls only fall away when she is there. He may be powerless to escape them without her help.

I need to be with her.

The next time she makes the walls disappear, he tries keeping them away, but they collapse inward, burying him, surrounding him again.

A fragment of a memory surfaces, and Dmitri snatches it to him before it can float away. He recalls a name, her name. *Elizabetta ... her name is Elizabetta. She is mine.*

Somehow he must help her shatter these walls. Determination to reach her drives him, and his continuity of awareness—away from the black void—is lasting a little longer each time. Her breath whispers silent words against his spine. The sudden desire to roll over and face her is thwarted by his body's refusal to move. He listens harder for her voice, her meaning, but fails to catch a single sound. Then the deepest memory he's experienced in longer than he can remember reverberates through every cell of his body.

Elizabetta is my light. I will endure.

CHAPTER 8: ELIZA

La Perfezione

At the airport in Venice, Eliza begins to worry when neither Sally nor Maria is waiting for Dmitri on the tarmac. *Pluck a duck—that witch promised one of them would be here to take him.* Her calls dump into their voice mail boxes. She sends another text message to both women, nervously pacing while the local driver, Antonio, sits in the nearby car with Dmitri. When Maria finally responds with a text, the reply settles like a sharp stone in Eliza's stomach: "He knows and is waiting."

Knows what? Knows we're plotting to overthrow him? Knows Dmitri is with me? Shit, shinola. Damn it, Maria, a little information would be helpful here. Eliza texts back a row of question marks, but it goes unanswered.

Antonio steps out of the car. "Miss Ross, Master is asking why we're delayed in arriving at the villa."

She startles and looks around in a panic, calculating the odds for running. It's impossible with the state Dmitri is in—he requires too much care and would slow them down. Any improvement she saw in Waiheke disappeared moments after they boarded their flight, and he's not resurfaced on any meaningful level since. *Nothing good will come of this.* They are out of time; there are no other options. She nods at Antonio and gets into the car.

In the backseat Eliza takes Dmitri's hand, needing strength and comfort, but his limp grasp leaves her feeling worse. Small talk with the driver won't help—she avoids talking to him. When they park in a private garage near the Santa Lucia train station, Antonio retrieves their luggage and leads them to an estate motorboat tied to a mooring pole while Eliza drags a clueless Dmitri along. Her eyes roam over him—she wishes she were in a stupor. This is not how she envisioned her arrival in Venice.

The estate is located on the Grand Canal in the San Marco District, which she longed to see, but the nearer they come, the more fearful she is—it prevents her from enjoying the sights and sounds of their passage along the canal. Shashenka is ruthless, she knows, and she can't help feeling she made a major mistake taking Dmitri from Novgorod. The only thing that may save them both is that Dmitri is out of his mind and this is her first screw-up.

When they arrive at the mansion, Antonio secures the boat to another mooring pole while Eliza helps Dmitri onto the stone platform in front of the villa, catching him when he stumbles. *Who will keep him from falling if Shashenka punishes me?* Once he's steady she looks up at the structure towering over them. She's been told about this estate, and focusing on it now distracts her from what is awaiting them inside.

Villa La Perfezione (Perfection) was built in the early sixteen hundreds, modeled after Villa Foscari "La Malcontenta." From what she's heard, the Palladian features are prominent inside and out. The limestone brick structure boasts five stories, with an ornate ballroom on the top floor; she sees a faint glint of light seep around the edges of the curtained windows. Matching single-story wings provide the living quarters for the villa's locals, she knows, and contain Shashenka's office, his personal library, and smaller music rooms. The canal-facing side has a split staircase, one set to each side of the Grecian-pillared portico. A breath catches in her throat as another déjà vu sensation prickles the corners of her mind—an overwhelming sense of being home.

"This way, Miss Ross." Antonio stuffs luggage under both his arms and promises to return for the remaining bags. The kind offer leaves Eliza's hands free to guide Dmitri. She knows he's been here before, but he shows no recognition of the place, let alone any sign of cognitive life. They walk up the stairs, Dmitri tripping over several steps before they reach the elevated main floor—the primary piano nobile.

Eliza's eyes widen as they sweep over the brilliant frescoes on the ceilings and the elaborate gold molding that lines the hallways. She's heard that the artwork is abundant throughout the primary and secondary piano nobiles, but it's more than the beauty that's capturing her attention. *I have seen this before—I know it.* Marble statues replicating the works of Michelangelo adorn each floor.

Oil painting reproductions—elegantly framed and prominently displayed—are reportedly found on all levels of the villa, and a few are within sight now.

La Perfezione is breathtaking—a step back in time. It's the one Belyakov residence with limited electrical fixtures and plumbing, and only a few modern upgrades. The furnishings are a mix of sixteenth and seventeenth-century Italian, French, and English pieces; each room or floor is defined by these styles. Heavily lined velvet and satin drapery in shades of red, green, or gold provides the needed barrier against the sun. The cut-block limestone of the outer walls matches the limestone plaster of the inner walls. Eliza notices how the white marble floors prevent distraction from the décor; the walls and ceilings are meant to be the focal point of the impressive villa.

She is so absorbed in the beauty that she fails to see four of Shashenka's personal guards waiting near the staircase that leads to the secondary piano nobile. Peter is the first to speak—it breaks her reverie—and the men with him move to surround Eliza and Dmitri. "Antonio, take their luggage to a storage room near the locals' quarters. Shashenka will decide later what to do with them."

The four guards grab her and Dmitri by the arms and drag them to a basement stairwell on the opposite wall. "Where are you taking us?" Eliza demands, but she already suspects where they are going. There's never anything good in the lower levels of a Belyakov mansion.

Peter snarls, "Shut up."

A musty odor wafts up from the lower level. The stairwell is narrow; when her foot slips on the stairs, Peter jerks her arm to keep her from falling. Seepage from the canal covers the last three steps, and when they reach the floor, the water level is a few inches above her knees. Eliza's eyes adjust to the dim lighting. There are no cells. *Why are we down here?* Peter and another guard drag her toward one of the large square support pillars that are staggered throughout the open foundation of the villa.

She hears the clinking of chains coming from Dmitri's direction before she sees the shackles attached to the pillar in front of her. In a futile attempt to flee, she slams her body into the two men holding her. Within moments they subdue her and force her back against the pillar, locking the shackles around her wrists.

Fear bubbles to the surface, and her tone becomes plaintive. "Why are you doing this to us?"

Peter answers her by backhanding her across the face. The force of the blow rocks her head to the side. "I told you to shut up."

You son of a bitch, you are so on my kill list now. Rage rises and climbs over her fear of being locked up in this place. She jerks against the shackles and tries to lunge forward, but the chains are short, and Peter easily steps out of her reach. The men laugh as they leave the basement without looking back. What little light followed them through the open door quickly retreats when they slam it shut.

The basement is a dark prison. *Typical, so freaking typical.* Eliza peers through the gloom for something, anything, that may help her escape or at the least get her above the water line. Nothing—nothing but putrid water, columns, and plenty of shackles to bind Shashenka's unfortunate victims.

A sob follows a whimper, and she knows Dmitri is crying. Matt's search results echo in her mind; she can't help wondering how many years Dmitri has endured imprisonment and torture beneath the Belyakov estates. *Was this why Dmitri only served part-time in the Druzhina after the rebellion?* Unless Dmitri answers that question, she'll never know.

In a soft tone Eliza calls out to him, "Dmitri, you're not alone—I'm here. I need you to stay strong with me." While it's her fault he's being punished this time, something tells her that Shashenka takes any excuse he can to further torment Dmitri. Her hatred for the devil vamp finds a new level to occupy.

Her words don't seem to soothe him, and when he continues weeping, Eliza decides to hum the song that calmed him on their last day in Novgorod. She doesn't know when or where she first heard it, or even its name, but she wishes she did—the melody's simultaneously simple yet complex score is haunting and beautiful. Dmitri's sobbing stills, and in between hitches of his breath he faintly hums a few notes along with her. She closes her eyes to listen to him; strangely, it comforts her too.

Several hours later Peter and another guard return to the waterlogged basement and unshackle Eliza, shoving her up the stairs. She's filthy and wet, so she is surprised they cart her through the villa with no regard to the soggy trail she's leaving behind. They take her to a semiprivate sitting area in one of the cubicula off the primary piano nobile's central hall. Shashenka sits on a divan and watches them enter the room. The malicious grin on his face triggers terror; she doesn't know when, but she is certain that she has seen him look at her that way before.

The men drag her to a stop a few feet in front of Shashenka and force her to kneel before their master. *Goblin king.* No, she decides, Matt's description is better. The depraved devil vamp rises and approaches her in slow, catlike steps, the sinister smile plastered across his repugnant face.

Eliza swallows hard and looks down. She recalls what Dmitri once said about Shashenka's perverse enjoyment of torture; defiance or outward response will prolong the ordeal. Somehow she must conceal her fear and not give her master any reason to drag out this encounter.

Shashenka's hand jerks her chin upward, forcing her to look at him. "Sweet Eliza ... sweet, sweet Eliza. Whatever am I going to do with you?"

The question is rhetorical, she knows, and his tone is calm, quiet. But instinct tells her this is a rattlesnake's tail—it stops rattling just before the strike. Not wanting to provoke him further, Eliza stares at him without a word, but it only seems to enrage him. He shoves her head to the side, and his claws rake her chin as he releases his hold. "Before I punish you, I need to know about your little holiday with Dmitri."

Eliza glares; her refusal to answer is met with a violent slap that knocks her to the floor. She groans but doesn't cry out.

"This will be unpleasant for you if you try defying me. I'll consider that very unfortunate—you normally please me so much."

Shashenka grabs her by the throat and wrenches her back to her knees, his hand poised to strike. "Why is Dmitri with you?"

She has no idea what he knows, or doesn't, and her mind works furiously to find an answer that won't jeopardize her plans or their lives. Drawing a steadying breath, Eliza puts a slight tremble into her voice. "I'm sorry, Master. I took him with me because he's not been on holiday since the end of our first month in Novgorod. I was trying to help him."

Shashenka's baleful laugh rumbles through the room. "I thought you hated him, despised the day you met him."

Eliza lowers her gaze to the floor, wondering if she can use that angle to get out of this predicament. She's still trying to decide when Shashenka bellows, "My patience is wearing thin."

"I'm sorry, Master." She looks up at him, thinking fast. "Do you recall our encounter after my first trip to London? I joked about being a monster—you said I wasn't one."

His eyes narrow, but he waits for her to finish. "You were right—I'm not a monster. I can't stand Dmitri, but I feel guilty for what I did to him. I guess ..." She pauses. "It's easier for me to hate him when he's not out of his mind."

Her reply seems to enthrall the despicable goblin king. *Another point to me—he's buying this load of bullshit.*

"Oh, sweet, sweet Eliza ... how you humor me. You're trying to fix what you broke, so you can what? Break him again? Delightful."

Her tone is flat. "No. I'm not a monster. I can hate him without breaking him. I just don't want to feel guilty about it anymore. The way he is now sickens me, and I can't stand to look at him."

He paces in front of her. "Tell me, did your little get-away help? Did you have fun?" His tone is back to quiet—dangerous. That means he's already formed a plan. She'd almost be impressed if he weren't such a detestable creature.

She pouts. "The last ten days were awful. It wasn't fun, and he's still out of his mind."

A full-throated laugh roars out as he tosses his head back. "You're a fool, Eliza. Dmitri is worthless to me. He can't even perform simple duties anymore. I wanted him left in Novgorod. What do you plan to do with him now?"

"I don't know, Master. I thought he'd be better and could go back to work, but he's not." She sighs and looks down at her hands. She honestly doesn't know how to reach Dmitri or restore his vacant mind. *He will never know how much I regret breaking him.*

Shashenka studies her for a long minute. "I've decided your punishment for going behind my back—for showing sympathy to your adversary."

"Yes, Master?" Fearful of what he may say next, she holds her breath.

"Maria also wishes to fix him, a useless endeavor, I may add, and while I'll admit that he brought me immense

pleasure before this mess, he's a waste of time and resources now." His wistful smirk turns into disdain. "Still, I
agreed to Maria's request, but only so long as we are here
in Venice. On the chance one of you succeeds"—he chuckles and raises an eyebrow in disbelief—"I think having
Dmitri in a special environment will prove the futility of
your efforts. You will learn a lesson about pitying others
and harboring guilt for someone not worthy of your con-
sideration."

"Excuse me, Master, I don't understand." *What is the
wretched devil vamp up to now?*

"The guards will deliver Dmitri to your quarters, where
he will stay until this little experiment is over. We shall
see if his mind is strong enough to withstand confinement
with a woman who despises him. That is, if his mind returns at all. Then, when you and Maria fail, Dmitri will be
put out of this coven."

Eliza ignores the threat of Dmitri's abandonment and
has to lock every muscle in her face to keep from smiling;
this is an unexpected gift, a chance to right her wrongs
against Dmitri. She keeps her tone appropriately sullen.
"Yes, Master."

"Oh, I almost forgot to tell you ... the rooms here are
different from what you had in the castle. There are no
shared suites, and only one bed."

"What?" Her heart races in a stampede of shock, fear,
and relief. "But Master, where is Dmitri supposed to
sleep?"

"Stuff him under the bed for all I care."

"But ..." Eliza gulps. Her duties often require bringing

men to her room, and the thought of anyone watching her have sex is repulsive. "What am I supposed to do with him when I'm entertaining someone?"

"Sit him in a chair, stand him in a corner, put him out in the hall, use him as a pillow. It's not my problem. Perhaps this will teach you to make better decisions in the future."

Eliza closes her eyes and shudders. "Yes, Master."

"Now, this is boring me." He looks toward the archway and signals to Peter, who is standing nearby. "Keep her here until I send one of the girls to show her to her room."

"Yes, Master." Peter bows his head.

"Oh, and sweet Eliza ..." She looks up, dreading to hear whatever may come out of his vulgar mouth next. "You need to clean up and get dressed into something more suitable. I expect your company tonight." He cackles. "In your room."

Mouth agape, Eliza watches him rise and saunter away.

CHAPTER 9: DMITRI

Lost in the Abyss

For the first time since Dmitri began trying to tear down the black walls, he manages to do it without Elizabetta's help. To his horror he finds himself in the dark, with water up to his knees and the cold, hard weight of shackles around his wrists. *Is this real?* The rough stones against his back are eerily familiar. *I should know this place.* His eyes clench shut as he tries to find the memory.

Images of torture, imprisonment, and unbearable torment saturate his mind. Echoes of the past flood through him; it's terrifying. The darkness around him mangles the fragmented images as he rushes to link them together. He remembers, but he cannot bear the return of these memories. This basement is one of many prisons he's been locked in before, and he knows what comes next—cutting, stabbing, slicing, beating, and whipping.

I have fallen from the void into the abyss. Is the void a black hole to the abyss, or is it the other way around?

Pieces of his life fell into the abyss one at a time long ago, but somehow he plunged into the void himself, became its prisoner, and he doesn't recall how it happened. He's lost so many things to the abyss—Elizabetta, his role as a Druzhina. But the void ... in the void he has lost himself.

Is this reality or the manifestation of a broken mind? Dmitri gradually becomes aware that he's been functioning on portions of a mostly absent brain for a long time, and the scrap he's using now is drowning in confusion. *I need help.* He searches the dark for a recognizable piece of himself, his life, even Elizabetta, but finds nothing. He is overcome by the overwhelming understanding that he cannot break free alone.

This is the abyss where I lost Elizabetta, and she is not here. This is the abyss where I lost everything, and nothing is here.

Memories taunt him—a certainty that someone will take him from this flooded basement for the next round of torture. Bile rises in his throat. He's not strong enough to endure it anymore. Past pain collides with this realization, the weight of it more suffocating than the black walls of the void. Tears spring to his eyes, and he's unable to hold back the cries twisting from his throat. The utter hopelessness of his existence swells inside him as the void tries to reclaim its prisoner.

Then through the weeping he hears a voice—her beautiful voice—humming a melody. He knows it well. Somehow, caught between this flooded prison and the blackness of the void, one ray of light has found him. Eyes closed, he allows her glorious voice to soothe his battered soul. "*Il mio tesoro"*—centuries ago he wrote it for Elizabetta.

The song stops abruptly, and Dmitri hears splashes and the rattle of keys. Someone is sloshing through the water. *I'm not ready for this.* His breath quickens and his pulse races—he expects their rough hands on him within seconds. A slight tremble down his spine explodes into uncontrollable shaking. But a clinking of chains comes from nearby instead. He's afraid to call out and draw attention to himself. *Are they taking someone away or bringing a new prisoner to these flooded depths?* Before he can make sense of it, the black walls of the void smash into him, and everything else ceases to exist.

Elizabetta, please, love, I need you to save me.

CHAPTER 10: ELIZA

Hurdles and Allies

Sally is the courtesan who shows Eliza to a bedroom on the third floor. The women say very little as Peter follows them; apparently Eliza is to be watched until Shashenka decides otherwise. Much to her annoyance, his presence leaves no opportunity to tell Sally what happened. An undertone of matching frustration is in Sally's voice as she points out the communal bathing room when they pass it on the way to Eliza's new bedroom. Wooden bathing tubs and buckets of hot water come to mind as she glances into the room. *Déjà vu ... am I Elizabetta?*

After Sally and Peter leave Eliza alone in the bedroom, her eyes sweep over the English furnishings and the suitcases near the armoire. Then her gaze drifts to the bed and freezes on it. *How am I supposed to do this?* Her mind whirls at the new developments as she unpacks. She must make this work somehow. A knock at the door disrupts her thoughts.

"Miss Ross, we are here for the luggage." A thin, dark-haired man and a blond teenage boy—local vampires—step into the room. She stands aside and watches them take the empty suitcases away.

She's still taking in her surroundings when Charles and Leonard—two of Shashenka's personal guards—deliver Dmitri to the room. She instructs them to seat him in a chair in the corner, but they rudely shove him forward and turn to leave. "Master says he's your problem. You make the idiot sit—we did our job," Leonard says and turns to follow Charles out into the hall. Both are laughing as the door slams shut behind them.

Dmitri stares at the floor, seemingly unaware of the guards' rudeness. His wet, filthy clothes drip foul foundation water onto the rug. He needs a bath as much as she does, and Eliza opens the armoire to select clean outfits for them. She stops when Shashenka strolls in unannounced. *Crap, he didn't even give me time to clean up.* The disgusted look on the goblin king's face tells her that she won't be allowed to help Dmitri right now. Shashenka lies across the bed, fluffs a pillow, and tucks it behind his back. Eliza grabs Dmitri's hand and starts toward the door.

"Where do you think you're going?"

She gulps. "To find someone who can help him clean up, Master."

"No, you're not. This will be his first test. We shall see if he's truly out of his mind still."

Can't he tell Dmitri isn't right? Ah, I see ... he's testing me too. Embarrassment over the disgusting implication delivers a lump to her throat. Her eyes dart around the room. There is no privacy—not even a dressing screen.

"You're wasting my time, Eliza, and I have no patience for you right now."

"I'm sorry, Master." Eliza guides Dmitri to the chair but turns it to face the wall before she urges him to sit. An odd gratitude for his detached state fills her, and she hopes that not one moment of her encounter with Shashenka registers in Dmitri's mind. *Not ideal, but better than him staring at the bed.*

But Dmitri's presence proves a huge distraction for her, worse than the baby monitor in Arecibo. Eliza cringes at the memory. *What is this, the next best thing to Internet live-streaming, you maggot?* Terrified that Dmitri will have a sudden lucid moment, she keeps darting her eyes his way, missing the cues that normally guide her through one of her sessions with the goblin king. Shashenka, of course, refuses to leave until she fully satisfies him in the many bizarre ways he prefers. It's midmorning before he leaves her—the room itself seems to breathe a sigh of relief.

When the door shuts behind him, Eliza grabs a nightgown and cleans herself as best she can using the pitcher of water and washbasin sitting on her dressing table. Her skin crawls with disgust—it's not enough—but shame and embarrassment keep her from going to the communal bathing room located on this floor. She can't face anyone else right now.

Dmitri. Eliza shoves the unpleasant thoughts aside, finds him a pair of pajama bottoms, and helps him change into them. One look at his disheveled appearance, and her guilt pushes against her other emotions. *It's my fault he's in this mess.* She seats him on the edge of the bed and washes the exposed areas of his body. His blank expression doesn't change, not even when she wipes the washcloth across his face.

Her eyes roam over his features. Even in this deplorable state, he is handsome to her. She allows a finger to trail over his high cheekbones and down along his jaw. *Why am I so drawn to him?* A long, slow sigh glides past her lips as she wonders if he'll ever be able to tell her the truth about her past.

The stress of the last few hours catches up with her, and she curls next to Dmitri on the bed and bawls with frustration. She is torn between wanting his mind back and hoping it doesn't return. *Gift.* She snorts. *A cursed blessing is more like it.* Having him so near could be disastrous for him; there's no way to know what his reaction will be if his senses return at an inopportune moment.

The thought of Dmitri becoming aware and watching her sexual encounters nauseates her despite his condition now. Then Eliza recalls one key phrase of the monster's command: "put him out in the hall." *Bingo! I will beat you at your game.* She will need help from the other courtesans and Maria to make it happen, but she will find a way to keep Dmitri out of the room when she's with a paramour.

With that decided, Eliza turns her attention to the man lying beside her. The planes and contours of his scarred body speak of strength beyond the physical power that is missing in his current mental state. As she did in Waiheke, she talks to him in a soft, reassuring tone hoping, begging for an answer—needing him in ways that she doesn't fully understand. Again her pleas fall on deaf ears, and exhaustion finally drags her into a fitful sleep filled with pleasant dreams and nightmares.

When she wakes it takes a moment to register that she's lying on her side—and for the first time, Dmitri is snuggled against her back. His right arm curls tightly around her waist, holding her, actually holding her against him. *This is really happening.* Eliza can feel his left arm under her neck, and her eyes follow it to the relaxed curve of his outstretched hand. It seems so right, so good—she doesn't want to wake him. Tilting her face up, she bumps his chin, which is touching the top of her head.

Dmitri appears to be soundly asleep. Eliza shuts her eyes, daring to enjoy the comforting sensation of his embrace. Compared with the men she's been forced to lie with as a concubine, and even to Matt, Dmitri is different; lying with him feels natural, though she's not sure he has any awareness that she is in his arms. It is that sense of naturalness, she realizes, that has always been missing from Matt's strong arms. *Is this because I am Elizabetta?* If not, it may mean that her physical attraction for Dmitri is stronger—or that she has fallen in love with him in spite of herself. Her fingers touch her lips, recalling the sensation of the few kisses they've exchanged. She can't deny she desires him, but within the chambers of her heart Eliza knows the truth—her feelings go much deeper than sexual attraction.

She must get up and ready herself for another night's work inside the inner lair. Not wanting to disturb him, she tries to pull away, but his grip tightens around her waist. Eliza rolls over and softly kisses his neck. Dmitri stirs. A brief smile appears on his face after his eyelashes flutter open and his gaze settles on her. But before the breath catches in her throat, his eyes go blank, unseeing. Her heart plummets just as fast. This time he doesn't resist as she sighs and moves off the bed.

Eliza grabs a clean outfit for herself and the clothes she laid out for Dmitri the night before and takes him to the bathing room. It's in the opposite wing, near the end of the hall and next to the staircase. She gapes as they enter— her mind wants to reject what her eyes see. Anyone bathing is fully exposed to all who may enter. There is no lock on the door. Four sinks with mirrors line one side of the room, and a single toilet is in a corner stall. Directly across from the main door stand four tubs with bare shower-heads—thin shower curtains hang as dividers between the tubs, but there are no curtains concealing the tubs themselves. Somehow she doubts that Shashenka uses a similar facility, and she wonders if he has a private shower located somewhere in the villa.

Eliza places their clothes on a bench in the middle of the room and leads Dmitri to a tub. To her relief he responds to her directions and begins to undress. After she turns his shower on, Eliza quickly slips around the curtain to the next tub, strips down, and starts her shower. The sound of the door opening and closing behind her freezes her for a moment, but whoever entered doesn't say a word. Several seconds later she hears the water running in the shower next to hers.

This is going to take some getting used to. After she rinses the conditioner out of her hair, she turns off the tap and wraps a towel around her body before peeking past the curtain at Dmitri. He's just standing there, and she assumes he's done—at least she hopes he washed himself. He accepts the towel she hands him, but his movements seem awkward to her as he rubs it over his body.

When they return to the bedroom, Dmitri's detached stillness indicates that he's already slipped away again. With a sigh Eliza combs his hair before doing her own hair and her makeup for the night ahead. She doesn't know what to do with him. She can't drag him along like a ball and chain all night while she goes about her duties—it may invite trouble from Shashenka—but she is afraid to leave him unattended. She must find someone to watch him.

They meander through and out of the villa, and Eliza seats Dmitri on a bench in the garden, hoping the high walls surrounding the perimeter will prevent him from getting lost while she returns to the mansion to find some of the other courtesans.

Sally, Stephanie, and Maria are sitting in a drawing room off the primary piano nobile when Eliza reenters the villa. "Good evening. Will you come with me to the garden? There's something I need to talk to you about."

Maria raises her eyebrows. "Is that something Dmitri?"

Eliza's unsure about involving the witch, but her choices are limited. She nods, and the women follow her to the garden; Dmitri is still sitting on the bench, the same blank expression on his face. *He hasn't moved an inch ... he's like a freaking zombie.*

"He doesn't look any better." Sally bends down to peer closer at his eyes.

Eliza tamps down the jealousy that pinches her insides when Sally sweeps his long bangs away from his face. "Improvement is minimal at best. He's doing a little better at following directions, but he's still mostly out of it."

"I had hoped your time together in Waiheke would be the turning point." Maria kneels before him and physically checks him over. For a brief moment her gaze seems to lock with his, but just as fast his empty stare returns. "How often does he exhibit awareness of things around him?"

"There's no pattern to it. It can happen minutes or hours apart, but it is happening at least once daily now." Eliza glances at the other women. "We need a system of watching out for him. I'm afraid to leave him alone and thought maybe we could take turns."

Maria nods. "It's a good idea. He shouldn't be left alone."

The others agree, and Sally offers to talk with Isabelle and Christina and seek their help. Given Stephanie's obligations outside the villa, her assistance will be limited, but Eliza is grateful nonetheless.

"I'll take a turn whenever I'm around, but I'm meeting Vincente tonight. I really need to go now." Stephanie pats Dmitri's leg. "You're in safe hands, and your friends miss you. I hope you feel better soon."

There is slight relief that he doesn't acknowledge Sally or Stephanie's gestures either. Chagrined, Eliza looks away to hide the resentment etched on her face. Jealousy has never been an issue for her before, but since she admitted the feelings she has toward Dmitri, it seems that a possessive streak has gained a foothold.

Impulsively she turns to the witch as Stephanie walks away. "Can you meet me here at the start of each night, Maria? I feel uncomfortable leaving him alone in the mansion or waiting with him where Shashenka is likely to come harass us."

"Yes, I think it's best we keep him out of sight as much as possible. There's no telling what Shashenka will do if Dmitri starts to come out of this state, and we don't need his progress set back—or worse."

In what alternate reality can this get any worse? Sally voices her agreement with the witch just as Charles hollers from the back door, "Master has a couple of men waiting for you ladies. It's time to get to work, girls."

"Let them know we're on our way," Eliza shouts back. She looks at Dmitri and reaches to brush his hair from his eyes again. "We'd better go, Sally. Thank you, Maria. One of us will give you a break soon."

Sally hooks her arm in Eliza's and rolls her eyes. "Shall we? Fix that smile on your face, and we'll go do what we do best."

Eliza groans. "There's other things I'd rather do best, but let's get this done."

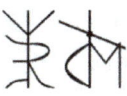

Unlike the foreign ambience of Novgorod, Venice sings to Eliza, and she quickly adapts to Venetian life. If it weren't for her duties in the inner lair, she would enjoy this city even more. She relishes strolling along the piazzas and prefers the gondolas over the motorboats for transportation; while drifting along the canals she can almost peel back the layers of modern changes and see Venice as it once was long ago. *Was this city my home in another era?* She tries not to think about the possibility, but the longer she's here, the closer the questions linger near the surface.

Within a few days of Eliza's arrival, she settles into her new routine with the help of the courtesans and Maria. Eliza is grateful that the arrangement keeps Dmitri out of the bedroom when she's working. To her surprise, Shashenka mostly ignores their efforts to look after Dmitri; he seems more interested in running his businesses and satiating his hunger for blood and women. Unexpectedly, it also frees her to enjoy outings with the other women whenever they have time to shop or take strolls in between entertaining paramours.

But it's the opportunity to further her plans against Shashenka that she appreciates the most. The nights away from the villa provide cover for Eliza to meet Vincente Falco two weeks after arriving in Venice. When Stephanie arranges a date for Eliza outside the inner lair, Shashenka doesn't question it; some of Stephanie's clients seek a second courtesan for themselves or an associate. Within minutes of leaving the estate, Stephanie pilots the motorboat to an unimpressive apartment building in the Dorsoduro District. Doubtless she's been here many times before; she ties the boat to a mooring pole and smiles at

Eliza as she announces their arrival via intercom. To Eliza's surprise—she expected Vincente to buzz them in—a short, stocky dark-haired man opens the door. Stephanie embraces him and the two exchange greetings before she turns to introduce Eliza.

"This is Vincente Falco—Vinnie, if you prefer. Vinnie, this is Eliza Ross, leader of the vendetta against Belyakov."

"*Ciao.*" He smiles and kisses the back of Eliza's hand before escorting them inside. "It's a pleasure finally meeting you. I've heard so much from Stephanie and Matt that it seems like we already know each other."

"Same here." *It's good to finally put a face to the name.* Eliza smiles as he leads them up the marble staircase to an apartment on the second floor, but she startles when she realizes they're not alone. Dark shapes stand in the shadowy hallways, and Vincente explains that this building is his pack's headquarters. It's her first glimpse at the potential supporters of her revolt against Shashenka—that is, if Vinnie agrees to help her.

Though the building appeared small and narrow from the outside, Vincente's apartment is spacious and comfortable. He motions for the women to sit as he opens a beverage console and mixes a drink from amaretto, coffee, cognac, and cream. Smiling, he raises the glass. "My weakness. It's too bad your kind lost the ability to appreciate fine food and drink, or I'd fix a beverage for you."

The last time Eliza tried human food was months ago, when she was held against her will in the psychiatric ward of a hospital in Bozeman, Montana. She shudders at the memory. "Trust me, for a vampire fine food and drink are not so fine."

For a while the conversation remains polite chitchat; then Vincente subtly turns the topic to the Belyakov coven. "So far my pack reports normal activity at La Perfezione. Your friend Matt and I are discussing ways to make their stay a little uncomfortable."

Oh, he's smooth. "How so?" Intrigue wrestles with concern—she's not sure making Shashenka uncomfortable is a good idea.

"Most of the vampires in this city are centuries old and prefer to keep their existence hidden. They often retreat to their lairs and don't venture out when Belyakov is in town—it's safer for them that way, since your coven's blatant feeding habits often attract the attention of the *polizia*. As the body count rises, the *polizia* get more nervous and spend too much time in our territories for our comfort." He pauses and sips his drink. "If the packs disperse through the city and help the unwitting *polizia* patrol by securing the residential sectors, the Belyakov vampires will have to go away from the city to gather their victims."

I wish Matt were here—I still don't get what he's talking about.

He smiles at her apparent confusion. "Should the *polizia* notice that large groups enter but do not leave the city, they will seek the location where the missing were last seen."

That is something Shashenka is smart enough to avoid, which means he may have to forego his weekly snack. *I wonder if this is Vinnie's plan or if Matt came up with this lousy idea?* "I think that will make him angry, not uncomfortable."

Vincente chuckles. "It will do both."

Now she can see where he's going with this. "And if they can't hunt within the city, it is easier for the werewolf packs to continue their surveillance."

"*Esattamente*—see, uncomfortable for Belyakov." Vincente pats Stephanie's hand. "You are correct—our new friend here is very sharp."

"Yes." Stephanie inclines her head in agreement and says, "Possibly smart enough to end Shashenka."

No possibly about it—I will end him. "Do you have the numbers to provide that level of protection to the humans and continue watching the villa?"

He grins and winks at Stephanie. "We've been proactive in helping you."

They have gained the support of neighboring packs within and outside the city. According to Vincente, those wolves will join the fight when she and Matt are ready to move against Belyakov. An unsettling thought arrives uninvited, and Eliza can't ignore it. "Won't this risk conflict between the Venice werewolves and vampire covens if the wolves are hindering their feeding too?"

"That little rogue Matt hired has also been helpful in that regard—when she's not off stalking somewhere. Teresina? Yes, that's her name."

Just how much has Matt shared with this guy? Eliza sits forward. "I understand she's a vampire. How does that help you with the werewolves?"

"She is calling in favors—local vampires will turn a

blind eye to the new werewolves in the city. Some of the smaller vampire covens will fight with us."

Stephanie says, "Venice is a unique balance of the shadow realms—there is less animosity and fighting between the vampires and werewolves here than in other locations around the world."

The comment piques Eliza's curiosity. *If I am Elizabetta, does that explain why I took to Matt when we met?*

Before she and Stephanie leave, Vincente introduces Eliza to his pack; they're a tough but suave-looking bunch of werewolves. She appreciates the chance to meet those who will fight alongside her when the time comes. Her only concern is their battle skills; she doesn't want another overconfident pack slaughtered because they've misjudged their enemy. The reminder of Josh's lost pack sends a quick, sharp pain through her. Still, Matt has done well in finding allies among the werewolves, and she's grateful for their support. *I really need to thank him next time I see him.*

As their conversation winds down, Vincente says, "When we meet next week, I think you'll be pleasantly surprised, Eliza."

She arches an eyebrow, still lost in her thoughts. Stephanie and Vincente exchange a knowing look. "Just tell her, Vinnie. The suspense will drive her crazy."

Vincente bows his head. "Your friend Matt will be joining us. He's taking advantage of being in the area and wants to see you."

"Seriously? Matt's going to be here?" A ripple of excitement courses through her. She hopes she'll have the chance to spend one evening, or at least part of one, alone with him—there are areas of Venice she'd like to share with Matt. Aside from enjoying the city nightlife together, they may have new information to discuss. Perhaps she'll finally understand why Venice seems to touch her soul.

CHAPTER 11: DMITRI

Ascending the Gates of Hell

Sounds and dim light filter in from outside the void; his nerves feel raw with sensory overload. Dmitri sits on a bed in a room that looks vaguely familiar, but again he doesn't know where here is or how he got out of the waterlogged prison. Painfully he searches through his memories and finds them a jumbled, unrecognizable mass of images; there are no reference points for when the memories were created or how much time elapsed between each one. Dmitri doesn't know how long it has been since his last coherent thought—it could be days or centuries.

His eyes roam the room. *Where am I?* He's motionless, afraid even to blink lest the darkness finds him again.

Sifting past the confusion in his mind, he locates the last complete string of memory he has: Eliza's explosion at him in the great hall at Novgorod. He can still feel the echo of pain, and his heart constricts. *My Elizabetta is gone.* It makes his disjointed memories suspect, as too many of them contain images of Eliza—the imposter—and he knows that she wants nothing to do with him.

Fractured images float like apparitions in his mind. Lying in his cell in Novgorod ... dents in the floor of the racquetball court at Big Sky ... standing in Eliza's room. Dmitri latches onto that image—he can't breathe. Even now he can feel the way her eyes blazed with an intensity that startled him. Echoes of her words come back: "... didn't destroy me ... ignited me." He doesn't know what that means. The nerves in his hands tingle with the phantom sensation of touch—her hands as she clutched his to her chest—and it pits hope and desire against dread and aversion. *Why did she ... what does it mean?*

More contradictory images and sensations flicker past him. Elizabetta talking softly, holding him, her arm around his waist. Eliza and her wolf friend, Matt, swimming in the ocean. Next a recollection of being towed to shore comes forth, but he cannot tell if it was Elizabetta or Eliza. *I would never swim with that imposter and her wolf lover.*

None of this makes sense, and Dmitri is certain that his tormented mind is mocking him. Rationally he knows Elizabetta and Eliza are not two people but rather a divide he created to separate who she was once and who she is now. Guilt drapes over him, its weight oppressive, the pain excruciating. His heart buckles under the weight of truth—there's no room to both love and hate her, to turn away and still be there for her. Dmitri has broken his pledges and promises to protect her and ultimately win her hand again. It is unacceptable and baffling that he's done this to her.

Where am I? Where is she? I need to find her. Dmitri steps into the hall outside the room. He doesn't know which direction to go, and though he recognizes the curved archways and marble floors, he can't place them. Their familiarity haunts him—he almost panics and retreats to the bedroom. Unsteadily he walks to a window at the near end of the hall and looks out. It's nighttime; the curtain is open and moonlight reflects off a canal. Gondolas and motorboats navigate the waterway. *Venice. La Perfezione?* Dmitri's heart begins to race. His hold on reality is tenuous at best, and he's not ready for it to slip away—not yet.

What am I doing here? How did I get here? Another memory tugs at his heart: this is where he stayed when he first brought Elizabetta into the coven.

"Dmitri, there you are!"

A voice he recalls—a new voice—breaks his precarious hold on the world outside of the void, and he tumbles back into the darkness. Only this time it's different; the black walls are translucent and outside images remain discernible, like he's looking through smoke-colored glass. The images become sharper, clearer. Sounds reach his ears; he understands some of what is being said, but he's unable to mutter a word himself.

A black haze shrouds his vision again. The void is trying to take him—he's oscillating between walls of nothingness and life. He pushes against a wall, holds it at bay. *I can't go back.* His body suddenly feels numb, heavy, but his eyes cling to the blond woman before him.

I know her. Sally! Her hand closes around Dmitri's wrist, and she tugs him along the hallway. He stumbles after her as they descend three flights of stairs. As she leads him outside to the pool house she says something about Maria, but he can't put a face to that name. He doesn't resist when Sally shoves him into a shower room and tells him to change and join her at the pool. Somehow he manages to do that much, but at the water's edge the battle against the void momentarily surrounds him in darkness, and the world falls away from him again.

When his sight returns he discovers that he is at the bottom of the pool. He lies there holding his breath as he tries to clear his head. The sudden appearance of a woman above him startles him. *The witch. Maria.* She grabs his arm and pulls him to the surface. *Where did Sally go?*

Maria touches his shoulder and encourages him to let go and float. "You seem better. Can you hear me?"

He still can't force words to his tongue. It's as if parts of his body have forgotten how to function or have disconnected from his brain. *What did the void do to me? How do I repair the damage?*

"On the outside chance you can hear me, I need to tell you to be careful. Shashenka is losing patience with this state you're in." She rotates to float and takes his hand in hers. "If you don't snap out of it, Shashenka may lock you up, kill you, or cast you out of the coven. I've done everything I can think of. I don't know how to help you."

Dmitri stares up at the night sky and tries to understand, but he doesn't have the strength to both fight the void and comprehend what she's trying to tell him.

"Many of the courtesans are doing what they can. Eliza is most at risk—her interactions with you have put her in a dangerous position with Shashenka."

Eliza, not Elizabetta. The latter loved him, but the other hates him. Dmitri's mind rejects that Eliza would risk anything for him. *Not possible.* Her actions backed her words and conveyed her feelings; it's unthinkable that she'd help him now.

Maria's tone oozes exasperation. "Can you hear anything I'm saying? Do you understand that you're going to get cast out or worse if you don't break free of this mental quagmire?"

Memories erupt and overwhelm him. His is a life of incredible loss and unbearable suffering. The recent images of Elizabetta—Eliza—cupping his face, swimming with him, holding his hand—must be false memories, imaginations from the abyss. *Eliza hates me. Elizabetta is gone.*

Dmitri sinks below the surface of the pool, recalling the agonizing hours spent in dark cells—too familiar, too comfortable, too terrifying. A solitary ray of light fixes a ghostly image of Elizabetta before his eyes. Torment, pain, the alterations of Elizabetta's mind, Eliza's hatred—

I've damned myself. He sought the void—it was the only way he could cease to exist, and now it's too late for him to escape. Deliberately Dmitri opens his mouth, fills his lungs with water, and stops fighting the darkness.

Instead of finding himself in the pitch-black stillness, he realizes that he's lying face down on the pool deck. Maria's hand strikes his back repeatedly as he coughs and sputters. "Stop acting like a gobshite and pull yourself together. We need you ... Eliza needs you."

Now he's sure this is another delusion born in the anguish of his devastated mind. Maria seldom swears or loses her temper, and he knows that Eliza doesn't want or need him. With this certainty in place he doesn't resist when imaginary Maria guides him to the pool house and instructs him to shower and dress. He marvels at how the hallucinations have displaced the nothingness of the void. But more than that, he wonders why.

When he exits the building, Maria is waiting for him—she's dressed, her red hair tidily coiffed. She takes his hand and walks him to the main garden, where several vampires are gathered. *I know this place.* Dmitri tries but fails to recall the exact memory as he watches the locals usher a group of humans toward Shashenka.

He must be insane from hunger. His mind flickers between the darker recesses of the void and staying in this memory a little longer. The vampires spring on their prey. Dmitri doesn't move. Maria thrusts a young woman toward him and commands him to drink. The burning ache at the back of his throat mixes with the scent of the human's blood, and his fangs part his lips. Instinct guides him even though his mind is shouting that this isn't real. Several long seconds pass before Dmitri realizes the woman is drained dry and nothing further will come from her corpse. He gently lowers the body to the ground and closes the woman's now sightless eyes. *Why does this seem ...* He shakes his head. *Is this real?*

Dmitri struggles to separate dream, memory, and reality, but the walls start to build and encase him within their layers again. A torrent of confusion washes over him; not for the first time he suspects that he has lost his mind. Then he hears Elizabetta's voice and tries to find her in the darkness of the void. *Elizabetta, where are you? I need you.*

A burst of bright light clears his vision for a mere second, but that is all he needs to see the horrific scene unfolding before him. A large group of vampires has assembled on the other end of the primary piano nobile. *What ... the garden. How did I get here?* Most stand motionless near a huddled form in the center of the crowd, but a few flinch in unison when the whoosh of a weapon slices through the air and hits its target. A vindictive smile spreads across Shashenka's face as his arm swings a downward blow with the perverted naval cat.

A dozen thin strands of razor-sharp wire hang from the baton instead of the traditional nine cords. It's a weapon Dmitri knows too well—even in his muddled state he can feel the shredded flesh and the echoes of pain the weapon inflicts. It is meant to torture, not punish.

Shashenka's eyes narrow and his nostrils flare—he's enraged. *I've seen that look too many times.* Shock ripples through him. *This is real.* It's not a delusion within the void. Blood splatters the room as another savage blow strikes the victim—a woman. Her screams tear Dmitri further from the darkness. *I know that voice. Elizabetta!*

Without thought he launches his body into motion, frantically pushing past vampires standing there watching the spectacle. *I must stop this.* He's within feet of reaching her when he slides to a halt, unable to move. Panic swamps his senses. *Elizabetta!* Maria approaches and places a hand on his forearm, and he realizes the witch has locked him in an immobility spell. Sympathy shows in her eyes, but she turns and walks back toward Shashenka.

Her movements catch Shashenka's attention. He pauses, his eyes narrowing as they rake over Dmitri from head to toe.

The weight of what he's just done crashes over him. No one dares interfere with another's punishment without bringing torture upon themselves. Horror sends shudders through him that never reach the surface of his frozen body. An expectant silence fills the room, and for the first time Dmitri sees the cowering form on the ground in front of him. It's not her—not Elizabetta—it's the imposter, Eliza. Their eyes lock, and he sees her astonishment that he of all people would attempt to protect her. *It was a mistake. What have I done?* Anger forces reason to the surface. It doesn't matter whether it's Eliza or Elizabetta; Shashenka shouldn't be assaulting any of the women like that.

He wants to shout or argue, but his pleas remain trapped inside his immovable body. *Please, Master, spare her.*

Shashenka's malevolent laugh breaks the heavy silence hanging in the room as he spins around and rushes toward Dmitri. Others murmur, their voices growing louder as Shashenka brings the weapon to bear against Dmitri's chest. Unable to move or recoil from the hit, Dmitri stands rigid, and searing pain lights his nerves on fire. A guttural cry echoes and dies inside him. His eyes remain riveted on the horrified expression of the woman on the floor. He's truly gone mad—all he sees is Elizabetta, and he knows it can't be her. *Eliza.*

She starts to move as if to crawl away. *Don't move.* She freezes in his gaze. More blows from the naval cat shred his flesh, and Eliza flinches at each blow. Then her eyes blaze with a murderous look he's seen long ago. *When? Why?*

She staggers to her feet—there's blood dripping from her torn blouse. "Stop! If you need to punish me, then you punish me, not him. He's suffered enough."

The naval cat clatters to the floor as their evil master reaches for Eliza. He grabs her by the throat and pulls her closer to his face, their noses nearly touching. "You disappoint me, sweet Eliza."

"Master, please don't hurt—"

Shashenka's tone turns deadly quiet, but Dmitri still hears what he says. "I will not favor your plea, Eliza."

Her legs shake as she places a trembling hand around Shashenka's wrist. "It's not his fault. Leave him alone ... please, Master."

Why would she defend me?

Shashenka lifts Eliza by the throat and tightens his hold. Spittle flies from his mouth. "Your mercy for him disgusts me. He will be punished for what you have done."

What did she do? What is going on here? His mind struggles to comprehend and accept the madness around him; no matter how hard he tries, he can't reconcile what he's seeing and hearing with the gulf he knows exists between Elizabetta and Eliza. *How much time has passed since that night in the great hall?* The woman defending him now is someone he doesn't know. He swallows hard and takes a deep breath. He needs Eliza to make eye contact—he needs to see the truth that may be hidden there. Elizabetta has never been able to lie to him. Her expressions and actions always give her away, and Dmitri needs to know if something of his Elizabetta remains.

Before any of it can make sense to Dmitri, Shashenka gives orders to his guards to take them both to the wine cellar. Their master's tone rings with contempt. "They want to stand for each other's punishment so much—then let them watch the other take their penalty." He orders one chained to a chair and the other placed in the shackles against the racks.

Now Dmitri's confusion battles terror; this is all too real, and this time the pain won't be visited solely on him. The woman—he isn't sure of her name anymore—has put herself in peril for him, though he doesn't understand why she's done such a thing. *Is she crazy?* Dmitri's mind mocks him—if anyone is insane it's more likely he.

He tries to clamp down against his rising fear as the guards drag the woman down the hall ahead of him.

She's resisting and trying to break free of their grasp. One of the guards strikes a savage blow across her face— Dmitri catches a glimpse of the malice in her expression as she turns her head and spits in the guard's face. A sinking feeling grows inside him, and it's a tragic truth he can no longer ignore—somehow a part of Elizabetta has returned to Eliza. But secretly his heart soars. *My Elizabetta!*

CHAPTER 12: DMITRI

Salvaging Wreckage

When Shashenka and the guards finally leave them in the wine cellar, there's no relief for Dmitri that the vicious assault is over. Elizabetta, unconscious, is hanging heavy against the shackles binding her wrists. One look at her gaping wounds—deep slices, a nearly eviscerated torso, and blood pooling at her feet—and his heart breaks with the reality of what he's done. He only just found her again, and this is the future he's brought her to.

New grief coats Dmitri's heart as time drags on—his selfishness has brought this upon them both. The darkness pulls at him until once again he's no longer sure what is real or fantasy in his broken mind.

Elizabetta is true. Dmitri turns to memories that are real, but he can only recall the tragic turns their lives took after the failed rebellion. Once again he regrets that Shashenka listened to Vladimir and Maria's pleas for mercy. Execution would have ended this miserable existence centuries ago, and neither he nor Elizabetta would have endured the nightmare their lives became.

It started with his punishment to reprogram her mind, something she never wanted and even fought against when her sentence was first pronounced. For centuries she endured a catatonic state, only to wake and have her mind completely wiped and reset. Dmitri was forced to reprogram her in Montana, far from the coven; her accusations that night at Novgorod are true. *I've ruined her, destroyed her life.*

It was worse for her, and for him, after she was brought to the estate at Big Sky. Nausea sweeps through him as he remembers the order to rape Elizabetta, to break her will, to force compliance to their master's demands; it sealed her fate and trapped her in the identity of Eliza Ross, concubine of Belyakov's inner lair. The incident is clearly etched in his memory. He couldn't do it—he'd never rape any woman, least of all her. They quietly agreed to stage the encounter, both understanding the consequences if they didn't comply with their master's demands, but it wasn't enough. That night she shattered—pieces of her fell through Dmitri's fingertips despite his efforts to hold her together.

Now Elizabetta has angered Shashenka again. The vile monster will target and punish her for even the tiniest infractions—Dmitri understands that ruthlessness better than most. *What have I brought her to?*

Everything has been his fault, from the very beginning. Elizabetta once pleaded for him to end her life, something he's considered before but always refused to do. *I can give her this much.* He may not be able to release himself, but he can set her free. He loves her enough to stop being self-ish and give her soul the freedom it deserves.

He looks forlornly at Elizabetta's slumped body hang-ing from the shackles and makes the decision to drain her. She cannot survive if she is bled out—it will allow her to gently slip away from this ruined life. Dmitri's hands shake as he caresses her cheek before wrapping his arms around her and lifting her weight off the shackles. For a moment he holds her tight, then turns his head and press-es a lingering kiss to her neck.

"Elizabetta ... *amore, ti amo e non smetterò mai di amarti.* I am sorry that I condemned you to this life. You were cursed the moment we met, and I will never forgive myself for destroying such a beautiful creature as you. Please forgive me, love. I will follow you as soon as I can."

His lips brush her skin once more. Then his fangs ex-tend to her jugular vein, and she moans as if he's about to tear her throat out instead of setting her soul free. The painful sound rips a larger hole in his heart. *I must set her free. I have to let her go.* He pulls back to look at her face one last time. Tears well in his eyes as she struggles to lift her head. *Oh God, not now. I have to end her suffering.* "I'm so sorry, love, forgive me."

Once more he positions his fangs and is about to break the skin, but her body tenses. Her voice carries a hint of fear. "Dmitri?"

He jerks back in surprise. The shackles go taut against her wrists as she gives a short cry of pain, and Dmitri's eyes widen with the realization that he hurt her more by letting go of her body. He's about to apologize, but her halting words stop him cold. "Dmitri ... is that ... you?"

"Y-yes, love." He steps closer and again positions himself to bear her weight. To be this close to fulfilling her request to die and having it interrupted batters his damaged soul.

Elizabetta's head tilts forward and rests against his collarbone. "Oh, thank God you're back."

He frowns—he's not certain he is indeed free of the void. Tenderly he places a kiss on the top of her head. He knows that he needs to end her life, but he doesn't want to do it while she's conscious. *I always fail her. I have to finish this.* He whispers again, "I'm sorry, love."

"Shh, don't." She clears her throat, but her voice cracks as she says, "It's my fault. I never meant to hurt you. I'm the one who is sorry."

A muddled memory of similar words comes to the surface, and he wonders if any of this is really happening. "You said that before?"

Elizabetta clears her throat again—this time her voice is stronger. "In my room in Novgorod. It was after you ... after that reprehensible night when I ..."

Muttering, mostly to himself, he scrambles to dig through disjointed memories that are so tangled he may never make sense of them again. But then another remnant of a conversation comes to mind. Confused, he says, "Didn't destroy you. Ignited you. You said that."

"Yes." Elizabetta takes in a raspy breath. "I was trying to protect ..."

"I don't understand, love." That has never been truer

for Dmitri than in this moment. It feels as if he's working with half a brain; there are gaping holes everywhere. Confusion and doubt erupt into uncontrollable tremors that wrack his body. Mere moments ago he intended to release her—take her life—and now that she's conscious he can't bring himself to do the deed. *What is wrong with me? Is this even real?* But if it is, he doesn't want her last memory to be of him murdering her. *What price will she pay if I allow her to live now?*

"At Big Sky I saw how fragile you were, and ..." She looks up at him in the dark, her eyes reflecting an intensity he hasn't seen in centuries. "I was afraid it was destroying you."

The world warps into an alternate version of reality that his mind staunchly rejects. No, he remembers her exact words: "I don't want you to touch me again—ever." He starts to back away from her, but she whimpers, and he remembers she's leaning on him for support. "I ..." Bewildered, he pulls his head back to look her in the eye. "I broke you, and you hate me. You sent me away."

"I don't hate you, Dmitri. I never have ... I'm trying to protect you."

Elizabetta lifts her head again. "God, Dmitri, we have so much to talk about, and I don't know if we have enough time. Trust what I'm saying is true. Seeing you like that ... it set me on fire! I accepted my role as a whore so that I can get close enough to kill that evil goblin king and burn his empire to the ground."

Dmitri's arms wrap around her as he dismisses her nonsensical words. *Impossible. This isn't real.* The past mangles the present until shock threatens to send him back to the void. He desperately reaches for something, anything, to keep him in this moment—keep him with her. Holding her with one arm, he raises a hand and drags it through his hair twice. He must fight against the return of the black walls; he must stay with Elizabetta, or he might be lost forever.

A breath catches in her throat—he thinks the movement inflicted more pain, and quickly he replaces the arm around her waist. But her soft tone carries a hint of relief. "I haven't seen you do that in months."

"Do what?"

"Hold your bangs away from your eyes. I've been sweeping your hair aside for you."

His eyes clench shut. *Nothing feels real.* "I can't—"

"Shh." Pulling her head back, she looks up, and their eyes meet in the dark.

"Is my name Elizabetta Rossellini?"

Those words strike a match which turns into a blowtorch that sets his mind on fire. *How did she hear that name? How does she know? Shit. Shit.* The answer can't be revealed—it's far too dangerous—but he's never wanted to acknowledge the truth more than in this moment. He lifts his gaze to the ceiling as the rational side of his brain argues with his heart.

She whispers, "Please ... tell me."

He needs to see her face to gauge how she'll react to the truth. But before he can decide what to say, he feels her lips softly brush a kiss at the base of his throat. *Elizabetta. Oh, my Elizabetta.* It burns away the remaining barriers that have separated them for much too long—he won't deny it anymore, and he doesn't care who knows. He lifts her body higher and his mouth finds hers. *She is mine! I will never let her go again.*

CHAPTER 13: ELIZA

Subterfuge

Oh crap. Eliza doesn't know what possessed her to kiss Dmitri, and she certainly didn't expect his response. The lingering sensation of his lips on hers merges with an explosion of questions in her mind. *Was that a yes? Am I Elizabetta?* Reason and logic cut through layers of pain and return her to her senses. She needs to focus. Shashenka could return any moment. Dmitri isn't in his right mind—he hasn't been for a long time—and he's merely mistaking her for a wife he lost long ago. Still, she can hardly ignore the way she intensified the kiss by parting his lips with her tongue. *What the hell was I thinking?* Now she's all too aware that his hips are between her legs; it's nearly impossible for her to fight the longing building inside of her. *Get a grip. He's doing this to help me, nothing more.* He's standing close, too close, but when he moved back the pain of the shackles cutting into her wrists was a clear indicator that he's been bearing her weight.

His lips press another kiss near her collarbone, and she's almost undone. *I'm not his ... don't feed his delusions. Focus, think.*

She doesn't understand her overwhelming need to protect him, or the longing she feels for him. What she needs are answers, but now she's hesitant to demand them. *What if I'm not Elizabetta, and I have to walk away from him?* The only certainty is that Shashenka will eventually take them from this cellar. If that deplorable monster discovers that Dmitri has recovered to any degree, he will do everything possible to break him again. More torture is likely in their future. Eliza can't bear to think about Dmitri suffering additional cruel treatment; he's already endured too much abuse.

Dmitri shifts; his grip loosens around her waist, but then his arms slide up her back, and she feels his hands lock around his wrists. His long, shaggy hair tickles her nose as he lifts his head. Eliza smiles and pictures the way he always pushes the hair from his beautiful eyes.

The sigh that whispers past his lips sounds almost relieved. He lifts her higher and uses his hips to brace her body and take more of her weight off the shackles. The movement sends another shot of pain through her. She tries not to moan, but a whimper escapes with a gasp. Her shoulders stopped throbbing some time ago, and she's lost feeling in her arms—they are beyond numb.

He starts to apologize, but she cuts him off. She's tired of hearing him say that he's sorry. "It's not your fault my flesh is torn like prayer cloths clinging to a tree."

Silence hangs heavy between them for a minute. *Crap, I*

shouldn't have said that. A dejected, almost guilty expression crosses his face as he looks down at her, but then she sees what looks like hurtful recognition in his eyes. *He knows he confused me with his lost mate.* She can only assume he regrets the kiss—she wants to take it back. *Can you say awkward? Great. All the more reason he needs to tell me the truth.* "Dmitri, I have to know ... am I—"

"Eliza ..." He grimaces but doesn't finish the thought.

Before she can push the issue, they hear a key turning in the lock on the door. She mouths, "Go" and feels her weight settle uncomfortably against the shackles again. It's not until the door swings open that she realizes Dmitri is crouched near the wall, his arms wrapped around his knees and a blank look on his face. *He's faking it, thank God.*

Warily she watches Peter reach up and unlock one and then the other shackle. There's a smirk on his face as Eliza drops to her knees, sending hot spikes of agony into every cell of her body. He gives her no time to get up on her feet but grabs her by the hair and jerks her upright. *I am really beginning to hate you.* She stumbles as he pushes her toward Dmitri and commands them to follow him.

Dmitri remains crouched and unresponsive—he's playing it well. Or is he playing it? She reaches for him, intending to give the appearance of dragging Dmitri along by his wrist, but her arms are useless—she can barely move them. He seems to understand that her weakened state threatens to expose them, and he clasps a hand over hers on his wrist to hold it there. *So he is aware.* Casting sidelong glances at him, Eliza tries to sift through whatever just happened between them. That kiss meant something, but what? The change in Dmitri leaves her baffled.

Is he well or not? Dmitri's not where he was before the mental breakdown, but he's not lost within that state anymore—at least he doesn't seem to be. Her stomach twists as she considers that truth and the awkwardness between them now. *I shouldn't have taken advantage of him when he's not himself.* She looks away, not wanting him to see her shame.

As they follow Peter through the villa, she notices Dmitri's eyes are taking in their surroundings. She tries to squeeze his wrist—he looks too alert—but the most she manages is a twitch in one finger. When Dmitri glances at her she shakes her head, squinting down at the floor. *I hope he understands.* By the time they reach the central hall, she is satisfied with his efforts—his head is down and his eyes focus on the floor just ahead of his feet. If she didn't know better, his behavior would fool her too.

Peter escorts them to their bedroom door and informs Eliza that they have fifteen minutes to clean up and return to the room; Shashenka will pay her a visit soon. After he leaves, her arms fall limply to her side. Dmitri's vacant gaze disappears as he rushes forward to seat her on the bed and asks where to find her clothes and toiletries. Without thinking, she says, "Your stuff is on the left side of the armoire and in the top two drawers. My stuff is on the right and in the lower two drawers."

Dmitri's eyes widen ahead of the confused look on his face. *Damn it, I forgot he doesn't know about our shared room.* "I don't have time to explain right now. Just grab our clothes so we can get cleaned up before Shashenka arrives."

Dmitri opens his mouth and closes it without saying a word. He avoids her gaze as he carries their clean clothes and toiletries to the communal bathing room. She's unsure how to take his silence and can well imagine what's going through his mind. She needs to figure out what to say about their shared living arrangements. *He's going to freak when he realizes we're sharing the bed too. What if he doesn't want to sleep with me? Shit, what if he does?* She's grateful to find the bathroom is empty at the moment. Dmitri turns the water on in the tub for her as she fumbles to undress—either his agitation is gone, or he's hiding it well. Briefly they argue when he tries to bathe her. She knows they cannot risk anyone seeing him take care of her, and such an intimate act would trigger too many conflicting emotions for her. *Double standard much?* She stifles a laugh; she's bathed him many times, but the thought of him reciprocating is oddly disconcerting.

When Dmitri ducks around the curtain and starts the water in the other tub, Eliza slumps to the bottom. She wonders how long it will take for feeling and control to return to her arms and hands; it will displease Shashenka if she's unable to touch him the way he prefers during their trysts. *Bet he'll yell at me or hit me for that too, even though it's his fault.*

Her wounds are still raw and healing—she bore the brunt of Shashenka's assault—and being shackled the entire time caused the near paralysis of her arms. She doesn't really know how long they were locked up, but it's obvious

Dmitri's injuries had enough time to heal. For once Eliza is grateful for Shashenka's sick weekly snack routine. At least Dmitri had enough fresh blood to speed his healing; she was denied the snack because her punishment for insolence was pending. *I'll show that devil vamp insolence on a whole new scale.*

Water swirls around her body, and her eyes close, but she tenses a moment later when someone enters the room. A familiar pair of hands settles on her shoulders. She recognizes the repulsive touch immediately—Shashenka. His hands slide down and fondle her breasts.

Can't he freaking wait five minutes? There is no way in hell I'm having sex with him in here. He can just put me back in the cellar if that's what he thinks he's doing. Shashenka bites her shoulder, gives a cruel pinch to her nipple, and tells her to hurry. Her heart races—Dmitri surely heard that—and she silently begs him not to intercede.

To her relief he doesn't move until after the devil vamp leaves the bathing room. Without a word Dmitri helps Eliza out of the tub. She blushes as he towels her off and dresses her before he reaches for his own slacks. *I was wrong. Helping him bathe and dress wasn't mortifying—this is.*

As he buttons his pants, he mumbles, "I can't do this ... I can't watch what he does to you."

Pluck a duck. She hasn't considered that this time he'll be alert enough to see the whole thing. *Oh, no.* She shakes her head yes and no, unsure what to do next. Aside from the humiliation of him witnessing what goes on with their master behind closed doors, she doesn't know if Dmitri is mentally strong enough to handle it or if it will enrage him to the point of interfering. Her fear spikes. *What if this drives him back over the edge? What if he goes batshit crazy and does something stupid, like attack the little maggot?* This is precisely what Shashenka intended, she understands—the perfect setup to give him a reason to torture Dmitri more. "Maybe you can get lost on the way back to the room. Watch for that monster to slink back to his hole, and then—"

"No!" His eyes are hard, cold. "I can't, I won't sit by and let him do this to you. Not now ... not ever again. I ... I can't."

She wants to agree, but to act now is too dangerous; all her planning will be for nothing. Her tone is harsh as she tells him, "We have no choice unless you're willing to expose that you're somewhat back in your right mind."

Dmitri says nothing—the way he glares at her speaks for itself. He snatches her hand and holds it around his wrist, half pulling her into the hall and toward the bedroom. She tries to resist—their argument isn't over—but he clamps down tighter on her arm and won't even give her a sideways look. Anger boils inside her, and she manages to move forward so that at least she's in front of him. *His mind may be back, but he can still act like a complete jackwagon.*

Then she sees Maria and Charles standing near the end of the hall, and a plan bursts into her mind. "Maria, Master is waiting for me. Will you take Dmitri and keep an eye on him for a while?"

If Maria is surprised to see them, she doesn't show it. "Yes, of course. I'll take care of him."

Dmitri doesn't show any sign that he's aware, but Eliza is certain he is angry at her. Whether it's for thwarting him this way, because he doesn't want Shashenka touching her, or for some other reason, she doesn't know. He can let her know what his problem is later—they must resolve this if they want to avoid a hostile sleeping environment, another situation they'll need to discuss.

The witch wraps an arm around Dmitri, but her eyes narrow as she glances over Eliza. "Are you all right? You look awful."

Thanks for stating the obvious. "I've been better, but I haven't regained full use of my hands and arms."

The witch purses her lips, then clears her throat and softly intones a spell in Latin. Eliza can feel a small measure of strength return to her body; she manages to flex and curl her hands a moment later. "Thank you, Maria." She nods at the witch and walks to her room with her back to Dmitri, not wanting to set him off should he decide to object again.

The spell Maria cast is just enough to allow Eliza to open the bedroom door. When she steps inside the room she finds Shashenka already sprawled on her bed and obviously very ready for her. She chokes back the bile that rises—she's never hated anyone more than him.

Shashenka doesn't hide his annoyance that she sent Dmitri away with Maria; his half-angry pout and narrowed eyes say it all. *Had you pegged right, didn't I, you little maggot-infested slimeball.* Eliza refuses to give him time to spring from annoyed to angry. Summoning courage and strength, she joins him on the bed as swiftly as her weakened state allows sprinkling in a few muttered apologies with her advances. It works to distract the repugnant little beast; soon he is selfishly lost in his own pleasure.

The sun rises before his bizarre proclivities are satisfied. *Lying there like a dead fish probably helped drive him off too.* By the time he leaves her room, Eliza is worn out and doesn't want to move, but she hurries back to the bathing room. Although many of her wounds are still healing, she relishes the ability to wash her hair and body. *I can't stand that monster's smell on me.* Her mind drifts to her long-range plans; she doesn't want to think about the conversation she'll have with Dmitri later.

Their earlier argument isn't as important as pressing Dmitri for answers. Eliza needs to know which way to go and whether he'll accept her plans or not. Either way her—their—best odds are in continuing to fool the goblin king. She must make him believe she is repentant. Dmitri needs to convince the evil creature that he is still out of his mind. A smile tugs at the corners of her mouth. At some point she needs to break the news to Dmitri that she's plotting another revolt. *I hope his hatred for Shashenka overrides any fear he may have to try again.* Aggressively co-opting the Druzhina is a priority, and his support will move her plans ahead faster. With his senses returning—perhaps holding intact—he may be able to help her regain lost footing there.

After Eliza dresses she goes to Maria's room to retrieve Dmitri. She is looking forward to spending the rest of the day with him, if they can get past the issue of their living arrangements. *Will he be okay about sleeping with me?*

Eliza isn't ready for sexual intimacy with him; she just wants the comfort of his arms for now.

But the possibility that a friendship or something more may develop isn't an awful thought. She knows something passed between them when they kissed in the cellar, and someday she'd like to explore the passion that hummed in its aftermath. Of course, if Dmitri has been celibate for centuries and mistook her as his lost mate, then it might explain the way he responded to her. She can only imagine how frustrated he must feel after centuries alone. *Probably another reason his mind went over the edge. Talk about self-control.* Then she dismisses the whimsical notion. Dmitri is far too good of a man, not to mention too good-looking, to have been alone for centuries.

Maria greets her at the door with a strange scowl on her face—Dmitri isn't there. "What do you mean, you don't know where he is?" Shock reverberates through Eliza—this isn't possible.

"I left him sitting here while I went to run a quick errand, and when I came back, he was gone. Before you say anything, yes, we looked—and, no we can't find him anywhere."

Eliza flees to start her own search. She checks every corner of the estate: each room, the flooded basement, the garden and courtyard, and even the boats moored along the villa's dock. *Shit! Shinola. Dmitri, where are you?* The rising sun scorches her skin, smoke rolling off the blackened blisters on her arms as she finally steps inside the villa. There is no sign of Dmitri anywhere.

No one has seen him—not Maria, not the concubines,

not the locals. Shashenka merely laughs at her concern when she informs him that Dmitri is missing. She doesn't know whether to feel relieved or horrified that the evil monster doesn't seem to care that Dmitri is gone.

Where did he go? Why did he go? Perhaps their time in the cellar together was enough to drive Dmitri away from her. Or maybe it came afterward, when they argued in the hall over Shashenka touching her. Does he think she's just a whore unworthy of him? Her heart constricts at the thought. *I shouldn't have said anything. Did I push him over the edge again? Did he run off to get away from me?* Dejection settles into her bones, and her feet drag in response as she walks back to their bedroom alone.

CHAPTER 14: DMITRI

Chasing Ghosts

Do I tell her? Can she be trusted? Dmitri glances over at Maria, who's busying herself at her potion table. The witch hasn't said a word since she led him to her quarters and settled him in a chair; it's obvious she hasn't perceived the change in him, and he's leery of revealing it himself. *Why isn't she curious?* Then he remembers the way Maria intervened when he tried to save Elizabetta from the beating on the primary piano nobile, and he grimaces—perhaps she is aware and is merely baiting a trap.

The witch's sudden motion to grab a bag startles him—she's about to leave the room. Maria hasn't said where she's going—doesn't even look at him—and they may not have another opportunity for a private conversation. *I have to free Elizabetta.* He's taking a risk in exposing the truth, but he needs to know if the witch will help him or doom him. "Wait."

Maria spins around so fast that the bag slides down her

arm and hits the floor. Her expression is cautious, almost as if she's uncertain that she heard him. He can see the questions in her eyes. Dmitri doesn't wait for her to speak first; he admits that he is aware and that he continues to struggle against losing himself.

"I would rather keep others from knowing ... at least until I'm certain that I'm capable of dealing with reality again."

"Understandable, given the circumstances." Maria locks her gaze on him but offers no other comment about the change. Her inscrutable expression leaves him even less sure of her trustworthiness.

No middle ground—all in or all out. Dmitri has already committed to this course, and it's too late to take it back. He dives straight onto the path that may be his undoing. "Can you tell me why Shashenka was punishing Eliza?"

The witch looks away and draws a deep breath. "He came to your room before twilight and saw her holding you. Eliza claims you still cry in your sleep, and she holds you until you calm down."

Our room. She holds me? There's so much he doesn't know, and it leaves him baffled. Sadness tinges Maria's words. "She argued with Shashenka over it—he disagrees with her willingness to help you." Her voice turns disgusted. "As usual, your master demanded an audience—everyone in the villa had to be present for the whipping. He told them she earned fifty lashes for insolence."

Dmitri gasps. The realization that his memories may not be as delusional as he thought is shocking. Then he remembers the bedroom he woke in when he first returned from the void. "Why are Eliza and I in the same room?"

Maria offers him the highlights, as she calls them, of his current circumstances. He doesn't know whether to celebrate the opportunity to be so close to Elizabetta or to run in fear. *Why is she helping me?*

His last clear memories are of her tirade in Novgorod, when she claimed to regret ever laying eyes on him. Everything else is too disjointed and tangled for him to sort reality from dream or delusion. He cannot comprehend how she went from hating him in Novgorod to caring for him now.

The witch is speaking again. "There are rumors that she began sleeping with you during your last night in Novgorod, and that it continued when she took you to Waiheke."

Dmitri digs furiously through his mind, searching for any recollection of being with her in Waiheke or sharing a bedroom here. Again it doesn't make sense to him; it seems unreal, impossible.

The dynamics of the situation have greatly changed since Novgorod, and a growing sense of urgency fills him. *I have to find a way to end this nightmare.* He pushes a hand through his hair, pausing at the crown of his head, and looks up at Maria. "Why did you stop me from protecting her?"

Maria's eyes flash in anger. "I'm trying to keep you from killing yourself. Your standing in the coven is the worst it's ever been. I saw the bloodlust in your eyes. Had I not stopped you it would have been worse for both of you."

Her words feel like a slap, and he winces. He wants to

destroy Shashenka, but Maria is correct—the explosive rage building inside is almost too much for him to contain. If he acts on the impulse to kill, it will put everything at risk. Despite their master's diminutive size, his lackeys are always within sight or shouting distance, the counterweight that tips the balance in a fair fight. The vile creature never hesitates to use his guards or Maria to neutralize a threat.

Dmitri looks hard at the witch; he can't figure her out. She acts like a friend and ally but then does all she can to follow Shashenka's bidding. He's not sure how Maria feels about Elizabetta, either. There was a time when she and Elizabetta were good friends, but he's noticed the strain in the witch's voice when she talks about her now.

What have I missed while I was in the void? As his thoughts settle on Elizabetta, his fear for her grows. *What is she up to? Shit, she's going to get herself killed. If I'm going to save her, I've got to get out of here.*

It takes every microgram of control he has to keep from bolting from the room. He's not quite ready to explicitly trust Maria. There's too much at stake—Elizabetta's life—and he's still pondering whether to go or stay, when Maria unexpectedly gives him the opportunity to escape. "Let's continue this in a few minutes. I need to collect some ingredients for the potion I'm working on."

Seconds after she leaves, Dmitri steps out of her room and sneaks through the villa. After liberating some money from the Druzhina safe in a main-floor office, he slips outside. Urgency drives him to action; for him this is an escape as much as it is a mission. *I have to get out of Italy.*

Dmitri bypasses the estate's boats and gondolas, instead leaping from decks to sidewalks to footbridges as he moves toward the mainland. Near *Fondamenta della Misericordia*—the place where he first laid eyes on Elizabetta—is the home they once shared. He tries to push the thought away and stick to his plan, but the pull is too much. Turning back, he races for their home—if nothing else, it offers a safe place to hide for the day. The sun will rise soon and prevent him from going much further until nightfall, but it's a start. At least he's out of the villa. *I will not fail her this time.*

The first rays of sunlight break over the horizon as he opens the front door. The furniture stands like abandoned sentinels in the brightening daylight. He and Elizabetta have owned this four-story villa for centuries, but the night before the botched rebellion was the last time Elizabetta was here; the place hasn't felt lived in since she was taken from him.

Dmitri pushes the depressing thought aside. In their bedroom he opens a cedar chest at the foot of the bed to retrieve the bedding, and the memories surge forth. As he makes the bed his mind drifts over the last time Elizabetta was here, the last time they shared a bed as mates—as husband and wife.

Optimism and euphoria filled their final moments together. The night before they were to launch their attack against Shashenka, they held a meeting with their comrades to go over the plans. The atmosphere was light—they were so sure victory was within their grasp. After Dmitri and Elizabetta retired for the day, they spent hours making love, the last time they would share that intimacy. That night they were ready to launch their attack when the guards and Maria seized them and changed their lives forever.

Dmitri runs his hand over the pillow on Elizabetta's side of the bed. He can't shake the feeling that something is amiss with her. The way she challenged Shashenka bothers him, and the glint in her eyes was the same one he saw centuries ago. She was telling the truth—she wants to kill Shashenka. He's sure of it. Yet Elizabetta's a weaker shell of what she used to be. *What does she know? What does she suspect?* Her recklessness will put her at greater risk of torture and even final death.

I have to find a way to get her out. If I fail ... He refuses to consider the outcome. Then he wonders how Elizabetta will react when she discovers that he fled La Perfezione. Dmitri knows he may not be able to return there unless it's to break her out—and first he must convince their friends in the Druzhina to help him cover their disappearance and keep them on the run after they escape. The idea is madness, but he can't see any other way out. Sorrow sweeps through him. If the Druzhina goes against him, he will have sacrificed the opportunity to spend his final days with Elizabetta. The risk is worth it—he has to keep thinking this, or what they have endured the last five centuries will remain a mockery of their lives.

Janek Novak, in Prague, is the first on Dmitri's list to help put his ideas in motion. The vampire is one of Shashenka's longtime business associates, but their rivalry is less than friendly; it is based on centuries of shoddy business dealings that have often left Janek cheated and without recourse. Janek always makes a point of watching Belyakov's people and often knows where they're at. Doubtless he hopes to use the information to get even with Shashenka someday.

Wherever Dmitri goes from Prague will depend on Janek's information and the Druzhina nearest to that area. Satisfied with his starting point, Dmitri closes his eyes and quiets his mind; exhaustion pulls him into a deep, dreamless sleep.

When the plane lands in Prague later that evening, Dmitri takes a hotel bus from the airport and catches the last tram of the night to Janek's neighborhood. It's located in an upper-middle-class apartment complex that allows the vampire to blend in as a businessman. Sunrise is a little over an hour away when he knocks on the door. He hears a chair slide across the floor inside the apartment, followed by light footsteps, and a slender, auburn-haired woman pulls the door open and looks up at him. "Janek, there's someone here to see you."

Stepping back, she sweeps an arm toward an inner hallway and motions for Dmitri to walk directly to what Janek calls his playroom. The room is a private disco with soundproofing to keep the noise from disturbing the neighbors. Loud music slams into Dmitri when he opens the door. A strobe light rapidly flashes white beams against every surface and vampire in the room, while a mirrored disco ball spins from the top of the ceiling, casting rainbows of color in all directions. A couple dozen vampires dance on the worn hardwood floor. On a raised platform in one corner, a disc jockey minds the music. Janek's odd taste still bemuses Dmitri; he doesn't know how any vampire can stand the bright, flickering lights. Personally, Dmitri was thrilled the disco era didn't last long, and he wonders if Janek will ever get over his love for it.

A hand clamps his shoulder, and Dmitri turns to his right—Janek smiles at him, inviting him to join the party. Shouting over the music, Dmitri declines and tells him that they need to talk.

When they're seated in the drawing room, Janek says, "It's good to see you ... I heard you weren't doing so well."

"I'd appreciate it if you'd keep thinking that. I was never here."

Janek nods, and they move directly to the point of the visit. The other vampire reveals that the Druzhinas are moving in strange circles and patterns these days; they disappear and resurface either all in the same location or scattered individually across the Belyakov estates. Dmitri frowns. It's contrary to how the Druzhina has operated for centuries, and he can't figure it out.

Janek claims he needs a few days to locate their present whereabouts, which means Dmitri has no choice but to stew inside a safe house, waiting for answers. *I need to get Elizabetta out of there sooner rather than later.* He buys a new cell phone and attempts to reach the Druzhinas on his own, but of course their numbers have changed; it's a typical Druzhina security tactic to prevent outsiders from tracking or spying on their operations. *Damn it, what are they up to?* Shashenka never allows the Druzhinas to disappear like that unless the entire force is needed for a multiple-target assassination or a coup d'état. The latter is rare and happens only when Shashenka is elevating people into positions of governmental power that suit his agenda and strengthen his dominion. Dmitri has seen and heard nothing to indicate that as a possibility; the global governments appear to be running the world as usual.

The wait leaves Dmitri too much time to think and reflect on the disastrous months since his life went to hell at Big Sky. The ever-present guilt over Elizabetta's role as a concubine eats at him like a cancer. Much of the blame lies on him—his repeated failures to honor the promises he made her. *Hell, I couldn't even get it right to end her life mere days ago at La Perfezione.*

That guilt and the time he spent in the void nearly destroyed him. He doesn't understand how he ended up there or how Elizabetta brought him out of it—only that she did. There's no way for him to know what Elizabetta feels for him, if anything, but she seems past the hatred. At least the kiss they shared suggested otherwise, and that change alone fuels his desire to protect her again. *It's my turn to save her.*

The confines of the safe house grow smaller as Dmitri paces and waits; he's about at his limit for doing nothing. He steps out for the rest of the night, wandering the streets almost until dawn. There's an ache in his chest—he misses Elizabetta. The brief moments they shared in the cellar aren't enough to make up for the years he's suffered within sight of her. *It'd be nice to hear her voice again.* He wishes he could call her. Then realizing that he's gone back to using her full name, Dmitri chides himself. *I've got to stop doing that—she's Eliza now.*

He pauses in the middle of the room. *No, she'll always be my Elizabetta. I miss her so much.* He can't linger another moment; he returns to the safe house with a decision made.

Plan B. I'd almost rather take another beating than go this route. Before he lost his mind, he remembers, Elizabetta kept sneaking away to meet her werewolf friend, Matt, but something about their relationship doesn't seem right. Dmitri doesn't know if they are just lovers or just friends, and he suspects there may be more to their interaction than appearances suggest. The mutt, obviously, has resources—he tracked Elizabetta down in Russia and has maintained contact with her since. Dmitri recalls increased werewolf activity near the Belyakov estate in Novgorod. There also seemed to be a heavier werewolf presence around the villa in Venice—he noticed the increased number of werewolves when he fled the city. *Too much coincidence. What are they playing at?*

His dislike for the mongrel makes it difficult for him to go in this direction, but if Matt and Elizabetta are plotting something together, it may be the ticket Dmitri needs to get Elizabetta to safety. What other option is there, with the Druzhinas in hiding? Perhaps it is time to pay the wolf a visit; at least he'd be doing something.

Dmitri places a few calls and arranges to take a flight leaving Prague after nightfall. He'll go to Montana and spend some time with the mongrel. He must try to persuade Matt that Elizabetta's life is in danger, that if she doesn't go into hiding, Shashenka will kill her. Dmitri is determined to stay there as long as it takes to convince the wolf that they can't wait to make a move.

He knows the idea is brash, even foolhardy, but every time he thinks about Elizabetta being subjected to the vile monster's sexual advances or more torture, he's pushed to the breaking point. But what if the mutt won't help him or Janek fails to locate the Druzhinas? *Should I return to Venice and kill Shashenka, even if it destroys me?* Regardless of what happens to him, once that evil monster is dead Elizabetta will be free. He smiles. Her freedom is the only thing that matters to him—he will get it for her one way or another.

When Dmitri arrives in Montana later that evening, he wastes no time, renting a car for the drive to West Yellowstone. The only piece of information he lacks is Matt's address, but perhaps someone from the area may be willing to give up the information. He remembers how the Druzhina followed the mutt and Elizabetta to the local bars. He has to grab his chest to soothe the ache still lingering there over that discovery—she was likely intimate with the wolf. *What if she still is?* His courage almost falters.

The first two bars turn up nothing, but Dmitri finds a man in the third bar who claims to work for Matt. The man is tipsy and says he doesn't know where Matt lives, but the scent he gives off tells Dmitri otherwise. He buys drinks for the liar as they shoot pool. The man is resistant to Dmitri's ability to influence his mind, but the alcohol works to loosen his tongue. Three games and a dozen drinks later, he finally provides Matt's home and office addresses. Dmitri shakes his head—only in a small town would an employee know that much about their boss. He excuses himself and slips out the back door.

There are no lights on inside when he pulls up in front of the small, square house, and Dmitri wonders if the mongrel is asleep. He knocks three times—no answer—and decides to pick the lock on the back door and slip inside.

Dmitri inhales for the fresh scent of wolf before moving with caution through the tiny one-bedroom home. There is no sign of Matt. Jealousy flares when he sees the bed; in his mind proof of a relationship between Elizabetta and the mongrel. It takes a moment to work past his feelings. *She kissed me—all is not lost.* He looks at the clock on the wall. Even if the mutt stays out until the two o'clock bar closing time, he'll arrive here before the bottom of the hour, but Dmitri has a little time left. He would be ashamed to admit it to anyone, but he spends that time searching for traces of Elizabetta—he won't leave whatever he finds behind. A relieved chuckle is the only sound he makes when he discovers nothing.

By four in the morning Matt still hasn't shown up, and Dmitri begins searching his papers for a clue to where he might have gone. On the kitchen table he finds a notepad with flight numbers and departure dates; the most recent date is two weeks past, and there are no return dates. Dmitri tries to access the Internet with his phone—no service. Then he looks for a computer, hoping to check the flight numbers, but fate thwarts him again. With no computer and no way to search, he tears off the piece of paper with the flight information, puts it in his pocket, and leaves.

It's too late to drive back into Bozeman to buy a laptop or find a public computer to use; he'll make an online search his first priority when the sun goes down again. There's nothing left for him to do but check into a local motel. Dmitri strips to his underwear, climbs in bed, and stares at the ceiling. His thoughts return to Elizabetta. He can't stop speculating what she's doing in the inner lair. How different their lives, or at least hers, may be once Shashenka is destroyed.

Dmitri's vampire existence has only ever known the chaos and cruelty of the Belyakov coven. It's difficult to imagine a life with no nucleus gathering, no torture, and no indiscriminate killing of humans. If he can convince Elizabetta they belong together, then whatever life that comes afterward he will enjoy—if he survives. Eyes closed, Dmitri lets sleep take him. His dreams that day are of a new life with her, and when he wakes at twilight he smiles. *Somehow I must find our future.*

The next evening Dmitri discovers the trip to Montana was a complete waste of time—the mongrel's flight information suggests he may be in London. Less than twenty-four hours later Dmitri arrives at Heathrow and takes a shuttle bus to the hotel in the Mayfair District the mutt stayed at before when he met Elizabetta in London. Disappointingly, the hotel clerk's search for Matt indicates that he's not there either. Dmitri knows he can't keep chasing ghosts. He finds a small hotel to check into for the day and places a call to Janek Novak, who has some news about the Druzhinas. *It's about damn time.*

"When they finally resurfaced a few days ago, each one was at a different Belyakov estate."

What the hell are they up to?

Before Dmitri can ask, Janek adds, "Whatever they're doing, it's not the typical holiday and doesn't match their normal check-in with Shashenka. The report states that they are dividing their time between talking with the locals and meeting others outside of your coven."

Very strange indeed. "Which estates?"

Janek asks him to hold while he gets the report. "Vladimir Jagr is in Prague. Anna Kachida is at Novgorod, Stephan Vasilou at Waiheke, and Victoria Edwards at Invercargill. Sofia Castillo is in Arecibo and Alexander Kozlov in London; Katherine Zervas was seen in Cusco, and Kees De Haan in Rio de Janeiro. Justin Walker was seen at Big Sky."

Justin is at Big Sky? Shit. Figures. Dmitri thanks him but tacks on a reminder. "You never heard from me or saw me."

Janek quips, "Seems I'm developing a pattern of talking to myself or seeing vampires that aren't there."

"There may be more of that in the near future."

A low, disgusted growl rumbles from Dmitri's throat as he ends the call. He missed the opportunity to see Justin in Montana, and now the nearest Druzhina is Alexander. Justin he trusts; Alexander is the one Druzhina Dmitri would rather not talk to first, if at all.

He counts his remaining money. There's enough to pay

for one more continental flight and a hotel for a couple of days. Taking a gamble, Dmitri books a flight to the next nearest Druzhina—Vladimir, in Prague.

He arrives in Prague after midnight. The first place he checks is the safe house; it's empty. He cannot risk being seen at the estate, but the shadows on this moonless night allow him to sneak into the villa. There's a strange sense of normalcy to the place without the presence of the inner lair. Given the locals and a few extras staying there, it takes him over an hour to search the premises. There is no sign of Vladimir.

Back at the safe house, Dmitri waits, holding on to the slight shred of hope that Vladimir will stop by this location before he leaves Prague. He isn't that lucky. When daylight comes Dmitri realizes that wherever his friend went, he is once more a step behind. He again counts the dwindling supply of cash and scowls. He's going to have to steal funds in order to fly back to Venice; he'll leave an IOU with his mark and pay it back someday. A slight smile lifts the corners of his lips as he recalls the one secret he and Elizabetta kept from the other Druzhinas—they always paid back what they stole. Still, Dmitri detests the thought, but he has no choice, and he doesn't know where to go next.

At the airport Dmitri books the next available flight to Venice. This flight won't arrive until after daylight the next day—he won't reach La Perfezione until after dark. *Is it my curse to always fail her?* The entire trip has been filled with nonstop disappointment and frustration. He hopes at least that his recent mental vacancy will lead

others to believe that he simply wandered off and mean-
dered around Venice for twelve nights. That is, if Maria
hasn't revealed his secret.

The only one who will not accept that excuse is Elizabetta. She's waiting for other answers too. He never
acknowledged the truth—she is Elizabetta Rossellini—and
he doubts she will let that issue go. Dmitri sighs. He hasn't
figured out what to tell her yet.

CHAPTER 15: ELIZA

Breaking the Law

Eliza is nearly out of her mind with worry—Dmitri is still missing. It's been well over a week since he vanished. She tries to focus on her job and push thoughts of him to moments when she's alone. *Why won't Shashenka allow anyone to go look for him?* She already knows the answer—their master doesn't care—and the truth spirals her anger higher with each passing minute. Her imagination whispers accusations that perhaps their master himself is behind the disappearance. *Did he order Dmitri killed? So help me, if Dmitri is dead ...* The thought trails off; she can't allow her building rage to push her out of control.

She struggles to pay attention to the paramour at her side, one of Shashenka's business partners. The middle-aged man is affable but bores her the same as any other consort. They are entering the garden for a stroll when a ruckus near the gazebo captures Eliza's attention. The vampires are crowding around something on the ground, and their voices are raised in a chorus of astonishment, curiosity, and bewilderment. When some in the crowd see her they step back; whispers carry her name regardless of how softly it's spoken. *What is this all about? Dmitri?* Her breath catches in her throat when an unobstructed path clears ahead of her. There, lying in a heap of torn and bloody clothes, his body battered and bruised, is Matt.

Oh my God! Eliza hisses and leaps over his body. She draws the horse-head dagger she always carries—the one Dmitri gave her—and defensively crouches over Matt's still form, pulling his ragged shirt aside to expose her mark. "I demand to know who touched him!"

Excited murmurs ripple around her as more vampires arrive from within the villa. Eliza touches a finger to Matt's neck—he has a pulse. A moment of relief merges with a memory. *Un-freaking-real. This can't be happening.* Nearly a year ago, during the battle at the Cleary ranch, Eliza stood over Matt this same way and defended him from vampires—vampires who wanted him dead. *Never again. Never.*

Fury blazes in her eyes as she looks around the crowd. "He bears my mark. Which one of you has dared to touch him?"

No one will answer her question, and the rage inside her looks for an outlet—she's envisioning slaughtering everyone near Matt. "Damn it, answer me!" Someone mentions getting Shashenka. She scans for a guilty face among the vampires, but no one will meet her gaze. *Cowards.*

When the goblin king arrives, his amused look turns to shock and then anger. "You marked him?"

"Yes." She doesn't back down. "I claimed him in Montana when you demanded the massacre of the rest of his pack. He is my property—he's protected. He's not to be touched by any vampire."

Shashenka's eyes narrow as he spins around and finds the witch in the crowd. "Did you know about this?"

Maria gives him a look that seems to challenge the devil vamp to defy vampiric law. Her tone is firm. "It was done by agreement of the Druzhina as a condition of Eliza's surrender. It was done according to law."

"They let her mark a werewolf?" Incredulity slides his nasal pitch up an octave.

"Yes." The witch's green eyes flash—Eliza sees both defiance and fear in Maria's expression. "The Druzhina allowed it. He was marked, Eliza surrendered, and he was left behind."

"If he was left behind, can anyone tell me what the hell he's doing here?" Shashenka hisses as if he's ready to attack as he looks around the crowd, but no one answers. The crowd falls so silent that other night sounds from the canal side of the estate penetrate the garden.

Eliza's never seen Shashenka come this close to being unhinged. *How dare he!* Matt wouldn't be marked if it weren't for his orders to wipe out Josh's pack. She pulls in her rage, but barely. "That's beside the point. One of our own has broken your laws and has insulted you by dumping Matt here."

She knows Shashenka cannot—without losing support among their kind—rewrite the law on a whim, and she pushes the issue. "He is my property, and I demand the

right of blood justice. I claim the lives of those responsible."

For the first time since joining the Belyakov coven, Eliza
sees true fear in Shashenka's eyes—it emboldens her.
"Master? Are you going to allow this insult, this affront to
your law? Will you deny me the blood justice I am due?"

Shashenka hastily looks at those around them. Too
many are watching this spectacle for him to ignore her
demands, and she knows it. Contempt and disgust are
etched across his face. His throat clears in a half-snarling,
half-strangled sound, and he yells at no one in particular,
"Summon the Druzhina."

In a flurry of commotion the guards carry Matt's body
to a storage room in the locals' wing of the villa. Eliza
holds her dagger at the ready and glares at those following
them. She doesn't know where the threat to his life came
from, and she won't leave his side until she finds out. *If it's
someone in this coven, I will kill them all.* When Maria
goes to retrieve what she needs to heal Matt, Eliza im-
plores her to hurry back. They're racing against borrowed
time—Shashenka is not going to tolerate this situation
much longer.

The crowd in the hall pushes and jostles each other as
they strain to get into the storage room. Eliza remains
crouched in a defensive posture over Matt's body, yelling
at them to get out. *Where is Maria?* She brandishes the
horse-head dagger at the crowd and levels one final warning. "I. Will. Attack. You!"

They take her threat seriously and drift away from the
storage room. When the witch returns, Eliza maintains a

split vigil, watching the door to keep everyone out and taking account of Matt's injuries as Maria uses a spell to vanish his torn clothes. There are numerous cuts and puncture marks, but most are confined to his upper body. "Did they bite him?" Vampire venom is poisonous, deadly, even, to a werewolf.

To her relief Maria assures her that his injuries in McAllister were far worse. "The punctures look to be claw and knife wounds. There are not as many this time—it should be easier to mend him."

Maria has barely begun to apply poultices to Matt's wounds when Shashenka storms into the room. His face is a mask of rage, worry, and fear; doubtless he is desperate to seek a way around enforcing the property law. *Catch-22, you son of a bitch. Just try wriggling out of this one.* If he skirts or ignores the law, it will bring chaos to his reign. If he upholds it, the ramifications are significant—it is a blow to the warring divide between vampires and werewolves.

"This werewolf is a threat to me, and I want him destroyed."

Eliza hisses, steps toward him, and points the dagger at his throat. "If you touch him, I will kill you. The law demands that I protect my property."

"You know that's impossible, Shashenka." Maria reacts to the rising tension, but her tone is smooth, diplomatic. "Your property law has stood fully enforced for over ten centuries. If you violate it now, despite what the werewolf is, no one will respect any law you claim the right to enforce."

The witch's comments enrage Shashenka. Snarling, he grabs boxes and supplies from the shelves and throws them about the room, tossing the empty shelving units at Maria and Matt. Eliza protectively moves between him and the other two, but Shashenka flies past her and snatches Maria by the hair.

"I forbid you to treat him." Shashenka's face contorts as he drags her away from Matt. *He's unhinged—he's lost it.* "He's a known threat to me. If you tend to him, I will consider it a violation of our treaty."

To Eliza's horror Maria bows her head and takes a step back. She has no idea what treaty Shashenka is talking about, but she clearly sees the impact of its reminder on Maria—the witch is terrified.

Invoking her right of property again, Eliza counters the devil vamp's obvious intent to allow Matt to die. "He is mine to protect. I will mend him."

Shashenka wheels around, his eyes bulging with raw hostility. "That is your right, but I will make you pay for this insolence." Spittle punctuates his words. "You will pay. Take that putrid creature away from here. I want him out of this villa. His stench is fouling my home."

Eliza is unsure what to do but remains defiant. "Where is he to go? How will I protect him? You haven't found the ones responsible for this."

She sees a slight spark in Maria's eyes. "I know where he can go, if Master permits."

Shashenka's head whips toward the witch, and for a moment Eliza thinks he may attack the other woman. "Where?"

Maria sounds cautious. "I have a friend with an unused apartment in Cannaregio. We can take him there."

"Will he be safe?" Eliza's not happy about moving Matt to an unknown location. "How do we know that whoever did this won't find him there?"

Maria looks from Shashenka to Eliza. "This friend is well protected, and no one bothers the property for fear of reprisal."

"Give me the address so I may tell my guards where to dump this mutt." He takes a threatening step toward the witch.

Eliza bristles, ready to move between them, and brandishes the dagger again. "Your guards will not touch him or know of his location. Maria can take us there."

"No." Shashenka's voice is deadly quiet. "She will not take you there. I forbid her any opportunity to heal this ... this ... this abomination."

"Maria, whisper the address to me."

The goblin king's eyes narrow, but he gives a curt nod of permission. Maria cups her hands around Eliza's ear as she relays the address and instructs her where to find a hidden key. Eliza only half pays attention; her mind races ahead to a different plan. *I need to get him to Vincente. He can protect Matt and take care of his injuries.*

Her tone belies the belligerent glare she gives Shashenka. "If you want him out of here, I will need to use a motorboat."

Shashenka flexes his jaw and his Adam's apple bobs as if he's trying to swallow something distasteful. A long minute passes while he seems to decide. It's obvious he doesn't like being cornered over this issue, but his evil mind has yet to figure a way around it. "Fine. You may take an estate boat and bring this mutt to wherever Maria told you. But I warn you, Eliza, take him anywhere else and I will hunt you down and kill you both."

Crap. He's probably going to send someone to follow me. I can't risk getting caught in the Dorsoduro area.

Eliza is about to speak when Shashenka adds, "I will permit you to stay with this abomination until the Druzhina arrives. They will track down the one responsible, and that lawbreaker will face justice." He pauses and sneers. "The Druzhina will protect him. You, my dear, will return to La Perfezione upon their arrival."

"Yes, Master." Even with the restrictions, this is more of a victory than Eliza expected. She turns her focus to departing the estate. "Maria, will you please ask one of the locals to ready a boat? I'll be waiting with Matt at the mooring poles."

"Yes." She murmurs as she passes, "Take care—you're playing with death or worse. This is dangerous ground."

Eliza ignores the menacing look Shashenka casts her way as she lifts Matt from the floor and walks out of the villa. Gently laying him on the stone landing near the boats, she waits for a local to arrive. Minutes later she sees Antonio; he darts nervous glances back toward the villa but quickly checks the gas and oil as he instructs her on how to pilot the boat. Eliza steps into the vessel and settles Matt across the cushions of a side bench. "Thank you, Antonio."

He manages a slight smile as he unties the bow from the

mooring pole and pushes the motorboat clear of the dock. "Be careful, Miss Ross. Master will hurt you."

Eliza nods but doesn't respond. Shashenka is the last thing on her mind. She puts the boat in gear and leaves, steering cautiously to avoid an accident on the way to the Cannaregio District. It's a relief to discover the area is as mystifyingly familiar to her as the rest of Venice—so much so that she has no problem finding the address Maria gave her. *I should change my middle name to Déjà Vu.*

Eliza leaves Matt in the boat while she scales the building to find the key Maria said was hidden behind a brick in the parapet on the roof. Panic sets in when she discovers it is not there—or anywhere on the roof. There is no activity inside the structure, and from what Eliza can tell, she's fairly certain that no one is home. *Hope they won't be upset if I break in.* Since she's already on the roof, Eliza decides the access door is the best option. She twists the knob until the lock breaks and the handle comes loose. Holding her breath, she pulls the door open and steps inside.

The place smells mostly of dust and stale air. Maria was right—whoever lives in this place is rarely here. Racing through the apartment to the main floor, Eliza unlocks the door and moves to bring Matt inside before any passersby notice the activity. A chaise lounge is in the first room to the left; it's the perfect place to leave Matt while she goes to search for a bedroom.

There are none on the main level, but she finds one on the second floor at the top of the stairs. The condition of this room is the first sign that anyone uses this home. The vague scent of vampire is discernible, but it's old and too faint for her to link to anyone she knows. *Perhaps Maria's friend is a vampire from another coven here.* What is oddest is that all the furniture she's seen in the home is under dust covers, except for this one bed that's been left unmade and clearly slept in. *I hope the owner doesn't come back.*

She finds another bedroom, a smaller room at the back of the second floor—it will do. Eliza locates linens and a blanket in a chest near the bed. The strong odor of cedar clings to the bedding and suggests they were stored for a long time. After she removes the dust cover and makes the bed, Eliza retrieves Matt from the chaise lounge downstairs. He's still unconscious—her worry catapults several notches. *Maria better be right about this not being as bad as his injuries in McAllister.*

Eliza pulls the sheet over his body before going to look for rags and medical supplies. She's surprised but pleased to find a bathroom cabinet well-stocked with salves and dry poultice ingredients that only need mixing with water for use. When she returns to the room she gently washes and dresses Matt's wounds; she's working on the last deep cut when his eyelashes twitch. Voice soft, she urges him to wake. She's done a lot of this type of encouragement lately.

"Baby vamp?" His eyes open and focus on her, but his voice is weak and breaks with each syllable.

She bends to place a kiss on his forehead. "Yeah, it's me. You're safe now."

He groans, wincing when he tries to move. Eliza's still binding another wound on his forearm. "Lie still. It's going to take a few days for you to mend."

"Where are we?"

I have no idea. Eliza glances around the dimly lit room. Everything about the place seems deliberate in its antiquated appearance—the curtains, rugs, and even the furnishings' classic design carry a hint of elegance, not unlike at La Perfezione. The owner clearly prefers period pieces to neo-modern décor. "It belongs to a friend of Maria's. She assures me that you're safe here."

Matt's eyes close as he adjusts his position, moaning softly with the movement. Eliza grimaces; this is too close of a repeat of what Matt barely survived at the McAllister ranch. "What happened to you? Who did this?"

"I had a message to meet Vincente at a restaurant in San Polo. I waited, but he never arrived. I was heading back to my hotel in Santa Croce when two gondolas pulled alongside me ... a bunch of vamps."

Eliza can't hide her shock. "Didn't they see my mark?"

"Yeah. It's not foolproof. They didn't care." He studies her. "How did you find me?"

"I didn't." Disgust and concern saturate her reply. "Whoever did this to you brazenly dumped you in the garden at Belyakov's estate."

"No way!" Matt struggles to sit up, but she gently pushes against his shoulders until he lies back.

"It doesn't make sense to me, and it really riled that vulgar goblin king. He wouldn't allow Maria to fix you up this time. Worse, he's bound by vampiric law to find and punish whoever did this to you. He is one pissed-off, unhappy demented camper."

Matt lets out a low whistle. "So how did we get here?"

"He didn't want you at the estate and allowed me to bring you here, but I can't stay." Eliza takes Matt's hand. "The Druzhina is coming in a day or two to solve this problem, and when they arrive I have to go back to the villa."

"You're just going to leave me here at their mercy, baby vamp?"

It bruises her heart to see fear in Matt's eyes, but there's nothing she can do about it. She shakes her head and looks at the window. "I won't have a choice. Maria is confident you can remain here, safe, until you're well enough to go wherever you choose." She brushes a hand across his cheek. "I'm really sorry this happened to you. I—"

"Crazy world we live in ... it wasn't your fault."

I can't seem to protect anyone I care about. Dwelling on the subject is depressing her—she's more determined than ever to end Shashenka and change their world for the better. She asks about the status of their plans, but Matt has little to add; everything is coming together for the take-over of Belyakov's businesses, and support from outside covens and werewolf packs is increasing. When he mentions that there's nothing new about Elizabetta Markov, Eliza locks her expression and tries not to react. *Yeah, and the one man who knows that answer I've managed to drive away.*

By the next day Matt is sitting up in bed—he wants to

get dressed and is ready to eat small meals. Eliza finds men's clothes in the apartment, but they're outdated by decades, if not centuries. Food is nonexistent, of course; it'd be rare for a vampire to keep it in their home. During Eliza's search of the apartment she finds money in a nightstand in the master bedroom. *Great, let's add robbery to breaking and entering.* She sighs—she has no choice. After she scrawls a quick note—"IOU 250€"— signing it with her mark, she takes the money and goes out to buy Matt some food and clothes. Given the apartment's age and lack of modern amenities, she sticks to fresh fruit, bread, cheese, and wine, along with a few jars of canned meat.

When Eliza returns with the goods, she looks over Matt's wounds, which are beginning to show signs of healing. He claims that aside from hurting all over, he feels better. The return of his sense of humor bodes well, and she rolls her eyes when he quips that she won't get rid of him that easily. *Yep, he'll live.* Her smile broadens—he's dodged death once again.

Just as quickly a frown reappears on her face. While trying to protect her, her werewolf family in McAllister was killed by her own coven. *I'm good at losing those I love.* The thought freezes her for a moment. Matt was the only survivor, and she loves him, but she isn't sure the feelings go deeper than friendship. Then there's Dmitri— she's sick with worry over him. *Is that love? Damn it, where are you?* Until Eliza learns the truth about Elizabetta Markov, she may never resolve the conflicted feelings she harbors for him and for Matt. She needs Dmitri to come back, if for no other reason than to untangle the mess in her heart and allow her to choose a direction for her life.

On the second night of their stay at the apartment, someone uses the front doorknocker. Eliza's nerves jump at the sound. It's likely one of the Druzhinas—her time away from the villa is up. Worry and dread course through her as she opens the door and sees Vladimir on the stoop, looking out at the canal. When he turns to face her, the glare he gives her is unexpected. *Great, here we go. This isn't going to go well for me.*

Eliza assumes Vladimir's sour attitude is because of the situation with Matt, and she doesn't want an argument. Quickly she shows him to Matt's room. It's impressive how serious and professional Vladimir becomes—a complete one-eighty from the way he greeted her—and as he lobs numerous questions at Matt, Eliza realizes he's seeking details about the attack. Matt gives an almost imperceptible nod when Eliza catches his eye. The information he provides is deliberately sketchy; they know the Druzhinas are still debating whether to take action against Shashenka, and she and Matt can't risk revealing their plot just yet.

Still, the vague information seems enough to satisfy Vladimir. The vampire nods and announces that Eliza is to return to the estate; he will follow her back to La Perfezione. It's not a courtesy, but an order, and Eliza realizes she's being taken into custody. He only allows her enough time for a brief good-bye with Matt. Seeming to understand her reluctance to leave, Matt flashes her a lopsided smile. "I'll be all right, baby vamp. Go on home to your devil vamp's lair. Don't need you getting in more trouble."

She ignores the disgusted look Vladimir casts their way and gives Matt a tight hug. "Just stay out of trouble yourself. I love you."

"Love ya too, baby vamp."

Vladimir follows Eliza out the front door and steps aside while she locks and closes it behind her. Then without warning he pins her against the door and snarls at her. "You and I will have a discussion soon."

The dark undertone of his voice matches his fierce expression, and she shrinks down. "W-what?"

"About Dmitri, your allegiances, and your loyalty to our master."

CHAPTER 16: DMITRI
Collision Course

When Dmitri arrives in Venice, he changes his mind and heads for his apartment instead of the estate. *There has to be something else I can do.* Something in his plans, the way this trip failed, is nagging at him—he needs to scrutinize the situation once more before he shows up at La Perfezione.

An uninvited thought stops him on the doorstep. He'd give anything to wind back the hands of time, if only to find Elizabetta waiting for him once more inside this empty place. Some of the happiest moments of his long life were spent here with her. For centuries it has stood as a testament to all he gained and lost—a shrine to the last vestiges of his life with Elizabetta. Even her clothes remain preserved in her trunks and armoire.

Dmitri takes a deep breath and pushes the broken dreams away, unlocking the door. He freezes and inhales. There's a hint of food somewhere in the house, and he catches the lingering scent of other vampires and— *What the hell is going on here?*

Soundlessly Dmitri moves to a console near the door and presses a button at the top back of its front leg. A hidden compartment lowers, and he reaches in and grabs the extra dagger he hides there. His eyes narrow. As silently as possible he searches the ground floor, peering into the shadows as he moves from room to room. Someone has left perishable and canned food on the sideboard near the table. *The Venice wolf packs wouldn't dare come here. Is it a rogue?* Dmitri skips every other step to quicken his ascent of the staircase, avoiding the stairs that creak. The smells are stronger toward the back bedroom—the heavy, pungent odor of a werewolf wrinkles his nose. With light steps he approaches the room.

The door is a few inches ajar. Dmitri flattens himself against the wall, craning his neck to look through the gap near the hinges, and freezes when a voice calls out, "I know you are there!" A low growl rumbles after the words.

That voice. How ... what? Why is he here? Dmitri shoves the door open, and it bangs against the wall as he steps into the room. "What the hell are you doing in my home?"

Matt's body trembles, and Dmitri recognizes it as the vacillation between completing the shift to wolf form and stopping it. The wolf blinks hard a few times, almost as if he's undecided whether to attack. Crouching in a defensive posture, Dmitri extends his fangs and hisses a warning, but his brows pull together as he takes note of the cloth dressings and bruises on Matt's chest, throat, arms, and face. *What is going on here?* "Don't lie to me, mongrel, or it will be your last mistake."

A crooked smile spreads across Matt's face but fades as Dmitri glares at him. The wolf's lips press into a tight line. Dmitri can smell the mix of testosterone and adrenaline— the sharp spike in those scents always precedes a were-wolf's attack. Shifting to an assault stance, Dmitri holds both daggers ready to thwart the mutt. "You don't want to try me. I will kill you."

"Shit." Matt mumbles something else under his breath and returns an icy stare as tension grows like a wild vine between the mortal enemies.

For the second time Dmitri finds himself in a standoff with Matt. But this time it's personal. The mutt's very presence here defiles the memory of Elizabetta. His odor taints the essence of her in this home, and the violation of something Dmitri considers sacrosanct is almost too much to endure. An overpowering urge to kill the mongrel wars with the need to find out why Matt is even here.

"I'm recuperating from a vamp attack." Matt's body re-laxes as his head drops to the pillow, and he phases back to his human form. "I didn't know this was your place."

"A what attack?"

"A vamp attack. You know ... your kind, four of them. They worked me over pretty good and left me like a gift on your devil vamp's doorstep."

Dmitri understands the severity of this statement. It doesn't bode well for Elizabetta; her limited memories leave her ignorant of the peril she's in because of this event. He can't believe one of their kind ignored Matt's mark. "Are you sure it was vampires?"

Matt taps his nose. "Whiffer works just fine. And before you ask the next obvious question—yes, they saw the mark, and no, they didn't give a shit. It seems the magic of vamp protection doesn't work on all of them."

Questions fly through Dmitri's mind—it's nearly impossible to snatch one thought. He takes in and exhales a deep breath to steady the torrent inside his head. *Why isn't he dead?* "If you were dumped at the Belyakov villa, how did you end up here?" Anger builds again, and he tightens his grip on the dagger handles.

"Eliza brought me here. She took care of my wounds and got me a little food before she had to go back to that devil vamp's lair."

It's Dmitri's turn to be confused. *Her?* "How did she even know to bring you here?"

"She said that witch gave her the address of a friend, that the owner was out of town ... didn't know you were that friend."

Why would Maria send them here? Is she trying to get us killed?

Matt seems to scrutinize Dmitri from head to toe—there's a peculiar expression on the wolf's face. "You look better than the last time I saw you."

A fragmented memory comes to mind—swimming with Eliza and Matt in the dark. *Was that real or a delusion?* His gaze meets the wolf's, and Dmitri realizes that the mongrel is waiting for a reply. "I'm feeling more like my old self these days." A menacing undertone carries the hidden threat Dmitri hopes to convey.

A nervous laugh rumbles from Matt. "I'm not sure

that's good news. The only time I've seen your old self, you were trying to kill me."

"Wish I would have succeeded."

"That's downright hospitable for an asshole like you."

I should just kill this mutt and be done with it. He can't—not yet, anyway. Dmitri ignores the comment and pulls a chair over next to the bed. He needs answers to what is going on here. Silence hangs between them a moment, and then Dmitri interrogates Matt about the attack. The mutt seems truthful and forthcoming with his answers, which only leads Dmitri to a bigger question—one the mongrel can't possibly answer. *What about the law?*

Dmitri can imagine the turmoil this has put the coven in. Given the nature of the property involved—a werewolf—there is no clear way for Shashenka to handle the matter. If the Druzhina was called, they will treat it like a typical property case. Otherwise this mongrel would already be dead.

The offending vampires are likely from one of the covens in Venice. The Druzhina will find out who they are, and will bring the guilty vampires to La Perfezione for punishment or execution. Dread climbs Dmitri's spine. He knows that no one told Shashenka about the terms for Elizabetta's surrender in Montana. *What kind of danger have we put her in? Nothing good will come of this.* "How long ago did this attack happen?"

Matt shrugs. "I'm not really sure. Days, a week ago? I've been here for four days, and I don't know how long I was unconscious before waking up here. Hell, I didn't even know they dumped me at the Belyakov villa until Eliza told me."

"Is she coming back soon?"

"One of your Druzhinas, Vladimir Jagr, arrived on the second day and took Eliza with him when he left. I've seen no one since. I've been trying to get on my feet so I can leave—it's been nerve-racking not knowing who or what may show up here."

It's Dmitri's turn to smile. His status as a Druzhina over the centuries, regardless of his removal from their ranks, makes this one of the safest homes in Venice. "No one comes here but me, and no one else will risk the wrath of the Druzhina by walking in here uninvited."

Matt shifts on the bed and sits up a little straighter. "Had I known that, I wouldn't have spent the last few days freaking out." He laughs. "Damn, could have had a party and a little fun."

Dmitri only half hears the comment as he analyzes the information. The offending vampires may already have been captured and may be awaiting their sentence. *If Shashenka follows the law.* It's obvious that Matt has no idea how much danger Elizabetta is in because of the situation. Because of him. *No, because of me ... the decisions I've made.*

He stands and pushes the chair away from the bed, feeling a strong pull, an overwhelming need to return to the villa to protect Elizabetta. Even the mutt's unwelcome presence here is a lesser priority for Dmitri.

Matt cocks his head to the side. "Going somewhere?"

"I need to get to the estate and make sure Elizabetta is safe." Dmitri deliberately uses her full name to diminish the mutt's inadvertent trampling on the sanctity of this home—and to preserve his most cherished memories of her here.

"You know she hates it when you vamps call her that."

Dmitri smirks. *If she ever learns the truth, she'll embrace it.* The thought makes Dmitri feel better, generous even, and he says, "I can't believe that I'm about to say this, but stay as long as you need."

The mongrel struggles to get off the bed, but he's too weak to stand and slumps against the headboard. "What do you mean, make sure she's safe? From what?"

Dmitri stops near the doorway and turns to look the wolf in the eye. "When we allowed her mark upon you, it was the first time in our history that one of ours claimed one of yours. We swore an oath of silence because the consequences for marking a werewolf may be severe."

"Shit. Son of a bitch! I sure wish you damn vamps would be straight-up with the truth one of these days. No one told me there were consequences for this crappy tattoo on my neck." A growl rumbles from Matt's chest, and Dmitri doesn't miss the murderous glint in the wolf's eyes.

"Elizabetta didn't know. We didn't foresee the two of you chasing each other around the globe and exposing it, either."

Matt's tone turns threatening. "I swear, if she's hurt because of this I will burn your coven to the ground."

Dmitri raises an eyebrow. It's the first thing the two enemies have ever agreed on, but the mutt's injuries leave him in no condition to help right now. A less-than-friendly smile curves the corners of his mouth. "I don't know when

I'll be back—lock up if you leave."

Dmitri bolts for the staircase without waiting for Matt's response. Given the situation, it's enough for now to learn that his assumption about Matt was right—the mutt will help him keep Elizabetta safe. *If Shashenka doesn't kill her first for owning a werewolf.* For now Dmitri's focus must be on this current mess; if everything goes as badly as he suspects it may, there'll be no need to seek Matt's help in taking down Shashenka later.

CHAPTER 17: ELIZA

Il Bacio Della Morte

Are we wrong about the Druzhinas? Eliza stands with her back pressed into the door, frozen by Vladimir's hostile words. She doesn't know what to make of him. Matt's last report indicated that Vladimir is rallying for Shashenka's removal from power, but the Druzhina's demeanor and tone suggest they may have bad information. Head held high, Eliza sidesteps him, walks to the mooring pole, and unties the boat, keeping an eye on Vladimir as he steps into another boat nearby. He doesn't make a move to leave—evidently he intends to follow her back. She starts the motor, puts the vessel in gear, and turns around in the canal to head back to the Belyakov estate.

Once they arrive at La Perfezione, Vladimir seizes Eliza by the arm and escorts her to the primary piano nobile, where Shashenka is awaiting them. She knows that look in the goblin king's eyes—anticipation shaded with malice—it is the same excited gleam he shows just before a sexual tryst or a torture session. Fear nips at the heels of her resolve to stand firm.

Vladimir says, "I've brought her back as requested, Master."

In a glacial tone Shashenka tells her to take a seat. He looks at Vladimir. "What did you find out?"

"The mutt's details are spotty. He never revealed what he is doing in Venice, but I suspect he was here to meet with Vincente Falco. The same day the wolf was dumped here, Falco and three of his packmates were found dead— their wounds are consistent with a vampire attack. Given the timing, it's likely that the same vamps are responsible."

Oh God, Vinnie is dead? Eliza's stomach twists in a knot, and she battles to keep a neutral mask on her face. *Did the vamps know he was helping Matt and me? Why did they let Matt live? Does Stephanie know?*

Her mind is in such turmoil that she barely hears Shashenka say, "He's lying." Their master's dismissive tone wraps each word in arrogance. "Werewolves are not known for their honesty."

"The mutt seemed truthful and even provided descriptions for these other vampires and the gondolas they were in when they attacked."

"And? Who are they?"

"The gondolas belong to Giordano's coven."

Shashenka's voice rises in pitch. "Pietro Giordano?"

"Yes, Master."

The goblin king's eyes smolder as he contemplates the news. Eliza doesn't know anything about the Giordano coven—she's never even heard of it—but she suspects there is a long, unfriendly history between the Giordano vampires and Belyakov's people.

Finally Shashenka gives Vladimir an order. "When the other Druzhinas arrive, you shall pay my regards to Pietro. Make sure you bring the guilty ones here—alive."

"In which manner shall we pass your regards?"

"*Il bacio della morte,* and same to his entire coven save the four you will bring here."

Il bacio della morte—kiss of death. *Oh God, he's just given the command to wipe out an entire coven. Why doesn't anyone fight back and take this evil, infected maggot out?*

"Yes, Master. It will be done." Vladimir casts another cold look at Eliza. "What of her—shall I leave her here or take her elsewhere?"

"I will deal with that after"—Shashenka pauses, looking repulsed—"after she gets her blood justice."

Eliza's eyes flash in equal measure of contempt and fear. There is no way to determine if the devil vamp merely means to use her in a vulgar manner, or worse. Shashenka's brutality is well known, especially by those within his coven; she's seen it meted out against others, and she's already borne it after crossing him twice. *All because I care for Dmitri and Matt.* Her pulse quickens. *What if Shashenka executes me right after I deliver justice for Matt?* She closes her eyes; the crushing weight of the mess her life has become steals the breath from her lungs.

Vladimir's voice pulls her away from her dark thoughts. "Will that be all for now, Master?"

"Escort her to her room and wait for my guards to re-lieve you. Then you may do what you wish until the other Druzhinas arrive."

"Yes, Master." Vladimir's hands ball into fists, and a muscle in his jaw twitches as he waits for her to stand.

Eliza takes several deep, steadying breaths as they climb the stairs and walk to her room. She asks the few vampires they pass if anyone has seen Dmitri—they haven't. *He's still missing?* She ignores the hostile look Vladimir is giving her, and refuses to give him a chance to speak when they reach her room. Without a word she steps inside and slams the door shut behind her, leaving him in the hall.

Her body trembles as she perches on the edge of a chair and stares at the bed, forcing herself to slow down and think through her predicament. Her biggest fear, she dis-covers, isn't for herself, but for Dmitri.

Why has no one seen or heard anything from him? Is he dead? She thought he was all right, his mind past its breakdown. Now she's not sure whether his mind snapped again or if something more sinister happened. She's terri-fied of what will become of him if he is still alive and she's not there to protect him. *Damn it, Dmitri, where are you?* She never got to ask him again about Elizabetta, and now the answer could be lost forever. Then her thoughts drift to Matt, and he settles at the top of her worry list next to Dmitri; if she's gone, there is no one to protect either of the men who mean the most to her.

I have to kill Shashenka. She considers the possibilities and understands there will be only one chance: when his goons bring her to exact justice against the vampires who harmed Matt. Likely Shashenka will be well protected by his guards, the Druzhina, maybe Maria. It's the worst possible conditions for rising against the goblin king. She doubts that she can harm one hair on the devil vamp's head before any combination of the others move to stop her.

Still, it may be the only opportunity she has, and she has to try. Eliza rehearses the moves in her head. There will be four of Giordano's vampires for her to execute; either she must attack Shashenka before she kills the Giordano vamps, or she'll need to move lightning fast to attack him before the fourth body hits the floor.

The quickest kill requires a sword to detach the head from the body. Granted, lopping the heads off the offending vampires won't kill any of them outright, but it will incapacitate them until their heads are burned to ash. After it bleeds out, a headless vampire's body will turn to something resembling brittle parchment that disintegrates once the head is destroyed. *I don't even want to know how I know that.* It's not a discussion she's had with anyone.

While Eliza repeatedly plays out the different scenarios, a nagging thought sneaks in and waits patiently on the side for her to notice. When she can't ignore it any longer, she turns her attention to it—it's taunting her with the fragment of a dream she had a few weeks ago. *I know how to kill a vampire because I'm skilled at it.* Eliza realizes the truth and gasps. *No, I'm good at killing.* The thought disturbs her, but her confidence boosts in equal measure—she will end Shashenka.

Two hours later she blanks her expression in haste

when Shashenka barges into her room. He stops just inside the doorway. "I thought you'd like to know ..." He can't seem to resist giving her a malicious smile as his pause builds tension. "After you've had your little justice, I am changing the property law. When it was decreed a thousand years ago, none of our kind would have considered using it to protect our mortal enemies. Thanks to the aberration that you are, the law must change—it will no longer protect werewolves. The modified law will be retroactive. Your repulsive pet will die."

In spite of herself Eliza blurts out, "You can't do that. You—"

"I can do that." Accusations fly off his tongue like poison darts. "You've left me no choice. It's your fault that I'm wiping out an entire vampire coven. Leaving that law untouched will only embolden the stinking beasts to kidnap our kind and force our marks upon them."

"But—"

"There is no but, Eliza! My coven is the keeper of the law, and if I'm to avoid threats to my rule, this perversion to the property law must be stopped."

"Please, Master, please don't hurt Matt. He wasn't here to see me. He's done nothing against you, and he won't harm you." She maintains eye contact, giving credibility to her lies.

A malevolent sneer stretches across Shashenka's face, and he laughs. "Oh, sweet Eliza, you can bet that pretty little ass of yours that I will make sure of that."

Before she can argue further he storms out and slams the door behind him.

CHAPTER 18: DMITRI
Point of No Return

I have to protect her ... save her somehow. Dmitri hears Matt call after him as he races down the stairs, but he doesn't slow or stop. Terror ripples through him. *What if I'm too late?* He'll exit through the back yard—he can't be seen leaving. He locks the front door from the inside and darts into the small garden behind the building, almost forgetting to lock the back door on his way out.

Logic and reason hammer fear and urgency; he can't just burst into La Perfezione. *They need to believe I've been out of my mind this whole time.* Stopping in the dark shadows of a copse of trees, he creates small tears in his shirt and slacks, then steps into the light of the walkway's lamp.

It's not enough—he's too clean. A quick scan of his surroundings provides the answer. Many Venetians place their garbage out for morning collection, and Dmitri takes advantage of the refuse. He slips down a side alley, rips open a bag of garbage, and pulls out a handful of discarded food. Holding his breath, Dmitri rubs the rotten refuse over his torso and legs. *Still not enough.* He sprints to the next bin and finds more waste to smear on his clothes. His face wrinkles in disgust at the awful stench—but he repeats the process three more times and finally takes a breath.

To complete the look, he heads down a few meters into a boggy area and adds mud to his slacks, shirt, and arms. Then afraid it may look overdone, he rolls in the grass to smudge the muck and grind it into his clothes. A block away is a dress shop with a large window, and the reflection of his appearance satisfies him; he swipes filthy hands over his head, disheveling his shaggy hair. *That will do.* Without taking a second look, Dmitri turns and heads for the villa. Now he must hope that no one will remember the exact clothing he was wearing when he left Venice almost two weeks ago.

Dmitri deliberately enters the rear of the estate by scaling the garden wall. No one is in sight; he drops to the ground and creeps up to the back of the mansion, slumping onto the steps. It's easy enough to mimic the stupor they believed he was in when he left—he simply keeps his eyes fastened on a crack between two paving stones.

Within an hour there's a flurry of motion, and voices surround him. When a familiar voice parts the crowd, Dmitri almost breaks his trancelike state, but he keeps his eyes unfocused, even when Vladimir orders the others away.

"Brother, are you all right? What has happened to

you?" Then Vladimir carries him inside to the bathing room near the second piano nobile, followed by two of the guards. *What the … I need him alone.* To Dmitri's astonishment his friend undresses him with care and places him in a tub. He doesn't know whether to feel humbled, embarrassed, or amused.

After Dmitri is dressed in a clean change of clothes—Vladimir's—and his hair combed, Vladimir guides him to the central hallway. There's a brief discussion of where to take him, and when it's confirmed that Shashenka wishes Dmitri returned to Elizabetta's room, Vladimir leads him there with obvious reluctance. Dmitri waits for the chance to lift his gaze. It's safest for him if most believe he's still in a diminished mental state, but he knows Vladimir will never betray him; their bond of brotherhood is too strong. If anyone can help Dmitri save Elizabetta, it is Vladimir. *I wish the others would leave.*

The guards remain while Vladimir escorts him into Elizabetta's room and instructs him to sit in a chair. He hears and sees Elizabetta in the periphery but continues the pretense of being out of his mind, staring at the floor without blinking and not moving a single muscle in his body.

"Oh my God, where did you find him?" She pushes past the guards.

Vladimir growls and positions himself between her and Dmitri. "Stay away from him."

"No!" Elizabetta takes two more steps, and Vladimir rushes forward, grabs her by the arms, and thrusts her across the room. "I told you to stay away from him."

"I need to make sure he's okay."

Vladimir's tone turns menacing. "You've done enough to him already. If you come near him, I will hurt you."

Shit! Dmitri can't reveal himself with the guards there, but he has to put a stop to this. Keeping his gaze on the rug, he rises and stumbles from the chair to the side of the bed nearest to where Vladimir has Elizabetta trapped in the corner. Shashenka's guards don't hide their amusement over his lurching gait and inelegant flop onto the mattress.

Elizabetta sidesteps Vladimir, hissing, "I'm trying to help him." She kneels in front of Dmitri, and her tone is soft as she takes his hands. "Dmitri, are you okay?"

He allows a muscle to twitch near his mouth. Fortunately she seems to understand, and he sees her relief, even the hint of a smile in her eyes. She stands and yells at the guards, "Get out. Get out of my room. You were assigned outside the door."

Vladimir orders them to stay where they are. He bends down and places a hand on Dmitri's forearm. "Brother, can you hear me?"

Dmitri resists the urge to answer; the guards are taking in every movement and sound. When he continues staring blankly at the floor, Vladimir tries again. "I need to know that you're okay, that you want to be in this room with her. I cannot leave you here if you don't wish to stay."

Blinking once slowly—he understands that the guards will not leave until Vladimir does—Dmitri allows his body to tip sideways onto the mattress. His eyes remain fixed as he lies there, silently pleading for them to go away.

"There's your answer. Now, get out, all of you," Elizabetta snarls. "You need to leave him alone."

Vladimir snatches Elizabetta by the throat. "You are responsible for this."

Then he switches the grasp to the back of her neck and pushes her to her knees; it takes every ounce of discipline Dmitri has to remain unmoving on the bed. Seeing them fight over him, knowing they care about him more than most, feels like an odd mix of surrealism and absurdity.

"Take a good look at what you've done, at what he's become because of you." Lowering his head next to hers, Vladimir hisses in her ear, but Dmitri hears what he says. "Someday I will make you pay for this."

No, you won't. Keeping his gaze fixed on the wall, Dmitri moves fast and locks his fingers around Vladimir's wrist. The sudden action seems to startle his friend. Vladimir releases Elizabetta and places a hand over Dmitri's forearm. One of the guards laughs, and the seething behind his friend's eyes tells Dmitri everything he needs to know; Vladimir intends to carry out his threat. Somehow he must find an opportunity to tell his friend what he is planning.

Moments later the two guards finally leave; to Dmitri's disappointment, Vladimir goes with them. As soon as the door shuts, Dmitri and Elizabetta collide, with him springing from the bed and her rising toward it. Without thinking Dmitri clasps her waist, pulls her close, and places kisses on her mouth, cheeks, and eyelids. To his surprise she doesn't reject his advances—she even seems to welcome his touch. Dmitri can't resist her walls being down.

My Elizabetta. He wraps her in a strong embrace. Gone is the awkwardness that settled between them after the kiss they shared in the cellar.

Whispering protests, she pulls back from him as her hands move to his chest. *I should have controlled myself. She's overwhelmed and not thinking.* He tries to hush her. They move to sit on the bed, keeping their voices low as they try to sort everything out. Elizabetta fires one question after another.

"Calm down, love, I'm fine," he says.

"B-but where were you? What happened?"

"It's not important. Are you all right? Has he harmed you?"

She shakes her head and presses her point. "How could you just leave like that? Do you know how worried I've been?" Her voice breaks, adding volumes of emotion to her pleading eyes.

That look burns through the layers of his resolve. Dmitri laughs and rakes a hand through his hair. "I was chasing ghosts. Turns out everyone I went looking for came to Venice."

Elizabetta's brows furrow, and she's about to speak, but Dmitri places a finger over her lips. He nods at the door. "I need to find a way to talk with Vlad, but I can't risk exposing myself. He needs to know his rage toward you is misplaced."

Her lips purse. "That's the second time he's threatened me in the last twenty-four hours. I think he means to kill me."

"I won't allow it!"

Lifting her head to look him in the eye, she says in a somber tone, "I doubt that the master of terror will, either." He clenches his teeth as she details her demand for blood justice for Matt, and Shashenka's order to wipe out the Giordano vampires.

While wiping out a coven isn't a favored move—it's a task he's been ordered to do in the past—Dmitri needs to learn the status of this debacle. "What else? I've already heard about the attack."

"What do you mean, you already know?"

He kisses her temple and whispers, "I ..." He catches himself from saying too much. "I crossed paths with that mutt of yours before I came here."

"Matt! Is he okay? Is he healed?"

His anger swells at her concern for the werewolf. While he realizes they may need the mutt's help in the future, he's not happy about her attachment to the mongrel. "He's fine, love," he says, clenching his jaw. "Now, tell me what is going on."

She explains Shashenka's plan to retroactively rewrite the property law so he can kill Matt. "I'm also to be punished after I extract justice from the Giordano vamps. It's the demented little maggot's idea of having the best of both worlds."

Dmitri tips his head back and closes his eyes. "We have to get out of here, love."

Voices from the hall send Elizabetta scrambling off the bed. Dmitri fixes his focus on the ceiling just before the door swings open and Peter and Leonard rush in, hoist him off the bed, and against Elizabetta's protests, drag

him out of the room. Once again he's shown the tour of the
bowels of a Belyakov estate and finds himself chained in
the knee-deep water of the basement.

Dmitri's mind is screaming. Somehow this madness
must end; he can't keep repeating the nightmare.
Shashenka must be taken out if Dmitri is ever to have a
hope of reclaiming his life. *I can't go back to the void. It
will destroy me.* There has to be a way—he must succeed
at protecting Elizabetta this time.

Many long hours later, he is brought to the primary
piano nobile, and with a guard to either side, stood near a
pillar in the central hall. He doesn't know how many
nights have passed since he was taken from their bedroom.
I've yet to have the chance to enjoy lying next to her again.
He struggles to portray a vacant state, but he doesn't want
to miss any details. Anna, Katherine, Sofia, Victoria, and
Stephan are present already; Dmitri suspects the other
four Druzhinas are bringing the Giordano vampires and
may arrive soon. He fixes his gaze on the statue behind the
chair sitting in the middle of the room. He's seen this setup before. Shashenka will sit there to preside over the
public punishment.

A few minutes later Shashenka strolls in with his full
complement of personal guards, who create a semicircle of
protection in front of him as he sits down. Maria takes her
place alongside their master. Then there's a commotion
from the hall, and Vladimir, Kees, Alexander, and Justin
lead four unfamiliar vampires into the room. Their hands
are bound, a Druzhina holding each one by the arms—the
classic Druzhina formation of the damned. The only one

not yet here is Elizabetta.

Like a preening peacock, Shashenka rises and slowly marches in front of the four captives, the baton of the naval cat held firmly in his hand. Its metal tails swing at his side. "Do you know why you've been brought here?"

One of the doomed vampires makes the mistake of playing dumb. "We've done nothing wrong and don't know why you've brought us here."

Dmitri flinches in spite of himself when the naval cat strikes the man across the chest. Shashenka's malevolent voice booms through the hall. "You are neither ignorant nor stupid. You have broken the law of property. You have insulted me by leaving that violation as a calling card at this—"

"We did you a favor by outing a marked werewolf," another of the Giordano vampires says. "That's a distortion of the law, and you know it." Dmitri's jaw drops open—no one in their realm dares interrupt Shashenka, let alone address him with such gall.

In an instant Shashenka is in front of the man and flailing the naval cat between each word that rushes out of his mouth. "That was not your decision to make. Do you know whose mark the mutt bears? Do you? That wolf is marked by one of my own, one who served among the Druzhina. Your ignorance of that fact makes your offense no less. You have broken the law."

Although he cannot see the doomed vampires' faces, Dmitri well imagines their surprise at this revelation. He himself is astonished Shashenka revealed that much to them. *What purpose does it serve?* He wonders if their master wants to instill more fear in the Belyakov coven members or if Shashenka is losing control and slipped up.

The other two prisoners remain quiet, but Dmitri knows Shashenka will remain true to his sadistic nature and refuse to be denied the opportunity to inflict pain on all four condemned before he allows Elizabetta to obtain blood justice. Moving from one to the other and back again, he strikes them in the face, chest, and legs with the naval cat. Vladimir, Kees, Alexander, and Justin maintain their firm hold against the writhing, desperate vampires. Shashenka moves past the line of men—none will meet his gaze, and their shoulders slump—and retakes his seat behind the guards. "Bring Eliza Ross. She shall have her blood justice."

Four of the locals escort Elizabetta into the hall. Dmitri sees the katana sheathed at her side, and he recognizes it as the same one he found her with at the wolf ranch in McAllister. They position her directly between the Giordano vampires and Shashenka's guards. Dmitri holds his breath. He notices her stance is tense but defiant; she shows no outward fear or panic. For a fraction of a second it reminds him of her look when she faced Shashenka on that long-ago day that he announced her reset punishment.

This is the strongest Dmitri has seen Elizabetta since the reset, and while she's about to commit a violent act—a penalty fitting this offense—a sense of pride surges through him. While she may not truly know herself, he is certain everyone in this room, aside from the newer Belyakov vampires and the condemned, is seeing this remnant.

Then he notices the briefest echo of fear spark in Shashenka's eyes, and he finds himself longing for the moment when, perhaps, that fear will be realized.

Elizabetta's bearing gives him hope that someday, even without her memories, she will be as strong as she was before. Their world demands such strength—only the strong survive in the shadow realms.

CHAPTER 19: ELIZA

The Price of Justice

Eliza just wants to get this over with. The waiting is wearing on her nerves; no one has entered her room since Peter and Leonard took Dmitri away three days ago, but she knows Shashenka's guards are just outside her door. Another part of her wants to escape, something she knows is impossible. She's barely slept and has spent endless hours pacing the small confines of her room.

Dmitri is a heavy constant among her fears. She doesn't know what they did with him or where they took him, and she's half out of her mind with worry. More troublesome is what Dmitri was up to during his absence. He never revealed where he had been or why he went away, and the fact that she didn't think about it until afterward only makes her angrier. He's very good at sidestepping issues, she's noticed—no outright lies, but it gives her reason to be suspicious of him. *What is he hiding?*

Her cheeks flush—he's certainly not hiding his attraction for her. She still can't believe the almost wanton way she threw herself at him when he returned. *What was I thinking? Evidently I wasn't.* It's cruel to feed his delusions. If she is Elizabetta, then it's one thing, but if she's not ... *I may have to walk away from him someday. I can't get too close.*

She's about to cross the room again for the thousandth time, when the door finally opens. Antonio walks into the room with a grave look on his face. Eliza swallows hard, unsure if she wants to hear what he came to say.

Ever polite, he gives her a small smile. "Miss Ross, you are to bring a weapon of your choice and come with us. Master has those who harmed your property, and the coven is awaiting your presence in the primary piano nobile."

Ready or not, this has to be done. She nods and steps over to the armoire, where she keeps the katana Josh Cleary presented to her. He wanted her to use it for her protection, but her presence cost him and his pack their lives. Someday she hopes to satisfy that debt—there is no one left but her and Matt to seek justice on his behalf. Perhaps today will be that day. She's planned her moves, and all she needs is for the evil goblin to be within her reach as the last of the Giordano vampires drops to the floor.

The biggest flaw in her plan is that she has no idea what will happen if she succeeds in decapitating Shashenka. A part of her hopes the others will rally and burn the head so no one can revive the devil vamp. But there's also a chance no one will lift a finger, other than to stop her. The latter will seal her fate. In some ways, Eliza doesn't care anymore. She's tired of living the life of a concubine, and final death is one ticket to freedom from Shashenka. Her maniacal laugh fills the quiet of the room. *I have lost my mind and have a death wish—just like Dmitri.* It shouldn't be funny to her, but it is.

Placing the sheath of the katana through the belt loop of her tunic, Eliza turns and gives a slight nod to Antonio. When they step through the door, she sees three others waiting to escort her, but notes they are locals and not the usual guards. Her thoughts don't linger on that fact; she suspects the Druzhina and Shashenka's personal guards are already waiting, and indeed every one of them is present when she reaches the primary piano nobile.

As they descend the final few steps, she spots Dmitri near a pillar and notices his wet and dirty clothes. *Oh goody, he's been in the basement again. I need to end this nightmare.* So far he looks unharmed, and that both brings her a sense of relief and adds to her determination.

Shashenka is securely seated behind his guards, with Maria at his side. *Spineless little coward.* Her mind races to readjust the moves in her head. She'll need to strike the final Giordano vampire, twist and leap past the guards, and hopefully succeed in delivering one final swipe of the blade through Shashenka's neck.

Twenty feet separate her from freedom from a life she's come to loathe. It's close enough that she doubts Maria will have time to cast the freezing spell, but far enough away that if his protectors are attentive, Eliza may not reach the rotten little devil. She is thankful the soon-to-be-dead vampires and the guards put additional distance between her and the Druzhinas, at least. Eliza draws a deep breath and firms her resolve—she has to try. She must succeed. Failure is no more an option than choosing to do nothing.

The locals move away from her as she stops in front of the offending vampires. She notices their torn and bloody clothing—obviously Shashenka couldn't resist terrorizing them. Eliza knows she is expected to make her charge and name the price they will pay, but it's a formality she refuses to be pompous about. She draws the katana from its sheath in a slow, deliberate motion. "You have harmed what is mine. You will pay with your lives."

Taking a step to her left, she stops in front of the first man and gives him a long, cold, hard glare. When he looks down she moves to the next vampire and stares at him until he makes eye contact with her. Her will to end these vampires wavers when the third vampire says in a hushed gasp, "It's you." His eyes dart back and forth, and his expression seems to convey urgency—not fear.

Damn it. Just my luck. Doubtless he knows something—he appears to recognize her—but she doesn't have the luxury of keeping him alive to find out. Killing Shashenka is more important than any secrets the man may hold; none of it will matter if she fails in her attempt to end the devil vamp. Eliza blinks to regain her composure and steps in front of the last man on the right. His look is arrogant, defiant, and it hardens her decision to finish her job.

Before she acts, her gaze slides once more toward Dmitri. His face is blank, and he seems to be staring past her, but Eliza knows that he's taking in every move she makes. Sorrow, pride, longing, and determination surge through her as she gives him a final look. While he's responsible for some of the misery she's experienced since arriving at the Belyakov coven, in his own way he's tried to do more to help and protect her than anyone else. Her self-confidence swells; she's finally taking control of her life. She owes Dmitri a chance at a life that doesn't include torture and heartache. *Do this for him ... for us. We will be free.*

Gripping the katana in both hands and holding it high over her right shoulder, Eliza rotates a half-turn away from the condemned and closes her eyes in final preparation for their execution. When her eyes open she exhales slowly and draws one deep breath—then explodes into action. Her body rotates, spinning toward the first Giordano vampire as her arms swiftly pull the katana around. The blade slices through the first vampire's neck and retreats over her shoulder as she steps and turns to the second.

The next body crumples to the floor, and Eliza continues to spin as she incapacitates the two remaining Giordano vampires. *No turning back. I will kill him.* Without stopping, she pivots toward Shashenka, and her left hand lets go of the hilt of the sword as she takes the first of the two strides she needs to launch herself over the guards. She's taking the second step when her body freezes midstride and she slides to an abrupt stop less than a foot in front of Peter. A look of pure hatred narrows his eyes.

Maria! The little cowardly son of a bitch anticipated

this move. Doubtless Shashenka had the witch muttering
the spell before Eliza even began the execution of the
Giordano vampires. Their master rises from his chair—in
the same embarrassing manner he did on the night she
eviscerated Dmitri in Novgorod—and claps slow and loud,
stepping past the guards.

A malicious grin spreads across his face. "Well done,
sweet Eliza." He puffs his chest out as he saunters nearer
and circles her. "You are a breathtaking and extraordi-
narily violent beauty to watch in motion."

With nothing to fear, he steps closer and wrests the
katana from the grip of her frozen right hand. She can feel
the bones in her hand and wrist break, but she can't even
cry out in pain. "You won't be needing this anymore." He
tosses the sword to the floor; it's still rattling there when
one of Shashenka's hands shoots upward and entangles
itself in her hair. He wrenches Eliza's neck back—more
bones crunch, splinter, break—and hisses, "You've had
your blood justice. Take her to the wine cellar and chain
her to the rack."

In her peripheral vision, Eliza sees the vile monster cast
a quick glance in Dmitri's direction. *Oh no, what now.* A
knot forms in her stomach. Without warning Shashenka
storms over to Dmitri and demands Maria verify whether
Dmitri is out of his mind again. To her tremendous relief,
Dmitri never moves or shows any sign that he's aware of
her presence. When the witch looks back at Shashenka,
she shakes her head and claims there's no way to tell.

*What the hell, Maria? Why would she sell him out like
that?* Eliza's blood goes beyond boiling—it's on fire.

Shashenka sneers. "*He* placed the mark on the mongrel. I don't care if he's aware. We need to ensure his mind is so broken that he'll never come out of it again." He looks at his guards and points to Dmitri. "Take him too and chain him to a chair. I'll deal with them soon."

Eliza can't bear the thought of returning to the cellar. A part of her longs for the chance to bring Shashenka here himself—to chain him in the flooded basement for days on end, then bind him to the wine racks for punishment. Afterward she'd like to see him dragged to the primary piano nobile for his execution. Inwardly she smiles at the thought.

It is pure fantasy, she knows—after everything the vile monster has put the human and shadow realm worlds through, there is too much risk to leave him alive once they overpower him. Unfortunately his execution must come at the moment of his overthrow. *Besides, I have to live through this first.*

The guards lift Eliza's frozen body and carry her to the torture room, and from the many footsteps following, she assumes that more than a dozen vampires are part of this procession. She is unable to turn her head, but she knows that more guards are dragging Dmitri behind her. Eliza can't hear any sound of resistance from him. *His strength and discipline are incredible.* Several sets of footsteps echo in the hall, and it makes her feel like she's part of a float in a perverted parade.

When they reach the cellar, the guards slam her back against a wine rack. Maria enters after Dmitri is hauled inside, and she waits until they have Dmitri chained to a chair before she begins reciting an incantation. Eliza can feel her broken and shattered bones right themselves and start to knit together—Maria is using a mending spell. Without a breath in between, the witch releases the freezing spell, and the men holding Eliza's arms notice the change in her body's posture and move quickly to position her wrists in the shackles and lock them in place.

Maria gives Dmitri a sympathetic look, then glances back at Eliza and mutters under her breath, "*Damnú air.*" The words are barely audible, but Eliza hears them and gives the witch a curious look as she leaves the room.

Gazing out the open door, Eliza notes the presence of the Druzhinas; they trailed the macabre little parade through the villa. Their faces show disgust and anger. All seem concerned for Dmitri, but the looks they level at her range from questioning to pitying. Briefly she wonders if they've changed their opinions about her or if they're reflecting their own hidden desires to take Shashenka down.

Then Leonard shuts the door to the cellar. Eliza can hear him urging the Druzhinas to move on, but they argue and refuse to leave. Next their voices rise as they confront Shashenka, who has evidently come to take pleasure in torturing her and Dmitri. It intrigues her to hear the Druzhinas push for Dmitri's release. "He's done nothing wrong," Katherine insists. Shashenka refuses to hear their pleas; his retorts are rude and haughty, reminding them that there is additional room in the cellar and basement if they continue to interfere with his plans.

That's it, you maggot—keep pushing them to our side. She doesn't care whether they like her, but she knows they are needed if she and Dmitri are to win. *Our side? Where did that come from? I'm freaking losing it.* She almost laughs aloud. Until this moment she hasn't realized that she considers Dmitri a critical member of their team. *We will do this together.* And like that, her mind is made up; whether Dmitri wants to be involved or not, she just signed him up for another revolt.

Her smile fades as the door opens and the vile monster steps into the room. Behind him she catches a glimpse of the Druzhinas still in the hall. They look perceptibly displeased. *Stay and listen. He was one of you—that camaraderie must mean something to at least one of you.* When their tortured cries begin, then perhaps—for Dmitri, at least—the Druzhinas will forge a united front and stand against the evil monster.

With a malevolent grin, Shashenka lays four weapons on a table near the outside wall. He takes his time looking from her to each weapon and back again, lightly stroking the baton, dagger, saber, and naval cat in turn. He finally decides on the baton and picks it up. The weapon slaps against his palm with each step he takes toward her.

"Your marking of a stinking werewolf embarrasses me." Disgust seeps into his tone. "I may have forgiven that, but your insistence on protecting that mangy beast and your demand for blood justice are insufferable. You coddle that imbecile, Dmitri, and provide excuses for the concubines too lazy to do their job right.

"You leave me no choice but to punish you. It's the only way you will stop making these mistakes. I take no pleasure in this, but you must learn this lesson. And mark my words ... you will learn."

Liar, liar, pants on fire. She knows he is suckling on every drop of joy he can find in her torment, and she draws a deep breath to brace herself against the first blow.

In one rapid movement Shashenka crouches and swings. The baton smashes into her shins, but before a cry escapes her, he backhands it across her legs again. The stinging blows force the scream lodged in Eliza's throat to burst through the room.

Dmitri's head snaps up. *No.* He must play his part and act as if he's in a stupor. She shakes her head, but then Shashenka strikes the baton across her ribs in forehand and backhand strokes, driving the air from her lungs, and she gasps, sputters, sucks for air. One part of her mind mocks her: *You don't need to breathe.* Before she can recover from the pain and draw a breath to inflate her lungs, Shashenka crouches and smashes the baton into her kneecaps. Tears, arriving late for the race, beat her lungs and scream to the finish line.

Shashenka continues to work the baton in a dizzying frenzy before he finally lays the weapon down and grabs the dagger. "This, sweet Eliza, is what happens to those who disappoint me."

She feels the sting of the blade as it slices the flesh above her breasts. Blood soaks the front of her tunic. Eliza wrestles against the scream clawing to get out, but it tears free and seems to go on forever. Somehow she must stop her cries—she can see what it's doing to Dmitri. The look of horror and pain in his eyes is too much for her to bear. Incrementally Eliza locks down her vocal cords, neck muscles, mouth, and tongue. *Being frozen would be perfect right about now.* The thought doesn't have time to linger. Shashenka slashes and stabs her arms, chest, and stomach in random, repetitive motions. Eliza manages to hold her screams hostage and uses their power to fuel the hatred that radiates from her eyes.

Her sense of time blurs as Shashenka changes from the dagger to the saber, and then to the naval cat. Then, with the first shredding blow of the naval cat across her face and neck, the monster rips the shrieks from the darkest recesses of her throat. Her internal dam breaks, and scream after scream rings out, flees the room, and leaves her behind. Eliza's ears go numb at the sound. Immense pain overwhelms her body and mind, and soon her only sounds left rush forth in bursts of guttural moans and hisses as her body hangs heavier in the shackles that bind her wrists.

Her head droops, and she looks down her body. There's a fleeting recognition that only tattered remnants of her clothing remain; blood seeps from hundreds of wounds. She fights to stay conscious, but her eyes roll against the effort to focus—almost as if they seek a place to hide from the horror they witness. Now her head feels too heavy to lift. Her eyelids seal shut, and somehow their weight pins her chin to her chest. Sound grows more distant, leaving her in silence. Her body barely twitches now as more blows from the naval cat land on the shredded remains of her flesh. Darkness finally comes, and Eliza wraps her battered body into its soft and welcome embrace.

CHAPTER 20: DMITRI

Kill or Cure

The guards bind Elizabetta, unconscious and battered, to the chair while the others push Dmitri face forward into the rack and lock his wrists in the shackles. He barely catches a glimpse of Elizabetta's bloody, mangled body when Shashenka's slight frame blocks her from view. *Damn the consequences—I need to see her face.* He's still trying to catch sight of her when the glint of a knife blade flashes ahead of its stinging slice across his cheek.

"It's so good to have you back, Dmitri. I've missed this pleasure more than you'll ever know." Shashenka buries the knife in the small of Dmitri's back.

Dmitri tries again to look at Elizabetta but sees the knife coming at him and reflexively turns his face away from the blade. The nearness to the rack leaves no room for the movement—his face smashes into the stout wooden structure. Blood spurts from his nose as his vision dims from the impact.

Shashenka unleashes a flurry of blows with the knife. Dmitri clenches his teeth against the onslaught, trying to withhold the screams that are tearing at his lungs to get out. He fails. Time becomes meaningless as he tumbles closer to oblivion. By the time Shashenka takes up the naval cat, Dmitri is barely aware that his clothing and flesh are being torn from his pain-racked body.

A vague sense of someone unlocking the shackles registers as he sags to the floor. Unseen hands drag him to a chair; he can feel the weight of chains wrapping around his body. His body rages against his attempt to think—he must fight the pain to remain conscious.

He's still struggling with that effort when a shriek follows a high-pitched scream. The sound ratchets his head up, and he freezes at the sight before him. Elizabetta's back arches and stiffens with each strike of the naval cat, but then she appears to slip into unconsciousness until the next blow. Many long minutes pass before Elizabetta's body finally slumps against the shackles. The demented, frenzied blows elicit involuntary twitches and spasms as her head lolls to the side and her chin bounces near her collarbone. Little is left of the tunic and slacks she was wearing, and blood pours from too many wounds to count, pooling around her feet. *How much blood has she lost? Is he trying to kill her?*

Dmitri winces with each blow—his heart sinks into depths of pain he'd forgotten existed. He cannot protest or cry out; if Shashenka realizes Dmitri is watching, the contemptible creature will draw out this abuse even longer. Dmitri slumps in the chair and focuses on a blemish slightly to the left of Elizabetta's bowed head. He allows his gaze to blur—his eyelids droop but do not close. An eternity passes as he waits for the horror to end.

Shashenka's rage dissipates, and he finally drops the naval cat to the floor. "Release them from their bindings and lock this room down. Spread the word that no one, and I mean no one, is to open this door."

Dmitri works to keep the blank mask on his face as Leonard and Charles unlock the chains and shove him off the chair. Peter double-checks Elizabetta's shackles; then with a smirk he delivers a hard punch to her stomach. A short, gurgling breath trickles out of her. Charles shakes his head and laughs, unlocking the shackles from Elizabetta's wrists. Her body hits the floor with a sickening thud. It takes incredible effort for Dmitri not to leap up and attack the cowardly lackeys—he's in no condition to take even one of them on, let alone the group.

The guards follow Shashenka out of the cellar and turn off the lights from outside the room. The moment the lock clicks into place, Dmitri crawls to Elizabetta's side. He gently sweeps bloody strands of hair from her face and takes inventory of her wounds as best he can in the dark—there are so many. *She has lost too much blood to recover from this without feeding.* Tears run over his cheeks and off his chin, leaving macabre streaks on Elizabetta's bloodied face and neck. With slow, careful movements he lifts her into his lap and wraps his arms around her nearly lifeless body.

The awful brutality she suffered carves a new hole inside him. Sorrow, love, and hatred rush to fill it. He murmurs, "I'm so sorry, love."

Hours slay minutes in the dark as an unknown number of days march silently past them. Elizabetta still hasn't stirred or regained consciousness, and Dmitri grows increasingly convinced that she won't recover—that Shashenka has all but bled her out and left her too close to final death. *Centuries of sacrifice, and this is what fate rewards us with?* Ignoring his own fatigue, Dmitri vows to hold her for an eternity if that will bring her back, but he's prepared to cradle her body until it turns to ash. He can't bring himself to let go or take her life—not now. Not when he's the closest he's ever been to getting his Elizabetta back.

Then an idea forms slowly, one that may work, but it's fraught with risk—and it may have severe consequences. *I have to do something to save her.* Lifting her higher, he repositions her so that her head falls back and gives him unobstructed access to her mouth. Her lips part; her breaths are shallow and ragged.

Dmitri extends his fangs, punctures the vein on his wrist, and brings it to her mouth. At first there is no response, but then he feels a slight movement in her lips. "Drink, love. You need to drink."

A faint smile spreads across his face as he feels her tongue press below the bite. He waits for her feeding instincts to trigger, but her fangs remain retracted, and after only a minute or two her head lolls to the side. He searches her face in the dark. Her eyes are open and rolled back in her head. A small trickle of blood drips from the corner of her mouth.

No! Oh no … no. Panic sets in—there are reasons vampires don't consume their own, and if any of the rumors are true, he may have just doomed her. Vampiric cannibalism is a crime punishable by death; as a Druzhina he executed many over the centuries for breaking that law. Some claim it causes insanity. Others say it creates a bloodlust so perverse that once a vampire's system is tainted with another's blood, they refuse to feed on anything else. There are also rumors that their undead blood lacks the necessary nutrients to sustain them, or that the blood turns caustic once ingested and eats away a vampire's body from the inside out. The only time their blood doesn't harm another of their kind is at the turning of a human, as it is essential to neutralize the venom and set the DNA changes.

What have I done? What if I didn't give her enough? He doesn't know if he's saved her or ensured her agonizing death. Dmitri leans his forehead against her neck. "I'm so sorry, love. I've failed you. I don't know what else to do."

CHAPTER 21: ELIZA
Bitter Truth

The blackness slowly lifts its veil. Internal alarms ring as awareness returns to Eliza's senses. The wrist she is drawing blood from does not belong to a human. The blood tastes sweeter, more pungent—a mix of flavors scented with overripe fruit, spices, honey, and a hint of metal. *Vampire blood.* She forces her heavy eyelids open. A blurred image of someone bending over her ... no, cradling her comes into view. Then she hears the angelic tone of his voice. *Dmitri.*

"Please, love, drink ... drink. Don't leave me. I need you to come back to me."

Eliza's mind shouts that vampires don't drink each other's blood—it is taboo, akin to cannibalism. *How do I know that?* The thinnest thread of a memory comes back to her, but it is gone before she can latch onto it.

Where am I? What happened? Eliza makes a weak effort to pull away, but Dmitri's left arm curls around the back of her neck, and his right arm moves to keep her fangs deep in his wrist. Her eyelids droop, a weak moan rises from her throat, and she pushes a sound off her tongue. "Mmm."

"Just a little more, and I'll let you stop. I won't let you kill me, love, but I need you to come back to me."

The comment strikes her as funny, but she's too weak to laugh. Not too long ago she said those words to him. A few more swallows of his blood give her enough strength to push against his grip on the back of her neck. "Enough," she mumbles. "Enough ... stop, stop."

Through half-closed eyelids Eliza watches him withdraw his wrist and lick at the small amount of blood trickling from the puncture wound. He moves his hand to cup her face. "I'm so sorry, love. I'm sorry you had to go through that again. Thank you for coming back to me." His shuddering shrug adds to the uncertainty in his tone. "I had to take the risk that my blood would revive you."

It's then she notices that his wounds are slight, or at the least he's had time for his injuries to begin healing. She assumes that she took the brunt of Shashenka's wrath. "You're all right?" she croaks with a hint of relief.

Shaking his head, he touches his forehead to hers. "Sometimes, love, I don't know if I'll ever be all right again."

A smile tugs painfully at the corners of her split and battered lips. "You will be ... whole someday." More to herself she whispers, "We're going to be okay."

Dmitri strokes a stray hair from her face. When he leans forward and places a featherlight kiss on the bridge of her nose, Eliza realizes that she's out of the shackles and he's no longer chained to a chair. She whispers, "What happened?"

He takes a deep breath and looks down at her. "I endured hours watching that evil, monstrous piece of shit torture you. I think my heart broke with each blow. But, you—you were incredible. Strong and brave. I couldn't believe the way you withheld the screams and let him see the full weight of your hatred."

Dmitri lightly kisses her again, and she's unsure if he means to reassure her or himself that she survived. "When you lost consciousness, I feared ... even your body refused to respond. He unlocked your shackles and let you drop to the floor."

He gulps as her eyes urge him to continue. "As you can see, the artifice of stupor minimized what he did to me next. He doesn't seem to enjoy an unconscious victim. But then he had another go at you." Tears well in Dmitri's eyes, and she strains to hear the choked words he whispers. "I thought I'd lost you."

Wanting to pull him close, Eliza moves an arm and winces against the pain, but a few seconds later her fingers touch his cheek and trail their way to the back of his neck. Weakly she tugs him forward until his lips settle on hers, but she is too battered and sore to express her feelings in a kiss. "Dmitri ..." Eliza can't believe what she's about to say, and she tries to stop herself, but something has shifted inside her. She knows this may well be the end for them—Shashenka may torture them further or execute them and be done with it. There may be no more tomorrows to express what she's denied for months. She clears her throat for courage and lets the words slip softly off her tongue. "I love you."

"*Ti amo, amore.*" Dmitri's head dips as if he's ashamed. "I'm sorry. I shouldn't have—"

She understands the words—"I love you, sweetheart"—but the retraction that follows stuns her. "Shouldn't have what?"

Dmitri shakes his head and refuses to answer. *I don't get it.* When his gaze meets hers, she says, "You make no sense to me."

He looks torn and uncomfortable. "I don't know how to answer that, love."

I have to know the truth. Eliza takes a deep breath; she's not going to let this go. "Am I Elizabetta Rossellini?"

His body tenses, and she tries not to wince in pain as he grips her tighter. Panic and elation spar for control of his expression. He swallows hard and on a breath he says, "Yes."

Sincerity bundles that one little word in layers of truth. *Oh my God, he's not lying. He's not delusional.* She expected Dmitri would dodge answering again, and it takes her a moment to collect herself and ask the next question. "Was I born in Padua, Italy, in the fourteen hundreds?"

She can feel the fear and excitement ripple off him. His heart beats louder and his breathing quickens. "Yes."

Her pulse matches the frenetic pounding of his. "And you turned me."

Dmitri gives a sad half smile that mirrors the pleading, apologetic look in his eyes. "Yes, love."

Eliza nods again and takes another deep breath.

There's no turning back now. The truth she's yearned for is coming at her like an avalanche, and receiving confirmation of what she's learned is the only way she'll be able to swim to the surface before the slide solidifies and entombs her. "Stop me when I say something that isn't true."

He's momentarily speechless, then tightens his arms around her. "I will."

Resting her forehead against his shoulder, she whispers, "We were Druzhinas. We led a revolt against Shashenka in 1513. It cost the lives of those who stood with us, and resulted in you enduring centuries of torture."

He stops breathing, and his heart pounds so hard it feels as if it will explode through his chest and slam into her. Eliza pulls back to look him in the eye again. Dmitri opens his mouth as if to say something, but the words never come.

Now. Ask him now. She already knows, but she needs to hear him admit the truth of their past. "Am I your mate? Are we ... married?"

The words seem to strike him like a thunderbolt—he pushes her to the floor and scrambles away from her with a horrified look in his eyes. Eliza's mind races like a brush fire. *Does he regret what we had? Was I a horrible wife?* She can't accept that—it doesn't feel right—but she never expected this kind of reaction.

It takes a full minute for him to respond. "Yes. No. We ... were mates and married, but—"

Bullshit. "Vampires don't abandon their mates! I will ask you again." She softens her tone. "Am I your ... are you my husband?"

Dmitri sits down next to her and gathers her back onto his lap, brushing his fingers along her jaw before placing his palm against her cheek. A cascade of emotions pours over his face: sorrow, shame, and guilt. Several tremulous breaths escape him before he says, "Yes, *amore*, I am your mate ... your husband." His head dips down and his lips brush her temple. "You are my wife."

The dam breaks, and Eliza sobs into his chest. All these months—believing lies, seeking truth—distort in the flutter of an eyelash, and the weight of unknown centuries crush her. *What have I lost? What did Shashenka take from me ... from us?*

"Please don't cry, *amore*."

Eliza pushes back to look at him again, sniffling. "What happened to me? Why can't I remember anything from before the apartment in Bozeman?"

His laugh is derisive. "The short answer is our nasty little goblin king."

"Dmitri, please. I need to know the truth about my life."

He draws another deep breath. The pain in his eyes tells Eliza that the ruination of their lives has taken its toll on him, and each word he speaks is saturated in truth and bears the hidden scars of what he withheld for far too many years. Eliza learns what happened after the revolt, and the roles Vladimir and Maria played in the mutilation of their lives. It's shocking for Eliza to hear that she was considered the mastermind. *Oh my God, this is all my fault. I think I'm going to be sick.*

Before she can take ownership of the blame, Dmitri

says, "Maria took your memories at Master's command."

Anger and hatred billow inside her, swallowing her guilt, swirling around in an ever-darkening cloud. *That damn witch!* Key phrases scream out at her: catatonic state, reset of her mind, reprogram. Coherent thoughts return when Dmitri begins talking about the recent past and the incident in Bozeman.

He gently strokes her cheek with the back of his fingers as he recounts the kiss they shared in the warehouse after he rescued her from the hospital. "Seeing you lie there in only a pair of panties, singing that silly little ditty, it was nearly my undoing. I wanted you so desperately ..." His voice trails off, thick with emotion.

I remember. She clasps her hand over his, holding both to her face a moment before brushing her lips against his palm. "I think that kiss awakened part of me. I started having these memory-like dreams, almost as if I was holding on to the few shreds of me and you that still existed."

"Impossible. Maria wiped your mind—your memories are gone, love."

But what about my dreams? Her eyes close tightly—she knows pieces of this puzzle are still missing. Perhaps in time her dreams will restore the memories she has lost. Her gaze locks on Dmitri's, and she can't deny the truth—it sizzles in every cell of her body. *He's mine.* If they survive, if there is to be a future for them, then there can be no more lies between them.

CHAPTER 22: ELIZA

No More Secrets

Unknown hours slip by as they cling to each other in the darkness of the cellar. The constant pain coursing through Eliza's battered body remains, but her mind suppresses it to a dull ache as long as she stays focused on something else. There's no shortage of topics to choose from, given what she's learned.

So many aspects of her life need reconciling that she hardly knows where to begin. She's still in shock that her suspicions have been confirmed. *I am Elizabetta Rossellini Markov.* The first hurdle she faces is acceptance that she has existed for over six centuries—not the almost twenty-four years she believed. Where she once assumed she and Matt were close in age, she now knows that he's the baby, not her. She's lived through historical events she has no memory of. And then there's Dmitri; it boggles her mind.

Dmitri was twenty-seven when Vladimir turned him, Eliza learns—four short human years older than she, but he had been a vampire for fifty years before they found each other. Eliza laughs quietly at the realization that he stalked her even then. Maybe he's always been a maniacal vampire stalker. *My stalker.* She misses not knowing when she fell in love with him, or why, and wonders if there is any way to regain her lost memories. There is an awkwardness in knowing that she is in love with Dmitri, loved him before, yet she doesn't really know the man—no, the husband—holding her now.

Shashenka stole five hundred years from them, but it was Maria who cast the spell that turned her into a blank slate. She wants to demand the witch restore her mind. Dmitri says it's not possible after a reset—he claims there is nothing left to restore. She can't accept that. Rage flares inside her; somehow that witch had better undo this mess, or Eliza will make her pay.

Of course none of it will matter until Shashenka releases them from this cell. *If he releases us.* But if he does, Eliza must be ready to go forward with her plans. "Dmitri, there's something I need to tell you."

He tenses but nods. "You can tell me anything, love. There'll be no more secrets between us."

This will freak him out—he probably won't like it one bit. She might as well jump straight into it. "Eventually Shashenka will either take us out of here to kill us, or he'll reintegrate us into the coven. I'm hoping the sick, sadistic war he's waging against us results in the latter, because ..." She notices his scowl and changes her approach to soften the blow. "I know you don't remember much, but Matt was in Venice to meet with me. He's helping me ... um ... us plot the overthrow of Shashenka."

"He's what?" Dmitri's deep voice rises an octave and his eyes widen in alarm. Sometimes she hates it when she's right—predictably, he's not enthused about her plan, but she's ready. Her jaw sets in determination to win him over.

"Trust me, this time will be different. Matt is doing a terrific job of bringing it all together. He's rather quite brilliant." Eliza puts forth a brave face to bolster her words, but guilt lurks just below the surface. The truth is that because of their plans, Matt's life is at risk now—Shashenka wants him dead—and it's too late to stop what they've put in motion.

Dmitri groans. "I really don't like that damn mutt."

"That's only because you thought he was stealing your mate. And you hate werewolves in general. And he's helping me plan this revolt." She laughs ruefully. "Look, Matt is my best friend, and he's a great ally. If you give him a chance, you may find you even like him."

"I doubt that," he says under his breath. "I'm supposed to be your best friend."

Eliza stands firm; she will not allow any division between her and Matt, or her and Dmitri. "Like him or not, he's my right hand in all of this. We will take Shashenka down—with or without your help."

A skeptical look clouds Dmitri's face as she details the progress they have made. Matt, she tells him, has allied with the werewolf clans near the various Belyakov estates, recruited at least one other vampire from the inner lair, and is even finding smaller vampire covens willing to help. Eliza notices a flicker of hope in Dmitri's eyes when she suggests that even some of the Druzhinas are turning against Shashenka.

"When this goes down, it will be a multipronged attack—we are targeting the goblin king's financial interests, allies, business partners, and estates."

Dmitri places a finger to her lips. In his eyes she can see pride and admiration tinged with fear. "But love, you don't understand how we failed last time. How can you know if you ... I can't lose you again."

She senses Dmitri's opposition is waning, and it boosts her confidence. "It's safe to say I have an unbiased and fresh perspective."

When he only grunts she says, "When we get out of here, I'll need to convince that evil son of a bitch that I'm contrite, repentant, and eager to please him again. You'll need to pretend that you're still locked within your madness."

"I don't want him touching you ever again." A feral glint flashes in his eyes. "Never. Again. Elizabetta, it sickens me to think of the ways he has already touched you, and I won't continue watching it now that you know the truth."

"You must. I must. If we are going to succeed, then we have to do this. We'll never have freedom or a life together if we don't do this right." She pauses, waiting for his reaction, but he says nothing—he just glares. *I hope that's his silent agreement look.*

She raises an eyebrow to show she's not going to budge on this point, and Dmitri finally relents. "All right." He looks defeated as he adds, "Knowing that I put you in this position ..." He shakes his head, but doesn't meet her gaze. "You'll never know how sorry I am, love, for failing you."

"We need to look forward, or we'll never know a future where this is behind us."

When he remains quiet, Eliza continues outlining their plans and lists those she believes they can co-opt and those she has marked or considered for execution alongside Shashenka. Dmitri finally speaks up, pointing out the strengths and weaknesses of her summation. He agrees with her assessment of the Druzhinas—she's awed by his quiet intelligence and suffers a twinge of shame that she ever thought him ignorant or simple minded.

When she mentions Maria, he says, "When the mole sprang the trap, it was Maria who stopped us. Her immobility spell ended our rebellion."

Immobility? Ah, the freezing spell. The reminder stokes Eliza's anger. "That bitch needs to go down with Shashenka."

To her surprise Dmitri shakes his head and urges Eliza to reconsider whether that extreme is necessary. Her mouth hangs agape as he goes on to defend the witch. *Maybe he's not as smart as I thought he was.* When she pushes back against his advocacy for Maria, he doubles down. If Eliza didn't know better, she'd swear they were talking about two different people—the witch is a riddle that she, at least, can't solve.

I can't trust her. "That witch hasn't changed one iota! And the immobility spell, well, she's already used it on me. Twice. The first was in Novgorod, and you saw the second time, when I killed the Giordano vampires. We can't trust her."

"What?" In a panicked motion he grabs her face. "In Novgorod?"

Gaze averted to the floor to hide the pain of his grip, she explains what happened the night after she left Dmitri in pieces in the great hall at Novgorod. He stares at her in apparent disbelief, and something in his expression triggers her doubt. Her tone becomes beseeching—she needs to unravel the truth about the witch. "That's also the night Maria revealed my true name. In her rant against me, she slipped and called me Elizabetta Rossellini. It set me on the right path to find the truth."

He lowers his face so their noses are almost touching, and his voice contains an edge of excitement. "Maria doesn't lose control, love. Everything she says and does is deliberate, always with purpose."

Blinking at him, she listens as he describes everything Maria said or did over the last year, and the subtle betrayals the witch has already perpetuated against Shashenka. There are only two possibilities in Eliza's mind: either Maria is setting them up for a final takedown, or she is orchestrating her own coup against Shashenka. She falls into silence as they puzzle over the enigma, but Dmitri reaches a conclusion before she does—the witch is an ally. She almost laughs at him. The thought of moving Maria to the top of the co-opt list, even ahead of the Druzhina, is sheer lunacy. *Brilliant—let's end this revolt before it even gets started.*

They are still debating the issue when the sound of someone unlocking the cellar door catches their attention.

Dmitri drops a quick kiss on Eliza's cheek before he stands and moves several feet away from her. She slumps on the floor near the table, and Dmitri leans against a rack—his arms hang down at his sides—as the door opens and the light from the hallway illuminates the dark room.

In brisk strides Maria crosses the cell and drapes a cloak around Dmitri's shoulders.

Mouth agape, Eliza blurts out, "Maria, what are you doing here?" A nervous surge of energy unleashes budding panic. *Did she hear our argument? Has she come to sell us out?*

Without looking at her, Maria places a hand on Dmitri's cheek and brushes his long bangs from his face. She says under her breath, "You look better than I feared." Then she turns to Eliza. "So do you, for that matter."

"What are you doing here?" Eliza tries not to scowl.

"I'm here to bring you both out."

Eliza's stomach churns. She gives a furtive glance at Dmitri, but his mask is in place; he doesn't show any obvious reaction.

"We have a meeting to attend in Paris." Maria's smile is actually mischievous. "I found your cell phone when we searched your room. I've had the most delightful exchange of texts with your friend Mattie."

Shit. Ice water runs through Eliza's veins, and its freezing chill seems to jar Dmitri from across the room. His head snaps up and his eyes turn hard, determined. Before Eliza can react or stop him, he closes the gap, slamming and pinning the witch against the wine rack. "What are you up to, Maria?"

Maria's words trip and fall over each other. "Y-you ... what? You are ..." She blinks and starts again with a laugh. "Yes, of course you're back. I should have known having you locked up together for so long would give Eliza enough time to reach you again."

Weak and shaky, Eliza pulls herself to her feet and steps between Maria and Dmitri. "You didn't answer his question. What are you doing here?" Her cold stare doesn't sway, but her body does. Dmitri wraps an arm around her waist to steady her.

The witch laughs so hard that they have to wait for her to compose herself. "I already told you, we have a meeting in Paris. I'm here to make sure you get to it."

Maria steps back and looks down the hall. When she reenters the room, her words tumble out in a rush. "This is neither the time nor the place for these discussions. It's daytime—we need to get you out of here before Shashenka or one of his lackeys notices us leaving. Now, either you come with me, or you're okay with staying put for the full year he intends on leaving you in here."

No way. "We're not going—"

"I think it may be prudent to go with her." Dmitri eyes the witch, seeming to convey a silent question. When Maria inclines her head and smiles, he doesn't allow Eliza time to argue. In one swift motion he lifts her into his arms and follows the witch out the door.

CHAPTER 23: DMITRI
Revelations

The witch leads them through the east wing of the villa, across the central hall, and into the laundry room in the locals' wing; everyone is asleep this time of day, of course, but Dmitri knows that the locals are also the easiest for Maria to manipulate should their group be seen leaving. *What is she up to?* Maria instructs them to climb into one of the large dirty linen carts. Dmitri gently lowers Elizabetta into the cart and cradles her on his lap once he joins her. Maria tosses a few rumpled sheets across their bodies, and the cart starts to roll.

Elizabetta whimpers in pain with the movement—her injuries are not healing. He adjusts his hold on her to prevent jostling her too much. *Is Maria really taking us to Paris?* Doors open and close. He can feel the cart moving from smooth to rough ground, and then onto another semi-smooth surface. Then another door opens, and Dmitri squints against the daylight illuminating the sheets over their heads; the brightness is blinding compared with the dark cellar. There's a brief sense of floating through the air before the cart settles onto a surface that moves and rocks. A motor purrs, and Dmitri recognizes the sound—they're on a boat. *Where are we going?* He insisted that Maria would be an ally, but she still hasn't said where exactly she's taking them. He hopes this doesn't turn out to be another one of his mistakes.

When the boat stops, Dmitri hears a mechanical rumble. *An automatic door?* Sounds of voices and cars suggest activity around them. Dmitri speculates that they are in the estate garage near the Santa Lucia train station in the Cannaregio District, but he resists the urge to look. He hears the distinct noise of a vehicle door just before the cart rises, floats, and settles once more on a solid surface. Doors slam shut, keys jingle, and the vehicle lurches into motion.

The engine's noise is the only sound for several long minutes. Dmitri's reluctant to say anything—he doesn't know if they are alone with Maria. His pulse quickens when the witch finally speaks. "You can get out of the cart if you wish, but you'll want to stay in the back—the sun is out in full force today. You'll also find a box of wet wipes, clean clothes, and your daggers in the lime-green bag by the side door."

Dmitri shoves the sheets aside and notices that Elizabetta also blinks rapidly against the brighter light—she looks terrified. He climbs out of the cart and extends a hand to help her over the edge. This is the closest they've come to freedom in centuries—he'd almost given up hope of getting out of the cellar—and he's grateful to have escaped with Elizabetta by his side. They sit together on the floorboards next to the cart and clasp each other's hands. *I can scarcely believe this is happening.*

After a few minutes he reaches for the wet wipes and gingerly washes the dried blood from Elizabetta's face. Fresh blood seeps to the surface. While his wounds are nearly healed, her injuries are slow to close because of the amount of blood she's lost. There's only one way she can recover. "Elizabetta needs to feed. We'll have to hunt when we arrive in Paris."

"I'll see what I can do."

The Venetian islands fall away behind them, and Dmitri takes a breath—the implications and possible consequences are too numerous for him to narrow down without answers. His tone turns harsh. "Okay, we're out of there. No more excuses, Maria. Tell us why you are doing this."

"We'll have time to discuss everything during the flight."

Elizabetta leans into Dmitri's side and gives him a worried look. "It's like the attack on the Cleary ranch all over again—something more is going on, and I know it."

That incident wasn't one of Dmitri's finer moments, and he's not thrilled by the reminder, but she has a point. Her body is trembling, and her eyes are wide with fear. He needs to push Maria for an answer. "I don't think we'll be getting on that flight with you if we don't have answers before we reach the airport."

Maria glances over her shoulder—she's scowling. "If

you must know, your little war against Shashenka is about to explode. I've waited centuries for this opportunity. You're going to have to trust me to control and direct the blast."

Dmitri's head whips around toward the witch, and he freezes midmotion, leaving Elizabetta with her head and one arm through the shirt he was helping her into. *Opportunity? Direct the blast?*

"What does that have to do with my meeting with Matt?" Elizabetta wriggles her other arm into the shirt. Her tone is cautious. "Did he know it wasn't me on the other end of the texts?"

"Matt? He?" Maria erupts into laughter. "Matt ... Mattie ... should have known." She glances back at them again. "You were always clever—I've always liked that about you. I thought we were meeting a woman. Imagine my surprise had we shown up and I discovered she's a he."

"Maria?" Dmitri is growing impatient.

"Yes, yes. Your meeting with ... Matt isn't going to be a secluded affair. As to the text messages, yes, he knew it wasn't Eliza."

Questions are written all over Elizabetta's expression, but Dmitri begins to understand; his face tugs into an amused smile. "Is this another of your complying while defying moves?"

"That's a fair assessment."

"What if Shashenka discovers us missing, and you're gone too?" Elizabetta still looks confused.

"He hasn't sent anyone to check on you since he stopped beating you, and he knew I was leaving for holiday. Odds are good that he won't discover your absence before we get back to the estate."

She can go back, but I don't believe we'll go with her. They ride the rest of the way to the airport in silence, and Elizabetta, he knows, is on the verge of hysteria. His heart drowns in guilt—she may never be as strong as she once was. As she draws her knees to her chest, locks her arms around her legs, and begins to rock, he smiles sadly. He's seen this before during her programming—she's teetering between a meltdown and holding it together. He repositions her and tries to pull her back against his chest, but she winces; there is no way to hold her without hurting her while her injuries are so raw.

He strokes her face with his fingers. "Shh ... hush, love. We're going to be okay."

Elizabetta's eyes fill with tears, and shudders ripple through her body as she begins to cry. *Damn it, I don't want to hurt her, but I need to get her under control.* Dmitri turns her around, wraps his long legs around her, and locks her in his arms until she shifts to rapidly rocking her feet and bouncing her knees. *If she keeps this up, she'll return to a blathering mess.* He grimaces and looks at Maria. "I don't suppose you have a sedative or calming potion in your bag, do you?"

"No. Whatever it is you're dealing with back there, you're going to have to handle it the old-fashioned way."

Dmitri pulls Elizabetta into his lap and gently untangles her blood-matted tresses. With his nose near her ear he begins humming, hoping that she'll recognize and react to the song. Yes, it should be familiar to her; if his hazy memory is accurate, she hummed the same song to him while they were locked beneath La Perfezione, and somehow it pulled him further from the void's grasp.

Slowly her body stills. Her head rests on his shoulder, and she looks up at him, a haunting curiosity in her eyes—almost as if she recognizes that she knows the answer but can't quite state it. "I've heard this before."

"Hmm ..." He drags a hand through his hair, unsure if this is the time to tell her. "It's a medieval song I used to play for you on the lira, and later on the violin."

"Who wrote it? What is it called?"

The hint of eagerness, as if she's discovered a major clue in her life story, is compelling, and he smiles. "I wrote it for you. '*Il mio tesoro.*'" Seeing her quizzical expression, he translates for her: "It means 'my treasure.'"

They're suddenly thrown forward into the side of the cart when Maria slams on the brakes. "Dmitri! Why are you telling her that? Does Eliza know?" The witch's tone matches the wild look on her face as she peers over the cart at them.

"Yes, she knows. And stop calling her Eliza—her name is Elizabetta." He ignores the confused look Elizabetta gives him and meets the witch's penetrating gaze.

Maria's tone is stern but cautious. "Now is not the right time. You should not force her to use that name when she doesn't even know who she is."

He places a kiss on Elizabetta's temple, his heart swelling with defiant pride and satisfaction. "She understands that her memories are gone and that she is my wife. That is enough for her to reclaim her rightful name."

"Trust me, it's a mistake." Maria shakes her head and resumes driving. "Still, the fact that she knows will make this easier."

Make what easier? Dmitri lets it go for now, since Elizabetta isn't questioning the comment. He hums her song again as the silence settles between them, and closes his eyes, remembering the countless times he played the melody for her on the violin. It's something he hasn't done for twenty-five years, not since his instrument went missing during an inner lair move. Now that he has her back, it is time to replace the lost violin, if for no other reason than to watch the delight on her face as he plays for her.

Maria pulls the van into the hangar. They board the estate jet—Dmitri will alter the pilot's memory to only recall seeing the witch—and settle into their seats for the flight to Paris. Dmitri is eager for answers, but when the witch seems content to dance around the issue with vague responses, his patience runs aground. *I can't take this any longer.* His tone becomes accusing. "You claim you waited for this opportunity, and yet you won't explain yourself. Your involvement in the first rebellion resulted in its spectacular failure. Secrecy isn't going to build our trust in you now."

"Had I known you two were going to try in 1513, I might have joined you then." Her angry retort dies on a deep breath. "Alas, when I learned it was coming, it was already too late. I was bound by agreement to protect Shashenka."

Elizabetta pins Maria with a hostile glare. "If you have to save his nasty butt, then how can you do anything to help us now?" She folds her arms across her chest; every cell of her body radiates distrust.

"There are very fine lines I must traverse in serving your master. If Shashenka knows he's in peril and requests my protection, I must—by oath and treaty—provide it. If something, shall we say, unforeseen were to happen, then it is not my fault if I am not there to protect him."

Dmitri scowls. "I thought you were a willing partner, his lover."

A hard look fills Maria's eyes. "I am no more his lover than Eliza, Sally, or any of the other courtesans, and in many ways even less so. He hasn't shared my bed in centuries." Maria looks sad, and for the first time Dmitri sees something he's never seen in her before—she's as broken inside as they are. "I'm not allowed to be with other men, and he prohibits any man from touching me."

Dmitri understands; she grew too powerful for Shashenka, but losing her as a mate was a weakness others could exploit; their master considered her more valuable as a weapon than as his lover. Dmitri's empathy for the witch grows with each word she says. "While I enjoy many freedoms those of his coven do not, I am no less a slave than the rest of you. I have only been held longer, long enough that most of the vampires from that time are no longer with us. Long enough that only Alexander and Sofia know the truth, and they were sworn to secrecy." She pauses. "Today the lives of four hundred people are at stake if I break the treaty."

She shakes her head. "There's so much you never knew about me. My ma and da were the most powerful witch and warlock in our village and took a stand against the vampires' invasions amid the tumult of the clan wars. It led to a standoff, which Shashenka brought to a swift end when Ivan found my baby brother. He was a wee little lad of three years. I was nine.

"Shashenka threatened to tear him limb from limb unless the village submitted to his demands. My parents didn't want to surrender, but their kin abandoned their defenses—it was a serious blunder. The vampires surrounded them, and Shashenka threatened to kill them as well as my brother if my folks didn't surrender."

Maria's voice becomes almost childlike, laced with pain. It's the first time Dmitri's ever heard her express such emotion. Her normally smooth, calm demeanor, is gone and her posture is curled in on itself. A quick glance at Elizabetta tells him that she finds this change equally unsettling. "Ma and Da hid me in a trunk before they went outside to confront him ... to rescue ... but then Shashenka's lackeys found me. It enraged and intrigued Shashenka that I, this little girl with furious green eyes, tried to kick and hit him."

She explains how Shashenka, always opportunistic, forced her kin into a treaty: he promised to rear her and finish her training as a witch, and in turn he would spare the village.

Maria looks out the plane's window, a vengeful glint in her eyes. "Liar. He spared everyone in the village but my ma, da, and brother. The vampires drained them and hung their bodies from the roof of our home. My kinsmen were forbidden from cutting them down for burial until a full month passed. Before the vampires left the village, Shashenka issued one final threat. They could not come after me; and if I ever failed to protect and serve him, the Druzhina would return and destroy the village, killing every living being. The oath swearing this allegiance was signed, and I was placed in his care—to do his bidding."

He hears Elizabetta gasp, but he doesn't turn to look at her—he meets Maria's devastated gaze instead. The witch's tragedy happened nearly four centuries before Dmitri joined the coven. *It's been lost to time, just like Shashenka intended to do to Elizabetta.* But this is Shashenka's pattern for control and power; the monster kills or ruins those who stand against him or get in his way, and manipulates those in power, directly or indirectly, to achieve his goals, holding whole governments and nations hostage to his demands. Those who benefit him are elevated in social status and wealth. Some of the wealthiest people in the world today are direct beneficiaries of Shashenka's controlling dominion.

Still, Dmitri marvels at the similarity between Maria's and Elizabetta's stories; Shashenka destroyed both women's families and unwittingly set the stage for their combined wrath. A wry smile curves his lips. *Poetic justice that they should finally come together to destroy that bastard.*

"I've waited a long time for both of you to be ready to try again." Maria flashes a warm smile at each of them in turn. "Neither of you will ever know the personal anguish I've experienced for casting my powers against you over these last many centuries."

Dmitri is nodding his understanding when Elizabetta's eyes blaze with sudden anger. "You knew! This whole time, you knew, and yet you let Dmitri suffer centuries of torture. You let me languish in this fake life. You took my memories and assisted that goblin king in torturing, controlling, and ruining our lives."

Her passion stuns Dmitri—it's a relief that she's too weak to attack the witch. Elizabetta's stare is powerful enough. Maria doesn't hold eye contact, but looks down at her hands as her face crumples into a mask of shame. "Unfortunately I'm still bound by oath to protect him from known threats. That's why it's imperative to move as fast as we can. As long as he doesn't learn of your plans, I'm free to help you."

The witch's words only seem to stoke Elizabetta's anger. "I want my memories back. You took them ... you stole my life! I'm sitting here next to a husband I don't remember or even know. My mind tells me that I'm a twenty-three-year-old American ... damn it, I'm Italian, and I don't think, speak, or feel like one. If I'm to die in an attempt to end Shashenka, the least you can do is give my life back to me."

"I did not take your memories, Eliza. In fact, they are partly to blame for the difficulties Dmitri had in controlling you during the reprogramming of your mind. As I told you before the first spell was ever cast against you, your memories are merely blocked."

They discussed this before? Why didn't Maria tell me? What else has she hidden or lied about? The anger he's kept in check is rising to match Elizabetta's.

"Then unblock them." Elizabetta stands and paces the cabin.

"It may be best if we wait until after the meeting."

Dmitri and Elizabetta say in unison, "Why?"

Maria breathes out a sigh. "It will overload your mind as the conflicting details of your personality, character, and past reconcile with your current memories and experiences. You'll be in no shape to address the coup council."

"The coup council?" Dmitri's long bangs flutter against his eyelashes, and he raises his hand and sweeps the hair back twice before lingering at the crown of his head. As a Druzhina he's aware of the council; they are the most powerful organization among Maria's kind, but they don't typically meddle in other realms' affairs.

"I wasn't lying about chatting with Mattie—Matt. I intercepted his text when he checked to see if Eliza was still meeting him in Paris."

Maria explains the series of texts that raised her suspicions that something more was going on than a friendly get-together. When she revealed herself and told Matt what had happened to Dmitri and Elizabetta, Matt sent an envoy to meet her in Tuscany. *So the mongrel is smart enough not to give blind trust.* He can feel Elizabetta's gaze but keeps his focus on the witch; he's not about to admit that Elizabetta may have chosen well when it comes to the wolf. Maria claims that she convinced Matt to solicit the help of the Orde de Maxia—the Order of Magic. She helped Matt petition them on Elizabetta's behalf.

"He did what?" The news sends Elizabetta into a tizzy, and she demands answers—she's clearly not happy Matt

made the move without consulting her. Dmitri takes the
lead and cuts the witch off. It's too easy for them to forget
that Elizabetta can't remember how the shadow realms
operate. *I'd better explain this to her myself.* All maxians—witches, warlocks, sorcerae, and wizards—fall under
the Orde de Maxia's jurisdiction regardless of where they
live. As a ruling body, the Orde de Maxia controls their
realm; he's also aware of the council's involvement in past
skirmishes, overthrows, and wars.

Dmitri gives Elizabetta the basics, then turns to Maria.
"I didn't know we or any outsider could petition them."

"They don't advertise it. They are quite happy to allow
non-maxians to think otherwise, but they will involve themselves through an outside petition if it's for the greater
good of the shadow realms."

Willing maxians could tip this endeavor in their favor ...
it might have made a difference before. Was it ignorance
or mere oversight that they'd failed to see this in their last
attempt to end Shashenka's rule? Dmitri doesn't know
whom he's angrier with—himself or the maxians. Then he
recalls the conversation he had with Sally at Big Sky, and
grimaces at the memory—at how wrong he was to think
that ones like her were of no use to their plans. *We erred
last time by not considering the histories of those in the
inner lair and outside our realm.*

The Orde de Maxia is calling for a coup council, Maria
tells them—a clandestine meeting of aggrieved and interested parties in advance of any shadow realm wars or re-
volts—and they will decide whether the Orde de Maxia
will back the venture or ignore it. If they support Dmitri

and Elizabetta, they will coordinate between the realms of vampires, werewolves, and maxians, and provide assets, logistics, and fighters to the leaders of the aggrieved. If they refuse, the dispute is classified as a revolt or a rebellion, and the leaders and their allies must take action at their own peril.

Maria is supposed to be helping us this time. Dmitri says, "I would hope they will back one of their kind going against a vampire as powerful as Shashenka."

"I plan to do my best in petitioning for the coup." A broad grin spreads across Maria's face. "I'm pleased to be at your service, Mr. and Mrs. Markov."

I never thought I'd hear those names again. He can't contain his joy—he wraps his arms around Elizabetta, pressing ardent kisses to her lips. She stiffens and lets out a painful groan. *Damn it.* He's forgotten to control himself. Tone sheepish, he draws back and says, "Are you ready to lead this war, Mrs. Markov? Will you fight by my side, love?"

"Yes, yes. A thousand times, yes!"

It's late morning when they arrive in Paris. Maria rents a windowless utility van to keep Dmitri and Elizabetta out of the sun; there is no way to bring them into the hotel until sunset. Matt, she says, is waiting for them in a double suite on the top floor. He will go with them to the Orde de Maxia meeting at midnight in the catacombs below Paris.

Maria fetches a bellhop with a cart for their luggage, which is loaded on top of the van. Neither Dmitri nor Elizabetta gave thought to packing when the witch sprang them from the wine cellar, but both are grateful that she had the foresight to do so. They hear her talking to the cheerful bellhop as they walk away. "Please take the luggage to my suite. I need to deliver fresh baguettes and red wine to a couple of friends."

For several minutes Dmitri and Elizabetta sit in silence. He surreptitiously pricks his thumb to make sure he's not dreaming or hallucinating—the sharp pain and drop of blood that pools on the surface prove he's not. He licks his thumb to stop the bleeding as his gaze returns to Elizabetta. *She's really here.* Then he says the one thing both have doubtless given thought to. "We're not going back to La Perfezione or any other Belyakov estate until this is over."

"What about the Druzhina? You know that demented little monster will send them after us."

"Let's hope we have more of them on our side than he does." Dmitri kisses her and tries to reassure her that this will work, but until contact is made he doesn't know for certain where each Druzhina stands.

A light knock sounds on the van's back door; Maria has two dazed human men standing with her. "I figured you're more than ready for a meal."

Dmitri makes a quick grab for the men to avoid the sun. He nods as Maria says, "Don't worry about the security cameras ... the van is parked in a blind spot. I'll take care of these when I return later."

Elizabetta sniggers. "Baguettes and red wine?"

The witch's smile looks suddenly sheepish. "*Bon ap-*

pétit."

As Maria closes the van door, Dmitri pushes the larger of the two men toward Elizabetta. His fangs lower at the scent of their blood. He'll make sure she is satiated first—she needs to heal. When she attempts to argue, he cuts her off. "You'll need more than I will, love."

Dmitri only half drains the man he feeds from, offering the remainder to her. Again she tries to resist, but he pushes her sleeve up to expose the gaping wounds beneath the thin fabric. An audible sigh of relief floats from him as she accepts the human, and when they finish she admits that the thirsting ache at the back of her throat is gone.

She can be so damn stubborn. Dmitri laughs. "There were times when I was programming you, making you believe you were human, that you resisted and refused to eat. It led to some strange sessions trying to balance a human nature with the need to keep you fed."

Elizabetta shakes her head and tells him what happened after she met Matt in Yellowstone Park. "I had just discovered that I am a vampire, and I didn't want to kill people. I was getting hungrier—the little bit of animal blood from meat packages wasn't cutting it."

Nothing like giving a starving man a cracker crumb.

"Matt tried to talk me through it with one of his brilliant analogies, but it didn't make sense until you brought that box of blood to my cell at Big Sky."

The affectionate way she speaks of the mutt grates on him, but for the wolf to make a difference where he struggled with her is too much to ignore. Dmitri asks, "How did he manage that without hypnosis and spells? There were moments you were very resistant to both."

"Matt has a certain country charm. He rationalized it this way"—she laughs and clears her throat—"he said it was probably the same as people who eat meat and those who choose some green label like vegetarian, vegan, what have you."

"I do not understand, love."

"The bottom line is that people have to eat to live. Whether they choose meat or veggies, they don't think twice about eating, or what life the animal or plant lived— they simply kill and eat when hungry. Same with us, he said. For us, humans are meat—other mammals are plants."

Dmitri arches his eyebrows and trips his long bangs into his eyes again. "It's not that simple; animal blood lacks the nourishment we need. Without human blood we risk falling into an incapacitated state that's nearly unrecoverable." He frowns. "The wolf's advice actually helped you?"

"Well, not much at the time, but it did later." Elizabetta shrugs. "We can't change what we are, and we have to have blood to live. I will admit that I do find humans more palatable and satisfying."

They laugh together as Dmitri pulls her into a hug. "We had a similar discussion after I turned you in 1426. You didn't want to kill humans, and you thought I had lied to you. It wasn't until you fell quite ill that you relented and allowed me to bring you a human."

Elizabetta leans back and looks at him. "I really was born in 1403?"

"Yes."

"When did we get married? What's our anniversary date?"

He's not certain how to interpret the eagerness behind her questions, but he's hopeful it expresses at least some level of desire for him. "We married on September 23, 1427." *Is she ready to accept me as her husband again?* She repeats the date aloud and smiles for a moment before a befuddled, shocked look settles over her face. "We've been married 588 years?"

Dmitri kisses the top of her head. Their next anniversary is a little over three months away. He wonders if they'll spend it on the run or if they will have succeeded in killing Shashenka by then—or if failure will have them imprisoned or dead when the date arrives. "Yes, love, but given our nearly immortal life spans, we don't quite mark the years the same way humans do. While the day itself remains special, we celebrate the anniversary once a decade; so when we celebrated our eighth anniversary— before the failed rebellion—in actuality we had been married eighty years."

Dmitri recalls the centuries of silent celebration while Elizabetta was catatonic. He would find a human with an exquisite bouquet, help her feed, and play the violin for her for hours on end. Not once did she know he was there, and the celebratory atmosphere he created while he was with her always led to a month of seclusion for him afterward. It was the only way he could deal with the heartbreak and prepare for another year ahead.

Elizabetta seems to understand his sudden sadness; she moves onto his lap and slips her arms around his neck.

"You marked fifty anniversaries without me even knowing. When we celebrate our fifty-ninth, it will be together."

He tries to smile; with such a volatile future hanging over their heads, Dmitri can only hope it will be so. For now, just having her back as his wife and mate is enough for him. *It will always be enough.*

CHAPTER 24: ELIZA

Coup Council

A few hours pass before someone raps on the van door; it barely registers with Eliza's distracted thoughts. It's not until Dmitri starts to move around her that she pulls away from the deep contemplation. So many aspects of her life have shifted in the last few hours that she's almost at a loss to sort through it all, but it's the change in her relationship with Dmitri that demands the most attention. Eliza doesn't know if she can accept the intimacy he may expect now that he's embraced their marital status. *I'm not even sure what to call myself. I may be Elizabetta, but I'm still Eliza, too.* She leans forward to open the door and finds Matt and Maria standing on the other side. *I have missed him.* Even in the dim evening light she can see relief and excitement in Matt's eyes.

Beaming, he reaches for Eliza's hand and helps her out. "Damn, it's good to see you, baby vamp. You look like shit. I was so worried. Are you okay?"

She laughs. "You really know how to make a woman feel sexy—it's nice to see you too." She doesn't hesitate to exchange their customary peck on the lips. Behind her Dmitri clears his throat with a low growl. *Seriously? I can't believe he just growled at me.*

Matt's head snaps up, and his lopsided smile seems trapped between frozen and falling away. Eliza steps back so the men can face each other. They've never officially met, or at the least not been properly introduced.

McAllister, Novgorod, Waiheke, Venice ... tried killing each other, wanted to kill each other, too confused to kill each other, and too distracted to kill each other. Yep, that about covers it.

Her lips quiver into a nervous smile as she takes her husband's hand. "Dmitri Markov, I'd like you to meet my best friend, Matt Wolfe. Matt ..." She pauses, unsure how best to introduce Dmitri. The last time she saw Matt, they were still searching for answers about Elizabetta. *About me.* Honesty is best, but it's going to hurt worse than ripping off a Band-Aid slow. "Matt, I'd like you to meet my husband, Dmitri Markov."

"Your what?" Matt's harsh, shocked tone leaves Eliza feeling as if she's been slapped.

She gives him an apologetic smile. "I am ..." *If I say it, I own it ... no more secrets, no more lies.* "Elizabetta Rossellini Markov, mate and wife of Dmitri Markov."

One glance at Dmitri's face tells her that he understands the message the introduction conveyed—deliberate, defined relationship status—and she squeezes his hand. He extends his other hand toward his natural enemy. "Pleased to meet you, Mr. Wolfe. Elizabetta speaks very highly of you."

Matt hesitates a moment before accepting and shaking it. "Yeah, um, sure." He looks around as if he's sizing up a vehicle to crawl under, and for a brief moment Eliza recalls hiding with him under the juniper bush in Yellowstone Park. *He didn't fit well there either.* In spite of herself she laughs out loud, stopping abruptly when both men frown at her.

She takes Matt's arm and turns toward the hotel. "So tell me, what kind of trouble are you up to in Paris?"

As they start to walk away, she gives Dmitri a reassuring smile, ignoring the seething look he casts in their direction. She knows he will remain at the van to help Maria dispose of the bodies, but if the fury radiating off him is any indicator, they won't be long. Eliza hears the witch try to soothe him: "Trust your wife. You've always held her heart." She's grateful for Maria's effort, yet she doubts it will placate Dmitri; it will take a lot more than a reassuring word to defuse the hostility between the men.

When they reach the hotel room, Matt explains that he made it out of Venice two days after Dmitri arrived at the apartment. His nerves couldn't handle staying there any longer, despite his injuries; he was on the first available plane back to London. Once he finished recuperating there, he returned to the United States. He laughs. "I think this whole thing is making me paranoid."

Her mind starts racing through justifiable reasons to be fearful, but Matt brushes aside her concerns. "When I got home to West Yellowstone, something just felt off, and I didn't want to stay there to regroup, so I went shopping—bought a rolling doghouse." At her confused look he adds, "A thirty-five-foot motor home. I parked it at the Cleary Ranch in McAllister."

She's missed his humor. "I don't know if that's a step up or a step down for you, Matt."

"That reminds me." He stands and opens his briefcase. "I've been working on these and wanted to see what you thought."

He pushes a few papers in front of her. *House plans?* Eliza notices recurring elements in the designs—metal shuttering systems, few south-facing windows, basic kitchens, and retractable roofs or skylights for watching the night sky. *Oh no, he's designed these with me in mind.*

His tone is sincere. "Which one do you like most?"

She doesn't want him building her a house, a reminder of his slaughtered dreams of a future with her. *Why would he show me these? Is he hoping there's still a chance for us?* "Where I'll live when this is all over is something that hasn't crossed my mind. I wouldn't know how to choose a favorite for you."

Undeterred, Matt says, "Well, you might want to tack that thought onto the edge of your revolt somewhere, because when this is done, I want to build your home."

"You're really serious, even now that ... that I'm married to Dmitri?"

"Baby vamp, you are my best friend, and while I may not live as long as you, I want your home built to last a millennium. I want it to be everything you ever dreamed of."

It's going to be okay. We're going to be okay. Grinning, Eliza jumps up and wraps her arms around his neck. "You're the best friend anyone could ever have. I love you to the moon and back."

The moment she gives him a quick kiss, Dmitri walks into the room with Maria. Before Eliza can drop her arms, Dmitri pulls them apart and slips between them, facing Matt. His fangs are showing, and his tone carries a clear threat. "What do you think you're doing, mutt?"

Matt looks past Dmitri's shoulder at Eliza. "I was trying to present your wife with a gift."

Afraid they may come to blows, Eliza steps alongside Dmitri and grabs his arm. She tries to pull him away, but he jerks her forward instead. "She doesn't need those kinds of gifts."

Shit ... not good.

Matt reaches back behind himself and grabs the house plans from the table. "I offered to build you a house. She was thanking me. I think."

Eliza tugs at Dmitri's arm again. "It's my fault, really. We've always exchanged friendly kisses. It doesn't ... I'm not ..."

Dmitri raises his hand and in an agitated motion sweeps his hair from his face. He still looks as if he wants to mangle Matt; the inferno of anger radiating off him is enough to force Eliza back a step. *Don't hit him. Don't do this.*

Maria makes an obvious attempt to redirect their focus. "This is a lovely suite, Mattie. Thank you for arranging it for all of us while we're here in Paris."

Eliza shoots her an annoyed glance, but Matt seems relieved to avoid a potential brawl. His tense posture relaxes as he maintains eye contact with Dmitri. "I booked this double suite when Maria said three of you were coming. I didn't think we'd have a problem or a need for separate suites—I thought you were back on the crazy train."

Jeez, Matt. Are you trying to start a fight? Again Dmitri growls and glares at him. Matt stiffens and draws a quick breath, and Eliza holds hers. *These two are going to kill each other.*

She exhales in relief when Matt says, "I'm sorry, man. No hard feelings?"

Dmitri's demeanor doesn't change, and Matt shrugs and wiggles his eyebrows. He glances at Eliza. "Does this vamp come with an instruction manual or a warning label? I never know what to expect—stalker, warrior, zombie, jealous husband."

"If the ladies will excuse us later, I'm sure we can settle this issue ourselves." Dmitri's tone is not a suggestion, but a challenge, and Matt seems to realize it too. The way he smiles and nods in acceptance sends a shiver up Eliza's spine. Her heart drops through the floor—she was wrong, foolish to think they'd give friendship a chance just because she loves them both.

When Maria suggests they settle the luggage into their rooms, Eliza is grateful to put a little distance between the two men. She tries to talk to Dmitri about Matt, but he rebuffs her and stalks off to the bathroom. He comes out minutes later; she gives him a hard look and then shuts herself in the bathroom. *Two can play this cold-shoulder game, jackwagon.*

Once they're showered and dressed in fresh clothes, they rejoin the others, pretending they didn't just have a spat. Eliza's decided to let this go for now, but at some point they are going to discuss Matt's role in her life.

The four gather at the suite's table to discuss the upcoming meeting.

"There's been some great developments for us, baby vamp." Matt flashes a wicked smile at Dmitri, and Eliza sinks down in her chair. "After the Orde de Maxia called for the coup council, we had to contact the vampire covens and werewolf packs that are interested in that devil vamp's demise. I've spent the last month rounding up more willing pack leaders from around the world. Teresina and Stephanie are still looking for more vampire covens."

"How many packs are going to help us?" Eliza asks. She still doesn't know how Stephanie took the news of Vinnie's death.

"Every pack in my employ near the Belyakov estates, and all the others bordering their territory. Rough estimate is thirty-two packs standing by, ready to fight. There are around 450 werewolves under their control."

The thought of that many werewolves fighting with them frightens her. *Is this still manageable if the allied vampire numbers are lower?* "How many vampire covens will stand with us?"

"Aside from those on the inside of Shashenka's coven, twelve other covens will take part."

"Only twelve? What are their numbers?" The disproportional vampire to werewolf ratio spikes her flight instinct—it's too much of a threat to her kind.

"It's not as bad as it sounds, but it's not great, either. But we still have time to find more." Matt, always honest, doesn't hold back. "Of the dozen we have, they claim 145 vampires are under their control. Their help will come at a price, though. They want territory in exchange, and I told them that you would work out those details before we move against Belyakov."

Matt looks at Maria, and a lopsided grin curls the corners of his mouth. "What about your kind? What do they do besides holding meetings and turning people into frogs?"

Maria wiggles her fingers and winks at him. "Don't tempt me, Mattie."

What the heck was that? Eliza looks at Dmitri, and the silent question seems to hang between them.

The witch says, "If the council approves the petition, then the maxians will get everything in place for the battle—people, weapons, containment chambers to hold those who aren't marked for execution. They will, at the Markovs' request"—she nods at Eliza and Dmitri—"provide maxians willing to fight and help ensure the overthrow's success."

"Maxians?" Matt, with his young werewolf years, doubtless hasn't heard the term before—though he knows magical beings exist.

"That is the proper term for our species, for all magic realm folk—witches, warlocks, sorcerae, and wizards."

Eliza swears she can see the wheels in Matt's head turn—as if he's trying to find a way to incorporate that information into his humor repertoire and use it later. She has to stifle a giggle. *I really hope Maria is ready for him. This could be fun.*

Their strategy session continues until it's time to head to the catacombs. Maria drives them to the Paris Métro and leads them to an abandoned tunnel near the Place Denfert-Rochereau public entrance for the catacombs. Together they clamber down an embankment and slip through a barely noticeable crack in the ground.

The hole requires them to crawl and then lie flat to squeeze through an opening slightly wider than their bodies. Maria mutters a spell that removes the soil from their skin and clothes, but when Matt quips something about the perks of not needing showers or doing laundry, the annoyed look she flashes him silences his attempt at humor. That shifts the mood among them, and the group becomes quiet, subdued. They follow the witch through a series of tunnels—remnants of the underground quarries that provided limestone for the monuments and older buildings of the city.

A din of voices grows louder as they near the meeting place, and Eliza's steps falter when she sees the nearly two hundred maxians, werewolves, and vampires mingling in the chamber. *Matt said our numbers had grown, but this shit just got real. What if someone rats us out?* On a dais fifteen feet above the floor, thirteen robed maxians—the council members, she guesses—sit on carved limestone seats and watch the crowd below. Eliza gulps, almost wondering if seeking their help is a mistake. Then one of the council members notices Maria and taps a wand on a metallic sphere that looks like the Flower of Life. A high-pitched ting resonates through the chamber. *They actually have wands? I wonder if brooms are myth or truth?*

When the room quiets, an older maxian with white-blond hair flowing past his shoulders stands and walks to the edge of the dais. "I am High Warlock Jacques Boucher, and I call this meeting to order."

His voice booms across the suddenly quieted chamber. "The Orde de Maxia has gathered you to hear the petition of aggrieved leaders Mr. and Mrs. Dmitri Markov of Venice, Italy. Please remain quiet while Miss D'Arcy presents their grievances against the Belyakov coven."

The warlock motions for their group to come forward to a raised marble platform in front of but slightly below the council's dais. Maria leads their group up the stone steps without hesitating. The only noise from the crowd behind them is the occasional hint of someone shifting their position. With rapt attention Eliza watches as Maria greets the maxian leaders with a bow of her head. While Maria is deferential toward the council members, there's an understated pride and sense of equality in her bearing that Eliza never saw her exhibit toward Shashenka.

"You may proceed, Miss D'Arcy." The high warlock bows to her and sits on his stone perch.

Maria clears her throat, thanks the council for hearing the Markovs' petition, and lays out their case. She tells of the first failed rebellion, and the years of punishment and torture Shashenka inflicted on Dmitri and Eliza. With precise details she explains the reset and reprogramming of "Elizabetta's" mind—the use of Eliza's full forgotten name is a stark reminder that the injustices against her started centuries before, not mere months ago.

Then Maria recounts the atrocities: the innumerable executions, the torture, the brutality. For centuries Shashenka has manipulated those in both the shadow realms and the human world. There's a noticeable reaction from the council members as she lists the many governments that he has brutally meddled with during his thousand-year reign.

It takes a little over four hours to lay out all the charges against Shashenka. As Maria brings the oral petition to a close, she pleads for the wisdom and guidance of the Orde de Maxia to aid the Markovs and their followers in a victorious war to end Shashenka Belyakov's control over the vampire realm.

When she steps back, High Warlock Boucher motions Dmitri forward. "Do you wish for your master's overthrow?"

"Yes," Dmitri answers without hesitation.

"What is your intended punishment for the wrongs Shashenka Belyakov has visited upon you and your wife?"

Dmitri reaches back and pulls her to his side. For a moment Eliza is confused—then she understands he's deferring to her, and it's sobering to realize he will support whatever she decides. Her voice is clear and strong. As much as she'd love to torture the monster for centuries, she understands the need to be merciful if they are to gain maxian support. "We will show more mercy to him than he's shown to anyone else. His death will be swift, and it will be at our hands." A surge of strength pulses through her as Dmitri squeezes her hand. *He will be at my side when the time comes.*

Then High Warlock Boucher asks a question she's unprepared for. "If your war is successful, what is to become of those living in the Belyakov coven?"

Dmitri whispers in her ear; she nods and gives their response. "Those who stand with, protect, or fight alongside Shashenka will be executed. The others will be free to choose their existence and join or form whatever covens they wish. We have no desire to rule Belyakov's dominion, let alone the vampire realm."

Murmurs and hisses erupt from the crowd. A chill raises the hairs on the back of Eliza's neck; clearly it was the wrong answer. The council members look to one another, some frowning, some bowing their heads together in discussion. High Warlock Boucher finally taps his wand like a drumstick against the sphere to quiet the crowd. The tinging noise blasts her eardrums, and she notices some of the vampires and werewolves in the crowd cover their ears with their hands.

"Belyakov's coven is the largest in the vampire realm. No other coven is even half the size of the network of covens he established and controls. It's a grave concern that you have not fully considered the aftermath of removing him from power. You mention nothing of the preservation or dismantling of those networks." The high warlock's stern look matches his serious tone.

Dmitri glances at Eliza, but when she gives a barely perceptible shrug, he seems to understand that it is something they must discuss further. Though she doesn't remember Dmitri from her supposed past or even know him well now, she finds it oddly comforting that he reads her silent communication so well.

Her chin lifts with pride as Dmitri speaks. She is awed by the power and strength in his posture—the way it carries in the tenor of his voice. *Eloquent, intelligent, strong, sexy ... yum.* For a moment she can see what might have attracted her centuries ago—it's attracting her now. Her heart swells with love, and a sense of disbelief rebounds through her. *That man ... he is my husband.*

Dmitri's words are measured. "While our team needs to discuss these matters in greater depth, I can offer with full confidence that our position will not allow anyone to rise and replace Shashenka or lead his coven in its entirety."

"If the Belyakov coven and its network collapse, such a disruption will create ripples of chaos that will affect the other shadow realms. You are too young, Mr. Markov, to know of or remember the tumultuous time before Shashenka Belyakov's rise to power. Your master, while vicious and cruel, at least brought stability and order to the vampires, their laws, and their way of life." The high warlock shakes his head. "What will you do to ensure there is no pandemonium once Belyakov's power structure is gone?"

Eliza's confidence plummets; she's been so singularly focused on destroying Shashenka that she's never considered any of this. *What kind of storm are we unleashing?* Without her memories, she cannot comprehend what a power vacuum in the shadow realms will do to their kind or how bad the chaos for control may become. The thought of someone else leading the Belyakov coven

doesn't sit well; while she certainly doesn't want the re-
sponsibility herself, she fears what type of monster may
rise to take Shashenka's place.

Dmitri is about to speak again when an idea occurs to
her. Touching his arm, she signals that she wants to address the council, and as his head tips toward the dais, she
tries to match the strength he displayed—her voice is
strong, unwavering. "We are early in the formation of our
plans, but I believe we can handle either possibility with
the help of the Druzhina."

High Warlock Boucher studies them for a moment.
"Mr. Markov, where does your Druzhina stand on this issue?"

Bluntly Dmitri says, "We have neither their support
nor their discountenance at this time. Recent information
suggests that half to three-quarters of them will stand
with us."

"What is their current number? Are they not severely
outnumbered by their counterparts in the Druzhinniki?"
The high warlock frowns, and Dmitri sweeps a hand
through his hair as he considers his response; he can't admit the skewed numbers are a concern.

"Not counting my wife or myself, there are nine."

Eliza misses the next question because she's marveling
at Dmitri's comment; although she knows they lost their
positions as Druzhinas, it is obvious that in some ways he
still considers them part of that elite group. *What if I
don't want to be one of them when this is over? What if he
does?*

When she tunes back in, Dmitri is saying, "Many of the

Druzhinnikis are corrupt, but there are those who want to get out from under Belyakov's rule." Eliza doesn't understand how he knows this, but she hopes it's true.

Dmitri adds, "I can only give you an estimate, but my past interactions with them suggests twenty percent, possibly fewer will break in support of us."

"Do you believe that eleven Druzhinas and what, fewer than two hundred Druzhinnikis are enough to keep order throughout the vampire realm if your plan to remove Shashenka Belyakov succeeds?"

"I do."

Eliza's mind is reeling. *I am ignorant and stupid. Matt and I didn't factor any of this into our plans.* In truth, Eliza expected to give the Druzhinas, and now however many Druzhinnikis that stand with them, the same opportunity and chance for freedom. *Will the Druzhinas have the desire to continue in that capacity afterward?* She has no intention of allowing the vampire equivalent to the mafia to remain intact. She leans in and whispers to Dmitri, "I think that first we need to find out where the Druzhinas stand."

Dmitri looks up at the maxians on the dais. "We need more time to secure allegiances before we can provide accurate answers to the questions you are asking."

The council members again murmur among themselves. High Warlock Boucher announces that the council also wishes to discuss the matter and evaluate the petition further. He adjourns the coup council until the following night at midnight. Eliza watches as their members rise and slip out of sight through a hidden exit behind the stone chairs.

The chamber erupts into a mix of laughter and excitement as voices float up from the crowd below the marble platform. When their small group steps down to the main floor, many in the crowd come forward with questions or comments of their own. "What is in it for us?" "What's going to happen with Belyakov's estates?" "Yeah, and what of his businesses?" "Dmitri, why won't you lead—you're respected." "What if you lose control?" "Will the Druzhina be disbanded?" "Yes, we need guarantees that we'll be protected if you lose."

The deluge of everyone talking over one another is too much, and Eliza grows increasingly uncomfortable when some of the strangers speak to her with a level of familiarity that she doesn't know how to respond to. She's grateful when Dmitri and Maria divert attention and conversation away from her. Matt also helps in that regard; he introduces the pack leaders as each one comes forward. It is far easier for Eliza to greet true strangers than those she supposedly knows.

Remarkably, many in the crowd voice strong support of their petition, some even pledging to fight with them regardless of whether the maxians get involved. While the council members will ultimately make the decision to participate or decline, Eliza recognizes that their revolt will have cross-realm support nonetheless. Going on the run is no longer an option.

The crowd begins to thin, and Dmitri, claiming that they have business to discuss before the next council meeting, excuses the four of them from those lingering in the chamber. Eliza smiles in approval. She never knew he possessed such magnetism and power, and she even sees a hint of respect and awe on Matt's face as he looks at her husband.

Matt whispers to her, "Do I need to add vampire king to your stalker hubby's list of special attributes?"

"He seems to be a natural leader, doesn't he?" Her heart lurches at the thought. It's humbling, like she's seeing Dmitri for the first time. *I'm so unworthy to stand by his side.*

Leaving the catacombs, the foursome quickly makes its way back to the hotel. While a couple of hours still remain before sunrise colors the sky and heralds another day, Eliza is exhausted from the information overload; she only half listens as the others discuss the council's questions and hypothesize how they'll go forward regardless of the maxians' decision.

Confidence oozes from Dmitri. "We can rely on the Druzhinas. Most, if not all, will be our allies."

"I agree." Matt looks across the table at Eliza as he pulls up the latest report on his computer. "Teresina followed them to another secret meeting in Venice. They're still debating, but there's been a shift in their numbers thanks to the latest antics of that devil vamp. Alexander and Sofia remain the sole holdouts against taking action—everyone else is on board. Teresina says they seem afraid to take the risk."

This gives Eliza the opportunity to address a nagging thought. "I don't think they like me very much." She can't forget the Druzhinas' faces as they stared through the open wine cellar door—their disgust, anger, worry, silent accusations. "I've not been one of them for over five hundred years ... and I've likely changed. A lot."

Dmitri smiles and kisses her forehead. "In some ways, love, you will always be a Druzhina. The goblin king can strip us of those ranks and duties, but he can never remove the bond of brotherhood and sisterhood we share with those we served with."

Maria says, "I believe that problem will self-correct once they learn of recent developments. We will obtain their allegiance."

"Even if we have their support, what if they don't want to continue being the enforcers of the law when Shashenka's gone?" Eliza looks to each of them in turn. They're not giving the Druzhinas any choice in their future, and she's uneasy about what will happen if they're wrong on this point.

Dmitri laughs. "Knowing them the way I do, I expect several will continue in the Druzhina after Shashenka is gone. They have too many centuries of that lifestyle to walk away from it."

Do you have too many centuries to walk away? She and Dmitri haven't discussed what they will do afterward, and her trepidation grows—they may want different lives. She assumed they would simply move on and leave this nightmare behind them. Now she must consider whether Dmitri shares her desires. "Is that what you want when this is over? To go back and be one of them?"

He takes her hand. "Yes, a part of me would like to do that, love, but we've yet to decide our future." Her heart constricts at the hopefulness in his voice—she knows he wants it—but she forces a smile to her lips.

Matt clears his throat. "You vamps live complicated lives. When our leaders go rogue, a pack member challenges and tries to kill them. Even fights over territory remain between the packs involved."

To Eliza's relief, Dmitri's tone conveys no disrespect. "I think that is due to your nature and limited life span. While the mutt gene slows your aging to a little more than twice that of a human, none of you live beyond two to three centuries. Vampires are ageless, nearly immortal, and our society is highly structured and defined because of it."

Eliza yawns; they may be ageless and nearly immortal, but she still needs her beauty sleep. "Speaking of immortal, I'm beat." She rises from the table and looks at Dmitri. "Are you ready to turn in for the day?" It's hard to ignore the way Matt grimaces; she can see what he is going through watching her and Dmitri interact as a couple. She's still trying to get used to it herself.

"Go ahead, love; I have another matter to attend to first." Dmitri's steely gaze locks on Matt, and she feels as if an iceberg pins her to the floor as he tells the werewolf, "I'd like to speak with you. Now, if you don't mind."

Matt shrugs but meets Dmitri's stare with equal intensity; he doesn't cast one glance at Eliza. "Sure, why not. This should be as fun as taking a rat for a walk."

Eliza's exhaustion flees to the corner as she looks from one to the other. A sudden rush of thoughts leaves her desperate to say something, anything to preempt whatever horrible insults they may hurl at one another, but she knows that she cannot even attempt to shape their discussion if she wants to avoid lasting problems between them. *I have to let them resolve this on their own. God, I hope they don't try to kill each other again.*

CHAPTER 25: DMITRI

Decisions and Boundaries

The kiss Dmitri interrupted when he first walked into the hotel suite sat on low boil all night, and his patience is bone dry. He is certain Elizabetta's behavior is a direct result of her brainwashing, which means he is in part responsible for it. Regardless, he cannot tolerate her physical affection with Matt; it's something he must put a stop to, or he may lose control and kill the wolf someday.

He sees the panic in Elizabetta's eyes and places a kiss on her temple to reassure her he means no harm to Matt. *Provided the mutt learns to keep his paws to himself.* Without another look at Matt, he strides out the door and up the stairs to the roof.

Dmitri's senses keep him alert to the threat behind him; the wolf's footsteps are synchronized with his. When they exit the roof door, Dmitri has Matt hold it ajar while he looks for something to prevent it from locking behind them. He finds a loose brick in the parapet, pries it out with his fingers, and places it between the door and the jamb. The mongrel gives him a guarded look as Dmitri moves past him and stops near a utility pedestal, his back toward Matt even though he's loath to expose himself to a mortal enemy. But he needs a moment to suppress the urge to attack, or he'll fail Elizabetta again.

"There was a time," Dmitri says quietly, "when I would have detached the hands or removed the lips of any man touching my wife. A werewolf"—he looks over his shoulder—"I would have killed on the spot."

He turns to glare at Matt, gauging the defiance in the wolf's eyes. "You are fortunate that these are not those times. I understand why you are my wife's friend, and that is mostly my fault—I cannot undo it. I understand you have feelings for each other, but—"

"Pah-dah-dum-dum." Matt chuckles, conveying no sense of nervousness or fear; it's clear the mutt believes them to be on equal footing. "There's always a but ... but it doesn't mean you need to be an asshole, unless you want to add that to your list of special skills."

Dmitri lets a menacing snarl erupt from his throat as he struggles to keep his anger in check. "You leave your hands and lips off my wife, mongrel! I want your word— swear that you will not touch her again. Your life depends on it."

A lopsided grin spreads across Matt's face. "I think I liked you better when I saw you in New Zealand."

Insolent fool—he doesn't know he's messing with death. Dmitri's eyes smolder with rage, and the instinct to kill his foe nearly propels him forward, but he manages to keep himself in check. The wolf's audacity and arrogance shock him.

Matt shoves his hands in his pockets. "Look, man, Eliza and I are very close. I love her and will always be her friend, and your threats aren't going to change that."

Her name is Elizabetta. Anger coils like a wild vine through his body. "Have you defiled her?"

"Defiled?" An amused look crosses Matt's face, and he roars with laughter. "Who in the hell talks like that? Damn, man, you need to get out more. If you mean, have we slept together ... it would depend on your definition of sleep."

Incredulous, Dmitri takes a step forward—his jaw is set, his fangs bared. He doesn't know how much more he can take before he attacks.

Two precarious minutes hang between them before Matt finally seems to grasp the severity of the situation and shelves the humor. The wolf's tone is curt. "Not that you deserve an answer, after what you did to her, but here you go. Slept, yes, many times. Naked, yes, once. Sex, no. The one time we came close to it, her ties to you stopped us before anything happened."

She's mine. The mongrel can go to hell if he thinks he's coming between us. Dmitri takes another step closer to Matt, leaving less than a foot of space between them. "You want her now. I can see it in the way you look at her, the way you touch her. I will never allow it."

The wolf shakes his head in what Dmitri interprets as a mix of dismissal and frustration. "It doesn't matter what I want! Vamps and their mate for eternity bullshit is an impenetrable barrier, if you haven't figured that out yet. Even when Eliza thought you were her enemy, she couldn't push against it. You may be vampires, but I'm telling you it's a short leash that keeps you tethered to one another."

"Stop touching my wife!"

In response to the unspoken threat, Matt leans forward on the balls of his feet. "I will not alter my friendship with her just because you're back in her life. If she chooses to change things between us, fine, but I will not do it for you. You haven't done much to earn my respect, and personally, I don't trust you to stop hurting her."

"This discussion is done. When our revolt is over, you will not be a part of her life." Dmitri nods dismissively and walks toward the roof door.

Matt's voice suddenly carries the authority of an alpha—it's enough to stop Dmitri in his tracks. "No! You wanted to air things between us. It's my turn, bloodsucker, and you're going to hear me out."

Dmitri takes a deep breath and turns slowly to face the wolf. A bloated pause grows between them as they stare each other down. Matt's canines lengthen, and for a moment Dmitri wonders if he'll attack. He doesn't want to break another promise to Elizabetta.

Matt punctures the tense silence between them. "You have no idea how pathetic and lost Eliza was when I found her in Yellowstone. She was devastated to learn monsters exist—and that she is one of them. She was in pieces, and it was your fault. I picked up every shred that you left in your wake. I put her back together. I stood by her, and you ... you continued ruining her life."

"I had no—"

"Bullshit! I don't care. I was there for her. You weren't. From the first day I met her, I've always been there. Eliza is important to me, and she always will be."

Matt looks away as if he's debating whether to continue his outburst. "I've spent countless hours thinking, feeling, wishing it were me with her instead of you. But none of that matters now. It never did." He looks back at Dmitri. "I never stood a chance because of you. She is yours, always was, and being vamps, you know damn well that will never change—ever."

"No, it won't."

Matt sighs and almost looks defeated, but he meets Dmitri's gaze with a hint of pride. "I want to tell you a little secret about werewolves that you vamps probably don't know. You think you're the only ones who bond for life with someone? We develop a similar emotional connection to others, only it's not exclusive or even reserved to our kind. It's a profound loyalty for those we hold dear, those we love, and it is as every bit as strong as a werewolf or vampire mate bond. I cannot, I will not ever abandon her. My friendship with her is for life."

Matt takes a step toward Dmitri. "I will stand with her ... I will die for her if I must. Unless she chooses to send me away, I am in her life until mine is over. If you have a problem with that, then you need to deal with it—it's your problem. Not mine, not hers."

Several minutes fall off the roof as they measure each other, the tension in the air around them so thick and heavy that Dmitri doubts a dagger could pierce it. In the many encounters he's had with werewolves over the centuries, he assumed that protecting, defending, and fighting to the death were the acts of a mate. He never realized there might have been something beyond that relationship, or that the bond was loyalty.

Matt is uncomfortably correct; the mutt was there when Dmitri was ruining Elizabetta's life. In some small way he is grateful for Matt's presence then—and even now he finds a strange comfort in knowing this werewolf cares enough to protect Elizabetta regardless of his unrequited feelings for her. Matt is also right that this is Dmitri's problem, and he'll need to find a way to deal with their friendship. The werewolf's loyalty to his wife may mean he'll be a part of their future for a long time to come.

His decision made, Dmitri extends his hand. "Thank you for your loyalty to Elizabetta. I will do my best to accept your friendship."

Matt hesitates, then shakes his outstretched hand. Doubtless they'll never forge their own friendship, but sidelining the problem will make it easier for Dmitri to reclaim his wife. With nothing left to settle between them, they return to the hotel suite with an understanding at the least.

Dmitri is surprised to see that Elizabetta—she's not yet recovered from her injuries—and Maria are still awake. When Elizabetta's worried and curious expression bounces between the men, Matt is the first to speak. His tone is cheerful—Dmitri raises an eyebrow at the abrupt shift in the wolf's demeanor. "Looks like the Markovs have a family mongrel, baby vamp. I'll try not to shed all over the house and chew up your shoes."

Elizabetta and Maria exchange a bemused look before they both burst into laughter. Dmitri stares at them, nearly choking as Matt moves alongside him and claps a hand to his back. He knows human families have pet dogs, and the ludicrous idea of vampire mates adopting a werewolf—one with a comedic streak—strikes him as funny. In spite of himself he joins the women in their laughter.

"Now, that's what I'm talking about!" Matt winks at Dmitri and intercepts Elizabetta as she starts to walk toward them. He picks her up and spins her around in a hug. "Don't worry, baby vamp. I may even come to like your stalker hubby one day."

A tinge of jealousy seeps to the surface as Elizabetta kisses Matt on the cheek before she leaves the wolf's embrace and looks at Dmitri. *Look at how she reacts—I have to follow the mutt's lead.* He takes his wife in his arms and tries to push his mixed feelings aside. "Promise me, love, that next time we'll discuss it first if you ever decide you want another mutt."

Elizabetta stands on her toes, smiles, and kisses him. "I promise." As her arms wrap around him for a hug, she whispers, "Thank you."

Those two words confirm he made the right choice, but Dmitri has had enough for now—he needs a break from Matt. He leaves one arm curled around Elizabetta's waist and looks toward their bedroom door. "We have a long night ahead, love. I think we should turn in now."

A chorus of good-mornings are exchanged, and Dmitri

leads Elizabetta to their bedroom. He's suddenly nervous—this is the first time in over five hundred years that they'll share a bed as husband and wife. "Allow me to put you to bed this morning." He draws her into a lingering embrace. *I've missed her touch. I've—*

Elizabetta pulls back, uncertainty stumbling across her face. His disappointment mounts—he recognizes her reluctant posture—but he's unwilling to give up so easily. "We can go slow, love. I'll be gentle. I know you're still healing."

She sits on the edge of the mattress and shakes her head. "It's not that. In some ways I don't know you." Her eyes roam over him. "Look, you're sexy as hell, and I'm tempted, but I don't ... before I can be with you like that, I need to remember us."

"I remember us." Sitting next to her, he pulls Elizabetta's head against his chest as he murmurs, "I miss you more than you can imagine. I need you, Elizabetta." Intimacy will restore and strengthen their bond; he knows this, but she's forgotten. "Let's just try. I will stop if you wish."

"It's not that simple for me." Her face contorts—disgust pierces every word. "Without my memories, I'm afraid that I'll ... I need to feel that I'm a wife making love to her husband, not a whore going on autopilot to turn a trick with one more man in a long line of men."

The reminder of what she's been forced into, what she has become, drowns his desire in sadness. To learn that his mate sees being with him as something akin to entertaining a paramour is a huge blow. He struggles to keep the pain out of his voice as he searches for the right words. Desiring her for nearly five centuries is making him crazy—it is testing the limits of his self-control. *Maria needs to unlock her memories soon.* "I understand, but I am not those other men."

"I'm sorry." Elizabetta strokes his cheek and kisses him once more before rising from the bed. "I'm going to put on a nightgown. We're both tired and need to sleep."

Frustrated, he doesn't tell her that the skimpy nightwear is a problem in itself. He could ignore it when it was Sally, but for Elizabetta to be so near and still out of reach is maddening. *My torment of Tantalus—will it ever end?* While Elizabetta's in the bathroom changing, Dmitri undresses and starts pulling on a pair of pajama pants, but changes his mind. *Damn it, she's my wife!* He's never liked the way pajamas tangle with the bedding; from now on he'll either sleep in his shorts or wear nothing at all. *She can at least give me that much, can't she?*

Disappointment has booted desire to the curb, and Dmitri won't allow her to see his anger. When she returns to the room, he's facing away from her side of the bed as she crawls in next to him. Soon her arm is around his waist and the feathers of her breath fall against his back, but Dmitri refuses to close his eyes and enjoy the embrace—he can't, or he will lose control. *She has no idea what she's doing to me.* Then her breathing slows and becomes shallow. She's asleep. He lets out a frustrated sigh.

An hour passes, and sleep still eludes him. Quietly he slips out of bed and moves to the chair to watch Elizabetta dream. Despite himself he smiles when her hands explore and turn his pillow, snuggling it against her chest. She may not remember, but some part of her never forgot. He keeps watching, wondering where her dreams take her, and hoping that by some small chance he's in them.

At twilight he leaves the chair to take a shower; when he returns to the room, Elizabetta is still asleep. He brushes a lock of hair away from her face and resists the urge to trail his long fingers over her body. Not wanting to disturb her further—this is the first time she's slept in a bed since she was tortured—Dmitri dresses in silence and steps out of the room.

He's not the only one awake. Matt and Maria are drinking coffee and laughing, and to his surprise, sitting together on the sofa. He lowers himself into a chair and bids them good evening, intrigued by their nearly human interaction. There's something about the way they respond to each other that fascinates him.

After six centuries as a vampire, Dmitri no longer recalls how he started each day as a mortal. *I wonder if those outside the vampire realm take this mundane routine for granted?* The two seem to share a similar sense of humor—they're both witty, quick with good-natured teasing as they banter back and forth. It's a side of Maria he's never seen before, but he must admit he's never really observed her away from the coven or outside of the company of vampires.

He's still pondering it when Elizabetta, showered and dressed, joins them in the living room. She rests a hand on his neck while her fingers play with his hair, and without hesitation she jokes with the mutt and witch; it seems she prefers to pretend this morning never happened. Dmitri briefly closes his eyes, enjoying the sensation of her touch and the end to tension between them.

Twilight surrenders to the night as the four steer the topic to their future plans, and how they'll proceed with or without the Orde de Maxia's support. Maria seems particularly concerned that they haven't reached those in the inner lair who may be willing to fight, a fair point; but when she suggests that she and Elizabetta coordinate their efforts at the inner lair, Dmitri gives his wife a knowing look. He is certain he speaks for both of them when he tells the witch they're not going back. "Shashenka left Elizabetta one step away from final death, and if it weren't for her taking my blood, she wouldn't have recovered. I won't give him another opportunity to kill her—we will take our chances on the run."

Maria scowls. "How are we supposed to prepare for a rebellion with you two outside of the coven?"

"Maria, has Master ever locked you up or tortured you?" Elizabetta asks with a new hardness to her voice.

"Not since I matured as a witch—he's too afraid of what I may do to him." The witch gives them a sympathetic look. "I still think going back is the best idea. Shashenka will remain ignorant, so I won't have to protect him—"

Matt gives an exasperated groan. "No way. Asking them to risk their lives like that is just plain wrong on so many levels."

"I can try to protect them better," Maria says flatly. "I've had over eight hundred years of manipulating that goblin king, as you like to call him, to serve my purposes, and I can do so again."

"Hate to tell you this, witchy-poo, but I'm not sure you've done such a bang-up job of that recently."

Maria folds her arms across her chest—the look is meant to intimidate—and Dmitri expects her to unleash a spell to teach the mongrel a lesson. But Matt won't budge, and Dmitri is silently thankful for his support. *Maybe having a mutt around won't be such a bad thing after all.*

Still, for Dmitri there will be no compromise—the witch can't guarantee total protection from Shashenka's wrath. "I will not subject my wife to one more moment of that demon's touch." Swift anger rises inside him as he struggles to tamp it down. "Being at the inner lair leaves neither of us the time and quick access we need to secure the Druzhina's allegiance."

Maria draws a slow breath through her nose and looks at each of them in turn. "Your points may be valid, but this could backfire—every day you're on the run increases the risk of Shashenka uncovering what you're up to, especially if we fail to get the support of the Druzhina."

Laughing, Matt throws his arms wide. "Have some faith, witchy-poo. I'm an awesome sidekick, and you know you're looking at two of the best Druzhinas that old devil vamp ever had. If we work together, Eliza can hold them down while Dmitri charms their socks off, and I will chew on their throats. See? End of problem."

"Are all werewolves as crazy as you?" Maria looks incredulous. "I'm thinking insanity might run amok among your kind."

"Naw, they broke the mold after me."

With that the tension evaporates, and Maria's tone actually sounds playful. "Perhaps we should consider a padded doghouse for you."

"Maybe, if you throw in a rawhide bone or two." He winks at Maria. "Admit it, witch, crazy, good-looking werewolves leave you weak in the knees."

Maria and Elizabetta burst out laughing. Dmitri appreciates the levity, but he wants to better prepare for the council's questions. *I need to get this back on track.* He refocuses the conversation, asking Matt for the status of his financial teams and their plans against Belyakov's businesses.

It works—Matt flips through a binder of notes, and the plans for their revolt begin to solidify. The failed rebellion becomes the benchmark of what not to do—avoiding its pitfalls boosts Dmitri's optimism that this time will be different. *We might actually succeed.* The hardest challenge ahead for him and Elizabetta will be staying on the run and out of Shashenka's reach.

Elizabetta scowls. "I'm not going anywhere, and neither are you, Maria, until you unlock my memories."

I want her back as much as she wants her life and memories restored. I wonder if she'll return to who she was or become some blend of the old Elizabetta and who she is now? Unease and determination flicker in her eyes—she's as nervous as Dmitri is, but as long as he has his Elizabetta back when this is over, then nothing that happens in between will matter. He takes her hand and gives her a reassuring smile.

Maria's nose wrinkles as if the choice offends her senses.

"We'll need to find someplace where you won't be heard. Often it's an unpleasant experience, and it's been known to drive some to the point of madness. In your case there's the added risk of Dmitri—he may not be strong enough to endure it with you, and if one or both of you fails to get through this process, it will have a huge impact on our revolt."

"We've always been strongest together." Cupping Elizabetta's chin, Dmitri pledges that he will never fail her again.

"If you're both sure about this, then I'll release the block as soon as possible following the council's vote."

Matt fidgets, displaying a nervousness Dmitri has never seen in him before. The mutt sounds almost timid when he asks, "Will it change her? I mean, will it make Eliza decide she loves cats and hates werewolves?"

"Unlocking her mind will allow her full memory to merge and reconcile with recent memories—it doesn't alter or change anything. You'll just have to hope that her love of you outweighs the decades of hate she held for your kind."

"Oh, great. You really know how to shoot a wolf down. I'm not sure I like you, witch." Matt seems to notice the horrified look on Elizabetta's face, and smiles. "Don't forget you have a lovable and loyal mongrel waiting when it's over, baby vamp."

When they arrive at the Orde de Maxia meeting, the questions from the council are brief—and this time Dmitri and Elizabetta are prepared to answer many of them. They assure the council that they will update them on the status of the Druzhina and develop a contingency plan to address a potential power vacuum.

Their replies seem to put several of the council members at ease, and High Warlock Boucher moves the council to vote. The room falls into an eerie silence, but soundless waves of eager anticipation and optimism swell through the cavern. The direction of their future will soon be known. Dmitri lowers his expectations to avoid crushing disappointment if the council votes against them. *We'll get through this with or without them.* He takes Elizabetta's hand, and when she in turn slips her other hand into Matt's, he nods in silent agreement; while officially it is the Markovs leading this revolt, starting this war, the truth is that Matt and Maria equally share in the effort. Dmitri reaches to take Maria's hand and smiles down at her when she squeezes back. The four of them stand united, waiting for the announcement of the vote.

The high warlock taps the sphere, and Dmitri squints against the ear-splitting sound. "In regard to the petition of the aggrieved—Mr. and Mrs. Dmitri Markov—what is your declaration, supreme maxians?"

None of the council members has given a hint to their position, and Dmitri freezes in disbelief as one after the other declares their support. Maria mutters that it's nearly unheard of—unanimous agreement among the Orde de Maxia is a rare event. The reality of what they are about to do settles over Dmitri, the ramifications exploding into a tornado of possibilities. He can feel the energy rippling off the crowd, though no one dares break the silence demanded by the council.

"By consent of the council, we declare our allegiance. We will back the Markovs and their allies in the overthrow of Shashenka Belyakov and bring an end to his reign of terror." The high warlock smiles down at the four standing on the platform. "You shall have your war!" He doesn't wait for a reply but speaks directly to Maria. "Miss D'Arcy, please notify the council when you know the date on which we move against the Belyakov coven."

"Yes, thank you, High Warlock Boucher." Her smile is radiant—she squeezes Dmitri's hand again.

"Miss D'Arcy, there is one other matter that must be addressed with this change of events. Belyakov's covenant binding you is fatally flawed—it incorrectly identifies you as a witch."

What is going on here? Maria's face scrunches into a mask of perplexity as she says, "I mean no disrespect, High Warlock, but I am of mixed blood. My ma and da were witch and warlock."

"You are misinformed, Miss D'Arcy. Your family's pure wizard lineage is fully recorded and archived in the Orde de Maxia Grand Library in Dublin."

Maria gapes but can't seem to speak.

"In light of that fact, we declare Shashenka Belyakov's contract and your oath to him null and void. The Orde de Maxia will protect your village if he moves against it. You will provide direct maxian support to the Markovs and this council during the campaign, and you are hereby ordered to never protect Shashenka Belyakov again."

Dmitri lets go of Elizabetta's hand and pulls Maria into a hug—they'll never have to worry about her turning against them again.

Soon Matt and Elizabetta are patting the newly discovered wizard's back, and a nervous, almost giddy laugh bubbles to the surface as she steps away from their group and looks up at the dais. "Thank you so much, supreme maxians, for granting my freedom."

The high warlock inclines his head. When he looks up, his gaze falls on Elizabetta. "Mrs. Markov, good luck. Do the shadow realms proud and win this war." He winks as the council members rise to leave the dais.

The chamber erupts in a cacophony of cheers, whistles, hoots, and hollers, with some supernaturals even pumping their fists in the air. Hope for freedom, for success, intensifies and almost erodes Dmitri's discipline to not move; he stifles a triumphant yell and holds his hands firmly at his sides instead of cheering along with the crowd. They never expected this level of support, let alone the unanimous vote. While they have yet to fight a battle, Dmitri recognizes that they have won their first major victory.

He wants to take Elizabetta in his arms and smother her in kisses until neither of them can take a breath. What the Orde de Maxia has given them is far more than he ever hoped for: the end of Shashenka is within their reach.

CHAPTER 26: ELIZA

Merging Divides

Eliza blinks and shakes her head to clear it. They are somewhere inside the tunnel on their way to the exit, but she doesn't remember getting past the crowd to leave the chamber—she was too busy fixating on the numerous ways she wants to kill Shashenka. The others didn't seem to notice. *I'm not going to tell them, either.* She tunes in to the discussion Matt's having with Maria.

Matt says, "What was all that stuff about birthright, wizards, and not a witch?"

Maria looks up at the wolf, a shy smile on her face. "In our realm, somewhat similar to yours, there are purebloods—or naturals, as you call them—and those of mixed blood." A pureblood, she explains, is someone whose bloodline has never been diluted by mating with another species. "Witches, warlocks, and sorcerae are the offspring of a maxian and someone from another realm."

Eliza leans forward to look around Dmitri. "You mean

the human realm?"

"No, not exactly."

Eliza's surprised to hear that maxians take mates from all realms—vampire, werewolf, human, and before they were wiped out, even the fae. Maria's new status changes the wizard's place in the maxian hierarchy, which is based on magical power—wizards are the most powerful.

"There are many witches and warlocks, very few sorcerae, and fewer still wizards," Maria says. "Once blood is mixed, all offspring from then on are witches and warlocks, or sorcerae—fae blood remains dominant." She further explains that wizards are the most powerful, and sorcerae are the next strongest—pure fae magic nearly rivals that of a wizard's. Witches and warlocks are the least powerful maxians, but she warns them never to underestimate a witch or a warlock. "They still wield magic force well enough to stand on their own against your kind."

Matt shakes his head. "Well, I'm still going to call you witchy-poo. Wizard-poo or maxi-poo just doesn't work for me. One sounds like a big pile of crap, and the other ... really, wizard ... wizard ... what?" A grin erupts across Matt's face, and he pokes Maria in the ribs. "Wizard-lizard!"

The surprised look on Maria's face seems to carry a hint of annoyance, and he quickly adds, "Something tells me saying that would get me turned into a frog."

Maria tries biting back the laughter but isn't able to contain it when Eliza starts to giggle too. Jokes about wizard-lizards and wolf-lizards fly between Matt and Maria while Eliza and Dmitri mostly walk on in silence. Maria's magic classification is huge news; still, Eliza can't help wondering if Dmitri is also preoccupied with the upcoming revolt and how it will affect those living at the Belyakov estates.

We're not going back to the coven. Maria plans to return to La Perfezione by the next evening, but the wizard will get little rest between now and then; the complex intermingling of spells she cast against Eliza leave her the only one who can successfully remove the memory block. Eliza looks at Dmitri out of the corner of her eye. *Is he worried about the return of my memories? What if I'm not the same afterward?* A shudder runs down her spine—she's scared witless herself.

When they reach the hotel room, they hurriedly prepare to leave Paris. Alastrina, a council sorceress who claims to have been an old friend of Maria's parents, has offered her sea cave home on the Scottish island Garbh Eilean for Eliza's memory restoration. Because of the island's remoteness, they will need to leave Paris after sunrise and then take a private charter jet from Glasgow to Lewis, Scotland, in order to reach the island by boat before sunrise the next day. But the secluded location is the perfect hideout, Alastrina says—isolated enough that no one will hear whatever torment Eliza faces as the two halves of her life merge into one.

Both Alastrina and Maria will accompany Dmitri and Eliza, but neither maxian will stay beyond lifting the spells. Alastrina has council business to attend to; Maria must return to Venice if she wants to keep her involvement with the revolt hidden. She will remain in contact with Matt while Eliza and Dmitri go through the memory reclamation together.

When they're packed and ready to go, Maria hands two objects to Dmitri: a half-inch-wide, three-inch-long blue garnet crystal and a black onyx gemstone recessed and fused into a two-inch-diameter bowl-shaped greenish-blue gem.

Both easily fit in the palm of Dmitri's hand. "What is this?"

"A redecrystapiezo. Like a cell phone, but for the maxian realm."

Matt leans in for a look. "A redecrys—what?"

"A redecrystapiezo." The sternness in Maria's voice kills whatever witty response was waiting to spring off Matt's tongue. "When you need to use it, slip the blue garnet into the onyx gemstone. You'll hear the gems sing, and the blue garnet and grandidierite colors of the base will shift and glow. Simply say the name of the person you wish to contact, and it will reach whomever you seek as long as they have a redecrystapiezo or a cell phone."

Eliza's eyebrows pitch up in surprise. "It can connect to cell phones?"

Maria nods. Deep within the earth, she says, is a geometric network of living, growing crystals with magical properties. When a redecrystapiezo is activated, its vibrations connect to the magic in those crystals, and it opens a channel for the two parties to speak.

"A rede ... redephone." Matt grins. "What? It's easier than chewing on a mouthful of letters. Redecrysta-ptooey. See, rede is much easier and doesn't tie a tongue in knots.

Tongues are meant for much better things."

He winks at Maria, and to Eliza's astonishment the wizard blushes. "Works for me," Eliza says with a laugh. She wonders whether he's flirting with Maria because he's on the rebound or because he's genuinely attracted to her. Less than seventy-two hours ago his hopes of a future with Eliza were destroyed—they're interacting as they always did, but there are boundaries between them now. Throw his bold flirtations with the wizard into the mix, and it leaves Eliza baffled. *Maybe his feelings for me weren't as strong as he believed. Ha. A man in love with the idea of being in love?* Deep inside she knows it's not so simple as that.

Cutting off the wizard and werewolf's banter, Dmitri says, "It's getting late. We should get going." Eliza catches the furtive glance he casts her way; it sets her nerves on fire, not knowing what to make of his subdued demeanor.

Matt draws Eliza into a long, tight hug. She tries to hide the trepidation roiling under the calm mask she's fixed on her face. "Be careful, baby vamp." He kisses her forehead, saying as he releases her, "Don't ever forget that I love you."

Eliza glances up at him, her voice soft. "I will never forget, but you be careful too." She sees Dmitri in the periphery; he's stone-still, and she can see him struggling to keep his own emotions hidden. But she looks into Matt's eyes, pecks him on the cheek, and says, "I love you too—always."

Dmitri's hand has begun to close around hers when Matt suddenly pulls him away into a bear hug. But Eliza hears him whisper fiercely, "Don't you dare miss picking up one piece of her when Maria restores her mind. I need to know I'll see my best friend again." The desperation in his voice sends another spike of fear through her. *This will change me. What if he doesn't like all the pieces of me after my distant past merges with the Eliza he knows?*

Dmitri looks freaked out as he draws back from the hug, and Eliza bites her lip to keep from laughing. She senses a subtle change between them. *I hope it means they don't want to kill each other anymore.*

The two men step further apart and Dmitri looks Matt in the eye. "I'll return her in better shape than you've ever seen her." Pride reflects in his smile. "She's a force to be reckoned with, and you may like that."

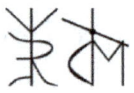

Even in the shadows of night, Eliza finds the small island of Garbh Eilean impressive. Gentle rolling hills and sheer vertical rock cliffs jut out of the Minch between the Outer Hebrides and the mainland of Scotland. It's a world unto itself—forgotten, yet not forgotten to time. It appears uninhabited, though she's certain the sorceress claimed to have a home here.

When they reach the island, Alastrina stops the bow of the boat directly in front of a cliff that rises one hundred feet above the surface of the water. She smiles at the three of them, caresses a red garnet crystal in the palm of her hand, and touches it to the rock wall. "*Revelabit.*"

Eliza gasps as the rock face shimmers and then disappears, exposing an olivine and crystalline cavern. A stone dock and stairs lead up to a deck in front of the windows and wooden door set into the cavern's wall. Alastrina smirks at her, then guides the boat forward to pull alongside the dock. Dmitri leaps onto the platform and ties the boat to the mooring hook as the sorceress shuts off the motor.

"*Occultaverant.*" Alastrina climbs out of the boat and faces the opening in the cliff wall. There's another shimmer as the rock face covering the opening turns translucent.

"Don't worry. We can see out, but no one can see in— and it is actually as solid as stone." The sorceress tosses the crystal in the air and catches it. "And no one can get in or out without this." She holds out the red garnet crystal for Dmitri to take, explaining that they must use the Latin words for *reveal* or *conceal* whenever they wish to take the boat to another part of the island to feed or explore.

If this works ... no, when this works, I hope we'll be too busy getting reacquainted. Eliza blushes at the smirk curling Dmitri's lips. *Jeez, he caught me checking him out— again.* To her relief Dmitri says nothing as he grabs their suitcases, and they follow the sorceress up the stone stairs to the wooden door. She opens it and nearly knocks them down the stairs when she unexpectedly whirls around, shooing a large rat out of the house.

Eliza gives Dmitri an amused look, and to her surprise a sly smile parts his lips. "That could have been a midnight snack, Alastrina," he says.

"No, I don't think Edward would like that much."

"Edward?" Eliza stares at the sorceress in disbelief. *She named the rat?*

"Yes, the rat is Edward. He's trained to fetch things for me and is quite an impressive little thief. I can only imagine the messes he's made inside. I thought he was out when I left."

"Oh." Dmitri looks at Eliza and licks his lips. His hand settles on her shoulder. "I know they're your favorite, but we'll have to take rats off the menu, love."

She laughs in spite of herself. *He's never going to let me forget that I tried to live off animals.*

Alastrina waves them inside and gives them a quick tour of her home, using magic to clean Edward's messes as they move through the small dwelling. Eliza wishes she could clean with magic—she'd never scrub a toilet again. The sea cave home has a kitchen, drawing room, bathroom, and two bedrooms, and each room overlooks the hidden cavern. A narrow hallway, illuminated by glowing green crystals, connects the rooms at the back of the structure. Everything about the hideaway screams otherworldly, and she speculates that its design and construction were fae influenced.

She's about to ask its history when Dmitri nods toward a circular white stone that sits flush with the travertine tiles near the door. "What is that?"

Maria and Alastrina both answer, "It's a mutaport."

A sci-fi transporter comes to mind, and Eliza can't resist. "What's a mutaport?"

Alastrina offers a lengthy scientific and mystical explanation that leaves Eliza and Dmitri baffled. Maria laughs at their glazed eyes and gives them the short version instead; it is a magical teletransport device that changes cells into faster-than-light particles, then bends space and time to send them through the earth to any destination the traveler selects. The biological matter restructures upon arrival at the destination.

The description excites Eliza's interest in space travel; she has to know more. It's like a sudden link between her unremembered past and the reality of her present. She can't help but feel that space fascinated her before too. *Can it go off-world? Was that how the fae came and went? How many can go through at once? What powers the device?* When it becomes clear that there is no end to her questions, Maria reminds her that time is against them; they can discuss it further after the war is over. Eliza's disappointed to learn that she'll likely not remember seeing the maxians mutaport, because she'll be under the start of the unlocking spell. It also means that Dmitri may miss it, as his attention will rightfully be on her.

The sorceress excuses herself to repack her bags—she claims that she's bored with her travel clothes—leaving Maria to brief Eliza and Dmitri on what to expect when the memory block lifts. Maria explains that because most blocking spells are short-term—in place for a few minutes to a few weeks at most—their release typically allows the mind to merge within a few hours. The longer a blocking spell is active, she warns them, the longer the merging process takes.

Maria's biggest concern is that Eliza's is a unique case. The block isolated and locked the memories in a protected part of her brain, which allowed Maria to wipe all other information and knowledge—making room for Eliza's reprogramming after the catatonic spell was lifted.

These life-altering spells began centuries ago, and the length of time the magic has been in place is unprecedented. It stuns Eliza to learn that when she became aware in Bozeman, Dmitri had already spent eleven months brainwashing her. She only knew about him for less than seven weeks before she ended up in the psych ward of the hospital.

Maria is unable to estimate how long it will take Eliza's mind to fully merge her memories, experiences, and knowledge—at the minimum it will be days. The wizard admits that she's unsure what impact the three incantations—catatonia, memory block, and mind wipe—used in conjunction with each other have had. Still, she remains optimistic that Eliza's past and present memories will, at the very least, merge. Both may aid in recovering some of the knowledge she's lost.

When Alastrina joins them in the drawing room, the maxians continue preparing Eliza and Dmitri for what they'll experience. Eliza speculates that she'll have an easier time of it than Dmitri. According to the sorceress, there is little he can do to actually help her through the ordeal, other than contain and control her when she goes out of her mind, something Maria says is necessary for the process to work.

When the spell lifts and Eliza is sufficiently recovered and ready to travel, they must alert the Orde de Maxia, and either Maria or Alastrina will return for them. The sorceress hands Dmitri an onyx stone, instructing him to cast it into the alabaster bowl on the kitchen counter and add a drop of each of their blood to send the signal. For now, she and Maria will use the mutaport to return to France; the boat will remain for Eliza and Dmitri to use should they need it.

With the instructions finished, Maria tells Dmitri to stand behind Eliza—he'll need to catch her when she collapses.

I am not ready for this. "If I'm going to black out, why not just have me lie on the bed or floor to start with?"

"It takes the pull of gravity to drain the blood from your brain as the spell starts to work. Alastrina has told Dmitri what to watch for—when it's safe to lay you down on the floor." She pauses, giving them a long, penetrating look. "Are you ready?"

Eliza nods and swallows a lump of fear. *Hell no.*

Placing her palm on Eliza's forehead, Maria begins the incantation. The wizard captures her gaze—Eliza couldn't look away if she wanted to—and as the last words are spoken, she blows a red powder from the palm of her other hand into Eliza's eyes. Dmitri flinches as the cloud reaches them, but Eliza doesn't stop breathing in time and inhales, then chokes on the dusty substance. Both of Maria's hands fall away and she steps back, her eyes never wavering from Eliza's.

At first Eliza feels as if it isn't working, and she is about to ask what went wrong, when a wall of red slams over her eyes. An intense burning sensation in her head rages like a wildfire, consuming all it touches as it sweeps through her mind. Then a wall of white crashes over and obliterates the red. Eliza gasps against the pain. A strange tingling begins at the top of her spine and spreads to every corner of her brain and body. It brings a different pain, one that numbs as it rips pieces of knowledge away.

Panic threatens to drown Eliza's resolve to endure the spell. Heat floods her body. She can feel understanding turn to confusion and ignorance, known things becoming unknown. *Am I going to recover from this? What if I lose my mind for good?*

A blue wall comes down, bringing a freezing chill. Whatever fragments of logical thought remain cede ground to her most basic primal instincts—hunger, survival, mating. Black mist seeps in and covers the blue wall. Her mental processes incrementally fail until only her involuntary responses remain active. The black mist penetrates every synapse in her brain, shrouding her remaining sensory perception.

Eliza has the fleeting awareness of being suspended outside of time and space, yet somehow she knows that only her consciousness and body are separated. Within this disembodied state her ability to think rationally returns in a bewildering rush. A kaleidoscope of colors crashes together and explodes throughout her entire being. For a moment she ceases to exist, and then it's as if every memory, thought, and feeling she ever experienced is shoved back into her body and mind in the same instant. Millions of conflicting fragments hurtle around her, within her, through her, and then the worst pain she's ever known rips her to pieces. Her body contorts against her will as her screams sear her vocal cords and deafen her ears. *Oh God, Dmitri, save me!*

CHAPTER 27: DMITRI

Trials of Endurance

When Elizabetta falls limp in Dmitri's arms, he almost panics—he's seen too many sightless eyes, heard too many final breaths, and many times listened to the last beat of a heart as another's life ebbed and faded. He can't lose her, not now.

Maria says, "It's done." She squeezes his shoulder. With a sympathetic look she joins Alastrina on the mutaport.

The white stone, its outer edges now glowing in what appears to be a burning ring, sends a burst of light that almost knocks Dmitri off his feet. Elizabetta's body convulses in violent twitches. His arms clench around her, and they nearly go down, but his quick reflexes help him recover his balance. *Damn it! I can barely hold on to her, let alone keep her upright.* Alastrina's warning ricochets in the back of his mind: he must not lay her down until the first fit passes and her body stills. Her head must stay higher than her body. He glances toward the mutaport—

whatever light shone from it earlier has disappeared, along with the maxians. He's on his own.

For several long minutes Elizabetta writhes and thrashes against him, and Dmitri wonders if this phase will ever end—if he can get her through the ordeal. Then abruptly and without warning, her body becomes dead weight in his arms. This is the sign he's waited for; he gently lowers Elizabetta to the floor and sits next to her, brushing the tangle of hair from her eyes. "I'm here, love. You're not alone—we're going to get through this together."

Just as he bends to place a kiss on her lips, Elizabetta's body spasms and jerks. Her flailing arms strike his head and chest, and as her legs kick against the floor, he scrambles back to avoid being hit again, following his instinct to give her room. Her body pitches sideways in a convulsive fit and crashes into a credenza. *Damn it.* Mortification puts him into motion. Alastrina said he must control her—keep her safe. He rushes to her side and drags her into the center of the room. "Elizabetta!" She shrieks, snarls, and hisses in reply. *Is this normal?* It's too late to ask the maxians now. Sitting on the cold stone floor, he pulls Elizabetta against him and tries to restrain her.

Elizabetta's claws and fangs fully extend, and a full-out scuffle ensues. He's still trying to subdue her when she begins biting and swiping at herself, at him, at the floor. Blood soaks into their clothes and smears on the floor—he's unsure whose and can't take even a moment to find out. He struggles to hold her wrists, but she manages to tangle her fingers in her hair, ripping it out in clumps. An unnatural strength—exceeding even that of an average vampire—combines with her wild and unpredictable movements, and it's nearly impossible for him to confine her actions. *How am I supposed to do this?* Whenever Elizabetta breaks free of his grasp, her claws rake her face, tear at her clothes, clutch her chest, and puncture any part of him that gets in the way.

Her screaming and wailing go from soft, subtle whimpers to ear-shattering shrieks and howls; each one leaves a new cut upon his heart. *What is this doing to her? Shit, will this ever end?* The more she struggles, the more determined he is not to let her permanently slip away from him—she's only just returned to him, and he can't lose her now. "Hold on, love, come back to me. We'll get through this. I'm here, I have you—I won't let you go." *This will work ... it has to.*

His words seem to fall on deaf ears; he can see she is suffering inside a bubble of unimaginable pain and horror, a barrier that he can't seem to penetrate by word or touch. He attempts to calm her by humming "*Il mio tesoro*," but any effects are blunted by whatever is going on in her head. He can't resist wondering which is worse—the way he silently disappeared into the void, or this hysterical and explosive hell that she has been plunged into.

For several hours Elizabetta remains incoherent, quieting only when a fit ends. The respite never lasts long enough—Dmitri has no time to collect his wits before another round of savage throes claims her. He is increasingly grateful that the furniture in this drawing room is sparse and lines the walls. He needs every inch of floor space to counter her efforts to break free and harm herself or him.

Then something changes, and the violent shuddering stops. Her body falls limp. *What have we allowed Maria to do to her?* He holds his breath, waiting. Confusion and worry rage through him as she goes from outbursts to stillness, sobs to laughter, grunts to jumbled words. Dmitri recognizes pieces of conversations from days to centuries ago, and she speaks in an odd amalgamation of every language she's ever known. Some of her comments, he surmises, must be from interactions with others. To his disgust and horror, Dmitri realizes that one string of broken dialogue may be from a sexual encounter with another man. His vision turns red—he can't let go of the suspicion that she's referring to Matt. *That damn mutt lied!* Bloodlust uncoils inside him. *I'm going to—*

Elizabetta says, "Stop. I can't. I'm sorry—I can't do this."

Worry pulls his brow into a frown as she mutters, "This is wrong ... so wrong."

What is wrong? Does she mean the other man—or what we are doing to her now? Dmitri can't ascertain if it's part of the replayed conversation or if she's having a semi-lucid moment. But then he sees the way she tries to cover her breasts when her arm breaks free, and he knows. *She refused him.* It provides a modicum of relief, knowing that if it was Matt she turned down, the wolf was telling the truth. The vampire mate bond was too strong for Elizabetta to break free of, even without her full memories.

Before Dmitri can absorb the implication—even as a concubine, she must have remained loyal to him—Elizabetta starts to wail, "I'm here. I'm in here. Somebody ... anybody ..." Her sob breaks with another ear-splitting scream. "I'm in here! Please help me—I'm trapped. Please let me out ... God, let me out. I'm in here."

Dmitri has no idea what she's ranting about, and his mind races down a hundred different paths as he tries to understand. For hours Elizabetta shrieks those same words over and over and over until he roars with the agony of it. He's desperate to free Elizabetta from whatever or whomever imprisoned her. Unadulterated bloodlust surges through him—a need to destroy the one responsible. Rage builds, and with it the desire to kill someone, something ... anything. He'll do whatever it takes to save her from this torment.

Then Elizabetta's body convulses in a series of explosive movements; her arms and legs flail as her body repeatedly rises and smashes down on the stone surface. Then her back arches until all but her head and feet leave the floor. His hands grasp and tear at her clothes, but he cannot pin her down. He's making another grab for her when Elizabetta's body pitches into the air. Before he can subdue or catch her, the entire length of her body smashes into the floor. *Damn it!* Dmitri doesn't know if the cracking sound he hears is her bones or the tile breaking. Once more he tightens his arms and legs around her. A pained scream wrenches from her throat and echoes through the room. *I'm hurting her, and this is killing me.* He grips her forearms as her body quakes again, and it takes every bit of strength he has to hold on to her until the fit finally subsides.

When Elizabetta's body goes limp and she falls quiet, Dmitri repositions her and cradles her in his lap, murmuring soft encouragements for her not to leave him. His heart aches over the agony she's going through—he loathes every wrong decision he made that led to this—and he doesn't know if anything he's done now has helped or made it worse for Elizabetta to endure. *Is the worst over?*

"I need you, *amore*. It's over ... come back to me." He begins to hum their melody again, and when the tune ends he places a gentle kiss on her lips. *Why is she still unconscious? Is this normal, or has something gone wrong?* "Elizabetta, please ..."

What if she never comes back from this? Despair settles deeper into Dmitri's bones as he rocks with his beloved held firmly in his arms. "Please, love, please. Don't leave me now, not like this ... I won't survive without you."

As if in response to his plea the whole process begins over again, and as the pattern repeats for countless hours, its never-ending cycle erodes his confidence that Elizabetta's mind will ever merge and survive this ordeal.

Hours fall to days, and days possibly to weeks—the sun has risen and set so many times that he's lost count. The redecrystapiezo has activated a few times now, but he's been unable to answer it. His need for blood is growing; the exhausting attempts to restrain Elizabetta are draining his reserves of strength and energy. *I know you're not the slightest bit hungry either, right, love?* She must be famished after what she has been enduring. *How much time has passed?* Increasing disquietude engorges his greatest fear—she may be trapped within the labyrinth of her mind forever.

Tears slide down his cheeks at the hopelessness that has claimed him. Endearments sputter off his lips, but the words become tangled around the lump in his throat. One plea repeats and falls into oblivion: "Please, love, please."

Dmitri presses his face against her neck as he rocks her limp body and weeps. Then she spasms and descends into the madness all over again, and devastation threatens to claim him once more.

CHAPTER 28: ELIZA

Hell Hath No Fury

Driven on a torrent of wind, a plethora of thoughts, memories, and sensations whirl in a cyclone just outside Eliza's reach. She leaps to catch even one of the shards hurtling around her, but as she reaches out the fragments splinter and pierce her body with lightning speed. Most tear through her without slowing down—their searing heat contorts her body. She lifts her arms to ward off the blows from the filaments slamming into her skull, but she is powerless to protect herself; the gesture only serves to slow their penetration. Unfathomable pain accompanies each fiery memory as it burrows into her brain.

There is no order to any of these fragments of thought—it's like trying to piece together a book that's been put through a cross-cut shredder. Extreme pain sears away numbness, and heat floods every cell of her body. It is the most excruciating experience of her life; even Shashenka's attempts to inflict pain seem feeble and pale in comparison.

The intensity of the storm increases, and the debris of her shattered life hurtles faster toward her from every direction. Hundreds of slivers push into Eliza's brain; thousands more rip through her body. A frenzied eruption of overlapping images, recollections, sensations, and sounds clamor for her attention. It is too much, too fast—she cannot access any rational thought or the slightest semblance of logical understanding—and Eliza feels herself slip into a suspended state that seems to greedily absorb the full-blown assault. There is no way to resist.

Little Eliza bounces on her father, Benito's, knee. A dagger pierces her heart, and an evil sneer curls Shashenka's lip. She places vegetables in her mother's basket. Her mother, Giuseppina, looks down and smiles as she tucks a loose strand of hair behind Eliza's ear. A beautiful, crooked smile spreads across Matt's face. She and her sister, Bernicah, play with dolls. Sergio and Dante—Eliza's brothers—beat up a boy who pushed her down and pulled her hair. She enjoys a long, passionate kiss with Dmitri as he makes love to her. Another sister, Paoli, kisses Eliza's scraped knee. She shares a moment of laughter with Maria, Victoria, Sofia, and Anna as they stroll through the piazza in Venice.

One after another these slivers of her life keep coming and entrench themselves deeper in her mind. She recognizes each one, but there are still too many missing pieces—and the unrelenting pain in her body barely allows her time to breathe, let alone process these broken images from the centuries of her life.

Eliza's sister, Melita, fights with her over a comb. A tall, handsome man steps out of the shadows on the piazza and somewhat shyly introduces himself as Dmitri Markov. Her sword decapitates a vampire, and she torches the head while Alexander and Vladimir look on. She's lying in Dmitri's arms as they look up at the stars. A shadow slinks through the apartment in Bozeman. She's frozen, unable to move, stretched out on a stone slab in an antechamber inside the Novgorod castle.

As words rush in, Eliza feels her lips move, silently reciting past conversations. She is close, so close, to making sense of one memory, but the cyclone's pitch increases yet again, and she loses the thought.

Dmitri's fangs puncture the vein on her neck. The pain of her mortal life ebbs as Dmitri rocks her in his arms. She wakes to the sensation of cool blood pooling in her mouth as she looks up into Dmitri's eyes.

Recognition seeps into her bones; the memories are starting to coalesce. More fragments merge and make sense, but everything is still a jumbled mess and out of order. Past conversations now roll off her tongue, whether she wants to say the words aloud or not.

"*Amore, ti amo e non smetterò mai di amarti.*" She mutters it again in English, "I will never cease loving you. Dmitri, *amore mio.*"

Dmitri ...

Then comes the moment where her true heartbreak began, and suddenly her memories flow together in a sequential order. The revolt had failed; as she and Dmitri awaited their punishment, she begged for death, terrified of their future, and yet Dmitri, Maria, and Vladimir urged her to live. *Why?* Eliza clearly remembers the conversation with Maria before the spells were placed—and the wizard's pledge, all those long-lost centuries ago, that after the mind reprogramming was complete she would find a way to remind Eliza who she was.

Now Eliza can feel the weight of the catatonic spell as it settled over her, stealing her life, claiming her future. All she was left were her memories, until they were isolated and locked away the moment the wizard cast the mind-wiping spell that allowed for Eliza's reprogramming five centuries later. Through the forefront of Eliza's thoughts flash the endlessly long years of the catatonic state—interminable hours trapped in herself, aware, alert, but unable to flutter so much as an eyelash.

During the tedious passage of years, Maria cared for and talked to her, providing updates on those whose lives went on without Eliza. Her friends among the Druzhina stopped coming to sit with her after the first few decades. It was just as well, as she quickly grew weary of their apologies and pity. But Dmitri—unshed tears burned through her during the long but always too few hours Dmitri spent with her. Not once could she utter a sound to let him know she was aware, or send the reassurance that she loved him. Over and over he brushed her hair, sang and played his music for her, or gently placed kisses on her face and immovable lips—so many times she lost count. She recalls the nights he brought her a human with an exquisite blood flavor to mark their wedding date. Always he'd puncture the throat and position the human over her mouth to prompt her ability to feed. She can still feel the way the blood trickled over her closed lips and down the sides of her face before her fangs came down and took the nourishment she needed.

Her mind screamed over and over, begging Dmitri to let her out. She doesn't know how many decades passed as she mutely shouted and pleaded for someone, anyone, to release her. Then insanity threatened to claim her—it was too much to bear. She was losing herself and sometimes even forgot her name. *My name—*

I am Elizabetta Rossellini Markov.

One after another the memories come. The sensations in her body change slightly as her past starts to merge with the false reality she's been living. A cooling tingle intermixes with spikes of white-hot pain. To her surprise, despite the torment of her body's reaction to the newest memories, her recent past seems to easily adapt to the truth that was buried in her brain. *God, I might survive this torture yet.* Eliza can now see the cracks and slivers of light where the locked memories broke through the barrier over the past year. The déjà vu moments when she recognized Dmitri's eyes or the way he swept his hair back, her sense of knowing the Druzhinas, and the innate awareness that she's seen most of the estates before—her mind, she understands, was trying to find its own way back together. It wanted its freedom as much as she needs hers from Shashenka.

Shashenka. That thought triggers a rage unlike any she's ever known. It consumes her, burning like hot acid in her veins. As each pulse drives it further through her body, awareness of her surroundings trickles forth, and in its wake the tension in her body vanishes. Suddenly Eliza can feel Dmitri's arms around her—can hear the words he murmurs.

"Please, love, please ..." All Eliza can do is lie there as his tears run over her neck. His voice breaks with the weight of centuries of suppressed emotions, neglected longing, and denied love—she can hear that and so much more in his few short words. She knows his heart as well as she knows her own.

Get up. Get up! Damn it, get on my feet. Dmitri is never going to hurt like this again.

The first semblance of bodily control returns—Eliza's finger twitches as she tries to flex and curl her hand into a fist. Next her toes wiggle, and she pushes harder to break out of the merging spell.

Get. The. Hell. Up. Dmitri is still holding her tightly and weeping. It rips her heart out—he has endured so much because of her.

Full control of her body bursts through her. Eliza leaps to her feet and clenches her fists as she spins to face Dmitri. She can feel the fury and determination blazing from her eyes.

May God damn you, Shashenka! I will send you to hell.

CHAPTER 29: DMITRI

Reclamation

Dmitri slowly rises, but he doesn't break eye contact with Elizabetta. She's on her feet, bloodlust pulsing in her eyes, and her chest is heaving—she's about to explode into a full murderous rage. He takes a cautious step in her direction, uncertain at the change.

"Oh, thank God you're here!"

He blinks at the unexpected words. *Is she relieved or about to attack?* "Elizabetta?" Then he startles as she launches forward, enveloping him in a fierce embrace. Her arms wrap tighter around his rib cage.

"Dmitri, I know who I am ... I remember everything! *Amore mio ... il mio angelo ... sempre ti amo.* I don't want to lose you—ever again."

It's really her! She came back to me. Dmitri gently curls a finger around her chin and lifts her face as his lips brush hers. "Welcome back, *amore.* I have missed you," he murmurs between kisses.

Her arms rise to encircle his neck, and she kisses him with a passion he's not felt from her in centuries. His emotions, already raw from the ordeal they just went through, threaten to overwhelm him; love battles loss, joy drowns sorrow, and reclamation conquers destruction.

He has no time to recover when she hungrily breathes out, "I want you." His breath catches in his throat as she rips his shredded shirt from his body. "This is going— gone." An excited tremor ripples through his abdomen. Elizabetta's fingers skim across his stomach and move between the waistband of his shorts and skin. "This won't do. These are history." Longing drenches each syllable that rolls off her tongue.

Her kisses trail along his chest and stomach. In a blur of motion she annihilates his slacks—the button flies off, the zipper teeth chase after it, and the very seams of his slacks disintegrate. Dmitri's pulse quickens as the last of his clothing drops to the floor.

It's been centuries since he shared this level of intimacy with Elizabetta, and his delighted but nervous laugh mocks his shaking fingers. Elizabetta seems eager but remains patient while he fumbles to unfasten the buttons on her tattered blouse and removes her clothes. When her last article of clothing is gone, she presses her body into his.

The sensation of her fingers and kisses exploring his body ignites him everywhere. For a brief moment Dmitri considers pulling her down to the floor, but he longs for a proper room and a comfortable bed. He's dreamed of this moment a million times—not once did he envision a stone floor in the quaint little drawing room of a sorceress's sea cave home. Determination to do this right wins over his desire to be rash. Unwilling to disrupt their contact—he never wants to let go of her again—Dmitri improvises. His hands slide down to grip her thighs, and he lifts her to his hips. Elizabetta locks her legs around him while her tongue flits teasingly against his shoulder and neck.

With half-faltering steps Dmitri navigates the narrow hallway. Her kisses and nibbles send shivers undulating through his body. Long-neglected passion battles reason, and he pauses in the hall, pressing her back against the closed bedroom door as he leans into her, tossing all logical thought away.

The sensory overload leaves him raw and desperate. Their hands, arms, legs, and lips are too far apart, too close together, everywhere and not there all at once. It's too much—it's not enough—he wants everything, but nothing more than this moment right now, later, forever as they float into a world where only they exist. *Heaven, this is heaven ... so pure, so right. She is mine forever.*

Their bodies tremble, and Dmitri slowly becomes aware that the strength in his legs is weakening. He's unsure how much longer he can hold out before taking them both to the floor. *I need to find a bed.* Somehow his hand reaches behind her to turn the doorknob. They nearly fall to the floor, but Dmitri's quick reflexes and long legs manage the few stumbling steps to the bed. Dropping onto the mattress, he loses himself to her touches and kisses. He's melting in Elizabetta's fire.

She first enthralled him nearly six centuries before; she

is doing it again now. *My wife, my precious wife.* Once more he surrenders to her, to their bond, as they simultaneously reclaim their lives as mates. Together they murmur affections and pledge their devotion to each other. Slowly the walls of this tiny bedroom fade away until there is no perception of darkness or light; there is only the two of them drifting in this abyss as their bodies merge and move as one. It's taken centuries to arrive at this moment, and he wants to remain here until the universe ceases to exist.

Uninvited seconds, minutes, and hours parade through the hallway and attempt to gain his attention with the changing light, but Dmitri ignores them. He doesn't care how many have lingered and left. Only one piece of time matters now, and it's the one he's been marking for centuries—the days since Elizabetta was taken from him. Lying with their limbs entwined, he murmurs, "Five hundred three years, ten months, and eighteen days."

Elizabetta leaves a trail of kisses from his chest to his mouth. "Hmm?"

"Five hundred three years, ten months, and eighteen days. My last confirmed count of how long I waited to reclaim you, *amore*, to know you again as my wife."

"I've always been your wife. That is how much time was stolen from us, and we need to make it up."

Dmitri chuckles. Nipping at her earlobe, he says, "We added to the delay, *amore*—you refused me in Paris." He laughs at the memory of that long day. "I pouted the entire time you slept. Now I am glad we waited ... this is extraordinary. You are so beautiful, exquisite, love."

Elizabetta murmurs, "There were times I wanted you, wanted you to come to me, and it drove me crazy that you never did."

Dmitri cups a hand over the back of her neck as her head nestles in the hollow of his shoulder. Voice thick with emotion, she says, "*Ti amo e non smetterò mai di amarti.*" Her breath brushes against his skin as her words penetrate his heart.

He kisses the top of her head. "*Ti amo, Elizabetta ... sempre, per sempre.*" A sliver of quiet sneaks between them, but he shoos it away. For centuries he's missed hearing her speak Italian, the way her words touched his soul.

Almost as if she read his mind, she says with a slight nervousness in her tone, "Italian feels awkward on my tongue."

The uncomfortable reminder of her false life and memories quiets them both. *I have so much to make up to her.* Dmitri struggles to form a meaningful apology. But what can he say to make up for the atrocious ways he failed her? What words can ever undo the horrendous experiences she endured because of decisions he made?

Elizabetta pops the bloated pause that hangs between them. "The only thing that matters now is that I know who I am again. We will end that despicable excuse for a devil vampire we call our master."

Tightening his embrace, he tells her, "I will be at your side—we will take him together. We will succeed."

Now her tears break free and spill onto his chest as she recounts the endless years trapped in the catatonic state. Dmitri's heart painfully constricts—shame and guilt threaten to choke him. *How do I ever set this right with her? How can she forgive me?*

"I couldn't see you, couldn't touch you ... I could hear you and was unable to speak. For years I screamed inside for someone to let me out, and no one even knew I was in there. Maria was sure that I wouldn't be aware, but I was, and it was interminable. For days, years, endless centuries I understood everything around me. All I wanted was freedom ... to hold you, to live our lives together, to be free from Shashenka's cruelty and control."

Dmitri's lips move, but the words lodge in his throat. A single, strangled sound falls in a whimper off his tongue as a tear rolls down his face. *If I had known ...*

"Hush, don't." She places a kiss on his trembling lips and wipes away the tear. When she pulls back he sees her tender smile. "The best moments were when we were alone, when you'd talk to me. You spoke as if you knew I could hear your words. It gave me hope and strength to see it through."

"I never knew—cannot imagine ... I'm so very sorry, love."

Elizabetta's hands frame his face, and she kisses him again. "I remember every word, every note of '*Il mio tesoro,*' every time you hummed or played it for me. I doubt my mind would have survived without you."

She presses kisses against his blemished chest. "I remember ,., these"—her finger traces one of the many scars over his heart—"were not here before. There are so many, too many ... you endured so much. Yet your face—he never marred it?"

"He needed me presentable, to not look like a monster in public."

"How many are because of me?"

The guilt on her face is too much—it is wrong—the last beating she endured left her scarred too. *It wasn't her fault.* He grimaces and shakes his head. "None."

"Please don't lie to me, *amore.*" She kisses another scar. "I know you were beaten and tortured because I defied your attempt to create my false life."

Dmitri cups her face in his hands. "It does not matter, Elizabetta. I would bear them all—I would endure every moment again just to have you back."

Tears well in her eyes, and he wipes them away with his thumbs. "I'm ... I ..." She draws a deep breath. "Forgive me. I am so ashamed of the way I treated you—for that awful night in Novgorod. I ..."

Both of us were forced to wrong each other. "*Amore,* you have no idea in how many ways I failed you when you were not yourself. For that I must beg your forgiveness. But you—there is nothing for me to absolve you of that you have done. None of it was your fault."

"There is one thing." Her gaze seems to search his, and Dmitri sees the slightest flush on her cheeks. Her eyelids close for a moment before she looks at him again. "In my heart I knew it was wrong to be with other men, even if I didn't understand why. Please forgive me, for I will not forgive myself, but I am sorry." Her voice falls to a whisper. "I feel ashamed that I have lain with others."

Dmitri tries to respond, but she cuts him off. "You were right—my heart never forgot where it belongs. Somewhere deep down I knew it was yours, and yet I never even attempted to fight back against becoming a concubine."

"If it helps you find solace, then I will forgive you." Dmitri wraps her in a firm embrace.

"*Ti amo ... mi dispiace.*" She murmurs the words—"I love you ... I'm sorry"— between every brush of her lips as she resumes kissing each scar she can find on his body, resisting his attempts to stop her, and he finds himself choking back the sorrow and joy warring inside him. A measure of absolution and acceptance seems to settle over both of them. Dmitri pulls her against his chest, and neither moves for what feels like hours.

At last Elizabetta pulls back and smiles up at him. "What has happened is behind us now. We did what we had to, to survive." She nods as though to reassure herself. "We're going to be okay, *amore*. We've always been stronger together than apart, and we shall not be separated again."

"In time we'll both be whole again." Dmitri jumps as she smacks his bare behind. "Ouch, what was that for?"

"Hesitation, pessimism ..." She pinches his bottom lip in her teeth. "No more of this moping and wallowing between us. I miss your laughter and your humor, your smile. Don't force me to drag them out of you."

His hands move to tickle her ribs. "I have not forgotten how to play, love."

"Instruments, games, me ... I would hope the hell not."

A mischievous glint sparks in her eyes. "Shall we race? It's time we took a shower break. Loser washes the winner."

Her friskiness lightens the burden he has carried for centuries. Laughing, tripping, and pulling one another back, they tumble out of the room and down the hall, but Dmitri reaches the shower first. He laughs triumphantly and pulls her close as they step into the shower together.

Steam swirls around them. Sheets of water rinse more than grime from their bodies, and with it go years of desolation and heartache. Willingly Dmitri surrenders himself to her as her hands slide over his body and the wondrous sensation of her touch courses through him. He wraps his arms around Elizabetta and kisses the top of her head, content to remain in this embrace until the hot water runs out.

She's the first to pull back, a naughty smile on her face. "Now, are you going to take me back to bed, or are you waiting for me to ravish you in this cold shower?"

The earlier urgency between them has subsided, and with kisses and nibbles they stumble out of the shower to the bed and spend hours rediscovering and reclaiming what they were forced to sacrifice and live without. Dmitri loses and finds himself again as they rise and fall, build and tear down, conquer and defeat together the scars inflicted during the years that were robbed from their lives. Their bodies entwine, rest, become one, until neither has any sense of the passage of time—they only desire to remain here forever. As the hours pass, the healing balm of these shared moments finally lulls them into the deepest and most peaceful sleep either has known in centuries.

Night and day blur together as they spend quiet minutes recounting memories of their past. Dmitri wants nothing more than to hide in this sea cave home with Elizabetta forever, but the urge for freedom grows stronger with each passing night. As their neglected hunger rises and desire for one another becomes thoroughly sated, he tries to push against the gentle nagging of his mind—they must leave soon. They can't avoid the unfinished business that lies ahead. Reluctantly he says, "We need to send the signal to the Orde de Maxia."

Elizabetta sighs, nodding in apparent understanding. She stands and holds her hand out to him. "You're right. Let's finish this."

They shower, dress, and tidy the home from its disarray. Dmitri notices that they move in unison, almost mirroring each other—further closing the gap on their forced separation. In the decades after they wed, it often was as if they read each other's minds, and he revels in the return of that connection. *I'd forgotten how closely we align with our bond.* She smiles at him—he smiles back with the contentment of knowing they fully belong to each other again.

At last Dmitri places the onyx stone in the alabaster bowl. Elizabetta extends a claw and reaches for his wrist. "*Ti amerò per sempre,*" she whispers, and punctures his finger. A drop of blood falls to the stone.

Taking her hand, he extends his own claw to pierce her skin. "*Ti amo, amore.*" When her blood falls, the stone shudders and glows white hot for a moment before it seems to cool to a translucent state. There is no sign that their blood was ever upon it. They share a look of wonder and join hands. Nothing appears, and there is no smoke or spark—it feels almost anticlimactic.

Together they go to the drawing room to wait in silence. Minutes later the mutaport activates without a sound, and a burning ring glows around the white stone in the floor. A shimmering light bursts forth, growing in size. Dmitri shields his eyes, and Elizabetta cringes away from its dazzling brightness as Alastrina emerges. The moment she is whole, the fiery ring disappears, leaving the white stone unscathed. *What a truly remarkable device.* He's surprised Shashenka hasn't discovered them and demanded Maria place them throughout his estates.

Alastrina smiles and circles them as she looks them over. "You look well. I was beginning to think you went on holiday or ran away or forgot to signal."

"It took a long time for Elizabetta's mind to merge." Images of what she endured flicker through his head; he has to stifle a shudder. Instead he says, "It was an exhaustive process. We needed to rest a few days when it was over."

Alastrina scoffs, her cackling laughter bouncing around the small room. "Vampires. I've never met one that can tell time very well."

Elizabetta's expression puckers the skin between her brows. "How long have we been here?"

The sorceress's answer leaves them speechless. *Thirty-seven days?* Dmitri is still trying to account for each day when Alastrina says, "A lot has happened while you two no doubt were making up for lost time."

It wasn't nearly long enough. He decides against relaying those sentiments to the sorceress; the sooner the matter with Shashenka is finished, the quicker he and Elizabetta can start a new life together. "Tell us what happened."

Alastrina sits in the chair facing them. "Shashenka got bored and sent a guard to retrieve Eliza from the cellar. Discovering both of you missing set off the alarm. That little imp has been pitching one helluva tizzy about it. Rumors of your escape are spreading through all the realms now.

"The Druzhina, to no one's surprise, is hunting you. The Druzhinniki is making sure that everyone knows Shashenka has placed a bounty on you both."

Elizabetta gives a dry laugh. "This ought to be good. Nothing like pouring a little more gas on the fire."

How much are we worth to that demon? Revenge will drive Shashenka's pursuit of them—the stakes couldn't be any higher now that they are officially on the run.

Alastrina seems to know what he's thinking, and tells them that Shashenka has offered one million rubles for each of them if their heads are sent to him as proof of capture—two million rubles each if they're brought to him alive. "Maria says he is planning a very drawn-out and public execution for both of you." The sorceress looks uncomfortable, shifting in her chair. "The only aspect he has yet to decide is which of you will die first."

Elizabetta gasps at the same moment he hisses. He squeezes her hand, and disgust and defiance saturate his tone. "Every bounty hunter and shadow realm thug will be looking for us. But this time we will not be stopped until that vile creature is dead."

There's a scratching sound at the door, and Alastrina walks over to open it. "With the cross-realm support you have, there are many who will keep their kind off your trail," she says. "Edward, there you are." She bends over and picks up her rat, who wrinkles his nose; he actually appears to glare at Dmitri and Elizabetta. "Oh, come now, none of that, Edward. I'm sure they forgot about you."

The look on Elizabetta's face confirms that she gave no more thought to Alastrina's pet than he did. *That rat looks as if he wants to bite us.* Dmitri says, "I'm sorry. We didn't mean to neglect Edward."

The sorceress's tone is pleasant but dismissive. "I didn't ask or expect you to care for him. Edward will get over it."

She sits back down in the chair and smiles at them. "Now, where were we? Ah yes, allies and enemies. Even with your supporters, there will remain some risk to you. If you'd prefer, you are both more than welcome to stay here until your shadow realm forces are ready to move against Belyakov."

Dmitri shakes his head, and Elizabetta's quick glance seems to convey that she stands resolutely by his side. They've only just returned to each other as rightful mates, and now they must reclaim the existence Shashenka stole from them. "As leaders of this war, we cannot and will not bring this effort together while hiding."

Alastrina looks down at their joined hands and takes a moment to scrutinize them. "Where do you wish to go?

We can use the mutaport to send you anywhere you like, though you may have a problem if you need to leave quickly and there is no mutaport on the other end."

Dmitri makes eye contact with Elizabetta and recognizes her unspoken answer. *What a blessing it is to have her back.* He nods at his wife and says, "Send us to one of the Druzhinas."

"I'll need to know at least a general location before I can send you anywhere."

Using the redecrystapiezo, Dmitri contacts Maria to update her on their plans and to ask for the whereabouts of the Druzhinas. To avoid raising the suspicion of anyone at La Perfezione, they keep their conversation brief. Once again the Druzhinas are scattered; the only known location Maria has for any of them is Belyakov's estate in Waiheke, where Justin Walker is on holiday.

Dmitri ends the call and takes Elizabetta's hand. Alastrina has already risen and is walking toward the mutaport. "Send us to Cactus Bay in New Zealand."

CHAPTER 30: ELIZA

Confrontational Reunions

That's it? Just blink and poof, and it's over? The muta-port experience leaves Eliza miffed. She expected to feel something—a pop, a tingle, dizzy, warm, cold, anything. Instead, transportation was nearly instantaneous; one moment they were standing on the device in Alastrina's home, and the next, they were here. The disappointed look on Dmitri's face tells her that he expected something more, too.

Eliza draws in a deep breath to smell the ocean air as they walk toward the shoreline. Last time she was here she strolled along this beach with both Dmitri and Matt. She wonders if Dmitri remembers, but he's already whispering in her ear that he does. It's hard to believe how much has changed in just a couple short months.

They walk in silence toward a hidden passageway in the low-lying hill that separates Garden Cove from Cactus Bay. A few trees stand sentinel between the edge of the beach and the grassy area beyond. The vegetation, while limited, is denser along the hill, and it helps obscure the entrance. The hideout, a small room carved out of the rock, used to conceal pirate bounty, but among humans it has long since been forgotten. Now it will provide them a place to stay, yet leave them close enough to watch the Belyakov estate for any sign of Justin. They will need to make contact with him as soon as possible; the risk of being seen by anyone looking to collect the reward is too high for them to stay in one place longer than a few days.

After inspecting their hideout, they sneak near the estate to wait and watch. It's just past one in the morning, and most of the activity seems routine—the locals attend to their duties, the neighboring properties are quiet—but hours pass with no sign of Justin. *I hope he hasn't left Waiheke already.* She wishes Maria knew where the others were—they need to move their plans forward. Then just before dawn, he returns to the mansion. Eliza squeezes Dmitri's hand—they have their chance. Doubtless Justin is in for the day and will not venture out again until nightfall. Eliza and Dmitri retreat to their hideout and make plans to intercept him when he leaves next.

Dmitri sounds anxious. "I don't want you out of my sight, but there is no way to watch both estate exits together."

Eliza wraps her arms around his neck. "*Amore*, I am back. I am no longer that pathetic excuse for a woman that Shashenka turned me into. I know how to do my job."

He sighs and runs a hand through his hair twice before pausing it at the crown of his head. "You're right, love, but it worries me that your skills may be tempered by disuse—I don't want you taken by surprise."

She gives him a petulant look as he explains the need to watch both exits of the estate and grab Justin as soon as possible. When he goes on to describe Justin's habit of alternating between social activities and fishing, she begins drumming her fingers on her crossed arms. Finally he assigns her the job of watching the main gate while he covers the cove—he's clearly convinced Justin will go fishing. *And we're back in 1426.*

His brows furrow. "What?"

"Nothing. Please continue." She smirks inwardly at Dmitri's plan—he's trying to keep her out of the action. *I'm sure that I don't need that level of supervision and protection anymore.* Still, she understands Dmitri's concern, and she doesn't object. It may take time before he can accept that she is the same person he married, not the dumbed-down shell of herself that she's been for the past nearly two years. In a way, Dmitri's cautious behavior isn't any different from when he first brought her into the coven; he was a nervous wreck on her first few missions as a Druzhina. For her, though, the return of her life, her potential, is invigorating, and Eliza can hardly wait to take action.

At least they both agree that they'll need to be well rested and ready to move once they make contact with Justin. Eliza curls against Dmitri's side and closes her eyes. Even though they will soon face the biggest challenge of their lives, this one small moment is perfect. She's smiling as she drops off to sleep, Dmitri humming their song. *I have come home.*

Dmitri wakes her before the sun sets. One look at him tells her that he didn't sleep at all. She frowns; he's serious about keeping her away from the action and is back to treating her like a rookie. "Don't coddle me, *amore*. You needed rest too."

His guilty smile doesn't mollify her. When she cocks an eyebrow to make her point, he laughs and pulls her into his arms. "Centuries of habit may be hard to break."

"I'm sure a few quick sparring matches will dispel that notion."

"Perhaps."

She shakes her head as he lets her go, and together they walk toward the tunnel. The sun is low on the horizon but not fully set—they'll need to expose themselves to its harmful effects if they are to be in position before Justin leaves for the evening. Keeping to the trees and shadows, they make their way toward the estate.

Dmitri embraces her as he cautions her once more to be careful. "I'll be fine, *amore*," she says as she pulls out of his arms. "If he comes your way, don't leave me sitting in a tree all night. Okay?"

"Shall we bet, love, gentleman's wager? I say he comes my way and we come to get you within the hour."

"You're on, and you are so gonna lose this bet." Eliza winks at him and runs off along the path to get in position.

He calls after her, "Don't forget to leave yourself an escape route."

She laughs and waves without looking back at him. *Easy-peasy. I should have upped the ante on our bet ...*

massages for an entire month. She thinks about his hands on her, and moans—that is one bet she wouldn't mind losing either. Her mood shifts as she pictures the numerous scars on his body, proof of what he's endured because of her. *I don't know how he survived it—survived me.* Her chest tightens with guilt. It will take a lifetime and then some before Eliza repays the debt she owes him for standing by her, for accepting her charge to never give up on returning her heart to him if he chose not to end her life. Silently she vows that she will find a way.

For now, it's time to refocus on the mission—there's a welcome strangeness to the word, to the idea of once more killing the real monsters among them. She pushes the sad thoughts aside and climbs into a tree near the main gate. *Yes, it is good to be back!*

She settles in to wait and watch. Within minutes of full dark, an estate car pulls out of the garage. Justin is behind the wheel, and as he drives toward her she smirks; Dmitri was wrong, and it will leave him out of the fun of capturing Justin. *I win, ha-ha.*

Once the car turns onto the main road, she drops out of the tree and runs after it, staying within the darker shadows. It's a short trip—within a few miles Justin parks near a bar. The sign above it reads "Paulie's Place." Another sign indicates they offer cold drinks, live music, and beach access. Eliza recalls seeing him out partying while they were at Novgorod—he seems to enjoy chasing women. He is out of the car and slips inside before Eliza can close the distance between them.

Damn it. Confronting him in public isn't the best option; there is no way to know if others will recognize her from Shashenka's bounty offer, and the less attention she brings to herself, the better. Eliza stealthily works her way from the shadowy outdoors to the inside of the small, crowded pub. Using the throng of people as cover, she searches the crowd for Justin. When she spots him dancing and flirting with a skinny blonde, her exuberance deflates; this could turn into a long night. She moves to a booth near a dark corner to wait.

For the next hour she watches Justin's every move. The blonde clings to him like Velcro, almost as if she's afraid to allow even an inch of space between them. If the woman were human, Eliza would chance walking up to him, but the untouched drinks on their table are a fairly good indicator that Justin's date is another vampire.

At least the time spent waiting isn't a total loss for Eliza—it gives her the chance to hone the influencing skills she hasn't used in centuries. As one man after another approaches her, doubtless seeking more than a dance partner, Eliza's body trickles out the pheromone that leaves her all but invisible to the crowd. Those who seem resistant or immune are easily turned away with a simple touch or a direct command sent through eye contact. She's forgotten how good it feels to do what they do best. *Perhaps becoming a Druzhina again isn't such a bad idea after all.*

Finally Justin leads the woman out the beachside door. Unwilling to let him out of her sight and possibly miss a chance to snatch him, Eliza slips out of the bar and follows them at a discreet distance. When they lie in the sand and begin making out, she settles in the shadows between a tree and bush to watch. *Come on, Justin, get done sampling this sweet-tart. I need to get you alone.* She has no interest in Justin's love life, and hopes this interlude is brief.

A surge of excitement rushes through her when the couple stops groping each other and Justin rises to his feet. He walks toward the water, but the woman soon follows and reattaches herself to his side. *Leech.* Eliza knows him well enough to recognize that this clingy vampire is the type of woman he'll never see again. Perhaps it may be enough to run Justin off soon and give Eliza a better opportunity to approach him.

Then to Eliza's dismay, Justin and the woman retreat to their earlier spot and lie down. She watches with increasing frustration as the two of them look up at the stars and talk. A few more minutes pass before Justin sits up and looks at his phone—he's apparently responding to a text message, but from this angle she can't tell whom he's texting. For a moment Eliza considers crashing their little party and demanding to talk with him alone. *Can just imagine the way he'll react to seeing me. Lead balloon, anyone?*

She leans against the tree and looks up at the night sky. It must be three or four in the morning—daylight will arrive in a couple of hours. *Is Dmitri still waiting, or has he noticed both Justin and I are gone?* Enough time has passed that Dmitri must know by now that he chose the wrong location. *Time—a luxury that I'm running out of here.*

A sound from behind her sets off Eliza's internal alarm, and she spins around to face the unknown threat. Two men rush toward her. Without hesitation she draws the horse-head dagger and assumes a defensive posture.

The men slow but continue advancing. Cautiously she backs out of the shadows toward the beach—if she has to fight, she'd rather be in the open than tangled in the brush. The men separate, an obvious attempt to divide her attention. Eliza keeps backing away in Justin's direction; her sudden appearance may surprise him, but if she needs help there's at least a chance he will come to aid her.

When the two men are within several feet of her, the one to her right lunges, and years of instinct and training take over as Eliza thrusts her dagger at the man. In the same instant she steps to the side to get out from between her attackers, moving to the left and avoiding the first man's knife just as the second man leaps into a low tackle. The force of his body sends her sprawling; she barely hits the ground when someone pounces on top of her.

Her fangs and claws extend, and she hisses, scrabbling for the hands now clenched around her neck, but another set of hands restrains her arms. In one fluid motion Eliza thrusts upward and swivels her hips to knee the man choking her. There's enough force in her blow to knock him away from her, buying her a second—maybe two. It's not enough. She tries wresting free of the second man's grasp, but he takes advantage of her rotation, and the next thing she knows, his arm is curled around her throat. His other hand clamps her wrist—he's trying to force her to drop the dagger.

Her mind races. *Dmitri was right—I'm rusty at this—but I'm still a better fighter than this jackwagon.* Adrenaline courses through her, giving her the boost she needs. Her chin drops to her chest, and just as quickly she tosses her head back and smashes the man's face.

It's enough to break his hold. Free of his grasp, she leaps to her feet and turns to face the other man, but he is already in a low, spinning crouch. Before she can jump out of reach, his leg sweeps hers, and Eliza lands hard on her back. The other man belly flops onto her as she hits the ground, and immediately he locks his legs and arms around her. Wrestling, kicking, throwing punches, Eliza manages to scramble to her feet again—she's almost clear of them when a third set of hands catches her arm midswing.

Before she can react to this new threat, her arm is wrenched in a twisting motion that pitches her forward. Using the momentum of the fall, Eliza tucks into a roll and leaps to her feet. She blindly claws, bites, and kicks, but within moments the three men take her back to the ground.

One man's hands are on her legs while another's knee is in her back before she can right herself. *Déjà vu—just like that cop in Montana.* She struggles in vain against their hold. The man astride her back tangles a fist in her hair and jerks her head backward before slamming her face into the ground. She half chokes on a mouthful of sand and writhes against them until they bind her arms behind her back. The battle is already lost, but she won't give them the satisfaction of taking her that easily.

"Good job, Viggo."

Oh, for Pete's sake—I know that voice. "You've got to be shitting me! Justin, what are you doing?"

"You're not quite what you used to be, Eliza."

She hears the triumphant ring in his voice, and as they roll her over, her gaze locks on Justin. "You don't understand. I have—"

Her words choke to a stop as Justin stuffs a wad of fabric—which she sees matches his torn shirt—into her mouth.

"You want this boss?" Viggo pulls a narrow case from his pocket and takes out a syringe. "She doesn't look too cooperative."

Justin grins. "I have ways of forcing others to cooperate with me. I'm sure she'll be no problem after we get her to the car."

Eliza strains against the ropes binding her wrists and ankles. *You need to listen to me.* She tries to speak around the gag, but her words are too garbled, and they ignore her.

Justin lifts her easily and starts toward the parking lot, Eliza writhing and squirming against his hold. *Damn it, Justin!* Somehow she must force him to put her down and listen. He simply readjusts his grasp and keeps walking.

When they reach the car, Justin asks the skinny blonde to fish the keys from his pocket and open a rear door. He throws Eliza on the backseat, then crawls in after her and straddles her struggling body.

Mental gears grind, and their teeth break off in Eliza's head as she tries to comprehend what is going on. Justin is, or was, one of her and Dmitri's friends—he is a Druzhina. The anger in his eyes has never been directed toward her this way before.

"I think that I will take that dagger you took from her, and that syringe you offered earlier," Justin says to Viggo as he reaches a hand behind him.

Eliza's eyes grow wide—she vigorously shakes her head. "No, listen ... listen to me." The gag strangles her words, but she keeps pleading even as she feels the prick of the needle on her neck. Her fading thoughts grumble away as the unknown drug pulls her down. *I wish the stories were true that vampire bodies are hard like stone.* Then the blackness takes her.

When consciousness returns, Eliza's head is pounding like an elephant is tap dancing on it. Slowly she realizes her arms are tied behind the back of the chair she is sitting on, and her ankles are tied to its legs. It's pitch black—there's a dark hood over her head. The gag is still in her mouth. *What the hell? Where has Justin taken me?* Fear creeps up her spine as she considers the worst. *Is this my execution at Shashenka's hands? Would Justin turn me in like that?*

Panic will not help her—Eliza breathes deeply to regain control of her emotions. She tilts her head one way and then the other, listening to the sound of soft movements in front of her. Not so much as a whisper comes from those she is certain are within feet of her. Squaring her shoulders, she looks directly ahead and waits for some indication of her captors' intent. She has no idea whom or how many she will face when they remove the hood—if they remove it.

Anger adds another stone to the foundation of her resolve. *What I wouldn't give for just one chance to go toe-to-toe with Justin. I will kick his ass for this.*

A hand settles on top of her head and jerks the hood away, taking a few strands of hair with it. Her eyes adjust to the light, and shock jolts through her. *No way. Un-flipping-believable.* For a moment she wonders if her mind is playing tricks on her, but a few blinks later she accepts it's true. There standing before her is every one of the Druzhinas except Dmitri, and nearly all of them are scowling—at her.

Vladimir clasps Justin's shoulder and congratulates him on a job well done. Then he steps forward and turns his furious gaze down on her. His proximity forces her to look up the length of his tall frame. If it weren't for the gag in her mouth, she would smile; of all the Druzhinas, he's Dmitri's closest friend.

The coldness in his dark eyes sobers her—she doesn't know what they plan to do, but she knows what they are capable of. "Eliza Ross, you have been brought to us because we need the truth. What happened to Dmitri? We demand to know where you have taken him. Depending on the honesty of your answers, we may let you live and return you to Master."

Oh, hell no. You either kill me or let me out of here.

He reaches to remove the gag.

"If you lie to us, we will kill you."

Eliza's eyes pop wide, then narrow at the threat; they're not considering letting her go. *We're on the same freaking side here!* The absurdity of the situation is overwhelming, and she bursts out laughing as he pulls the gag away. Without warning Vladimir backhands her and commands her to be quiet. She tastes blood in her mouth. Movement catches her eye, and she pries her glare away from Vladimir just long enough to look around the room. *Alexander.* His presence reminds her how precarious her position is. If she reveals too much, he will likely report it to Shashenka. If she reveals too little, Vladimir will make good his threat and probably deliver her himself.

She eyes Vladimir with caution. "What do you want to know?"

"Those of us who have seen Dmitri understand the condition he is in. We know you took him with you when you escaped La Perfezione. What did you do to him? Tell me where he is, Eliza!"

Shit. She has allies here, she must, but she'd have to reveal the return of her memories to gain their support. Given Matt's last report, she can no longer trust Alexander and Sofia—as far as she knows, there's been no change in their position.

"I'll tell you what you want to know, but on one condition." Her tone is stern. "Alexander and Sofia must leave the room before I say another word. If they stay, I'll tell you nothing."

In a moment of déjà vu they argue among themselves just as they did during the standoff over saving Matt's life at the Cleary ranch. Then Vladimir shouts over their bickering, "Enough. Alexander, Sofia, please go upstairs and wait for us."

Eliza notes the hurt and confusion on Sofia's face and the petulant look on Alexander's as they storm out of the room. After the door closes behind them, she waits a moment to collect her thoughts before looking back at Vladimir. "I know what you're up to here." Vladimir's dark-brown eyes smolder, but she meets his look with equal intensity, putting as much power as possible into each word. "I know you're trying to gain intelligence to further your plans against Shashenka."

Gasps and hisses erupt from the group as Druzhinas look at one another in horror. Eliza doesn't relent. "If you implement those plans, you will fail and ruin everything."

Vladimir tightens his neck and flexes his jaw, but his tone is cool. *Go fish.* He says, "Just what plans are those?"

Time to let him catch the big one. "I know that you, Anna, Kees, and Katherine favor ending Belyakov's rule." She looks at each one as she names them. "Justin, Stephan, and Victoria just recently committed to joining you. Alexander and Sofia are against you—the only thing holding you back."

She watches their surprised faces and waits for Vladimir to quiet their outburst. When he does, he takes another step toward her. "You seem strangely informed. What makes you think that is our plan?"

"I know you. You've not been as clandestine about this as you may think."

"Trust me, Eliza, you don't know us at all. We faithfully serve our master."

Vladimir's dismissive tone makes her laugh outright. *Faithfully serve, my ever-aching butt.* Still, she can't resist toying with them a little longer to bring impact to what she'll reveal. She needs to gauge their loyalty to the goblin king.

Shifting in her seat, she pulls against the ropes restraining her. "I hurt Dmitri while trying to protect him from that evil goblin king you are so intent on destroying. Dmitri willingly left La Perfezione with me, and we went into hiding. We intended to snatch Justin"—she glares at him—"so we could arrange a meeting with all of you."

Her words stun them into silence. *One, one thousand, two, one thousand.* She keeps counting until Vladimir snarls at her, "What kind of game are you playing, Eliza?"

Twenty-three seconds. Took them long enough— maybe we can get down to business now and stop this bullshit. Tone defiant, she says, "One I intend to win."

Confusion rains over their faces. Katherine says, "This is a waste of time. Shashenka has her mind so twisted that she's useless. It's clear she's screwing with us."

Victoria mumbles, "I knew this was a mistake—we're going to have to kill her. We can't risk sending her back to Shashenka now that she knows—"

Waste of time? Kill me? Wrong. Not going to happen. "I thought you wanted my answers! Honest and straightforward? What the hell do you think I'm giving you? Trust me ... you're on the wrong damn path—both where Shashenka's demise is concerned, and about me."

Kees growls through clenched teeth, "We know you well enough, Eliza."

She looks down, draws a breath, and raises her eyes to them. "No. You. Don't." Her chin lifts in pride. "You know full well that I am not, nor have I ever been Eliza Ross."

The room again goes quiet. Stephan is the first to speak. "What did you say?"

"I am not Eliza Ross. I am Elizabetta Markov, and you will release me. Now."

None of them moves—they stare with mouths agape. She doesn't give them time to recover. "You will not over-see the crusade to end Shashenka's rule. The Orde de Maxia has already approved our petition and decreed their support. Dmitri and I will lead this war."

The Druzhinas look as if they were quick-frozen. Several moments pass as Vladimir eyes her warily, his conflict etched across his face. "You lie. Dmitri is in no condition to petition anything."

"Our plan is in place." Eliza measures their uncertainty as she looks from one to another. "You've been under my team's surveillance for months, and we have eavesdropped on you during your not-so-secret meetings. You will not proceed. You will follow my orders, and we will not fail this time."

Suddenly Anna is at her side. "Elizabetta? You're back? I mean, it's really you—you have your memories?"

Smiling, Eliza nods. "Yes ... I know and remember each of you very, very well."

In the next moment, against Vladimir's objections, Victoria, Anna, and Katherine untie the ropes and haul Eliza to her feet. The women envelop her in a hug, laughing and talking all at once. In their excitement they ask so many overlapping questions that they barely wait for her answers. Until this moment she hasn't realized how much she's missed them. These women—her sisters among the Druzhina—are her best friends.

Vladimir asserts his authority again to remind them that Eliza still hasn't answered his questions about Dmitri.

With her arms around Anna and Victoria's shoulders, she says, "Dmitri returned to his senses shortly after we arrived in Venice, back when Shashenka first tortured me."

Again she regards each reaction, but when she looks back at Vladimir, she bursts out laughing. "Dmitri was fully in charge of his faculties when you bathed him following his brief disappearance and return to La Perfezione."

"What?" Vladimir's eyes grow wide.

Between chuckles she says, "He was pretending to be in a stupor and actually found it awkwardly entertaining that you bathed and dressed him."

The others begin to laugh, but Vladimir grows noticeably angrier. "And neither of you saw fit to say something?"

Eliza matches his icy tone. "You insisted the goblin's lackeys remain in the room. Remember that? We had no opportunity to tell you before we were taken to the cellar for more torture."

Vladimir reaches up and massages the base of his neck. Shame douses his embarrassment, and he gives her a quick nod.

She looks at those gathered around her. "I realize that we have a lot to discuss, but Dmitri is going to panic if I'm not back to the tunnel before sunrise."

Kees clears his throat and shifts uncomfortably. "Justin brought you from Waiheke two days ago ... Dmitri is probably doing a three-foot hover."

What? "Two days ago? Where the hell are we?"

"Melbourne, Australia."

Shit. Shinola. This is just flipping fantastic. "I have to get back to Waiheke right now. You have to take me back." Eliza moves toward the door. The glare she gives Justin intensifies with each step. *He's first on my dance card for an ass-kicking.*

Katherine says, "It's daytime. We'll have to wait until dark."

Eliza spins around. Their haughty, arrogant expressions are gone; even Vladimir looks sheepish. She scrubs her palms over her face. "Do any of you have Maria's number? We need to call her."

"What does that witch have to do with any of this?" Vladimir snarls.

Eliza huffs in exasperation. "First off, she's a wizard, not a witch, and secondly, Maria is our ally. She can contact Dmitri, tell him what happened."

Victoria gives a shy but firm smile and shakes her head. "We've already ruled her out as an ally." She holds out a cell phone. "You can call Dmitri."

"No, I can't." She shoots Victoria a frosty look. Voice flat, she says, "Dmitri left Venice without a phone, and mine was on me when Justin's goons jumped me. Thanks to his pal Viggo, it was smashed to smithereens."

They stare at her. "I realize that you don't know this,

but Maria's the one who helped Dmitri and me escape and petition the Orde de Maxia." She raises a hand to cut off their questions. "It's a long story. I'll tell you about it later, but first we have to let Dmitri know that I'm okay."

Her frustration kicks up another notch as she looks at the dumbstruck faces staring back at her. *Break out the crayons—it's time to draw a picture.* "Maria is the only one who can call him. He has a redecrystapiezo—that's the magic realm's equivalent of a cell phone."

Her words are met with more confusion. *Unbelievable. How hard is this to understand?* "Look, Maria gave one to Dmitri, and she can reach him on it. Call her. Now."

Victoria swipes the screen of her phone and hands it to Eliza after placing the call to Maria. The wizard assures them she'll relay the message to Dmitri—she'll instruct him to stay put and let him know that Eliza will return with the Druzhinas after nightfall.

Irate, Eliza tosses the phone back to Victoria and turns on Justin. "If you would have just listened to me, this whole mess could have been avoided."

His posture is guarded. "You should know that once we set a trap, we spring it."

"Since when do we spring traps and not pay attention to what a captive may say? Is that a new policy, or am I not getting my memos?" *Great, now I'm channeling Matt. I hope Maria is keeping him updated.*

Stephan seems to notice her tension and takes the opportunity to redirect the conversation, asking how the Orde de Maxia will contribute to the overthrow of Shashenka. Eliza tries to avoid answering. She won't risk details as long as there are any uncommitted or opposed Druzhinas, and even when Vladimir insists the Druzhinas have sworn a blood oath to remove Shashenka, she's not convinced—loyalty to a master can break a blood oath. She also informs him that she doesn't trust Alexander and Sofia to violate their fidelity to Shashenka.

"You're wrong. Come upstairs, talk with them." Vladimir cocks an eyebrow. "You'll need all of us." Reluctant, but left with little choice, she follows the Druzhinas up out of the basement to the living room, where her eyes immediately settle on Alexander sitting on a couch. *That filthy, rotten son of a bitch.* Enraged by every trick and dirty game he played with her—and the despicable order he gave Dmitri to break her—she flies across the room before anyone can stop her.

"You dirty bastard." She snatches him off the couch and slams him to the floor as her claws come out and both hands lock around his throat. "You're responsible for what Shashenka's been doing to us. Instead of breaking me, you nearly destroyed my husband. Why should I trust you instead of killing you right now?"

Obviously startled, Alexander looks to the others. "What's going on?"

Eliza lifts him by the neck and bangs his head into the floor. "You are not listening to me, Alexander." Her voice changes to a low, threatening growl. "I know what you've done—the ways you've betrayed us—and I don't trust you."

Kees and Stephan pry her hands from Alexander's throat, urging her to calm down—it only angers her further. Her claws leave deep scratches as they pull her away. She screams at Alexander, "If you rat us out to that little son of a bitch, I will kill you. You got that? You're never going to cross me again."

Vladimir steps between her and Alexander and orders them both to sit down—Eliza refuses to move until Alexander takes a seat. Then over her objections Kees explains to Alexander and Sofia that the Markovs are leading an Orde de Maxia–sanctioned war against Shashenka. Their reactions—Alexander's gaze shifts around the room, while Sofia, mouth agape, trembles—don't reveal where they stand. Eliza clams up when Vladimir gives her the floor. *This is a mistake.*

She levels a cold stare on Vladimir when he prods her to divulge more. Looking again at the two Druzhinas, she weighs her options. Alexander makes her the most nervous; he's too often done Shashenka's perverted bidding, and the way he's fidgeting now suggests he's hiding something. Sofia mostly seems terrified—that in itself is problematic, as she could turn them in to save herself. But it's Kees who nudges her to a decision. "You failed the last time without our help," he says. "Don't make the same mistake again."

Damn his analytical brain—he always makes too much sense. Against her better judgment she relents and provides the specifics of their plan.

Eliza takes in their body language as the details unfold. Disgust, horror, skepticism. Shock, curiosity, disbelief. Fear, uncertainty, and distrust ooze off the Druzhinas when they learn the number of covens, werewolf packs, and maxians joining her campaign. The mix of allies surprised her at first, too—she's had time to adjust. But they haven't experienced friendships with mortal enemies, and it takes a few hours for them to get past centuries of hating werewolves to even consider accepting them as allies.

When she finishes telling them what they need to know, Vladimir demands that they renew their allegiance to each other by blood oath; the coming war, he says, requires a loyalty to each other that only a blood oath can bind them to. A chorus of ayes and yeses spring forth as the Druzhinas draw their daggers. Eliza doesn't share their faith that such a bond can't be broken. To her surprise, there is no hesitation from Alexander or Sofia—they slice their palms and exchange handshakes. *Yeah, I'm not buying it.* Then all faces turn to her, and she isn't sure why.

Anna's smile is encouraging. "We are waiting for your oath, Elizabetta."

My oath? "I haven't been one of you in over five hundred years."

"We've never accepted your removal—or Dmitri's, either." Kees extends his hand, his eyes holding hers. When she doesn't move, he says, "Once a Druzhina, always a Druzhina. Do us the courtesy, sister—pledge your oath."

Borrowing a dagger, Eliza slices her hand deeply enough for it to bleed and solemnly states the words they are waiting to hear: "I swear allegiance to my brothers and sisters of the Druzhina and this just cause. I will sacrifice my life to protect you, as you will give your lives to protect me. We will bring justice to our realm and freedom to our coven."

She moves through the line to clasp their hands and bind her blood oath with theirs. Sofia and Alexander are at the end, and Eliza hesitates as her eyes rake over them. Even as they firmly grasp her hand when she finally offers hers, she can't let go of her doubts. She wishes she could know for certain if they are true allies or whether she just looked into the faces of Shashenka's newest moles.

CHAPTER 31: DMITRI
Bonds and Oaths

Dmitri waits as long as the fading shadows allow before he retreats to the tunnel between Cactus Bay and Garden Cove. By now he is confident that if Justin left the estate, it was probably through the main gate—and his worry ticks up a notch as he thinks about Elizabetta confronting Justin alone. Unwilling even to entertain the thought, he tries to convince himself that the night was equally uneventful for her; Justin must have remained at the mansion. *She will rejoin me soon.* The sky is growing lighter by the minute.

When the sun is just about to rise above the horizon and Elizabetta still hasn't returned, Dmitri races to the other side of the estate with a growing fear that something went wrong. A quick search along the drive where she was supposed to be reveals nothing but rocks, bushes, and trees. He's out of time—the sun's rays are strong enough to damage him now—and he must seek shelter.

Where is she? What happened? Agitation and misgiving occupy his every thought as he paces the tunnel and small hideout throughout the day. *Damn it. I never should have allowed her to go alone.* At twilight Dmitri runs for the Belyakov estate and resumes searching for any clue to Elizabetta's whereabouts. He finds none. Circling the estate in wider arcs only increases his panic. He's checked every rock, shrub, and tree within five miles of the estate, but there's no trace of her.

Cautiously he sneaks inside the mansion, slipping noiselessly from room to room; perhaps the locals' gossip will provide an answer. The only thing he learns is that Justin left before sunrise and won't be returning for a few days. New fears take root. Justin's departure and Elizabetta's disappearance are connected—he's certain of that. *Justin wouldn't deliver her to Shashenka, would he?* The thought sickens him. The centuries-long friendship he's shared with the other Druzhina is one of mutual respect and loyalty.

The sun rises again and forces Dmitri to settle into the tunnel for the day. He uses the redecrystapiezo to contact Maria; the wizard has heard nothing, but promises to get in touch if that changes. *Shit, shit, shit.* Until he learns something, anything, he doesn't dare leave Waiheke to look for his wife. Pain spirals through his chest at the thought of losing her so soon after their reunion; the ache won't stop devouring his insides. The more it feeds, the faster his mind plunges into reckless territory. He's half-tempted to fly to Venice, march into La Perfezione, and kill their repulsive master himself.

Another full day and night pass without any sign of Elizabetta. Maria doesn't call. Dmitri doesn't know how long he can tolerate being stuck in this seaside hideout—he's not had a minute of sleep since Elizabetta's disappearance.

On the fourth day he startles when the redecrystapiezo vibrates against his thigh. In his haste to grab the device from his pocket, he drops the blue garnet crystal. *Shit, slow down.* Dmitri snatches the crystal out of the dirt and sets it in the onyx and grandidierite base. Nothing happens.

Does this thing take messages? Fearing he missed or disconnected the call, he turns the device over in his hand and nearly drops it again when Maria's voice suddenly comes through as clearly as if she were standing next to him. "Dmitri?"

"She's still gone. Justin hasn't returned. I've looked everywhere and—"

"Dmitri, calm down. I have news." Maria cuts off his panicked rush of words. But the next thing she says drives his heart through the floor. "Justin captured her and took her to Melbourne for interrogation."

No. No. This can't be. "Maria—"

"It's not what you think. Now listen to me. Eliza is with the Druzhinas, and she asked me to relay a message. You're to stay put—they are coming to you."

Dmitri's mind explodes in a tangle of thoughts and questions, but before he can form a single word, Maria says, "They'll leave Melbourne this evening and meet you at your hideout before sunrise."

All of them? What do they want with us? He knows that Matt's surveillance indicates a shift in the Druzhinas' position, but after what happened during the failed rebellion, he can't blindly trust any of them to take a stand against Shashenka. A shudder runs down his spine—he can still see the faces of those who were executed and hear the echoes of their screams before they died. The Druzhinas stood by and watched, not one going against their master. *It's possible they are doing his bidding again. This feels like a trap—Elizabetta is the bait.*

Dmitri won't fall for such a ruse. Staying inside the hideout will play into their hands. *They're not going to box me in.* At sunset he leaves the tunnel and takes his position in a tree on the Cactus Bay side of the hill, watching the night shadows blanket everything around him. The only light is from a sliver of the moon—it's just enough for him to see into the dark.

Sometime after two in the morning the Druzhinas emerge from the tunnel, Elizabetta in their midst. Dmitri's anger has festered for four days, and Justin's cocky smile is the spark that ignites his pent-up rage. When they are within a dozen paces, he leaps out of the tree and tackles Justin to the ground, pressing a dagger to his friend's throat. Dmitri's tone says what his words won't—he will kill to get Elizabetta back. "Release my wife."

Heavy, stunned seconds fall around them. No one moves or says a word until Alexander begins to laugh in his typical arrogant manner. The others join in, and rattled, Dmitri chances a quick look at his wife. To his astonishment Elizabetta is shaking her head, smiling. She walks over and kneels next to him and Justin. "*Amore?*" When Dmitri doesn't move, she firmly grabs his wrist and pulls the dagger away from Justin's throat.

Dmitri hears laughter in her voice. "He deserves to have his ass kicked, but they're not holding me, *amore*. They are with us."

He looks at her, ready to reposition the dagger at Justin's neck, and then at the Druzhinas gathered around them. Amusement shows in the set of their mouths and in the mirth in their eyes. Even Justin is grinning. Dmitri doesn't know whether to feel foolish or relieved—or remain suspicious. But it's Elizabetta's relaxed posture that eases his concern. If something were wrong, he'd see it in her eyes. He sheaths the dagger and extends a hand to Justin.

The other man clasps Dmitri's forearm as he's pulled to his feet. "You're looking better than I've seen in a long while. Welcome back, brother." Justin, smirking again, claps Dmitri on the back.

Dmitri's distrust still ripples below the surface; his mind is torn between believing his eyes and ears and the fight or flight instinct still raging inside him. "*Amore*, what is this all about? What's going on here?"

Elizabetta places her hands on his hips as Justin steps aside. Dmitri tries to return her kiss and ask questions at the same time. Between kisses and laughter she repeats, "They are with us."

Elizabetta's excitement doesn't calm him. He's about to ask another question when Vladimir's taunt cuts him off. "When this war is over, I will get even with you."

The hair on the back of Dmitri's neck prickles. "Even for what?"

"For tricking me into bathing you."

Dmitri closes his eyes to block the memory, but in spite of himself a chuckle erupts from his throat. He rakes a hand through his hair. "You'll never know how embarrassing that was, Vlad—at least I find humor in it now." Then he recalls the threats his friend made against Elizabetta, and his tone turns serious. "But if you ever threaten my wife again, you and I will fight."

"Had I known what you two were up to, I would never have threatened our ferocious sister." Vladimir smiles and hugs them both. "I cannot tell you how good it is to have Elizabetta back and see you both together again. It has been far too long and cruel a punishment."

In the next moment the Druzhinas press around them. He's unable to avoid the throng; every turn finds him grabbed by another of his friends as they exchange hugs, laughter, and friendly backslaps. The bombardment of attention is too much—he's not ready to let go of his suspicions. A smile finally finds its way to his face, fading when Alexander approaches him.

Alexander grins, his tone uncharacteristically sincere. "It is good to see you found your way back to us, dear brother."

The years of animosity between them reignites Dmitri's anger. "No thanks to you."

"We all do what we must."

"What you've done is beyond that, and we both know it." Anger boils Dmitri's blood.

Alexander shrugs and smiles. "Perhaps, but only because you entertain me so."

Stephan mutters, "Great, here we go again."

The conversations around them come to an abrupt stop. Everyone understands that this running feud between Dmitri and Alexander must end. Dmitri catches the scornful look Elizabetta casts at Alexander—it bolsters his determination to retaliate. *He will pay for what he's done to her.* "It seems to me that you wanted to settle a score between us back in Montana. I say we settle it now."

"Both of you need to stop this." Vladimir moves between them.

"I intend to. Step aside, Vlad." Dmitri's words allow no argument; the confrontation is long overdue. Vladimir groans and places a hand on each of their chests. "As you wish. But there will be no weapons, claws, or fangs, or we will intervene. Make it a clean fight, gentlemen."

When Vladimir steps away, Alexander sneers at Dmitri, and his mocking tone returns. "Go ahead—make the first move. Take me ... if you think you can."

That is all the invitation Dmitri needs, and in two quick strides he's thrown the first punch. The jab catches Alexander in the nose with a resounding crack. Alexander dodges Dmitri's next strike as he wipes the stream of blood away from his nostrils with the back of his hand. "This should be fun."

In the next instant Alexander launches forward and bends to catch Dmitri around the waist. The movement is so fast that Dmitri's fist misses its mark. Lifting Dmitri off his feet, Alexander tosses him to the ground and lands on top of him, expelling the breath from his lungs. Dmitri grunts and throws a left hook, and with his knee he catches Alexander in the hip, knocking his foe off balance. As Alexander attempts to pull him back to the ground, Dmitri scrambles to his feet.

Alexander is up in a flash. The two men circle and close the gap between them. *Bring it on.* Dmitri throws a jab, but Alexander connects with Dmitri's cheek at the same moment Dmitri's fist slams into the other vampire's stomach. Dmitri flexes his jaw and blinks to clear his head.

Seeing Alexander wind up for another series of hooks and crosses, Dmitri drops his shoulder and throws an uppercut that catches the man under the chin. The blow staggers Alexander back three steps, but Dmitri presses forward and maintains the distance between them, landing multiple jabs to his rib cage. Defensively Alexander draws his elbows into his sides to ward off the blows, and Dmitri drives the other man back one step at a time. He's caught unprepared when Alexander dives to the ground, using a low roundhouse kick to sweep Dmitri's legs out from under him. Alexander is quick to follow through with downward kicks, and Dmitri has to rotate to avoid the blows and set up his counterattack.

Those around them watch from a safe distance, but Dmitri barely notices their presence. Over the next few minutes he and Alexander scuffle on the ground, both grappling for a headlock. *I've got to get on my feet.* Dmitri breaks free and scrambles three steps back before motioning with his hand for Alexander to reengage. The other vampire doesn't hesitate; their fight resumes in a furious exchange of hooks, jabs, and crosses. A gap opens between them, and Alexander is quick to take Dmitri's legs out from under him again, but this time Dmitri's ready to react. With his palms against the ground, Dmitri pushes up and swivels his hips as his legs thrust into a scissor kick. It's his turn to catch Alexander off guard; one leg strikes Alexander's midriff while the other catches his opponent behind the knees. The move takes Alexander down hard.

Both men spring to their feet and circle again. Dmitri assesses the situation—he's inflicted some damage, but so has Alexander. Each sports a split lip and bloody nose, and Dmitri suspects his opponent has bruises that match his own. His gaze shifts to the cut above Alexander's left eye—that's one injury he doesn't have.

Alexander drops his shoulder—his intent to tackle is clear—and again Dmitri uses the opportunity in an attempt to gain the upper hand. As Alexander tries to wrap his arms around Dmitri's waist, Dmitri's elbows slam into Alexander's back and his knee delivers three sharp blows to his opponent's side. Then Dmitri steps back into a spin kick and sends his foe flying twenty feet. Alexander lands face down, and Dmitri rushes forward and pounces on him. In one swift move he hooks an arm around Alexander's throat and rolls them over, tightening the choke hold as his legs lock around the other vampire.

Alexander's hands scrabble at Dmitri in a frantic attempt to break the hold around his neck. The muscles in Dmitri's arms flex as he uses his other hand to wrench his grip tighter and apply more pressure. Alexander tries to wriggle free, but his movements are limited to rocking them from side to side. Even from underneath, Dmitri has him pinned in an unbreakable hold.

Dmitri growls through clenched teeth, "I don't want to kill you. Yield the loss."

"Go to hell."

"I've done my time there, as you well know and delighted in." With his forearm under Alexander's chin, Dmitri applies upward pressure. It's an unmistakable signal; he will detach his opponent's head. "Yield or die."

Alexander writhes once more before his body relaxes. It's barely audible when he says, "I yield."

Dmitri releases his hold and shoves Alexander off him. The other man is on his feet first, and without hesitation he offers his hand to Dmitri. When Dmitri doesn't move to take it, Alexander reaches down, grabs him by the elbow, and hauls him to his feet. "I will not deny that at first, dear brother, I did enjoy it ... our little game. But it lost its appeal after what happened at Big Sky."

And which incident led him to grow a conscience? If that's even possible. The cold look Dmitri gives in response seems to spur Alexander along. "When ... I saw what it did to both of you"—he shakes his head—"I have never regretted giving an order more."

The reminder of that night—the order to rape Elizabetta, and Alexander's threat to do the deed—reignites Dmitri's rage. "And yet had I refused it, you would have raped my wife!"

Alexander's eyes dart toward the other Druzhinas. "I ... I ... um ..."

Dmitri's fists clench as he takes a step forward, hatred

and anger radiating from him. His hand moves toward the dagger at his waist. Alexander takes a step back and hangs his head in defeat. "Yes, at the time I would have likely followed Master's orders." He quickly adds, "But I would have taken no pleasure in doing so, and I will never follow or give such an order again."

Disgusted, Dmitri spits on the ground and points at Elizabetta. "She is a Druzhina. By blood oath you owed her your protection, and instead you participated in destroying her life. For that I will never forgive you."

Alexander squirms and looks up to meet the disapproving faces of the Druzhinas around him. Doubtless most, if not all, never knew about the ugly incident at Big Sky. Clearing his throat, he approaches Elizabetta with apparent humility. "Elizabetta, as a Druzhina, I have wronged you. Dmitri is right. I should have protected you, and I can offer no excuses for my failure." His shoulders sag.

Her eyes are hard, cold. "No, you can't. What you did to me, to Dmitri, is reprehensible." She looks at the other Druzhinas. "Now do you understand why I question his loyalty to our blood oath? Do you see how far he will go in carrying out Shashenka's orders?"

Alexander gulps hard and bows his head, his hands clasped behind his back. He draws a ragged breath before he speaks. "I am not a perfect man. I allowed my jealousy to become an excuse for what I was doing. I have no defense ... Dmitri and Elizabetta are within their right to claim justice for the ways I have wronged them. I have broken my oath as a Druzhina."

Vladimir looks from Alexander to each of the others.

His tone is layered in ice. "Alexander, you have violated our trust, the pact of our bond as brothers and sisters of the Druzhina. I concur that the Markovs have the right to claim justice, but I will not decide your fate. I propose leaving that decision to those you have wronged. Druzhinas, what say you?"

Somberly one after another nod their consent. Dmitri takes Elizabetta's hand and they step away to confer.

Dmitri himself is torn; the Druzhina has never cast out or punished one of their own. He's willing to spare Alexander's life, but he wants justice for what the vampire has done to Elizabetta. She agrees to give Alexander one last chance—though it's clear she won't hesitate to kill him herself if he steps out of line. *I won't stop her.* When they return to the group Dmitri looks Alexander in the eye. "We have no wish to kill you, Alexander. The fight between us is over. You will, however, stay away from my wife. And you will apologize for the wrongs you've done her."

It almost stuns Dmitri when the other man walks over and kneels before them. Alexander swallows hard and clears his throat again. "Elizabetta, dear sister, I humbly beg your forgiveness. I have wronged and failed you, but I swear on my life that I will never do so again." He extends a hand—she gives it one abrupt shake.

"I will set it right between us," he says. When she steps back Alexander takes out his dagger and slices his own palm before offering his hand to Dmitri. For a moment their gaze locks. Alexander's tone is solemn as he recites the blood oath with his bleeding hand extended, and

Dmitri detects his sincerity; he draws his dagger without hesitation. The blade makes the cut and the two shake hands.

"I accept your bond to this oath and pledge my life in return."

Releasing Alexander's hand, Dmitri turns to affirm his oath to the others. "Sisters and brothers of the Druzhina, I swear that I will sacrifice for you as you sacrifice for me in the coming war against Belyakov's empire. I will give my life to protect yours as you will give yours to protect mine."

Predawn colors tinge the sky as the remaining Druzhinas make their covenant with Dmitri and the group retreats to the hideout. There, plans fall into place; the Druzhinas only recently swore their blood oath and were still determining how best to proceed, but they have already begun the recon and co-opting of the estate locals. As Dmitri listens to the discussion, he realizes now why the Druzhinas were traveling outside their normal patterns when he made his fruitless trip to find them.

During their recent recall to Venice to wipe out the Giordano coven, the Druzhinas made initial contact with a few locals there, but a true assessment must wait until the inner lair moves on to its next location. Of the thirteen other estates, only four are left to probe: A Coruña, Spain; Bogor, Indonesia; Adelaide, Australia; and Xi'an, China. Unfortunately the inner lair will leave for Xi'an in the next few days, and the timing of this move will delay their efforts to discover the loyalties of the locals there. If Shashenka's stay there is typical, he will remain in Xi'an for at least six weeks before moving on to another estate.

Kees is quick to detail the loyalties of the other compounds, breaking them into three categories—supporting, divided in support, and unlikely to support. The latter he terms hostile estates. Dmitri isn't surprised to learn that the hostile estates are Prague and Novgorod; they are expected to provide Shashenka with additional resources and fighters when the war for his dominion begins. Confidence is high, according to Kees, that the estates with divided support will rally to their side or be a negligible threat.

When Kees finishes his analysis, Stephan pitches a plan to lure Shashenka and the inner lair to one of the Western hemisphere estates for the main battle, since the seat and bulk of Shashenka's power lie in the Eastern world. Sofia recommends Machu Picchu, Peru, as the ideal battleground given the proximity of the supportive villa in Cusco. Her suggestion draws Elizabetta's ire—she outright accuses the woman of setting a trap. Dmitri isn't sure where Elizabetta's distrust is coming from, and he watches Sofia for any sign of duplicity. Sofia, unruffled by the accusation, lays out her reasons for choosing that site. Her argument is sound—minimal population and mountainous terrain will provide cover and allow their infiltrating forces to keep the human world ignorant of the supernatural realms' battle. After several minutes of discussion, Sofia's recommendation gains support from everyone but Elizabetta. Her disappointment is palpable when Dmitri ends the debate; he'll notify the Orde de Maxia's supreme council to ensure they're at that location when the time comes.

Not one to be thrown off by losing an argument, Elizabetta is quick to propose that the other Druzhinas be in charge of coordinating with a local point person at each estate when the war begins. To further her argument she claims that their allies among the werewolf packs will need that contact when they move in to help take over the estates. All movement from the others ceases.

She either doesn't notice or ignores it. Then Elizabetta pours gas on the fire, suggesting that each of them maintains direct contact with Matt and the other pack leaders as their plans move forward. Dmitri's lips twitch—this is the woman he fell in love with.

The discussion erupts into a shouting match, and Dmitri watches it unfold in silent fascination. It's hard enough for them to accept the involvement of werewolves at all, but the idea of closely working with over a dozen of them is more than they're ready to handle. Their friends seem to have forgotten that Elizabetta was a leader in her own right centuries ago. One by one she wears their arguments down and brings them over to her side. The biggest point of contention is the alliance with their mortal enemies. They've already lost on this point too—they just don't know it yet. *So, apparently, have I.*

Elizabetta leans against Dmitri's chest as the group debates where to meet in the meantime. After hopeless centuries without her, he is still adjusting to having her back. He's most grateful for the restoration of their near-silent ability to comprehend and communicate with each other. As Elizabetta looks up over her shoulder now, Dmitri sees a mischievous spark in her eyes and gives her a knowing smile before brushing a chaste kiss to her lips. If she does what he suspects she will, then the other Druzhinas are about to be floored once again.

Elizabetta announces that she has an idea and needs to borrow someone's cell phone. Several minutes pass while she talks on the phone—she avoids revealing whom she is talking to, but it's obvious she is developing a plan and making arrangements to move them. It's what she's not saying that confirms Dmitri's suspicions of who is on the other end of the call. He struggles to keep a grin off his face as he wonders how the other Druzhinas will react. They're watching her, their expressions curious and unsure. *Wait for it. Wait ... this is going to be good.*

When the call ends, she doesn't disappoint him. Her words light the fuse and set off the bomb: Matt is sending a chartered jet to pick them up in Auckland. They will fly to the United States, and the werewolf will take them to the luxury retreat that he's recently purchased in Oak Creek, near Sedona, Arizona.

Amused, Dmitri watches the reactions to Elizabetta's announcement. The Druzhinas have only just gotten used to the idea of allying with werewolves, and they're clearly perturbed at the thought of going anywhere to meet with the mongrel. As Elizabetta defends Matt's role in their war preparations, Dmitri realizes that the maxians were correct: restoring her memories did not alter her affection for the werewolf. *We really are stuck with him now.*

He hides a rueful smile behind his hand. He's come to accept Matt's friendship because of the affection and loyalty between Elizabetta and the werewolf, and now it's a package deal the Druzhinas will have to accept, too. It's difficult to believe that a mere eleven months ago the Druzhinas were debating killing Matt during the standoff at the McAllister ranch. He almost laughs out loud when he realizes what Matt's reaction to this turn of events will likely be. *There'll be no living this down for any of us once the mutt puts it all together.*

Noting the Druzhinas' uncomfortable glances, he says, "Love, did you forget to tell our sisters and brothers that we now have a mutt?"

She laughs as her arms wrap around his neck. "It may have slipped my mind, *amore.*"

CHAPTER 32: ELIZA

Strategic Decisions

When the group arrives in Sedona, Arizona, after sunset, Matt and Teresina are waiting on the tarmac with two seven-passenger vans. Eliza barely notices the view from the little airport atop the mesa overlooking the town; her joy over seeing Matt again claims her full attention. As she throws herself into Matt's embrace, she almost doesn't catch the way Dmitri scowls at them, but she's too happy to be dissuaded from exchanging her customary hug and kiss with Matt. Recovering her memories, her life, didn't change how she feels about Matt—he'll always be her best friend.

"Damn, it's good to see you, baby vamp." Matt grins, takes a couple steps back, and glances at Dmitri before settling his gaze on her again. "Maria said you came through the Vulcan mind-meld without a scratch, but not hearing from you for so long was making me a little wacko."

Eliza punches his arm. "You had that market cornered long before I met you."

I think that I was most nervous that we'd lose this between us. A devilish smile curves her lips, and without warning she launches herself at Matt, knocking him to the ground and straddling his body as she grabs him by the shirt collar. She leans in until their noses touch. "Maria is right—you're certifiable." She's only half-joking. "If I had been in my right mind in Yellowstone, I would have killed you without so much as a second thought. Do you know how crazy and dangerous it is to just walk up to a vampire and be like, 'Oh hey, I'm cute and funny. Let's be friends.' Damn, Matt, what were you thinking?" His smirk fails to melt her heart this time; there is no humor in her voice as she says, "Looking back, I can honestly say that you scare the crap out of me. I don't know how you manage to stay alive."

His grin broadens as he grips her by the waist and sets her on the ground beside him. "I was thinking life was too boring; why not spice it up a bit?" He stands and extends a hand to help her up. "Besides, I wasn't getting all my memos back then ... that one finally caught up with me in Venice."

Eliza rolls her eyes and laughs with him as a collective murmur rises from the Druzhinas. Still holding Matt's hand, Eliza leads him over to the group of perturbed vampires and provides proper introductions.

After everyone exchanges guarded pleasantries, Matt smirks and gestures at a small, slender woman standing off to the side. "Druzhinas, this is Teresina De Luca, rogue vampire extraordinaire. She's been tailing you for months and could even teach Dmitri a thing or two about stalking."

The diminutive vampire beams with pride as he says, "Teresina has eavesdropped on your not-so-clandestine meetings and successfully dogged your every move around the world."

A snap of his teeth follows a wolfish yip, and Eliza laughs at his blatant pun. The others seem to find it less humorous, given how effective Teresina's efforts were. *He's doing this to rile them, and it's working.* Another ripple moves through the Druzhinas. To be bested by a rogue at stealth and spying is unsettling to them, she knows—they are supposed to be the best in the world.

Their initial shock, however, gives way to respect for the sly little rogue, and the Druzhinas greet Teresina with various levels of warmth and awe. Eliza finds herself taken with the woman—she herself had the same impact on them centuries ago, and she recognizes the sheer talent and skill required to best the elite body.

With the introductions over, Matt looks at Dmitri. "It's good to see you too. Thanks for bringing my baby vamp back in one piece."

Eliza holds her breath, wary of his reaction—they haven't really discussed Matt. But Dmitri's smile appears kind and sincere, and she exhales in relief as he says, "I promised I would. You'll find she is a force of nature now. She may even manage to keep you in line, mongrel."

"The wolf den awaits—I even got rid of the fleas. Shall we go?"

Splitting in two groups, they leave the airport for the drive to the mansion that Matt bought in the village of Oak Creek. Eliza's excitement grows beyond the reunion with Matt as the importance of gaining the Druzhina's support settles over her. When she first solicited Matt's help, such a possibility seemed bleak. Now it's a reality that will mean the difference between victory and defeat.

She looks over her shoulder at Dmitri in the backseat and knows he feels the change too—the renewed hope, their potential for a future without Shashenka. *It will be different this time ... we will not fail.*

Riding in the front seat with Matt, Eliza briefs him about the Druzhinas but detects a nervous undertone in his replies—he's understandably tense about this impromptu gathering. He says, "I thought about asking a few friends along, but it's a full house, and you vamps didn't do so well around a pack of wolves the last time we all got together." She doesn't miss the barb. This is the same group of vampires that tried killing him not too long ago.

Taking Matt's hand to send silent reassurance, she says, "Granted, they still need to work past their own prejudices, but I expect everyone will get along just fine. Thanks for flying us here ... giving us a chance to regroup and advance our plans."

"I'd hang the moon for you, baby vamp, except I don't know how to be around the moon in human form." He laughs, but Eliza can tell he's uptight—his jokes are falling a little flat, and he's unfocused, jumping from one topic to another.

She squeezes his hand again as they pull up to a sturdy

steel gate. Eliza notices that there are no other homes in the canyon—she appreciates the advantages of such an isolated location.

"This is it?"

"Yes," Matt says with a hint of pride. "Welcome to the doghouse."

An audible growl comes from Dmitri, and Matt looks at him in the rearview mirror. His smile vanishes. "Before I, uh, knew about your past, I bought it with Eliza in mind. It reminded me of our time together in Montana, and I wanted her to have a safe retreat to enjoy far away from that devil vamp of yours. Now since ..." He doesn't finish the thought. "I just hope she'll still want to come here."

Eliza doesn't breathe; Matt's unspoken words are like a neon sign glaring into the night. Dmitri has likely filled in those blanks, but to her relief he remains tactful. "I'm sure Elizabetta will love it."

A smile returns to Matt's face. "And as you can see, baby vamp, there are no near neighbors and nothing on three sides of the property. Just a lot of wide open-countryside."

Eliza's gaze roams over the rugged canyon as they stop in front of the house. This dwelling dwarfs the tiny one-bedroom home she stayed at with Matt in West Yellow-stone—that was a shanty compared with this place. "I'm so proud of you, Matt. You've really done well for yourself."

"For us." Matt waves in a circle, including Dmitri. "All of us. I know it has a lot of glass, but don't panic about the windows. I had a shuttering system installed to protect you during sunlight hours. You'll love it at night, though—great view in the moonlight."

Eliza glances back at Dmitri and sees the twinge of jealousy in his eyes. She knows he's trying—for her—but she'd rather see him let go of his misgivings altogether. *Time for a little nudge?* "I'm sure we'll enjoy spending time here with you," she tells Matt.

Matt and Teresina park the vans and everyone heads toward the front entrance. Eliza's never been in this part of the United States before, and she finds the landscaping—a mix of cactus, red rocks, and desert shrubs and flowers—lends a natural appearance to the two-story adobe structure with its rock walkways. A garden terrace wraps around the base of the sprawling house.

When Matt opens the door, she pauses in the entryway in awe of the interior. Tile floors, in shades of burnt-orange adobe, host an array of trees growing through the floor. Some of the trees are built into the support of the structure and staircase—she's never seen anything like it. Winding timbers stand like silent sentinels around the doorways and create the banister rails.

A raised garden pond, hemmed by small boulders and various agave plants, is the focal point of the great room. There's even a juniper bush near the pond—Eliza smiles at the reminder—and river rock pillars and a stone hearth adorn the interior of the room. The open floor plan allows her to see the additional cobb hearths tucked into the adjoining rooms.

Eliza walks over to the pond for a closer look at the juniper. "Is this ..." *No, it couldn't be.* She bends down and looks under the branches. A small patch of bark is gone, the exposed wood etched by claw marks—hers—exactly where she picked at it months before. She clamps a hand over her mouth. "Oh my God, Matt ... you stole this bush from Yellowstone Park. I mean, this is the bush. The one we hid under?"

"Yeah, it is, and yes, I did. It felt like this house was missing something, and general reminders weren't quite enough for me. So I snatched it from the park and carted it here. I thought you'd get a kick out of it, and on a bad day you're always free to crawl under it and feel safe from the world."

His hearty laugh and unabashed tone remind Eliza why she came to love him as a friend. She rushes over and throws her arms around his neck. "You're the best. Thank you—I love you for this."

"I love you too, baby vamp." She follows his gaze to Dmitri and smiles as Matt says, "She'll need to tell you the story about this bush, but I'll leave it for her to decide whether she allows you to hide under it with her. If she won't, just lift a branch and make funny faces at her— she'll eventually let you in."

While Eliza and Matt laugh at their inside joke, the others simply look on with a mix of curiosity and concern over the familiarity between the two of them. Dmitri's tone remains polite. "Given Elizabetta's reaction to it, I'm sure it's an interesting story."

She gives her husband an appreciative smile. "Interesting, perhaps, but it's actually the story behind why we now have a mutt, *amore.*" Dmitri nods in reply, and Eliza moves to his side and takes his hand. There is so much she still needs to tell him—tell all of them—but now is not the time. Those are conversations better left for later, when they're not under so much pressure. Deliberately she shifts their focus and asks Matt to give them a tour of his home.

Eliza notices that Teresina stays well behind the group, almost as if she wants to blend in with the shadows. The Druzhinas seem to almost forget she is there; they are too busy watching the werewolf. *Matt and I have our work cut out for us if we want to put this bunch at ease.* She grins at him. "Your home is spectacular. I love it, Matt."

Matt beams with pride as she gushes on about the property and how happy she is for him. When she quiets he turns to Dmitri. "You haven't said much."

Dmitri's expression remains serious, but she knows better—the slight curve to his upper lip gives him away. "While it's not the padded doghouse Maria recommended for you, I suspect it is now firmly settled on Elizabetta's list of favorite places to go on holiday. I'm sure it will grow on me."

Matt hands Dmitri a set of keys. "Good. I'm not sure how often I'll be here, but you two are welcome to use it anytime you want."

"Really?" Eliza's face lights up with surprise.

"Yes, really, baby vamp. As they say in these parts, *mi casa es su casa.*"

Over the next few days the Druzhinas purchase new cell phones and exchange numbers. Communicating with a Belyakov-provided phone is too risky; they'll need the freedom to coordinate the war effort behind Shashenka's back. They'll also continue with their assigned duties so as not to draw attention from any outsider or coven member. For now their current missions will buy them precious time and won't create suspicion if none of them check in with the inner lair for the next few days.

When Matt quips that Teresina is a shadow Druzhina, it sparks an unexpected discussion that gives way to a lively debate. *Should we add her to our ranks?* Eliza isn't sure. Their numbers have not changed in several hundred years because of Shashenka's tight control over them—something that may be coming to an end. With the new blood oath between the Druzhinas and the possibility of their evil master's demise, some argue that they are now an autonomous force.

Teresina stays out of their debate, and when they press her to gauge her interest in joining them, she seems uncomfortable, claiming that her entire vampire existence has been solitary. She's leery about tying herself to them, it's clear. Eliza suspects that as a rogue Teresina has spent decades working for the highest bidder across the shadow realms—that is how she became involved with their plans—and she's reluctant to give that independence up.

Justin, busy staring at the rogue, has been unusually quiet until now. When he finally averts his gaze his suggestion is blunt. "She's already been spying on us for months—she may as well finish the job from the inside." When he offers to partner with her, Eliza detects an underlying motive.

Justin was the newest Druzhina among them before the

last failed revolt, and Eliza worked with him a scant five years before she was placed in a catatonic state. She recognizes now that she's never seen Justin look at, much less interact with another vampire in the same manner. Hundreds of years ago he was reserved, almost shy, but since her return to the coven she's noticed he's become quite the ladies' man. *Is he crushing on her, or does she just make him nervous?* Although Eliza doesn't know a lot about the rogue, she does notice that Teresina seems to gravitate toward Justin too. Eliza backs Justin's proposal; she can't resist playing matchmaker. *These two could be great together.*

When Teresina accepts the offer to work alongside Justin, Vladimir delivers their first set of orders as a team. Because co-opting the estate locals is the primary step before they initiate a move against Shashenka, Justin and Teresina will resume probing the loyalties of those in the inner lair and of any coven members at the estates showing divided support. The task seems well suited to Teresina's skills. She's unknown, an outsider, and the locals may be more willing to talk to her than to someone who's closely linked to Shashenka. The other Druzhinas offer to help cover Justin's assignments from Shashenka in the month ahead; as long as Justin checks in on schedule, Shashenka will never know.

Vladimir offers to seek appointment from the Orde de Maxia to work as the liaison between the realms for those taking part in this war. Eliza nods her approval. She can't believe the difference between this time and when they failed five centuries before. If Justin and Teresina complete their assignment by the end of the month, Dmitri may be able to provide the Orde de Maxia with the intelligence they need to begin moving logistical support to Machu Picchu. Her optimism soars—this nightmare could be over within months.

Kees probes their plans for flaws and contingencies not considered. He encourages Matt to notify his mergers and acquisitions team and have them initiate takeovers of Shashenka's businesses now. The financial targets will take the most time to complete, given the complexity of international business laws, and they'll provide a much-needed distraction to divert Shashenka's attention elsewhere.

"I believe a realistic time frame for engaging in the ground battle against Master and his forces could commence within ninety days," he says.

Eliza sees she isn't the only one with her mouth agape; Dmitri is so stunned he's not even blinking. Murmurs ripple through the Druzhinas, their faces shocked, fearful, and excited.

"Are you certain that the unfinished tasks can be accomplished that quick?" Matt voices what Eliza is wondering—her tongue is still disconnected from her brain.

"Yes." Kees makes eye contact with Matt. "You've been quite an asset and have made more progress on this endeavor than you may realize. I think the biggest mistake would be to wait too long. Each day that passes raises the risk of Shashenka discovering that there are forces gathering to end his reign."

That comment seems to bear its own weight, and several

minutes pass before Kees continues his summary; he be-lieves more needs to be done to avoid a potential power vacuum. The biggest problem is that though they know the vampire realm will suffer to some degree once Sha-shenka's ironclad control is removed, no one really knows what such upheaval would look like. Realization settles like a mist around them—if they fail to keep the fallout contained to their realm, they may not be able to stop it.

Eliza watches Dmitri rake his hand through his hair twice, holding the crown of his head as he thinks. Her mind drifts over the countless times she's seen this ges-ture—it's his tell when he's upset or deep in thought. She's so lost in reminiscing that she startles when he says, "I have a plan."

Dmitri proposes that the Druzhina becomes the ruling body—no single leader—with advisors from all realms to support the decision-making process. He reasons that the Druzhina is already keeping the vampire realm under con-trol and should be able to stabilize it in the aftermath of Shashenka's demise. While it's not a full contingency, it's at least a foundation they can work from.

Deciding what to do with the estates once Shashenka is destroyed is a simpler problem, one Eliza and Dmitri have already discussed at length. Eliza explains that the Dru-zhinas will have first pick, and the remaining properties will be awarded by lottery in the Orde de Maxia chambers after Shashenka is gone. "This will throw a bone to the allies who want something out of the deal," she tells the group. Her canine pun doesn't go unnoticed, and for the first time since Josh Cleary's pack was wiped out—by these very vampires—Eliza feels as if she has come home. *This is my family—they were my family for decades before this nightmare began.*

All find the plan acceptable, and for several minutes the Druzhinas discuss which estates they will lay claim to. Dmitri and Eliza select La Perfezione since they already own property in Venice. The Prague estate will go to Vladimir and Anna. When Stephan and Victoria ask for the estate in Adelaide and Kees and Katherine choose the villa at Invercargill, Eliza notices a pattern developing—most are taking property in their home country, or they're selecting their favorite vacation estate. The next two Druzhinas prove her point; Justin selects Big Sky and Sofia takes A Coruña, the locations nearest to where they lived before becoming vampires.

The only real surprise is Alexander's choice. At first he doesn't want any of the estates, but then he changes his mind. "I think that I'd like to select one after all, but I have a question first. Once this war is over and we own these estates, they are ours to do with as we choose?"

"Yes," Dmitri says.

Alexander grins. "Then, dear brother, I'm going to take the villa at Waiheke, but I'm not keeping it ... instead I want to give it as a gift to the both of you." He nods toward Dmitri and Eliza. "It is but a token that I hope will help you forgive the ways I've wronged you."

A swollen pause settles over the room. Eliza is unsure how to feel about his gift—he's still not shown himself worthy of her trust. "That's a generous offer, but I suggest we wait and see how this war unfolds." *And whether you prove yourself or betray us again.*

The tension in the room is rising, and once more she's grateful when Matt deflects their focus. "You know you vamps are bad for my business? How am I supposed to build houses for any of you if you're going to stay in your old vamp lairs?"

Dmitri rolls his eyes. "Don't worry, mongrel, we'll let you build us a new home and may even allow you to put a doghouse on the property when this is over."

Eliza laughs. "*Amore*, Matt is housebroken, and I think he can stay in our home whenever he's not off wandering the global neighborhood. Besides, what good is a guard dog—correction, guard wolf—if he's forced to sleep outside?"

"Yeah, what she said." Matt laughs and leans toward Dmitri, his tone conspiratorial. "I'm not sure if you know this about your wife, but she can be quite stubborn if she doesn't get her way."

Dmitri shakes his head, but he's smiling. "You have no idea, Matt, no idea how stubborn Elizabetta can be."

"You are both stubborn, and that brings up a concern I have." Vladimir looks from Dmitri to Eliza. "You two have a giant bull's-eye on your backs, and with Kees's extended timeline, it leaves you at considerable risk. You need to go underground until this war is launched."

Eliza and Dmitri have also discussed this, and the glance they share confirms their decision. She speaks for both of them. "We've been offered a safe place to stay if we need it, but it's too isolated—we need to be involved in the final stages of bringing this coup together. We're going to take our chances, stay on the run."

"That may be suicide." Stephan pushes the issue. "Perhaps you should reconsider."

"There is equal risk in not being hands-on during these final stages." Dmitri's tone carries a note of finality; there is no room for debate on this point.

Sofia looks at Katherine. "Your mate can handle your current assignments without you," she says. "Perhaps we should stay with the Markovs and act as bodyguards."

Matt growls and points to himself. "Uh-hum, guard wolf sitting right here."

Dmitri rolls his eyes again. "Down, boy. As to the rest of you, Elizabetta and I are not children that need looking after."

Eliza laughs in spite of herself. *Those two might be okay yet.*

"I think we're going to overrule you on this one, brother," Vladimir says, and he speaks with authority. "You're both too valuable to risk." He suggests the Druzhinas prepare to leave Sedona and resume their regular duties by the next night. The one exception will be Katherine and Sofia—they'll stay behind to protect Dmitri and Eliza.

He looks at the other Druzhinas. "Our workload is about to go into overdrive, but I want two to three of us with Dmitri and Elizabetta at all times. Protect them where we must, hide or move them when we need to, and help them win this war."

A chorus of "Aye" and "Yes" echoes through the room, leaving Eliza and Dmitri no choice but to accept that they may not know another moment alone until Shashenka is gone.

CHAPTER 33: ELIZA

Full Circle

Eliza's grateful when Matt, recognizing that she is at her limit for nonstop seriousness, turns the remainder of their last full night together into one of music, singing, and dancing. She can't stop laughing when he declares, "My doghouse, my rules. No work, mistrust, jealousy, or crankiness—violators will be staked in the sun." For good measure he tacks on two rules: no hating the werewolf, and everyone must have fun. His humor and charm succeed—the entire group welcomes a night of levity.

When Matt dedicates a song—"Hush"—to Dmitri and Eliza, the room erupts in cheering and clapping as they dance. They haven't danced together in centuries, and she's impressed—Dmitri has kept up with the times. *Damn, he's fine.* She doesn't take her eyes off him as their bodies sway and move together. Not to be outdone, Dmitri announces he has theme music for Matt—"Stuck In The Middle With You." Matt sings along while dancing a few seconds with each of the women before he grabs her and Dmitri, dancing with both of them. *And here we are, stuck in the middle with a werewolf comic.* Matt's craziness sets the mood for the rest of the night, and it's well after sunrise when the merriment ends and everyone turns in for the day.

Dmitri and Eliza are about to head up the staircase to their room when Matt asks for a few moments to talk with her. Somewhat reluctant—she sees the longing in his eyes flare and dim—Dmitri nods and kisses Eliza. "Take your time, love." Awed by his chivalry, she watches him ascend the stairs.

When Dmitri is out of sight, Matt takes Eliza by the hand and leads her over to the juniper bush. "Crawl under there, baby vamp."

Chuckling, Eliza shakes her head but complies. She's still smiling at the memory when he slides in next to her. *We've come full circle in so many ways.* He slips an arm under her neck—just as he did before—and takes her hand, placing a kiss on her temple. "I've wanted to do this since we arrived."

A chiding voice from the loft filters down to them. "Did you forget you have guests trying to sleep up here?"

Matt and Eliza laugh, and Eliza shouts, "Shut up, Justin."

"Stick your fingers in your ears and do some humming," Matt calls out. "Damn, we didn't have noisy vampire neighbors in Yellowstone. I may have to fix that problem."

When their laughter dies down, Eliza takes in every

feature of Matt's face, particularly his eyes—many unspoken words lie in those hazel-green depths. Although he's not said anything, she knows the doubts are weighing on him. She's seen it in his actions and expressions since they arrived in Sedona. She needs to assure Matt that their friendship is as strong as ever.

The nostalgia of this precious moment sparks an idea. "Psst. I know what we are. I'm a bloodsucker, and you are a werewolf. So ... is it my turn to ask why we're hiding under a juniper bush in the middle of the day?"

"Under this bush is the first place where things felt right between us, where our friendship started. Now that you have your memories and life back, I guess I wanted to make sure you're all right ... that we're okay."

"You'll always be my best friend, Matt. That will never change." Eliza shifts her body to look up at him. "I feel whole again—that's the only thing that changed for me."

Matt studies her face. "So that bloodsucker hubby of yours treats you well? You're happy?"

For the first time in a very long while. "I am, Matt. Dmitri is a terrific husband, a true gentleman—he makes me who I am. I would never have survived these last centuries without him."

"I about went batshit crazy for that month you were gone, not knowing if you were okay. I think I drove Maria nuts too, checking daily to see whether she had any word about you." He laughs. "She threatened me, no, swore to turn me into a frog next time she saw me. I'm a little worried she meant it."

Eliza sniggers. "Be afraid. Maria's an exceptional wizard—you shouldn't provoke her. Besides, I don't know what I'd do with a guard frog."

"Oh, ha-ha." He makes a ribbitting sound. "Who knows, maybe I could leap tall vampires in a single bound."

I've missed you, moments like this. She can't imagine her life without Matt. "The biggest issue I've had to come to terms with is guilt for the many werewolves I killed centuries ago ... I keep wondering if I missed out on having a friend like you."

"Hey, now, none of that. Besides, I'm one of a kind." He laughs and wiggles his eyebrows. "This is our time, and we're about to rock the shadow realms together. We're like this totally badass superhero team of the preternatural world."

Squeezing his hand, Eliza says, "I wish we would have met five hundred years ago. If you had been working with me the way you are now, we could have ..."

She can't keep the regret from her voice, and Matt groans. "Seriously, Eliza, what is with you and the would-haves, could-haves, should-haves, and what-ifs? You should know this already, seeing as how you're an ancient, decrepit, grandmotherly old woman, but life is too short ... even if you are practically immortal. You need to learn to live in the moment, appreciate what is around you, take each night as it comes."

She does know, but everything she's gone through—what Dmitri was forced to endure—makes her mistakes hard to live with. Perhaps she can better explain this to Matt when her emotions aren't so raw. She shuts her eyes tightly and takes a deep breath to calm herself. "I think it's just my way of saying how important you are to me."

"Maybe I should talk that witchy-poo friend of ours into turning you into a spider or something. That'd give you a new perspective on life."

"You wouldn't dare," Eliza hisses—she hates spiders. "I'd kick your little frog ass with all eight of my legs."

For hours they banter under the juniper bush as the daylight shadows move across the room. When they last shared time under this bush, life was simpler, even if traumatic for her. It astounds her how complicated everything has become since. It's nearly twilight when soft, familiar footsteps descend the stairs. Moments later a pair of legs stops near the juniper bush, and a hand lifts the branch.

Eliza pulls Matt back, pressing against the trunk of the bush in mock fear. "Uh-oh, looks like my stalker found me."

"Something tells me he'll always find you, baby vamp."

I know he will.

CHAPTER 34: DMITRI

Despicable Compromise

After most of the Druzhinas leave to resume their official duties, the others continue working on the plan to bring down Shashenka's financial empire. By the third day the mergers and acquisitions team has notified the boards of directors of Belyakov's targeted businesses; Matt expects the daily updates will reveal little until the responses arrive.

It leaves them killing time in between, and for Dmitri it's a welcome chance to spend time alone with Elizabetta and explore the canyon behind Matt's property. The sultry looks she's been giving him for the last hour are too much to ignore. Dmitri asks Matt to show Katherine and Sofia the nearby lake; the wolf flashes him a lopsided grin and ushers the women out of the house. *Maybe the mongrel isn't so bad after all.*

Dmitri takes his wife's hand and leads her toward the West Fork Trail. They follow the winding creek for a few miles before scaling a cliff to take in the view at the top of the mesa. Looking out over the rugged terrain, Dmitri wraps an arm around Elizabetta and pulls her tight to his side.

Soon they are lying on their backs, staring up at the moonless sky. There is little light pollution here, and the darkness blanketing the area allows them to observe the hazy outline of the Milky Way; it's nearly as perfect as the nights they shared centuries ago in Arecibo. After what Shashenka put them through during their last visit there, neither is eager to go back.

Dmitri's tone is soft, quiet. "When the war is over I'd enjoy taking holidays here, if for no other reason than to watch the stars with you, love."

"Mmm ..." She squeezes his hand. "I'd like that, *amore*— it's been far too long since we experienced moments like these."

Dmitri rises onto his elbow and brushes a hint of a kiss across her lips. "I say we make this place our own," he murmurs, trailing kisses under her chin, along her throat, and down to the opening of her blouse.

Elizabetta's fingers slowly stroke his shaggy hair as he unbuttons her shirt, and together their hands roam and explore while their clothing is discarded haphazardly around them. As their bodies entwine, Dmitri pulls Elizabetta on top of him, the emotion shining in her eyes conveying more to him than words ever will. *I'm so grateful to have her back, to share this life with her again.*

With a hand cupped around the back of her neck, Dmitri pulls her in for a deeper kiss. Together they lovingly murder minutes and hours as they move as one. Tender endearments—spoken and unspoken—fill the cracks in the silence around them.

Determined to make this moment last as long as possible, Dmitri takes and gives everything he can to please her. Although there is no need, he recommits every feature of Elizabetta's face and body to memory. His hands touch, caress, and move over her lithe figure with gentle fervor while his tongue tastes the sweetness he breathes in. *All of her, all mine ... now, forever, always.*

As the stars dance along their path in the sky, Dmitri willingly loses himself, surrendering to Elizabetta's movements. Her kisses ignite him as her hands tease the flames that lift them higher and higher, settling them among the stars themselves. Hardly caring that the world has fallen away, Dmitri holds her tighter—urgency builds, consuming them, sweeping them into a universe where nothing else exists.

My eternal beloved. Dmitri doesn't loosen his hold on her as they drift in the aftermath, trying to ignore the faint lightening of the predawn sky as it heralds the coming day. He wishes this night were infinite. When the sensations subside, he hums "*Il mio tesoro.*" *She is forever my love, my treasure.*

With great reluctance they acknowledge the late hour and return to Matt's home before the sun rises. When they hurry through the back door, the shutters are already closed against the rising sun. Katherine, Sofia, and Matt are playing an animated game of cards. *The way that wolf charms his way into a vampire's good graces is remark-*

able. A few days ago they wanted to kill him on sight. While it would be easy to join in their fun, one look at Elizabetta tells Dmitri that she'd rather hold on to the shreds of their night together. Taking his wife's cue, he bids the others good morning, and he and Elizabetta retreat to the solitude of their bedroom to allow their night to claim the day.

At twilight they slowly descend the stairs, stopping to kiss on every other one. Matt clears his throat. He appears anxious and is waiting for them with the news that there were unusual developments during the day regarding one of the acquisitions. An influential board member with Stern-Grenze Shipping in Saarlouis, Germany, has requested a meeting to discuss the matter. "Milo Kohler." Matt frowns. "He claims to have leverage against the other board members, and if we give him what he wants, he'll force enough votes to allow for a fast and friendly takeover. Otherwise—"

Dmitri scowls. "His terms?"

The wolf shrugs. "Milo won't reveal them unless we meet with him."

While Milo Kohler is on their list of corruptible executives, the timing of this contact doesn't set well with Dmitri. *This isn't the way these deals are done.* He wonders if Shashenka is behind this or whether it is an innocent request.

"Is this shipping business vital in the grand scheme of Belyakov's downfall?" Elizabetta looks at both men.

Matt nods. "It's an international shipping business directly tied to seven other smaller businesses—copper mining, textiles, spice, and tea production—and collectively they could be the linchpin to unraveling the biggest components of Belyakov's financial empire. If we lose Stern-Grenze, our odds drop for acquiring the bulk of the devil vamp's businesses."

Katherine says, "Kees is near that area—he's dealing with a territorial coven feud in Frankfurt."

"Milo is insisting on a meeting with the three of us." Matt shakes his head and waves toward Dmitri and Elizabetta. "He'll only give his terms to us—in person—and he won't accept a subordinate to go in our stead." He pauses. "Mr. Kohler"—disrespect wraps around every letter of the man's name—"expects us to come alone."

Is Milo being duplicitous? How does he know about our involvement with Matt? Dmitri grimaces—he can't dismiss the possibility that Milo may have sensitive information that he's afraid will end up in the wrong hands. "Where and when?"

A ripple of distrust goes around the table when Matt tells them they're to meet at a hut near the Cloef Overlook on the Saar Loop the following night.

"I'm not comfortable with that idea." Sofia shakes her head. "I think it's best if Kees checks it out first and give us the go or no go. If it's a go, Katherine and I will arrive ahead of you at the overlook and wait in the shadows in case there are any problems. There are bounty hunters all over Europe looking for Dmitri and Elizabetta."

Dmitri silently agrees. Shashenka is likely on alert now

that takeover notices are out; even if he doesn't know who is behind the acquisitions, he will be out for blood. Dmitri's still considering this when Matt claims that the communication from Milo seems opportunistic, almost as if the man seeks to better his position once the acquisition is done. Matt's assessments are often correct, and Dmitri's worries ease somewhat.

"I'll call Kees, and I'll scout the area myself before dark tomorrow and let you ladies know the best locations to conceal your presence." The wolf's smile is apologetic as he glances at Elizabetta. "Sorry, baby vamp, your honeymoon at the doghouse with your stalker hubby is over. It's time to get to work."

Kees finds nothing noteworthy on Milo. The executive appears to be an ordinary middle-aged man with an average human life. The following afternoon Matt's search around the hut turns up nothing either, and Katherine and Sofia move into position shortly after dark. Just before midnight Matt, Dmitri, and Elizabetta arrive at the hut on the Saar Loop. They exchange wary looks as they approach the door; there is no sound from anyone inside. Pushing the door open, Matt enters first.

But for a gray-haired middle-aged man sitting on a bench, the hut is empty. The man rises, his gaze darting from one to the other as Elizabetta closes the door behind them. With a heavy German accent, he introduces himself in English as Milo Kohler. "You must be the American werewolf, Matt Wolfe."

After he shakes Matt's hand, he turns to Dmitri and Elizabetta. "And you are the Belyakov vampires, Dmitri Markov and Eliza Ross, correct?"

I don't like this already. How does he know our association with Belyakov? Dmitri keeps a wary eye on Milo as they sit opposite him on a bench along the hut's wall. "Let's get this over with. What do you want, Mr. Kohler?"

Milo keeps glancing at a manila envelope on the bench beside him. He swallows twice. "As I told your people, I can help or hinder this acquisition." He sits up straighter and squares his shoulders. "If you give me what I want, all will be settled quickly. If not, there may be setbacks or lawsuits. I have many methods at my disposal."

"Go on." Dmitri's distrust and dislike for Milo climb with every word that comes from the man's mouth.

"I want to chair the board when this is over, my salary doubled, my enemies on the board removed, and ..." There's a gleam in his eyes. "I want immortality."

Power and immortality? That's what this is all about?

"Get greedy much?" Matt snarls.

Dmitri scowls at Matt. The first and second terms are possible, he knows, but the third and fourth ... he suppresses a shudder. Turning a human, condemning them to this existence, is monitored and controlled by all vampire covens; it keeps their numbers from exceeding their food source. Dmitri has only turned one human—Elizabetta— and that was an act of love. But Milo would be a violation of law and a repugnant task. "Why should we give you immortality?"

A muscle twitches under Milo's left eye as he returns

Dmitri's hostile look. "I've watched and worked with your kind enough to know that the real power comes from the shadow realms, not the human world. I'm tired of being your pawn."

Dmitri notices that Elizabetta's reaction to the man seems to mirror his own, but she hides her disgust better and sounds almost friendly. "And how do you propose we remove your enemies?" she asks.

Milo shrugs. "I don't really care as long as they are gone. I cannot manage Stern-Grenze in a profitable way if my enemies remain. Fire them, consume them, or simply eliminate them and be done with it. You're the skilled killers, so I'll leave that detail to you."

The comments cement Dmitri's initial impressions. *If anyone needs to be neutralized, it's you.* "If we agree to this, when do you wish to be turned?"

"Oh, no way." Matt looks appalled. "His kind isn't needed in our world."

"Milo, answer my question."

The man's eyes shift between the vampires and the werewolf. "I'm not sure of the process, but the sooner we get it done, the quicker I can manage a successful transition for you."

"If we refuse to meet your last two demands?" Elizabetta arches an eyebrow.

Milo sneers. "You're not the only ones with spies and leverage. If you refuse me or try to kill me, then you will be exposed to the human world, and everyone will know what you are planning against Shashenka Belyakov."

Both threats are a death sentence for them, but more

disturbing for Dmitri is Milo's arrogance. *He'll carry out his threats.* Dmitri asks Matt and Elizabetta to join him outside to discuss the matter. It's an effort to remain polite and keep the raw hatred inside himself. "We'll need to confer for a few minutes, if you'll excuse us."

Once they've moved out of hearing range of the hut, Dmitri speaks before Matt can raise his objections. "I do not like that man one iota, and I will like him even less as a vampire. He's corrupt and greedy, and he will pose a risk to us later."

"It sounds like he's a risk to us now." Elizabetta looks at Matt. "Do we really need him to finish this takeover?"

Matt grimaces and nods. "Last thing we need is to create a Shashenka wannabe. But unless we want months of legal wrangling and risk losing some of the other businesses, we have no choice but to deal with him."

What little Dmitri has seen and heard of Milo tells him that the man has an evil streak just waiting to be unleashed. He proposes they give him what he wants, but as soon as Shashenka is destroyed they'll need to end Milo Kohler. They can't give him the opportunity to terrorize the shadow realms.

There's tension in Matt's voice. "I'm not afraid of fighting, but I've never killed anyone in cold blood ... never gone out of my way to murder anyone."

The faint smile on Elizabetta's face signals that Matt is about to learn something new about his "baby vamp." Dmitri looks on with pride as his wife speaks.

"Milo called me Eliza Ross, so he may not know as much as he thinks he does. If he knew that I'm one of the best assassins the Belyakov coven ever had, I doubt he'd so glibly threaten us. When the time comes, I will take him out."

"Damn, you're scary, baby vamp." Matt shudders.

Dmitri chuckles. "She's very good at what she does, and yes, she can be terrifying when she needs to be." He takes a deep breath. "I'll turn that cockroach tonight, but we'll need an extra set of eyes on him until Elizabetta can eliminate the problem." Dmitri glances toward the hut. "I'll ask Katherine and Sofia to look into that when we regroup with them later. Let's get this done."

They reenter the small building, and Dmitri forces himself to say, "We'll meet your demands." His eyes smolder with anger. *He will pay for his choice.* Dmitri plans to make Milo's transformation as miserable as possible. While no turning is completely pain free, the amount of suffering between the injection of the venom and the drinking of vampire blood—to complete the change—is always up to the vampire doing the deed. Dmitri would prefer to allow Milo to suffer the full three days, and he finds it unfortunate that this needs to be finished before sunrise.

"I knew you'd see it my way." Milo's smile is smug as he picks up the manila envelope. "Inside this envelope is a list of my enemies, and another smaller envelope that I need you to deliver to a board member we need on our side. Call it an insurance policy, if you will. He's at his mistress's apartment in Mettlach."

Simple blackmail—or a peace offering? The man isn't on Milo's hit list.

Matt barks, "We're not your errand boys. Deliver it yourself."

"If it were possible ..." Milo shakes his head, obviously terrified. "He'd just as soon kill me as look at me, so let's just say he won't be too cooperative with me until he gets that envelope." He refuses to budge on the demand; something in his posture says there is more to it, but Dmitri isn't sure what.

"Fine, we'll deliver it. Let's get this done. We have better things to do." Elizabetta cuts off any further argument, and Dmitri's nose and upper lip quiver. Only years of discipline hold back the rage he feels as his fangs come down and part his lips.

"You are sure you want immortality?" he hisses.

Excitement gleams in Milo's eyes. "I've waited a long time. What do I need to do?"

Not bothering to answer the question, Dmitri launches himself across the tiny room and pins the despicable man against the wall. He bites down on the human's throat with force enough to cause pain but not break his neck or puncture his windpipe. *You will suffer your damnation.* He expresses more venom than necessary and doesn't relinquish his crushing bite until the man begins to shake and writhe from the spreading venom. *Unfortunate ... this won't kill him outright.* Disgusted by what he's just done, Dmitri unceremoniously drops Milo to the ground and joins Elizabetta and Matt on the other side of the room.

Matt's expression is a mix of horror and curiosity. "Damn! Shit ... shit. I don't think I ever want to see that again." Then he glances between Dmitri and Elizabetta, appalled. "What the hell is wrong with you?" He looks incredulous. "Were you freaking insane? How did you fall in love with this guy after he did that to you?"

If the mongrel weren't in shock, Dmitri would make him pay for insulting Elizabetta like that. But she just chuckles and slides her arm around Dmitri's waist. "This may not have been the best example of how to turn someone." Her eyes tell Dmitri that she's not offended, and he relaxes. "*Amore* did not turn me in such a harsh manner—it was a beautiful and loving act."

"We can choose to be kind or cruel in turning a human." It bothers Dmitri that Matt thinks he was unkind to his mate—he's spent her entire vampire existence trying to keep her from harm. "When I turned Elizabetta, I was already deeply in love with her. My bite to her neck was as gentle as a kiss—I used a minimal amount of venom, and I immediately offered her my blood. Granted, a body's unnatural death is never an easy passage, but *amore* completed her transformation in under an hour."

For several minutes they watch Milo squirm and claw at his throat. The wolf's brow pulls down into a fierce scowl as the man groans and slurs incoherent words. "The point of this"—he gestures toward Milo—"is what, then?"

Dmitri's response is cold. "To make this vile creature suffer his choice." He smiles inside—a little bit of retribution for manipulating them into this agreement. If it were possible, he'd only offer his blood in the final hour of the third day to complete Milo's change. *This worm will get my blood far sooner than I wish to give it.* A twinge of bloodlust pulses inside him. After dragging out Milo's turning, Dmitri would thoroughly enjoy the brutality of killing the man upon its completion.

Dmitri picks up the manila envelope and stalks out of the hut, knowing the other two will follow and leave Milo to suffer his agony alone. They stop near the edge of the overlook. Matt and Elizabetta are talking, but Dmitri tunes them out as his gaze settles on the view of the hills surrounding the Saar River. Low, misting clouds swirl around them, shrouding them and hiding the river from view. The night matches the black mood churning inside him. Dmitri is skilled at keeping his bloodlust at bay—he's only ever lost control once, centuries ago, on the night the still-human Elizabetta was attacked. Although she disabled the man and fled, Dmitri released his bloodlust and meted out gruesome justice as he ripped the man's body apart with his bare hands. A gratified smile curves his lips at the memory.

Two hours before sunrise they reenter the hut to finish with Milo. He's still lying on the floor, moaning, doubled over in pain. Through gritted teeth he wails, "I'm dying ... you're killing me."

"Duh. Hence the term undead, you jackass." Matt still looks uncomfortable.

"Shut up, Milo," Dmitri hisses. "If I wanted you dead, I would have drained you hours ago. It's time to complete your change." He extends a claw and punctures the vein on the inside of his wrist, then grabs the man by the neck and hauls him into a sitting position. "Drink."

Milo's terrified eyes dart between the three of them, and he pauses a moment before clasping Dmitri's forearm in his hands. Placing his mouth over the wound, he begins to drink—somewhat hesitantly at first, but soon he's suckling like a greedy pig.

Dmitri knows the man must take his blood for at least one full minute, but it's a challenge to remain calm with the man's detestable mouth and tongue on his skin. When the time is up, he shoves Milo away and wipes his arm against his pant leg in disgust. Normally Dmitri would lick the wound to seal it, but he'd rather keep bleeding than taste that man's scent a second time.

The final phase of Milo's transformation begins with a fit of violent shudders. They watch as the man's eyes roll back in his head and begins to make choking sounds. Soon he is gasping for air in between agonized screams. Dmitri has to rein in the impulse to kick him over when Milo's body becomes rigid and contorts with the strain on his dying body.

Matt squirms at the sight. "Please tell me this isn't normal. I don't want to think my baby vamp went through this."

The alarmed look on the mongrel's face is priceless; his reaction, mingled with Dmitri's desire to kick Milo Kohler, makes the situation suddenly hilarious. It seems to strike Elizabetta the same way, and the two cannot contain their amusement.

She regains her composure first and reassures Matt that this is quite normal for this phase. Dmitri reminds the wolf that this will only last tens of minutes, not hours or days.

Matt looks aghast nonetheless. "Okay, you know what—this is just way too much information for shit I never wanted to know about ... don't want to know about now. Shit I never want to see again. I think I'll go wait outside. I may have to throw myself off the cliff to get these images out of my head."

"I'll go with you and keep you from jumping." Elizabetta starts to follow Matt out, but winks at Dmitri. "I don't want to look for a new mutt, *amore*." She blows him a kiss and closes the door behind her.

He scowls. *Thanks for leaving me with this nasty creature.*

Another half hour passes before Milo's body finally begins to quiet, and Dmitri recognizes that the first death is upon the man. Milo's eyes close and his mouth gapes like a fish as he struggles to take in the final few breaths of his mortal life. *One minute ... two minutes ... three minutes ... four minutes ... inhale.* The count lengthens between breaths. Then Milo's lungs expel air one last time, and for the next twenty minutes there is no sign of life—neither that of a mortal man nor of a nearly immortal vampire.

Suddenly Milo's mouth flies open, and he sucks air as if it's life-giving—a useless but common reaction among the newly turned. Dmitri watches with contempt as the new vampire's claws and fangs begin to grow. Moments later Milo opens his eyes and looks wildly around the room. *I ought to end him right now and be done with this mess.* When Milo's gaze settles on Dmitri, the new vampire leaps to his feet.

Go ahead, attack—give me a reason. To Dmitri's disappointment, the neophyte doesn't move. In a dry tone Dmitri says no more than he must. "It's done. There are rules and laws for our kind, and I suggest you learn them—fast. The only one I will bother to tell you is this: you will not expose our kind with injudicious killing or dumping of human remains in public places. Break the law, and you will deal with the Druzhina—they are ruthless and deadly, and they are not known for compassion or giving of second chances. Don't doubt me on this, for I am one of them—and our justice is swift."

Milo's hand clutches at his neck. "My throat—it's burning."

"You're thirsty. Feeding is your problem, not mine. We're done here. I suggest you stay out of the sun if you want to live." *Enjoy your short tour of immortality, asshole ... your days are numbered.* Without another word Dmitri leaves the hut.

CHAPTER 35: ELIZA

Dance with the Devil

In the darkness Eliza sees the storm clouds building to the west, and she shivers—they seem portentous of what may be coming. *Did we make a mistake?* Amid Matt's discomfort and Milo's transformation, her concern for Dmitri is increasing by the minute. She's noticed subtle hints that his bloodlust is near the surface, and she fears what will happen if he loses control. *Could Matt and I even stop him?* Her contemplation ends when Dmitri finally steps out of the hut and announces it's time to leave. He'll get no argument from her or Matt—both are more than ready to put this night behind them.

After leaving the overlook, Eliza's group meets up with Katherine and Sofia. Neither Druzhina reports any unusual activity in the area during the hours they were at the hut with Milo. On the drive back to Mettlach, Katherine calls Kees and asks him to pass word to the others—Milo Kohler just signed his death warrant. They are not removing Shashenka Belyakov only to create the next millennium's monster.

Matt drives them to the apartment building where they need to leave the small envelope. Eliza sighs. Looking up through the windshield, she notices the night sky is beginning to pale—the sun will rise soon. *I hope this doesn't take too long.* She's grateful when Dmitri offers to deliver it to Milo's rival while the others wait in the car.

To kill time, she tells the women about Matt's freak-out over seeing someone turned, and it evolves into a three-against-one teasing session.

Good naturedly Matt threatens them with their wizard. "Yep, I have it figured out. When Maria arrives to turn me into a frog, I'll talk her into making baby vamp into a spider, Katherine into a grasshopper, and Sofia into a fly." His tongue juts out and retracts for extra emphasis. "We'll see who gets the last laugh then."

"I think Maria should turn you men into frogs, and we ladies will have frog races. It will put you on equal footing with our kind." Sofia smiles and winks at Matt.

If I didn't know better, I'd swear she's more than charmed by Matt—she's acting like she wants to jump his bones. The effect he has on women is too much—Eliza sighs. "Kees and Matt can be frogs if you want, but I'll keep my prince charming just the way he is, thank you very much."

Katherine laughs. "Are you afraid we'll see Dmitri's sexy little naked frog butt?"

Cringing as he half turns in the front seat, Matt says, "Ew ... what is with you vamps and always providing too much information? The last thing I want to think about is any vamp's naked ass, and I don't care what form it's in. That's it—I'm not playing with you girls anymore. I'm going to take my toys and go home."

When the laughter quiets, Eliza looks up at the sky again; they are running out of time to seek cover. "I wish Dmitri would hurry up. We're going to be playing beat the sun if he's not here in the next few minutes."

Sofia yawns and taps her watch. "If all he is doing is dropping off an envelope, he should have been back by now. If we sit here much longer we'll be forced to hide inside the apartment building all day."

"Maybe he's on a roll for making ugly baby vamps tonight." Matt glances at Eliza. "Should we go in and see if we can drag him away from this mystery rival?"

Matt and Eliza leave Katherine and Sofia in the car and take the apartment elevator to the penthouse suite on the top floor. Compared with the average appearance of the lobby, this level is for someone wealthy—obviously the rival's mistress has money. *Maybe the envelope is a bribe or blackmail.*

Matt's reaching for the doorbell when Eliza thrusts herself forward and clasps his wrist. *What was that?* She taps her ear and shakes her head. Matt doesn't hear as well in human form as he does in wolf form, and she sees his questioning look, but she holds a finger to her lips and closes her eyes to listen.

Voices float from behind the apartment door. "This will go a lot easier on you if you tell us where Eliza Ross is hiding."

"Go to hell! I told you, I came here alone."

"Hit him again, Rico." There's a pause followed by a loud thump, and this time even Matt seems to hear Dmitri's rasping groan.

They exchange a quick look and come to the same decision. Matt's body trembles and shifts into wolf form as Eliza draws her dagger and kicks the door open. They burst through it together but barely breach the interior when the contents of a curio cabinet hurtle toward them.

Son of a bitch. Eliza ducks and dodges the flying objects as she races over to Dmitri's bound and prone body. He lifts his head, his eyes widening. "Elizabetta, no!"

She is about to plunge the dagger at Dmitri's captor nearby when the weapon tears itself from her grip and sails across the room to another man standing near a sliding glass door. *What the hell?* Matt charges toward Dmitri and Eliza but stumbles and yelps in pain. Her momentary confusion clears as Eliza spins around and takes in the man near the glass doors. Urgency rings off her words. "Spread out ... he's using magic against us."

"Elizabetta, run!" Dmitri's voice is tinged with fear. "He's a greater sorcerer, get out ..."

Yeah, not happening. She scans for a nearby weapon and in a diving roll grabs a porcelain vase to throw. The sorcerer shatters it in midair before it reaches him. Then with a wave of his hand he lifts Eliza's body and tosses her into the wall. In that same moment Matt leaps and takes the second man down—his jaws clamp firmly around the man's neck, ripping his throat out. The sorcerer whirls around with a murderous glare and shoves both hands outward. Scrambling to her feet, Eliza watches the impact of the invisible blow—Matt yelps and howls as he rolls over twice and tries to regain his footing.

Damn it, we're getting our asses handed to us here. The sorcerer's gaze is still fixed on the werewolf as she launches herself across the room to stop him. Without removing his eyes from Matt, the man waves an arm in a backhand motion—the invisible force hits her with enough thrust that her body lifts and crashes through a glass case and the interior wall behind it. Pain bursts through her. Her breath comes in sucking gasps, and she blinks away the tears blurring her vision.

"Elizabetta!"

She sees Dmitri's reflection in a window and focuses on him as she tries to draw a steady breath, but before Eliza can respond she hears panic weave into his voice. "Elizabetta, are you all right?"

The look on his face indicates growing fear and frustration. He's lying hog-tied, and she hears his menacing snarl as he strains against the ropes. *He should be able to break through ... unless ... shit!* The sorcerer must have used enchanted ropes, which means they are in serious trouble.

Through gritted teeth she yells, "My leg is broken." Then she says, "Where's Matt—is he okay?"

Before either can answer her, the sorcerer cackles from somewhere in the other room. "Keep fighting me, and none of you will be okay," he calls out. "I will collect the bounty Belyakov has offered for Dmitri Markov's hide, dead or alive. Granted, the wolf is worthless, but I suspect Shashenka will throw in a little extra for my effort ... not to mention a bonus for the she-vamp."

Her mind races, but it's hard to focus around the pain. *Shashenka ... bounty ... thug or lackey? Shit!* It makes sense to her now. *That maggot set us up—I'm going to stake Milo out in the sun.* Milo works for one of Shashenka's businesses, and it's clear he set up a fellow board member—a maxian, at that—to collect the reward. *Must be their get-rich-quick scheme.*

Matt's reflection comes into view as he crouches and edges closer to Dmitri—the two exchange worried glances. Then Eliza sees Dmitri mouth something at Matt, but she can't quite make it out. She manages a weak smile when she hears the low growl rumble from Matt's chest.

I hope that creep didn't hear that. Where is he? She scans the room but can't see the sorcerer or his reflection anywhere. Looking back at the men's images, Eliza notices Matt's ears twitch forward as he looks from Dmitri to the hole in the wall. Dmitri mouths something again—this time she can read it clearly: "Get the women."

Jeez, Dmitri, you don't send a werewolf running through an apartment building. It's obvious that he isn't thinking straight—supernaturals go to extreme lengths to hide within the human world. Still, the circumstances leave them little choice, and Matt will have to risk exposing his wolf form or being seen streaking in human form. If it's the latter, then any observers will just think he's crazy— she hopes. They need Sofia and Katherine's help if they are to defeat or escape this sorcerer.

Matt lets out a snort and dashes out of the room. She holds her breath, listening for any indication that the sorcerer is going to chase him down.

"The mutt has abandoned us." It's Dmitri speaking—
he's stalling for time. "You have me, and that woman in
there is not the one you seek. Let her go."

What? No. Shit, maybe. Eliza would rather stay with
Dmitri, but gathering the Druzhinas to rescue him is a
better alternative.

"I am nobody's fool, Markov. I will not release your mate
or give her the opportunity to avenge you."

How does he know that? Dmitri doesn't respond, and a
sick feeling grows in Eliza's stomach. Something about
this entire incident feels off. She's sure her initial assessment was correct, yet she can't shake the feeling that
there's something she's missed.

"Many of us in the magic realm are older than most of
you vampires. While you may not remember me, I remember you and your mate very well."

The sorcerer's reflection moves into her view. Leaning
over Dmitri, he points toward the room where Eliza is
slumped against the wall. "While she may not be this Eliza
Ross that Belyakov wants so badly, she is your mate. If the
rumors are true, she's been missing for over five hundred
years. I'm certain Belyakov will be more than a little interested to reclaim his lost property."

Eliza tries to come up with a solution, but her brain
feels sluggish. Even with Katherine and Sofia, their fighting skills may be useless against this sorcerer; if he is as
old as he claims, then his magic-craft is probably far
advanced and makes his already enhanced powers more
deadly. *I wish Maria were here.* With Dmitri trussed like

an animal and her leg broken, the best she can do is buy time and provide a distraction.

Eliza grimaces at the femur bone poking through her jeans. A compound fracture; even for a vampire such a serious injury takes a few days to fully heal. *I'm not walking out of here, not today.* She grabs the broken leg above the knee and pushes, then straightens the leg until the exposed bone retracts from view. Her jaw clenches against the agony as she runs her fingers over her injured leg. The bone is still protruding inside her jeans; she'll need to shove it far enough to align it. Eliza blows out a pain-filled breath, and quelling a scream, she pushes her lower leg further to clear the jagged ends of bone and align the break.

The bone grinds, crunches, and finally slides into place. The pain is incredible—it takes a moment for Eliza's wits to return. She shifts her focus to helping Dmitri stall for time. Through gritted teeth she snarls, "Who are you?"

"It's not important who I am."

"It may be of importance to the Orde de Maxia," she hollers back, venting a pent-up scream.

The sorcerer's laugh is haughty. "The realm of magic is not that structured or controlled—we don't need supervision like vampires do. There are many things your kind will never know about maxians. We are the true power in this world, free to do what we please, regardless of what any organization within our realm may do or say."

Eliza doesn't know if he's lying, but the ploy to keep him talking is working. "In other words, you're too chickenshit to tell us your name."

A fraction of a second later, the sorcerer is standing over her. His gaze quickly shifts to the bloody tear in her jeans, and a sadistic grin lights his eyes as he places his foot on top of the broken bone and pushes down. The air is sucked out of Eliza's lungs—it takes two sputtering gasps before the scream in her throat bursts like a wailing banshee.

Seeming pleased with her reaction, the sorcerer moves to bear more weight against her shattered limb. The pain is so intense that Eliza barely hears what he says next. "I am Guillermo Sanchez. I am the maxian who will go down in your vampire history as the one who brought an end to the once-great former Druzhinas known as Dmitri Markov and Elizabetta Rossellini."

Eliza fights the waves of pain that flood her eyes with tears. Desperate for relief, she takes a swipe at the evil creature, but he's gone before her claws make contact.

"You vamps are fast, but not fast enough." He reappears several feet away from her. An unseen hand closes around Eliza's throat and lifts her from the floor. She claws at the grip around her neck, only to inflict injury on herself. Unable to break free, she floats out the door and back into the room where Dmitri lies bound. The sorcerer follows her but stops several feet away from them, an evil smile creasing the corners of his mouth as he looks from one to the other. Then in a rapid twisting motion he stacks his fists one on top of the other and rotates them in opposite directions.

Eliza's body contorts like a wrung dishrag. Her inhuman screams bounce off the surfaces of the room, joined by

Dmitri's agonized yells as her spine snaps in several places. Sporadic images of the room slip through the volley of darkness and blazing white light clouding her vision.

"Stop! Stop hurting her! Let her go." Dmitri emits a series of low, guttural growls. She captures glimpses of his face pinched into a mask of terror and rage as he writhes and thrashes against the ropes binding him.

An evil grin spreads across Guillermo's face as he pulls Eliza toward him—with her flickering vision it's a macabre sight. His arm whiplashes in the same moment the invisible grip throws her into the wall near the suite's broken main door. Just before the impact she hears him say, "There, I've let her go—she only needs to crawl a few short feet. Shall we make a wager?"

Eliza lands with a sickening thud. Harrowing cries rip from her throat, and her vision bursts in shades of crimson red. Awareness surfaces in slow increments—she is unable to move. Her eyes clench shut against the scorching heat of the pain as she tries to gain control of her breathing. She must push past the unimaginable burning sensations that desiccate each miniscule cell of her body.

The welcome sounds of Katherine, Sofia, and Matt penetrate her pain-clouded thoughts. Eliza's vision is still blurry, but she hears Dmitri's deep, terrified voice. "Get her out ... damn it, Matt, save my wife. Get her the hell out of here!"

Mumbling, she tries to protest, but the words lodge in her throat when Matt's wolf teeth sink into her shoulder and he drags her from the room. She hears crashes, hisses, and screams—Katherine and Sofia are now engaged in the fight. Eliza's traumatized body ties her tongue into knots. "P-pl ... ple-ple ... please."

Save Dmitri! For a moment Matt's eyes meet her beseeching gaze. The slightest shred of hope settles in her when he leaves her near the elevator and turns back to the sorcerer's suite. Eliza tries to focus on the sounds—Dmitri hisses between curses, Matt's growls punctuate snapping teeth, and the women shout, trying to direct their assault.

Eternity seems to pass. Unable to move, Eliza can only lie there and watch the open doorway for signs that the women and Matt are neutralizing the sorcerer and freeing Dmitri. Then a bright light and loud boom precede a shockwave that slams into her. *What the hell was that?* Ears ringing, Eliza blinks rapidly and looks on in horror as seconds and minutes fall into oblivion. Silence. Not so much as a breath or heartbeat can be heard. Fear plants a seed deep inside her; panic and loss grow and crush her heart. Then the sound of someone moving through the apartment reaches her ears. She catches and holds her breath until she sees Sofia and Matt—he's naked and in human form—stumbling through the door. They are packing Katherine between them. Eliza cannot tell the extent of Katherine's injuries, but it's obvious the woman is out cold.

When they reach the elevator, Sofia jabs the button to open the doors. *They're not going back for him.* Hysterical, Eliza starts screaming, "What about Dmitri? Is he okay? Oh God ... someone tell me he's okay."

Matt kneels next to Eliza. She can tell by his light touch and slow movements that he's being as gentle as possible with her numerous injuries. It's a wasted effort; every jostle reignites the fire along her nerves. Tears glisten in his eyes as he cradles her against his chest. "I'm sorry, baby vamp. Dmitri ... I'm sorry, he's gone."

No! He isn't ... can't be ... Eliza searches his face; his words don't make sense. "No! No. No, no ... he can't be ... go back. Somebody go get him. Dmitri!"

"Hush, hush. Not that kind of gone." Matt's trying to soothe her, but it takes a moment before his words register. "I mean that evil sorcerer threw some kind of infernal glowing ball that exploded, and when our senses returned, he and Dmitri were gone. Disappeared."

Oh God, he's taken him to Shashenka.

Sofia steps into the elevator ahead of Matt and Eliza, Katherine in her arms. "I think it was a maxian version of a stun grenade. Did it knock you out too?" She pushes the basement button and the elevator descends.

Eliza can barely form coherent thoughts—she blinks against a swell of tears. "It felt like it busted my eardrums, and I couldn't hear for a few minutes, but I didn't pass out."

"Did you see them leave?" Sofia sounds hopeful. "Did you see which way they went?"

"They didn't come out of that suite."

"What do you mean, they didn't come out?" Matt scowls. "We searched the entire place before we left—I couldn't even find a pair of pants or a robe to put on."

A memory sneaks up and whispers in Eliza's mind. *Oh crap.* "Did you see a circular white stone anywhere on the floor?"

Matt looks puzzled, but Sofia's forehead creases and her eyes narrow. Then she nods and affirms there was one near the kitchen.

I wonder if it was a mistake involving the maxians. One of them is already fighting against us. She clenches her eyes shut—she wants to shake her head but can't. She knows. "It's a mutaport. They went through a damn mutaport to God knows where, but I'll lay odds that they are in Xi'an right now."

"A what?" Matt and Sofia say at the same time.

The elevator doors open, and Matt steps out, looking in both directions before he turns toward the darker end of the hall. Eliza waits to explain until Matt and Sofia settle her and Katherine on the floor. "A mutaport is a magical transportation device the maxians use." She draws a ragged breath and winces but manages to slightly adjust her shoulders. It's not much movement, considering her broken spine and leg, but it eases the pain just a little. "They can go anywhere in the world they want with it."

Sofia takes out her cell phone and tries to place a call, but the cell signal is too weak to connect. "I'm going upstairs so I can call Maria. If she can come or send someone, perhaps we can use that muta-whatever to get out of here too."

She doesn't wait for a response but runs for the elevator. *At least one of us came through that encounter largely unscathed. Just a coincidence, right?* While Sofia is gone, Eliza inquires about Matt's and Katherine's injuries—the Druzhina still has not regained consciousness, and it's beginning to worry her.

Matt claims his biggest wound is to his pride—the werewolf genes will repair his minor injuries soon enough. He tells her that Katherine was hurt when the sorcerer threw her through an archway and her head tore a large gouge out of the opposite wall. She'll recover without permanent damage. A closed head injury on a vampire is not fatal, but depending on how bad it is, Katherine could be out for days.

Matt looks worried. "What about you, baby vamp—you took quite a beating. You look like you're in bad shape."

Eliza grimaces. Her spine is broken in at least two places, her right leg has a compound fracture, and she probably sustained some internal injuries, but it's nothing permanently disabling. She takes a painful breath. "My body will mend, but even for a vamp I'll be out of commission for a few days."

Matt gently strokes a loose strand of hair from her face, and his eyes glisten with tears. He lowers his forehead to hers and says under his breath, "I thought I lost both of you back there. I'm sorry that I didn't get Dmitri out too."

This is the first time Eliza's heard Matt speak fondly of Dmitri, and it touches her, deepening the affection she holds for her best friend. "Matt, I know you tried ... and I know Dmitri is grateful you at least got me out of there."

"You said that sorcerer took him to Xi'an?"

"The inner lair should be there right now. I'm sure the sorcerer turned him in for Shashenka's bounty."

Matt turns a shade whiter. "What do you think that devil vamp is going to do to him this time?"

Eliza was avoiding that thought, and the mention of it

is enough to free the tears she's been holding in check. "It's different this time. I don't know if that nasty goblin king will be content to merely torture him or if he'll exe—" She's unable to finish.

Matt tries to assure her that they will get Dmitri back, but the sick thought has taken root and is growing like a noxious weed, strangling her from the inside out. Her breath quickens, and her heart tries to smash out of her chest. *Oh God, he's going to die. He's gone. No!* Rage runs through her already seared cells, driving her pulse up until it feels as if her eyes will pop from their sockets. *I'm going to kill Shashenka ... in ways he's never imagined.* The most hideous keening she's ever heard echoes around her, and Eliza wishes someone would shut the woman up. Matt is cupping her face and yelling at her, but it's not until Sofia comes running that she realizes it's her own voice.

Several minutes pass while they calm Eliza down. No one says a word about her meltdown—they don't have to. Tears still trickling down her face, Eliza watches Sofia toss him a pair of slacks the Druzhina stole from a dry cleaning delivery girl. The slacks are a little large and hang low on his hips, but he says it's better than hiding naked or streaking in public. Eliza looks at the crooked smile on his face and realizes he's going to be okay—his humor is back.

"I made a couple of calls." Sofia checks on Katherine—she's still unconscious. "Maria is sending Alastrina to get us and will let the Druzhinas know what happened. We'll use that mutaport to get to a safe house in Xi'an. The rest of the Druzhinas will meet us there."

Eliza blurts out, "A Belyakov safe house?"

"Oh, good heavens, no. An Orde de Maxia safe house. According to Maria, it's filled with spelled protective wards—no one will be able to touch any of us there. You and Katherine will be able to recuperate, and the rest of us will plan Dmitri's extraction from Shashenka's dungeon."

"He is there, then? Maria confirmed that?" Eliza searches Sofia's face for answers, but she already knows what she'll say. There's no reason for the sorcerer to keep Dmitri.

Sofia nods. "Maria saw him minutes after he arrived. Seems old Guillermo was brazen enough to pop right into the middle of Shashenka's chambers with him."

Eliza can't restrain the snigger that jolts her battered body—she can well imagine what the unexpected arrival may have interrupted. She doesn't know whether to laugh or cry. That Dmitri is once again at Shashenka's mercy chills her, but there's a twisted sense of pride that he of all vampires was there to ruin the goblin king's fun. After the months she spent submitting to that monster's bizarre proclivities, it feels like a pinch of payback.

A few minutes later Alastrina arrives. Her normally cheerful expression turns grave when she sees Eliza and Katherine. "You're fortunate he left you alive." The sorceress mutters healing spells, and Eliza winces as her bones turn into place and the heated sensation of their mending begins. Katherine takes a little longer to respond, but after a few minutes she finally opens her eyes. When Alastrina seems assured that both women are stable enough to move, she directs Matt and Sofia to assist them, but with caution; Eliza and Katherine are in a fragile state and are still healing.

They take the elevator up to the penthouse suite, which is wrecked beyond imagination. The walls and windows are cracked; the furniture lies in broken chunks of material and wood. Eliza equates it to the aftermath of a tornado—the stun grenade was that devastating. She marvels that it didn't rip Matt and the Druzhinas to shreds.

Matt helps Eliza and Katherine to what's left of the divan, then joins Sofia and Alastrina in gathering everything that may be a clue to Guillermo's whereabouts. The sorceress won't activate or send anyone through the mutaport until she's certain nothing of value remains. Eliza watches in morbid fascination as Alastrina stuffs items into her bag—shredded papers, ripped photographs, toenail clippings, a broken brush with hair tangled in it. The sorceress keeps muttering in a singsong voice, "You cannot hide ... I will find you ..."

Matt says, "What happened to the dead guy's body?"

"Doesn't exist anymore. Guillermo probably used an obliterate spell." When Alastrina sees their questioning faces she adds, "It completely vaporizes a body, down to the last cell. Guillermo doesn't like leaving a trail of bodies that will lead back to him—it's his go-to cleanup spell."

How does she know the sorcerer so well? Eliza's speculation halts when Matt finds her dagger and returns it to her. She clutches it to her chest, hoping it's not the last gift from Dmitri she'll ever hold—she feared that she'd lost it to the sorcerer. *Guillermo must have discarded it during his assault.*

Her finger traces her mark on the blade. *Algiz ... pro-tection. I failed to save Dmitri.* Her mind drifts over the memory of the night he gave this dagger to her, the same night Matt found her in Novgorod. A priceless gift, one that moved her to tears when she first saw it—one that carried the love of a mate even before she knew who Dmitri was to her. Eliza chokes back a sob, and determina-tion storms through her. *I will not lose you now, amore. I will save you.*

Alastrina kneels in front of Eliza and says, "I'm taking this matter to the council. Guillermo is dead wrong about one thing. The Orde de Maxia doesn't like being trifled with, and whether he knows it or not, he just put a huge wrench in their alliance with you. They will strip him of his powers should he ever be captured."

"Should? You don't sound optimistic about that." Eliza studies Alastrina's face; there's something she's not telling them.

Frowning, the sorceress replies, "You caught him on a good day. He is a murderously evil sorcerer. I blame the fae in him—his mother was pernicious. I've never seen an-other as sick and twisted as he." She shakes her head. "The Black Death—that was his little baby. Guillermo cast a spell to mutate a bacteria and infused it in the fleas that he then scattered among the rats."

"He did that?" Eliza's horrified—Guillermo makes Sha-shenka look like a choirboy. "You are talking about the bubonic plague?"

"Yes, and in total it killed more than four hundred mil-lion ... half were human, the rest from the shadow realms and the fae world. Well, all but the vampire realm—being undead left them immune. History only records the human deaths, but it killed scores of maxians and werewolves and wiped out the fae. At least they are believed to be extinct; no one has reported seeing a fae since."

"Sweet bejeezus." Matt lets out a slow whistle. "And your kind allows him to live?"

Alastrina's eyes blaze, and her tone turns curt. "No. That worm has been on the run for centuries. He's among the oldest and most powerful of our kind—we've yet to find one that can defeat him. He has perfected magic that some of us never even discover in a lifetime."

When Alastrina is satisfied that they've not missed anything of importance, she has Katherine and Sofia stand on the mutaport to go through first, then motions for Matt and Eliza to step onto the white stone. Eliza sees the nervous look on Matt's face as he lifts her, and she squeezes his forearm in encouragement. A split second later they are standing in the safe house in Xi'an.

Moments after their arrival, the sorceress appears, and her cheerful disposition is back. "This is Mei-Hau—she'll help you get settled." Alastrina introduces them to the young woman standing near a silk screen door. "I have to return to Paris and meet with the supreme council over these developments. You'll be safe here, even from Guillermo—he cannot break the protections. I'll return in a few days." With that she winks and smiles, steps onto the white stone near the front door, and mutaports away.

Matt shakes his head. "Damn. I think Maria should give us one of those, and a few redes, and whatever other great toys they have and we don't know about yet."

Everyone but Eliza laughs; the full weight of the last few hours has settled into her bones. Her mate has been stripped away from her again, possibly dooming their rebellion to failure before it starts, and now she's learned there's an even greater evil in the world than Shashenka. Her heart drags against hope like a deep-sea anchor.

CHAPTER 36: DMITRI

Condemned

Helpless, Dmitri watches the chaos of the fight between the sorcerer and his friends. Great relief rides waves of irony as he welcomes the sight of a werewolf dragging off his mate. *Never thought I'd see that day.* After Matt pulls Elizabetta's broken body from the room, Dmitri watches the wolf rush back into the fray. *I hope he got her to safety before he came back.* With Katherine hurt and unconscious, Sofia certainly needs the help; she is no match alone against Guillermo. Matt and Sofia are doing their best, and although they don't know each other well, they are trying to coordinate their movements. They've separated in an attempt to divide the sorcerer's attention; now they alternate their attack, with one feinting while the other lunges forward, but Guillermo sidesteps them, delivers blows, and dodges their efforts. Dmitri can tell the sorcerer is toying with them. Then a blinding white light explodes, and Dmitri is slammed into darkness.

When he begins to regain his wits, a slow, horrifying reality sets in—he is lying hog-tied on the floor of Shashenka's quarters in Xi'an. The bed looks as if it was recently used, but no concubine is present. Shashenka is handing a case—presumably with the bounty—to Guillermo. But neither man is smiling, and both look tense, unhappy. *Is it because Elizabetta wasn't captured?* At least he doesn't think she was—she's not here. Through clenched teeth Guillermo reminds Shashenka that he's not one of his minions, and storms out of the room.

Anger pours off the demented monster as he paces his quarters, and Dmitri expects the next round of torture to begin soon. Then Shashenka's eyes narrow; he sits on the bed bench and scrutinizes Dmitri instead. "I was told you recovered from your madness."

"Yes, Master."

"How fortunate for you." Shashenka sneers and repositions himself; his body twitches and shifts as if he can't decide whether to attack or flee. The odd behavior is uncharacteristic, and Dmitri doesn't know why the bastard is so on edge. "Yes, very fortunate that the idiot Guillermo didn't realize your precious Elizabetta is Eliza Ross, or I'd be executing both of you right now. Neither of you amuses me anymore. I've come to think of you as the blight on my existence."

In their long, tormented history this is the first time that Shashenka has desired their deaths over torture. *I'm sorry, Elizabetta.* Dmitri gulps despite his resolve not to react. There were moments during Elizabetta's reset and his time within the void that he longed for death, but now that he's reclaimed his mate, he wants to live. He wants to end Shashenka Belyakov, to know freedom. He's too close to realizing that dream to lose it now, and his heart sinks, knowing it may never happen.

When Dmitri remains silent Shashenka spits out his next question. "Do you care to tell me why two of my Druzhinas were there fighting for you?"

Of course—Guillermo. His mind works rapidly to formulate a believable response. Against a rising sense of fear, Dmitri forces himself to maintain eye contact to add credibility to his lie. "I assume they were trying to carry out your orders to capture us."

Shashenka looks unconvinced. "I've recalled Katherine and Sofia to explain themselves. They should be here tomorrow; seems they were injured and need a day to recuperate."

Only two were injured before Dmitri lost consciousness—Elizabetta and Katherine. He wonders if Matt and Sofia were hurt when the blast of white light knocked him out. *I hope they're all right.* "What are you going to do with me?"

Shashenka's lips curl into a snarl. "I will not deprive myself of the pleasure of an audience. At the moment you are also most useful to me alive—you will be the bait that will snare your beloved Elizabetta."

Dmitri's eyes follow his master as the demented monster circles him again. Shashenka stops and looks down at him. "I will take great pleasure in executing both of you. I will take each of you one exhilarating piece at a time—you will experience your demise together."

The thought sickens him. Now that her mind is whole, Elizabetta will stop at nothing to get him back—she will take the bait, and he doesn't want her to try if she has no solid plan to get them both out alive. There is no way for any plan to succeed once they are both under Shashenka's control. Dmitri mulls it over as Shashenka's guards take him to a cell and toss him inside without removing the bindings. *She needs to stay away; this can't be done from in here.*

For several hours Dmitri lies uncomfortably bound in the dark—he can't break free of the enchanted rope. The ache in his arms, shoulders, hips, and legs dulls when he loses feeling in his limbs, but the pain in his heart increases as he accepts that they have already lost—he's lost everything this time, including Elizabetta.

Sometime later the door opens, and Sally rushes over to kneel beside him. In swift movements she cuts the rope, then helps him sit up and sweeps his bangs from his eyes. Stretching and flexing his freed limbs, he asks, "Does that evil monster know you're here?" Her friendship, so unexpected, is one more thing he will soon lose.

Sally envelops Dmitri in a tight hug. "I think he was tired of the grumbling from Maria and the concubines. Maria gave me a spelled knife to break the magic in the rope. The whole coven is in an uproar. I'm only supposed to be here long enough to untie you."

She smiles up at him. "It's good to see you back to normal. I mean your mind and all, not normal as in back here in a cell." She looks over at the cell door—he knows she can't stay much longer. "I was so worried about you."

Sally hugs him again, kisses his cheek, and is turning to leave when he says, "Wait. Have Maria pass on a message." *Trust her friendship.* He finishes in a breathless whisper. "Tell Katherine and Sofia they were there to capture us. They'll understand."

Before Dmitri can say anything else, she is gone, and he is once more left to ponder his fate in the dark—a routine that is all too familiar. He sits in a corner and rests his head on his knees. Mocking hours traipse through the tiny room, and he can feel the passage of time but doesn't know how far ahead it's gone without him.

He wraps his arms around his legs as his thoughts return to Elizabetta. They've sacrificed so much—time, blood, marriage—and it's difficult to accept it was destined to be a long prelude to final death. Then he thinks of Matt, the Druzhinas, and even Maria—he knows they'll help Elizabetta. She can still win their freedom. The strength he draws from her has always been key to his survival, more so now than before—but if doing so dooms her chances, he will sacrifice his own strength to save her.

He's so lost in his thoughts of her that he almost fails to notice the sound at the door. Maria is standing in the hall, smiling. *Elizabetta!* "Is Elizabetta—"

"Calm down. She's fine." He catches a hint of mischief in the wizard's eyes—her hands are behind her back. When he rises and walks forward to greet her, she coyly sidesteps him and moves to the other side of the cell. *What is she up to?* Maria is full of surprises lately, and Dmitri tries not to smile in anticipation.

"I brought you something."

"Oh?"

With a dramatic flourish she pulls out the object hidden behind her back and holds it out for Dmitri to take. He stares in stunned silence—a longing sigh escapes his lips. Her exuberance doesn't dissipate, and that makes it even more surreal. "I know you thought this was lost to you, but I've kept it safe and ready for you these last couple of decades."

Is it really mine? Dmitri looks closer at the Stradivarius violin in the wizard's hands. Indeed, he thought it lost forever, but he recognizes the fine instrument as his own. His chin trembles, and his eyes blur with tears as he takes the violin and bow from her, gently brushing a hand along its smooth wood as he tucks the violin under his chin. A slight smile reaches his lips. He tests and adjusts the tuning of the seventeenth-century instrument, and music comes to mind—the Allegro from Arcangelo Corelli's Twelfth Concerto Grosso. Dmitri closes his eyes as he remembers an earlier time, and the way he used his vampiric influence on Corelli to learn from the master composer himself. Fingers in place, he pulls the bow across the strings.

Maria claps softly as he plays. The upbeat tempo reacquaints his nimble fingers to playing, and Dmitri's spirit lifts at each progression—no note is forgotten, nor a single beat missed. It revitalizes a spark of life inside him that he believed died long ago. When the song concludes, Dmitri transitions to Capriccio detto, "Il Molza," by Giovanni Battista Vitali. The haunting slower portions of the melody touch him deep inside, and tears run down his cheeks. When he first heard it, Elizabetta was about 150 years into her catatonic state; the song echoed his heartache and hope, the lowest and highest of his emotions at that time. After the last note fades Dmitri uses the back of his bow hand to wipe the tears away.

The reunion with his cherished violin leaves him unable to speak past the lump in his throat. Still clutching the violin, he wraps Maria into a tight hug.

She seems to understand and pats him on the back. "You promised Elizabetta that you'd play '*Il mio tesoro.*'"

Blinking, he looks up at the ceiling to prevent new tears from falling; the promise was made on their way to Paris. When Dmitri looks down at her he can only say, "Thank you, Maria ... thank you." Then a thought strikes a sharp blow, and he winces. "If ..." He takes a steadying breath. "If Shashenka succeeds, I doubt there'll be a chance for me to honor that promise."

Maria brushes aside the implication. "I don't have to protect him anymore, but I will protect you. We're doing our best to thwart his plans. Elizabetta will not walk into his trap. We are all scrambling to arrange everything so it springs in reverse when the time comes."

At the reminder, he asks about the others; it's a relief to hear that their injuries have healed. Maria also tells him that Sofia and Katherine convinced their master that Guillermo interfered with their attempt to capture him and Elizabetta. *Thank heavens they didn't end up down here with me.*

"Where is Elizabetta at now?"

"A safe house here in Xi'an." Maria is quick to add, "Not a Belyakov safe house—a maxian safe house. It's heavily warded and well protected. The Druzhinas are also rotating through, with at least two to three of them staying there with her at all times. I had to add a ward that prevents her from leaving the safe house property, though—she is dead set on making Milo Kohler pay."

Only if she beats me to it. "That son of a bitch tricked us into turning him, and he deliberately sent Elizabetta and me to Guillermo Sanchez. I don't want the others touching that slug—I am claiming the right of justice. I will finish him."

Maria promises to pass on the message. "The Druzhinas are monitoring Milo and say that he's already showing a deadly bent to his character. He's murdered some of his rivals with cold, calculated brutality, but he is moving the acquisition along as he promised—so at least Milo's done one thing right."

I should have just killed him. "Whether the acquisition is complete or not, I will hunt him down as soon as I'm able."

Maria nods and assures Dmitri they're doing all they can to protect him here, but she can't risk breaking him out until they are ready to move against Shashenka. "I must go before my absence causes suspicion. Enjoy your violin."

He thanks her again for returning it to him. "Be careful, Maria, these are dangerous times."

Maria will never know how this simple pleasure calms him; the return of the violin is like reuniting him with a long-lost friend. After the wizard closes the door, Dmitri cradles the violin under his chin again and plays "*Il mio tesoro.*" The song has been an unfailing mercy for both him and Elizabetta; she'll understand the meaning behind each note now that her memories are restored.

> My treasure, my light,
> O golden gleam in darkest night.
> For where the bleakest hour stands,
> Love makes the fortress where we shelter.

> My treasure, my heart,
> Shields of truth no guisarme shall part.
> From greatest strength, my love, arise,
> Vanquish fear, despair, keep faith alive.

> My treasure, my home,
> Eternal day, forever night.
> Entwined for now, beyond all time,
> Of two halves, one soul, and bound for life.

> My treasure, my—

He can't finish—it's too painful. *I hope I'll get to play this for Elizabetta once more.*

The next several days and nights fall into a pattern: he plays the violin for endless hours, sleeps for a while, and tries not to think about how quickly time is passing.

He's so lost within his music one night that it's not until the last note falls away that he realizes Sally has entered the cell. "That was beautiful!" He smiles and tries not to laugh at her exuberance—she's bouncing on the balls of her feet, something she often does when happy or excited. Dmitri thinks of it as one final piece of innocence she has held on to.

He sets the violin down. "So, what brings you to my dark and gloomy concert cell today?"

To his surprise Sally announces she's an inner lair spy now. Her bubbly tone becomes serious as she says, "I spoke with Anna—Justin and Teresina completed their assessment for the remaining estates. Support is growing at the divided estates. But big surprise, Novgorod and Prague will go down hard. Vladimir says those locals have sealed their fate."

"And what of those in the inner lair?"

"There are a few fence-sitters that seem inclined to wait and see how the battle goes, but they're keeping their mouths shut. We have all the concubines—they want their freedom—and some of their favorite patrons are indicating support. Master has a lot of enemies among his supposed friends."

Dmitri wishes Kees were here; doubtless the Druzhina has a better perspective on the numbers willing to fight for or against them. Still, he believes the overall numbers may have shifted in their favor regardless of how many Druzhinnikis stand with Shashenka. While Dmitri doesn't look forward to the lives that will be lost to either side, the path to independence is always coated in the blood of tyrants and of those willing to sacrifice their lives to achieve freedom.

Sally is one of those willing to die for it. A memory surfaces. "I never forgot what you said when we were at Big

Sky. You were right ... overlooking those of the inner lair was a huge mistake last time."

Sally lays a hand on his arm. "I'm glad we're not being left out."

He wonders what she looks forward to, if she's already made plans for her future. Many lives will change regardless of their success or failure, but if they win, those like Sally will know a better future. "Have you decided where you will go when this is over?"

Her exaggerated shrug is followed by a quick bounce. Then excitement lights her face. "I'm still trying to figure that out. Some of the girls are tired of coven life and want to go rogue, but I don't think I'd like that lifestyle. I guess I'm the kind that's always needed family in one way or another." She pauses. "I've considered joining the Markov coven, if you'll have me."

The statement is unexpected, and he's not sure how to react to her request—establishing a coven goes against his and Elizabetta's desire not to lead. But there's such hopeful anticipation on Sally's face that he can't bring himself to tell her. "That is something we haven't decided yet, but if we form one you are more than welcome to join it."

"Good! It will save me from being that annoying next-door neighbor who never gives you a moment of peace."

Dmitri can't help laughing. "Is that a threat?"

"Nope"—Sally pops the *p* and sniggers—"that's a promise."

"It's nice to see you're aspiring to be the neighborhood menace."

She does a little dancing wiggle. "Yes, that will be me,

and I'll blame it on your bewitching violin playing. Speaking of, play again for me, please."

Dmitri plays another song and is still chuckling when she closes the door. Resuming his isolated concert, he lets his mind drift with the music. It's been centuries since he's played for more than one or two people, and he misses sharing music that may hold meaning for others. When this war is over—if they survive—he'd like to entertain their guests at La Perfezione.

For now, though, he can only play the violin, pace, sleep, and try to count the seconds until he sees Elizabetta again. Maria, Sally, and a few other concubines take turns sneaking down to his cell to keep him company. Their visits are few and always too brief, but at least they keep Dmitri informed of new developments; the upcoming revolt is nearing the final stages, and the rebels will soon launch their attack. It gives him hope that even without his direct participation they will succeed this time. The darkness robs him of knowing precisely how much time has passed, but from his scattered conversations with the courtesans and Maria he knows that at least two months have gone by.

I wonder when someone will take me from this cell. It's been more than four months since he fed last, and the burning ache of hunger is growing inside him. Granted, a vampire cannot starve to death, but being deprived of blood long enough may leave him in an unrecoverable state. If Dmitri isn't freed soon, one of the women will have to sneak a human in for him. He will need his strength when the time comes to fight.

Then Maria arrives with bad news: Shashenka is increasingly agitated that Elizabetta is not walking into his trap, and his patience has run out. "He announced to the inner lair last night that he's set your execution date and plans to make a public spectacle of it."

Dmitri swallows against his rising fear. "Are you sure that you can protect me?"

"I'm not going to let it happen."

"When?"

The wizard grimaces. "Within the week, whenever the Druzhinas arrive. He's demanded their presence and requested the head local of each estate attend. He wants to make sure everyone in the vampire realm knows how he deals with traitors."

Shashenka is doing this to force Elizabetta out of hiding—Dmitri's sure of it. "This is the trigger of our war. Are we prepared to fight here in Xi'an?" He would give anything to have this discussion with Kees, Matt, and Elizabetta. He doesn't know if they planned for this contingency or if it's even possible to launch a counterattack.

Maria looks disgusted. "No. The Orde de Maxia has all their assets ready at Machu Picchu. The war must begin there. Guillermo's resurfacing has complicated matters by dividing the magic realm's attention."

This is beginning to sound like it will end badly for us. Dmitri shudders at the thought. "Has Shashenka caught on to the forces against him?"

"No, thankfully, he has not. Depending on what happens in the next few days, our time"—she points to herself and Dmitri—"here inside his lair is rapidly coming to an end."

Dmitri rakes his hand through his hair and shakes his head. He understands the implication and the wizard's unspoken fear—it leaves her ancestral village open to a retaliatory attack. Questions race off his tongue as fast as Maria can answer them. It becomes clear that the others have yet to figure out a way to lure Shashenka to Peru. A plan begins to form—one that's ludicrous but just may work. They'll need to move fast. Breathlessly he outlines the plan and gives Maria instructions for key members of their team.

She nods. "I'd better go and see if I can put this ball into play. Hang in there, Dmitri—this will all be over soon."

That's what I'm afraid of. Maria is about to close the door when Dmitri remembers the violin in the corner of the cell. He rushes over and picks it up. "Maria, please. I do not want to risk losing it here regardless of our success or failure. Please give it to Elizabetta ..." A lump forms in his throat. "I know she'll care for it."

After the wizard leaves, Dmitri sits on the floor with his back against the wall. He'd give anything to have Elizabetta in his arms right now—to spend one last moment with her. The thought that he may never see her again hollows out his soul. Dmitri understands that he has sealed his fate, but he doesn't know if he's ready to face his destiny. There's no turning back now. *Elizabetta ... ti amo e non smetterò mai di amarti.*

CHAPTER 37: ELIZA

At What Cost

Eliza is going stir-crazy cooped up in the safe house. More than eight weeks have passed since she arrived, and the only time she's left the premises has been when Alastrina or Maria has taken her to meet with the Orde de Maxia council in Paris. Those meetings are brief and often perfunctory, giving no clear sense of where the maxians are in their planning for the upcoming war. Although the council members offer routine assurance that everything is going smoothly and that her campaign will begin soon, she needs specifics, not generalities.

More bothersome to Eliza is the council's obsession with capturing Guillermo Sanchez—and their concern for her safety as long as his whereabouts are unknown. Her escape from him made it personal; the sorcerer is offering his own bounty now, and she doubts it's to turn her over to Shashenka. *As if it's not bad enough I'm in hiding from a devil vamp, now a four-thousand-year-old sorcerer wants me ... dead ... alive?* The only certainty she has is that it's diverting the maxians' attention from her revolt.

Eliza flings open a courtyard gate and slams her fist against the invisible barrier preventing her from leaving—Maria's solution when Eliza insisted on going after Milo Kohler. "Damn it, Matt, you could have at least taken me with you!"

She knows Matt meant well, but at the moment he is on her least favorite list. When Eliza objected to remaining there in Xi'an, even Matt spoke against her desire to leave. The reasons he gave run through her mind now—Shashenka's bounty hunters, Guillermo's reward, and the Druzhinas' claim that they can no longer adequately protect her. It matters little to her that Matt had valid points; she's still angry with him.

The architecture here is clearly influenced by principles of Confucian order and Feng Shui, but this place doesn't bring her peace. *It's just pissing me off.* The four connected houses—the main, opposite, and both side houses—surround an inner courtyard with two walkways that intersect in the middle of the yard. Trees, plants, and ponds mirror each other in the open quadrants divided by the walkways, and long benches line the walls of each veranda and provide a sheltered place to sit and reflect. *I don't need to find my Zen moment. I need out of here!* All she does is think, and she's had enough of it—she wants to do something useful.

The shoji screens creating the doors and interior walls are covered in magic-craft runes, symbols, and words providing the protection wards for the dwellings. The silk tapestries are a combination of traditional Chinese designs and additional maxian spells. It should bring her comfort that the protection spells cast on an individual staying here are not easily broken or defeated, but she has no appreciation left for them. They are a constant reminder that she is one of those things being controlled and blocked, and the beauty that fascinated her at first now only aggravates her further.

Maria and Sally send regular text message updates about Dmitri, and Eliza finds his continued confinement disconcerting. The only time Shashenka avoids the opportunity to torture a prisoner is when an execution date is set—when he's building anticipation for the deed. The clock doubtless is running against Dmitri's life. Maria constantly reassures her that she will get Dmitri out if necessary, but the wizard's time away from the inner lair leaves gaping holes with no protection for him.

A laugh rings out; Eliza hears the familiar voices of the two tasked to babysit her. She pushes the gate shut before she turns to face Justin and Teresina. Eliza is at least thankful for their company. *I'd go completely nuts if they weren't here.*

If frustration and fear weren't her primary focus, she'd be more curious about the budding relationship between the two. She watches as Teresina playfully punches Justin's shoulder. In response he hooks an arm around her waist and nips at her neck. The reminder of what she's missing with Dmitri grows another vine of sadness inside her. *Get a grip. It's not like they've bonded. It's not the same.* The subtle hints for such a connection are missing; no marks, no telltale ring of matching color around the iris. Thinking about the thin golden-brown ring around her eyes and Dmitri's, she smiles to herself. *Only those who look closely will see it.*

Justin gives her his usual irrepressible grin as they stop in front of her. "Hey, Elizabetta, I thought we might find you out here."

Not hard to deduce when you consider I can't go anywhere. "Anything new or exciting going on?"

"Yeah, it sounds like there might be." She perks up as Justin continues. "Vladimir called a little earlier and said Maria needed us to gather for an emergency meeting. The maxians are making arrangements to bring the Druzhinas and Matt here by tomorrow."

A prickle climbs the back of her neck. *Has something happened to Dmitri? Oh God, let him be all right.* The fact that Maria called for the meeting unsettles her, but speculation will get her nowhere—she's already on the verge of panic. Eliza exhales a heavy breath. Unwilling to dwell on the unknown, she asks, "Has anyone done anything yet about that slimeball, Milo?"

Teresina crosses her arms. "Matt and Vladimir still have a no-touch order on him. As soon as he outlives his usefulness, he will be put down."

"Put down? Seriously? We're not euthanizing a favorite pet here, Teresina. When his time comes, he is mine—I will make him pay."

Justin laughs. "Don't stress over it. Dmitri has first dibs on him when this is over, and you'll have to sort that out between the two of you."

Eliza cocks an eyebrow—she finds no humor in letting Milo live. As the conversation drifts toward unimportant topics, she tries to enjoy the distraction, but her mood doesn't improve. Later she spends most of the day tossing and turning on the mat in her room. Her mind is filled with too many possibilities—none of them good.

It's late afternoon when Anna slides the shoji screen door aside and enters Eliza's quarters. "I thought you might be awake. Everyone is here but Maria and Matt. They should arrive within the hour."

Anna has no idea why Maria called for the meeting. A shiver passes through Eliza. "I'm scared, Anna. It can't be good news. The longer Dmitri is detained without punishment, the more convinced I am that Shashenka has set his execution date."

"Try not to think about that. Shashenka is still waiting for your capture, and it's unlikely that he'll do anything before then." She walks over and pulls Eliza into a hug.

Eliza grimaces. She hopes Anna is right, but the bad feeling inside her grows stronger by the minute.

Victoria, Sofia, and Katherine arrive next—they have nothing new to report either. At twilight the women go to the courtyard, where the rest of the Druzhinas are waiting for Maria and Matt's arrival. Eliza has no interest in their banter; she wants to get this meeting over with, if for no other reason than to ensure Dmitri's safety. Every minute Maria is away from Belyakov's estate leaves Dmitri unprotected that much longer. *Wouldn't put it past the little maggot just to end Dmitri out of boredom.*

A huge grin breaks across Matt's face when he steps into the courtyard and sees Eliza. He grabs her into a hug and spins her around. "Good to see ya, baby vamp."

She frowns as he sets her down. "I'd say likewise, but until I hear that you're going to spring me from this jail, you're still on my shit list."

Matt laughs as he leads her over to one of the benches. "We may have a parole date for you by the end of this night."

You'd better. "Don't mess with me, Matt. I have no patience, and my humor is more than gone."

He looks her in the eye—she knows he wants to tell her but won't. "I'm not ... that's partly why Maria called this little get-together."

She growls. *I hate it when I'm right—this is going to be bad news.*

Eliza doesn't miss that Maria bypasses the greetings and goes straight to one of the ponds, steps onto its rock rim, and turns to face the Druzhinas. "I know everyone is anxious to hear why I called you to this meeting, but I need to ask your patience for a few more minutes. High Warlock Jacques Boucher will be joining us momentarily, and I don't want to lose time repeating the information."

Murmurs ripple through the small crowd, but Eliza stares at the wizard, trying to ferret out whatever secrets Maria is holding back. *Must be big news if the high warlock needs to be here.*

When he arrives, Jacques Boucher seems to take over the meeting—he vanishes the décor of the courtyard and produces a table and chairs. Because of the informal nature of this meeting, he requests that all use his first name, not his title. Eliza looks between Jacques and Maria, wondering if her team has now abdicated all control to the maxian council.

That question is soon answered; Maria looks at each of the faces gathered around the table. "I've called you here because of developments at the inner lair."

The wizard's gaze locks on Eliza, sending a current of dread pulsing through her bones. *It's something bad—I knew it.*

Several start to ask questions, but Maria raises a hand and continues without pause. "Eliza, I'm sorry for being blunt, but I don't have time to sugarcoat this news. Shashenka is no longer willing to wait for your capture and has set Dmitri's execution for three nights from now. If you Druzhinas haven't received the call to report, it will come very soon—your master expects you to bear witness."

Oh, hell no. "I can't believe you left him there unprotected. Why are you even here wasting your time to tell us this? You get my husband out of there right now!" Eliza's voice rises as the implications drive spikes of terror through her mind. She can't help feeling that her whole world is about to collapse.

"Calm down, Eliza." Maria tries to admonish her further, but when Eliza continues shouting—she's had it with the others making decisions for her and Dmitri—the wizard mutters under her breath and magically gags her. "I'm sorry, Eliza, but you need to listen—we don't have time for debates."

How dare she! Fury rages inside her—she keeps trying

to force out the words that the wizard has silenced on her tongue. The sympathetic look Matt gives her angers her more. *Why don't you say something? Stop this. Do something.* She glares at him—in response he offers her a faint smile and turns his attention back to what Maria is saying.

The wizard explains that Dmitri is the one who laid out this plan—and it may be the only way to prevent the collapse of their campaign and the war. "The question is, can we get Shashenka to take the bait?"

"What is the plan?" Kees darts a glance in Eliza's direction.

"The first possibility is for us to bring our war here. While the coup council assures me that they can pull our assets from Machu Picchu in time, there's too much risk for this to go wrong and expose us to the human world. Great amounts of magic are required to blind the public to a full-scale battle, and it will mean less magic available for the fighters on our side."

It's not the earth-shattering pronouncement Eliza expected—she's waiting for the other shoe to drop.

"The better plan, in my opinion, is to use Shashenka's arrogance, greed, and hatred to snare him in the trap we've set at Machu Picchu. The bigger risk there, besides failure, is that it may mean sacrificing Dmitri's life."

What? Are you freaking nuts? Eliza stands and slams her hands on the table. Everyone turns to look at her, but she's too busy glaring daggers at the wizard to notice their reaction. She can't speak, but the vehement shaking of her head relays her opinion. When Matt reaches up to grab her arm, she pulls away from him, picks up her chair, and throws it into the wall of the opposite house.

I'm going to strangle her. Eliza leaps onto the table, but she's only halfway across when Maria mutters another incantation, one Eliza knows and hates—the immobility spell. "I am really sorry to have to do this to you, Eliza, but you need to be still and listen. We don't have time for hysterical antics or drawn-out debates."

Body frozen but emotions boiling her insides, all Eliza can do is mentally scream with raw contempt. Growing hatred for Maria duels with worry for Dmitri—it's almost impossible for her to pay attention. Eliza recognizes the signs as the heat of her rage surges through her. Bloodlust—it won't abate until she kills something, or Dmitri is safe. *Damn you, Maria. If you condemn him to this fate, I will find a way to kill you alongside that devil vamp.*

The wizard is saying, "Shashenka knows that some outside entity is trying to take over his business interests, but he's been willing to let others handle the problem because he's more focused on Eliza's capture. His number one priority remains Dmitri and Eliza's execution.

"What Dmitri proposes is that we use this"—Maria pauses and looks at Matt—"unknown entity to give Shashenka what he desires most." She briefly glances at Eliza.

"Matt will send word to Shashenka and claim to be the alpha of a werewolf pack that is orchestrating your master's financial ruin. He'll also make it known that his pack has captured Eliza in retribution for the mark she left on him.

"These are the terms Matt will present: in exchange for

Eliza, he will demand the bounty Shashenka has offered, as well as half of the businesses that are being targeted for takeovers. Matt will sweeten the deal by promising to cease the acquisitions against the remainder of Shashenka's businesses. If Shashenka refuses, Matt will threaten to keep Eliza alive and out of Shashenka's reach forever. His proposal will insist that Shashenka meet him at Machu Picchu, where he supposedly is holding Eliza captive, to formalize the agreement."

Alexander says, "You know Shashenka will show up with forces exceeding a few Druzhinnikis, if he even agrees to meet with Matt."

Maria nods. "Yes—in fact, we're counting on it. The more that come to the battlefield, the fewer local allies we lose in the separate skirmishes at the Belyakov estates. Our forces will be ready to take him down ... hopefully with minimal loss of life."

How does Dmitri factor into this plan? Oh, that's right—he doesn't!

Maria clears her throat and casts another glance in Eliza's direction. "If Shashenka's greed drives him to accept Matt's terms, there's a sliver of an outside chance that he will bring Dmitri along and make use of the audience he will have readily available at Machu Picchu. He may also make plans for after, when he believes he can execute both together."

Their guilt-ridden faces won't look at Eliza, but the bloated silence speaks to everyone's understanding—the sacrifice they will be forced to make is Dmitri's life.

"I don't dare tip my hand—Dmitri doesn't want me to

expose my duplicity in your master's downfall until it's too late," Maria says. "He's asked me not to stop Shashenka if he executes Dmitri before he leaves for Peru." She gives Eliza a sad, apologetic look. "Eliza, Dmitri does not want you to go against his wishes on this."

Bullshit! This is complete bullshit.

"Can't any of the maxians snatch Dmitri if he's left behind?" Victoria looks at the high warlock. "We can't just leave him to die. Not all of your people are going to be at Machu Picchu. You've already pledged at least one maxian for each estate to help take those properties."

Jacques shakes his head. "We will have a presence at each estate, but those maxians may be engaged in fighting against hostile locals and Druzhinnikis loyal to Shashenka. Releasing Mr. Markov from a cell is a lesser priority."

Lesser priority? Un-flipping-believable! If they don't rescue Dmitri first, then they can fight this war without me.

Matt says, "I think we can pull this off—it just might work. Shashenka is already unhappy that I bear a vampire's mark." He smiles. "That devil vamp is conceited enough to believe that he can wipe us out and save all of his businesses. He'll think his Druzhinnikis and Maria are more than enough to eliminate the threats against him. Shashenka will never see what's coming until it's too late."

Kees looks around the table. "I'm not sure he'll take many Druzhinnikis, and those on our side may be forced to reveal their loyalties before this goes down. Shashenka will likely order the Druzhina to go with him."

Maria nods. "I'm counting on that. In fact, I expect that is how the Druzhinas and I will end up at the battle site—

Shashenka will take us there."

It's mind-boggling—they seem more concerned about the Druzhinnikis than Dmitri—and Eliza is certain she's missed something. The dots just don't connect. What Matt and the others have said has merit, but she is enraged over the idea of sacrificing Dmitri to achieve their goals. Internally she's still seething when Maria releases the immobility spell. "I'll free your tongue if you agree—nod your head—not to go ballistic."

Eliza nods, but the wizard raises an eyebrow. "Careful, Eliza. I won't hesitate to quiet you again."

Eliza draws in a deep breath and battles to cool her fury as Maria releases the spell. It's all she can do to keep the roiling bloodlust from taking control. "To say I'm upset about this harebrained plan is an understatement. I will stop at nothing to protect Dmitri. Ending Shashenka at any cost—including my husband paying the ultimate price to set him up—is something that I will never agree to."

"The risk may be worth it." Matt reaches for her hand, and she jerks it away from him.

"Don't you say that to me—ever! If you want me to be the bait in this trap, you'll have to force me by using Maria's magic against me. I won't cooperate ... I won't unless we rescue Dmitri."

Her outburst ignites the debate Maria said she wanted to avoid. To Eliza's dismay, the Druzhinas agree to Maria's plan—Eliza can't bring herself to admit Dmitri wants this. Her heart sinks further when even Matt takes their side. *I thought they were our friends.* Eliza storms off to her room. *I will never forgive any of them if he dies.*

It's hours later when someone knocks on her shoji screen door, and she hears Matt's voice—it's laced with regret. "Baby vamp?"

Eliza doesn't answer him. Then she hears the screen slide open, and she rolls onto her side to face the wall; she doesn't want to look at him. "Eliza, I know you're mad at me, but I just wanted to tell you—"

"Tell me what, Matt?" She turns over, her fists clenched. "Tell me how little I mean to you? Tell me that Dmitri's life is worth nothing in the big picture? That if our roles were reversed and it was me sitting in that cell, you'd make the same choice and sacrifice my life? Matt, you took a stand against me, against Dmitri. What can you possibly say to me?"

Anger and defiance flash in his eyes. "That's not fair, Eliza, and you know it. I love you, and I will always do what it takes to protect you."

"You have no idea what love is! I don't want to hear your lame-ass excuses ... just shut up and go away, Matt."

The way he clears his throat after several seconds of silence tells Eliza that her words have hurt him, but she doesn't care anymore. She's already planning ways to avenge Dmitri should he die because her so-called friends sold him out to Shashenka.

Matt's voice is saturated with unspoken words when he finally speaks. "I came to tell you that we leave in one hour for Machu Picchu. Your devil vamp accepted my invitation to parlay."

Tears spill down Eliza's face as his footsteps fade in the distance. She should never have trusted a werewolf—he proved himself as much of an enemy as those serving Shashenka. *It's done. There's no going back now.*

CHAPTER 38: ELIZA

The Fog of War

Eliza is still lying on her mat when Jacques enters her room. She glares at him—he betrayed Dmitri too. "What do you want?"

"Maria had to return to the coven before we sent Matt's message to Belyakov. I remained to prepare you for transport to Machu Picchu."

Before Eliza can say another word, Jacques intones an incantation that once more binds her tongue against speech. "Your people thought it best for you to travel in silence. I'm sorry, but I agree with them."

Somehow she's not surprised—they don't want to hear what she thinks of their betrayal. *Damn maxians. They must really get off on wielding their power against others.*

Anger burns in her eyes, but the warlock seems nonplussed. "Mrs. Markov, I have been around far longer than Shashenka has existed. I have seen many, many things come and go in this world and across the shadow realms.

Never discount someone whose life is in peril. There is no greater leader than one who is willing to put himself first in line and ask no more of another than he is willing to sacrifice or do himself. Your husband is such a leader. While it would pain me greatly to see Mr. Markov fall before this war even starts, I will not disrespect his wishes. It is because of him that I will fight to see this through."

And I will find a way to kill you if he dies.

"The shock of your husband's orders has left you too close to see objectively—to see the gift he's given to those of us fighting on your side." Jacques takes Eliza's arm and escorts her to the main house. He wipes away the tears hanging at the corner of her eyes—she was content to let them run. "Remarkable and miraculous events often happen to change the direst and most hopeless situations. Dmitri's willingness to take his stand has cleared the way for a plan that has high odds of success."

She's not buying his pep talk. Jaw clenched, she makes her unspoken reply a cold, hard glare. *I wonder how they'll react if I sit down and refuse to fight when the battle starts?*

"I do not believe Mr. Markov has chosen a lesser mate, but a true equal—a woman who is a leader in her own right. A leader who can rule alone if that is what fate decides." The high warlock positions Eliza on the mutaport. "I'm sending you on to Machu Picchu now, but know that I will be there waiting in the shadows before Belyakov arrives. Do not judge or turn against those who stand by your side ... give them the chance to prove your husband right. Make the shadow realms proud, Mrs. Markov. Go lead them and win this war."

Before Eliza can process his words, the mutaport activates, and she is whisked away. A moment later she is standing inside the ancient ruins of Machu Picchu, surrounded by four rock walls.

Two wolves with umbrellas step forward to shelter her from the sun beating down from a cloudless sky. Eliza opens her mouth to speak, but nothing comes out. *What the hell? Are they seriously going to leave me gagged this whole time?* Her jaw clamps shut as she glares at Matt standing nearby.

"I know what you're thinking, and no, you won't be silenced for the battle." He looks hurt. "I also know you're mad at me and may never forgive me, especially if Dmitri doesn't make it through this, but I love you, Eliza, and I always will. We will make our stand together whether you want me by your side or not. I will fight for you and I will die for you—Dmitri would expect no less of me."

He turns to one of the werewolves holding an umbrella. "Tami, will you take Eliza to your tent until we're ready to reveal her?"

Tears threaten to well again as Matt leaves the stone enclosure without a backward glance. Nothing about this is what Eliza ever envisioned. A part of her doubts that Dmitri expected anyone to take his plan seriously, let alone carry it out. *How do we ever come back from the damage this has done to us?* She feels betrayed, and betrayal always comes with a price.

Numb, Eliza follows the young wolf to a small tent set up near an outer wall. Tami doesn't say a word as she zips

Eliza inside, leaving her isolated and alone—just like in the false life she lived a short while ago. She didn't have any family or friends then either. *I need my family—my friends. I need Dmitri.*

As the daylight shadows pass slowly, Eliza tosses and turns in a relentless attempt to quiet her mind. *Is Dmitri alive or dead?* The bloodlust that fills her prepares her for battle more than anything else ever could. As her eyes roam the seams of the tent, she can't stop thinking about the failed rebellion. *Were we always fated to lose? Will Shashenka perish at the expense of everyone I care about? Is that the price I'll pay for freedom?*

Even now she can hear the deep resonance of Dmitri's voice as he said long ago, "Fate, *amore*, is the choices we make that put us on the path to our destiny. Destiny is the result of those paths of fate that we choose along the way."

"What is the difference, *amore?*"

"Destiny is where we leave this life behind—it's where our soul's journey begins. The most noble act any of us can do is accept the fate we choose and be ready to embrace our destiny when it finally calls to us."

I wonder if he still believes that? Is he prepared to meet his destiny now—like this? In her heart Eliza suspects Dmitri is more than ready; he has always embraced this idea. But she is not. There are too many unfinished elements in her life, and number one is seeing the end of Shashenka Belyakov.

Another night and day pass, and no one comes to see her—not even Tami, who is supposed to be staying in this tent. It's just as well; Eliza doesn't want her company. Her thoughts return to Jacques's words in Xi'an. Whether she wants to admit it or not, his speech had more impact than he'll ever know. Eliza is anything but at peace with herself, but she is ready to see this war through. *I will be worthy of you, Dmitri.* There are supernaturals waiting for her to lead them in this war, and she will—even if Dmitri is not by her side.

Tami finally returns at twilight on the third night; the wolf is there to escort her to the battlefield. Eliza draws a deep breath, closes her eyes, and exhales slowly. *It's time.*

Outside the tent she scans her surroundings from a tactical perspective. Blood will soon be spilled here, and she intends to do a good portion of the spilling. She takes in the steep, terraced terrain and the crumbling ruins of Machu Picchu. The sheer cliffs that border three sides are high enough that a fall from any of them would kill a werewolf or maxian—vampires would receive serious injuries but would recover over time. While an abundance of mountainous ground surrounds the site, the flattest areas are scattered among the terraces that sit in a saddle between two peaks. The walls of the ancient buildings will offer cover during the battle.

For the first time she takes in the beauty of the area. The tranquility seems almost sacred—to desecrate these ancient ruins with a violent battle feels wrong. Eliza isn't sure this site was such a good idea after all. *I hope the maxians are prepared to rebuild these ruins if we damage them during the fight.*

Matt is in the middle of the widest terrace, surrounded by almost two dozen werewolves—he's only wearing a pair

of old, tattered jeans. *A quick shift, and he's ready to fight.*
She assesses the area around him, and her nerves jump at
what she doesn't see. Aside from the werewolves, still in
human form, there doesn't appear to be anyone else present. Eliza looks closer at the ground; the grasses aren't
trampled by the hundreds of feet that would have trod
there if their fighters were at Machu Picchu. Only the
well-worn paths used by tourists show any sign of use, and
she's sure those paths couldn't have accommodated the
number of combatants expected for this battle. *Where are
our fighters? Our backup forces?* She can't even detect the
scent of maxians or other vampires. *Have we lost before
it's even started?*

Matt steps away from the group of werewolves as Eliza
approaches. He doesn't smile—it bruises her heart, even if
she does deserve it. Taking her by the arm, Matt guides
her toward a terrace wall along the west side. Panic claws
at her throat. She opens her mouth several times but still
can't utter a sound.

After a heavy sigh Matt says, "The others took a vote
and decided to leave your gag in place until the fight
breaks out—they think it will be more convincing. For
what it's worth, I voted against it."

He winces as she scowls at him. "I'm sure a hundred
thousand different questions are going through your mind,
but we don't have long—Shashenka may arrive anytime
now. It's more important that you're up to speed.

"We're going to offer you to Shashenka when he arrives. We have reports that he's rallied Druzhinnikis and
followers from the lesser covens in his network, but it ap-

pears that he will arrive ahead of the greater numbers of his fighters. We expect the Druzhinas and Maria will be with him. If we can launch our assault right away, we may be able to take him with minimal effort."

Eliza doesn't believe it for one moment. Shashenka would never go into a potential fight without his full force—it's a ploy. She shakes her head, imploring Matt with her eyes. *That evil creature has something up his sleeve, and we have not accounted for it.*

He looks down at her but doesn't seem to understand. "Sally waited to send a message until after Shashenka left the estate in Xi'an. Dmitri is alive and still locked in his cell. Looks like he gets to sit this one out."

Matt grips Eliza's shoulders. "We're going to win this, Eliza, and when it's over we'll get you to Xi'an to free Dmitri."

Free Dmitri. Those two words do more to calm her already frayed nerves than Matt's other assurances, but she can't shake the feeling that they have missed something of great importance. All she can do is nod in acknowledgment. *I hope they're right, or we're going to get our asses handed to us.*

"Now, if you're ready, we're going to rejoin the group."

Matt turns to walk back, but Eliza grabs his arm and pulls him into a hug. She's still very angry with him, but if anything goes wrong—she can hardly bear to think of it— she can't allow their last exchange to be marred by bitterness or hurt. It's humiliating enough that in a moment of irrational anger she silently accused him of being her natural enemy, when all he's ever been is her best friend.

When Matt pulls away he presses a kiss to her forehead. "I love ya, baby vamp. Let's go get this done."

I love you too. She tries to convey the message with her eyes, but he is already looking at the group of were-wolves—they have grown suddenly tense, and some begin to shift.

He's here. A breath catches in her throat as she watches Shashenka's guard approach. *Equal footing?* There are just under three dozen Druzhinnikis with the goblin king, tightly clustered at his sides and back. Not surprisingly, Maria stands next to Shashenka, and the Druzhinas form a semicircle at the outer edge of what he always sets for a safety zone.

Shashenka saunters toward the werewolves as he looks Eliza over; clearly he believes that he'll soon have her. His lips are curled in a smirk, and smugness oozes from him. "Let's get this over with, mutt."

Matt takes a deep breath. "I need more than your word that you'll relinquish the businesses I've asked for. I'll also need a guarantee that once I hand this she-vamp over, you won't retaliate in the future."

Eliza glances at the Druzhinas and Maria. Their solemn faces belie the apprehension they must be feeling. None of them will meet her gaze. *Something is definitely wrong.* Rage surges again as she considers whether they are about to deliver the ultimate betrayal—stand with Shashenka while he wipes out Matt and the werewolves.

"How stupid do you think I am, dog?"

The evil gleam that lights Shashenka's eyes sends splinters of fear through Eliza. The goblin king is up to something, she knows it—he is too confident in his approach.

As if to confirm her assumption, he snaps his fingers. The air shimmers behind the Druzhinas, and a dozen of Belyakov's business associates—those helping Matt's team with the mergers and acquisitions—come into view. Their hands are bound behind their backs, and two Druzhinnikis flank each one. Terror haunts their faces.

"Traitors, Mr. Wolfe. Duplicitous traitors." Shashenka nods at the Druzhinnikis, and to Eliza's horror they sink their fangs into the helpless humans and drain them. She swallows against the growing lump in her throat. The Druzhinas and Maria made no move to save these poor people—her mind screams that Dmitri was wrong, but she still can't accept it. *Have they betrayed us?*

A faint tremor rises in Matt's voice, but he says, "I don't need them. Are you going to waste my time with these theatrics, or do we have a deal?"

"Let me tell you something, Mr. Wolfe. I am nobody's fool, least of all yours." Shashenka snaps his fingers again, and another shimmer of air brings forth Teresina—only she's not alone, and she doesn't appear to be held captive.

Silence engulfs them in a cruel reality that shouldn't exist. Eliza's jaw drops in shock. Standing next to the rogue is Milo Kohler.

Shashenka's tone is deadly quiet. "Come forth, you two." He casts a triumphant grin at Matt and Eliza. "You thought you had these two in your pocket. You actually did me a favor by rewarding Milo with immortality. He's been one of my most loyal servants for the last three decades. As for our lovely Teresina, there's a reason she's the best rogue our realm has ever known—she's always on the winning side."

"Teresina?" Uncertainty coats each syllable as Matt looks questioningly at her.

"It's nothing personal, Matt. Business is business. Your fee fell a little short."

Eliza doesn't miss the shock and horror on Justin's face or the pain that washes over him a moment later. His heart is breaking at the betrayal. Treachery on this scale changes someone, and not for the better—he will never be the same fun-loving man again. She tries to scream out, but her tongue is still silenced. *You bitch! I am going to kill you.*

Maria appears nervous now, looking around as if trying to find something, someone, in the shadows. *If Maria isn't unveiling these surprises, then who else is helping that demented monster?* The devil vamp obviously knows more than he should. *We're doomed.*

Shashenka struts closer, cackling with each step he takes. "Don't look so surprised, mutt. There's a reason I've led my realm for ten centuries, although I will admit it's been a while since I've had this much fun."

Matt, seeming bored and unimpressed, hooks his thumbs in his jeans' front pockets. But he's nervous—Eliza can smell the fear wafting from him. The other werewolves dart glances around the plateau as if looking for a way to escape. *We're dead. If our forces don't show up and act soon, we are all dead.*

"Underestimating a foe runs two ways, you devil vamp.

Do you really think that I failed to do my homework and came here unprepared?"

A sinister smile curls Shashenka's lips. "To be precise, that is exactly what I know and believe. Shall I show you how wrong you are? Are you ready to learn a deadly lesson, pup?"

Again Shashenka snaps his fingers, and Eliza's heart seizes and stops beating. Dmitri, surrounded by four of Shashenka's henchmen, shimmers into view. A Druzhinniki is holding a cutlass to Dmitri's throat; another has a dagger pointed at his heart. For a brief moment she and Dmitri lock gazes, then instinct to protect her mate propels her forward. The werewolves standing beside her tackle her to the ground before she takes more than three strides.

Tongue still bound, Eliza struggles under the wolves and mouths out, "Let me go ... get off me, let me go." She raises her head as her eyes sweep over their supposed allies—the Druzhinas and Maria stand there thunderstruck and unmoving. *What are they waiting for? Have they abandoned us too?*

"Bring him." Shashenka points at Dmitri. Eliza watches in horror as her husband is marched over and forced to kneel before the evil monster. A malicious grin twists Shashenka's mouth. "You really thought you could get away with this again, didn't you, Eliza? Or should I call you Elizabetta?" His face wrinkles in disgust—he makes her name sound like a hate-filled slur.

"Let him go!" Matt growls. Tremors ripple through his body—he's about to transform.

Several Druzhinnikis step forward, blocking Dmitri from view. "Not so fast, pup!" Shashenka hisses. "I told you that you have a final lesson coming. You will watch all of your friends die before I execute you." There's a slight pause, and Shashenka holds an arm out to the side. "Dmitri Markov, I hereby sentence you to death for treason. Maria, my sword!"

CHAPTER 39: DMITRI

Victors and Losers

For a fraction of a second there is no sound or movement from anyone. Dmitri's heart is pounding so hard in his chest that it threatens to break his rib cage. He's lost sight of Elizabetta—the werewolves had her pinned to the ground the moment Shashenka ordered him brought forth. *Where are our forces? Why aren't they engaging?*

Shashenka's face contorts with hatred and vengeance. "Maria! I want my sword."

Dmitri sees Maria blink at the vile vampire standing next to her—her expression reveals nothing. She nods and takes a step back. Hand out, palm up, she mutters an incantation, and a sword quickly materializes; her fingers curl around its grip. "*Fág an Bealach! Fág an Bealach!*"

Before her words register on anyone, Maria lunges forward and buries the sword in Shashenka's chest. At the same moment a brilliant white light ripples across the night sky, revealing hundreds of vampires, werewolves, and maxians visible on the terraces surrounding them. An astounded shriek comes from Shashenka—he's demanding the rest of his forces. Another flash of light unveils hundreds more fighters, bringing the combined numbers into the thousands.

In the confusion that ensues, Dmitri rolls clear of the Druzhinnikis standing over him and leaps to his feet, straining against the shackles on his wrists as he sprints over to the werewolves surrounding Elizabetta. By the time he reaches the group, none of the werewolves remain in human form. Some are already rushing toward the fight.

"Elizabetta!" Dmitri recognizes the ferocious look on her face as she leaps to her feet. "We fight together—don't leave my side."

She opens her mouth as if to say something, but no words come out. Dmitri turns his back to her. "Get these off me."

In the next instant, before she can touch the bindings, the shackles fall off, and Elizabetta is shouting, "Watch out—move."

A few Druzhinnikis are running toward them with claws and fangs extended. Dmitri and Elizabetta crouch in a defensive stance as the enemy closes the last few feet between them. The first one reaches for Elizabetta's throat, but her body drops as her arms shoot upward—the Druzhinniki sails over her head. Dmitri, blocking his adversary, doesn't see what happens next, but he is confident Elizabetta can hold her own against Shashenka's thugs.

He dives and rolls to the side. When he comes up, two

Druzhinnikis are advancing their attack. He feints a low roundhouse kick, and as he returns to full height his hands find their targets. His left fist pierces the chest wall of one vampire as his right grasps the neck of the other. The time when they were all on the same side is long gone, and he has centuries of retribution to deliver for all he's suffered at their hands. White-hot rage consumes him. Many will die this night, and he doesn't intend to be one of them.

Dmitri darts a quick look between the Druzhinnikis as he simultaneously tears the heart out of one and rips the throat from the other. Their bodies fall in a heap like marionettes with the strings cut. Dmitri spots Elizabetta—she's standing over the body of her second attacker. Pride swells within him as she decapitates the vampire with her claws and dagger. *That's my Elizabetta—deadly, gorgeous.* She looks up at Dmitri, reaches behind her back, and holds out his horse-head dagger—it will be useful in the fight ahead.

Where is he? Dmitri scans the bedlam, but he can't see Shashenka anywhere. The werewolves are attacking in pack formations—powerful jaws sever the heads of enemy vampires. The Druzhinas are engaged with the Druzhinnikis but are easily defeating their opponents.

Magic bursts and sizzles in the air around them. "Shit!" Elizabetta cries out as a bolt of red light sears her shoulder. She's looking at the wound and shaking her hand out, but Dmitri's attention is drawn to the one who threw the bolt. Realization dawns; the magic they expected to be one-sided isn't, and among the fighting vampires and werewolves, several maxians battle their own kind. *When did Shashenka form an alliance with them?*

Elizabetta bumps into him as another Druzhinniki leaps at her. Dmitri grabs him by the shoulders and falls back into a roll that tosses the man to the ground several feet away. As he jumps to his feet he sees three more Druzhinnikis wrestling Elizabetta to the ground, and a pulse of bloodlust rips a menacing growl from his throat. Before he can reach her, a large werewolf with light-brown hair and furious hazel-green eyes plows into the vampires clawing at her. *I'll be damned—guard wolf indeed.*

With Elizabetta between him and Matt they advance on the enemy; their movements are synchronized, as if they've fought together before. The Druzhinnikis nearest them move back, seemingly intimidated, and Dmitri is able to assess the scene around them. Stephan is fighting near Victoria's prone body—she's not moving, and her chest is soaked in blood. Vladimir and Anna, together with Katherine and Kees, are taking swipes at the maxians fighting for Belyakov's side. *Where are the others? Where is Shashenka?*

Dmitri's head whips around when Elizabetta grabs his arm. Unadulterated terror amplifies her voice. "Sofia!"

His gaze follows her finger, and then he is sprinting alongside Elizabetta as the blade of Sofia's adversary finds its mark in one fluid move. Sofia's body sways and crumples to the ground. A guttural cry rips from his throat as her head rolls in the opposite direction. If Sofia bleeds out before they can reattach her head, her body will harden, and she may not be able to recover. They're nearly upon her when another Druzhinniki lowers a torch and sets Sofia's head on fire. *God, we're too late. Sofia ...*

Sofia's body is already disintegrating as they reach her killer. Even though it's been centuries since Dmitri and Elizabetta have fought together, they move in concert with one another now. Elizabetta jerks the Druzhinniki's hips to the left as Dmitri's claws sink into his throat and shoulder, pulling him to the right. The man's body rips in half, its two portions landing several feet apart.

Elizabetta kneels by what is left of Sofia's burning head. Her hands shake as she reaches forward, but she withdraws them to avoid being burned. Raw hatred mixes with profound grief on her face. "Damn you, Shashenka!"

Dmitri is reaching for her, to pull her into his arms, but she springs to her feet and spins in a circle. Her eyes move from combatant to combatant. Dmitri knows whom she's looking for—their master. There is only one way to stop this bloody battle before they lose any more of their friends.

An eerie howl pierces the sounds of battle, and Dmitri turns to look at Matt; the sound came from him. Matt's snout wrinkles into a snarl. Following the wolf's line of sight, Dmitri sucks in a breath. "Elizabetta, look—Maria."

The air is alive around the wizard. Sparks fly from Maria's fingers as she lobs volley after volley of green lightning at three of her kind. Her body flinches and jerks each time she's hit with her opponents' blue bolts of energy. White orbs explode around the quartet of fighters, but it's Maria's face that draws his eye—Dmitri has never seen such a determined or deadly look on her. He freezes in awe of the spectacle.

When Matt springs into motion, Elizabetta is right on his heels; it's enough to jar Dmitri out of his trance. As they rush across the terrace Dmitri realizes other were-wolves are racing in Maria's direction too. *Matt's howl must have been a rallying cry.* The wolves tear into three of the rogue maxians—limbs, a head, and chunks of flesh hurtle out of the melee—rendering them unrecognizable masses of flesh and bone before he, Elizabetta, and Matt can even reach Maria's side.

The wizard is turning her head to look at them when a red ball of energy strikes her in the chest. Her feet fly out from under her. Matt lunges forward, shifting into human form, and slides on his back to catch Maria before she hits the ground. Dmitri is stunned by the werewolf's speed. He's never seen a werewolf shift that fast—didn't even know it was possible.

Dmitri scans for the fourth maxian whose red blast of energy hit Maria, but he doesn't see any others nearby. *How could he have just disappeared like that?* When he looks back to make sure Maria is all right, he sees Matt cradling the wizard in his lap and brushing the hair from her face. Elizabetta is kneeling beside them.

Matt says in a protective tone, "She's going to be fine."

Maria's face is covered in grime. Her eyes still haven't opened. "Damn it, don't you make a liar out of me, witchy-poo." Matt throws back his head and gives another soul-piercing howl. Some of the nearby wolves join him, and it sends a shiver up Dmitri's spine.

Dmitri and Elizabetta exchange a quick glance—he knows that she is thinking the worst. After losing Sofia the way they just did, Dmitri can't blame her. He isn't sure himself that Maria is going to be okay. *How many more do we have to lose?*

"As soon as I catch my breath, I am going to turn you into a frog, Mattie. You're breaking my eardrums with that infernal howling."

Elizabetta giggles. "She's okay."

Once the wizard returns to her feet, Matt shifts back into wolf form—this night is far from over. They are winning individual battles, but victory will only come if they destroy Shashenka. It's Maria who spots the little demon first. "There he is! Let's finish this."

The four take off, fighting their way through the swarms of combatants, but Maria quickly falls behind—she can't run as fast as vampires and werewolves. Matt seems to realize they're racing off without her and slows his pace. Dmitri darts a glance at Elizabetta. They keep running at full speed—they are not going to allow Shashenka to slip away and avoid the justice he is long overdue.

Terrace by terrace they fight their way to the level directly below where Shashenka is standing surrounded by about a dozen Druzhinnikis. He's directing his forces and shouting orders—he's yet to notice Dmitri and Elizabetta making the rapid climb over the lower terraces toward him. Dmitri grabs Elizabetta and pulls her to a stop before they go over the final wall. "There's too many for us to take alone. We need to get the other Druzhinas up here."

Their eyes sweep the chaos of the battlefield around them. Three terraces below, Matt and Maria are still heading their way. The Druzhinas are scattered over the battlefield, helping other vampires or maxians fight Shashenka's forces.

"I don't want to risk that maggot-infested slimeball getting away. I doubt any of the Druzhinas will hear us if we shout for them, and that will only give away our element of surprise."

Elizabetta rises to her feet, but Dmitri pulls her back down. "*Amore*, we can't do this alone. Shashenka and his lackeys are trapped up there—they'd have to come through us or bail off the side of a cliff to get out of here."

The wolf and wizard clamber over the wall of the terrace and join Dmitri and Elizabetta. Maria is winded and bent over with her hands on her knees—she's going to need a moment before she's ready to fight again. Matt is panting too, but Dmitri suspects he'll recover faster. He places a hand on the wolf's shoulder. "Matt, I need you to do another rallying howl. Maria, see what you can do with magic to alert the Druzhinas to get up here."

Elizabetta spins toward him and hisses through her teeth, "Matt's howl will alert Shashenka."

"He'd still have to try to get past us. If he makes a run for it, we can slow him down." Dmitri looks at Matt. "Get as many werewolves headed our way as you can."

Matt's head arches back as he lets out a wolf cry so loud that Dmitri feels as though his eardrums will rupture. Maria squints against the sound and sends her voice on the wind. "Druzhinas, hear me ... come now."

There is no sign of Shashenka or his Druzhinnikis near the terrace wall, but Dmitri can hear them fighting. He directs Elizabetta to keep watching the upper terrace while he scans the lower battlefield for their reinforcements. One by one the Druzhinas look their way and start running—all but Stephan and Victoria. *I hope we haven't lost them too.* Matt's call seems to have worked—several wolves are also racing in their direction—but the few minutes it takes for their allies to reach them feel as if hours are passing.

Alexander reaches them first. "I told Stephan to stay with Victoria. She's badly wounded and will need protection while her chest injury heals enough for her to move on her own." An ounce of dread leaves Dmitri—they're both alive.

Anna looks around as everyone gathers on the terrace. "Where's Sofia?"

Elizabetta's shoulders tense. Without looking at any of them—her eyes are riveted to the terrace wall separating them from Shashenka—she says, "They killed her. She's dead."

"Are you sure? Maybe she's just ..." Justin trails off as Dmitri shakes his head.

"The Druzhinniki decapitated her and torched her head before we could reach her." Dmitri's tone is curt—he's still grieving.

The shock and horror on the faces of the other Druzhinas match his own. For the first time in their long history they have lost one of their own in battle. Sofia was the oldest Druzhina next to Alexander; she was in Belyakov's coven when the elite group was formed. *She never knew freedom.*

"We don't have time to mourn," Elizabetta snaps. Dmitri sees more than anger and grief in her eyes—a long minute passes before he recognizes it. *Guilt. She thought Sofia and Alexander were going to betray us.*

He reaches for her, but she shrugs him off and points to the terrace above them. "There are enough Druzhinnikis up there to keep most of us and the werewolves busy. Maria, I need you to watch our backs—Dmitri and I are going after Shashenka. Let's end that son of a bitch!"

Dmitri nods at Vladimir—a moment of unspoken determination passes between them. The werewolves and Druzhinas run forward and leap at the wall. Several of the wolves shift to human form to climb the precariously steep paths that lead up through the ruins. Dmitri grabs Maria by the arm and swings her onto his back as he runs past her.

When the Druzhinas crest the top of the wall, the Druzhinnikis are waiting to launch a counterassault. Shashenka stands well behind his lackeys, shouting commands as Dmitri weaves his way through the fighters. When he's fifty feet away from Shashenka, Maria says, "Put me down and do what you need to. I've got your backs."

Dmitri barely slows enough for Maria to drop down without tumbling—his focus remains riveted on Shashenka, and the brief flash of fear in the evil monster's eyes delights him. He's only two paces behind Elizabetta as she feints going left and then drops her right shoulder to ram into Shashenka. Disappointingly, the little devil is ready and manages to sidestep her. *Oh no, you don't.* With not a second to lose, Dmitri leaps to tackle Shashenka the moment the repugnant bastard gets clear of Elizabetta.

In the span of a single heartbeat, the world around them contracts until all sound and movement from the battle raging around them fall away. *Gotcha, you son of a bitch!*

For a few moments they tumble and roll across the ground, but Shashenka breaks free and bounds to his feet before Dmitri can lock his foe into a hold. Their master's sword is drawn, but his words are empty of the bravado and arrogance he used for centuries while torturing Dmitri. "If you surrender right now, I may let you live."

Cold hatred resonates in Dmitri's reply. "There will be no surrender—not from us and not from you."

Together Dmitri and Elizabetta back Shashenka toward the edge of the terrace. *He's going to try making a run for it.* Dmitri throws himself at Shashenka—it's now or never. His arms come up empty, his hands finding no purchase except for a scrap of fabric from Shashenka's shirt. The nasty little devil spins away from him, only to end up in Elizabetta's arms with his back to her. *You're the best, amore.* Her mouth opens—she flashes a quick glance at Dmitri—and her fangs bury deeply into the side of Shashenka's throat.

Try to get away from her now. Raw hatred burns in Dmitri's eyes as his hands clamp around Shashenka's wrist. It takes a few seconds to wrest the sword from the evil vampire's grip, but the moment he does, Dmitri throws it with all the force he can. The sword tumbles and spirals through the air and drops out of sight over the edge of the steep mountain. *The predator turns prey as the victim becomes vanquisher. Poetic justice.*

Elizabetta readjusts her hold—one hand pins Shashenka's arms behind his back while her other hand clamps tightly around his throat. Blood trickles down where her claws pierce their master's neck. Her gaze rises to meet Dmitri's, holding the promise of freedom for all their tomorrows. "*Amore*, would you like the honor?"

Dmitri's eyes roam over the creature who has tormented their lives for centuries. The forced heartache is at an end. Dmitri will never know another moment of torture at this monster's hands. Elizabetta's family will finally have justice—and she will never suffer the touch of this vulgar pervert again. "Yes, *amore*, I think I would."

Steps deliberate, slow, Dmitri veers left, right, left, as if determining the best move to make. But his mind is already made up. No, this slow procession is calculated to bring Shashenka as much terror as possible before Dmitri ends his life. His eyes catch the quiver in Shashenka's bottom lip. *Reap what you sowed.* He notes the tremble in the monster's hands—the very hands that inflicted so much pain and horror that there were moments Dmitri didn't want to live.

A dark, wet patch spreads across the front of Shashenka's trousers. "Look, *amore*, it seems our cowardly master has lost control. I think he's afraid of us now." A smirk draws up the corner of Dmitri's lips. It's strangely gratifying that fear has pushed their once-powerful master beyond his limits.

Elizabetta wrinkles her nose. "From the smell of it, he did more than that."

"Please! Please don't ... I'll give you anything. I'm begging you. You can have whatever you want if you just let me live." Shashenka whimpers pleas, his nasal pitch fluctuating as he snivels. His small stature diminishes with each sob. "I promise—anything. Name your price ... money, estates, businesses. I'll give you whatever you ask."

Dmitri leans forward and grabs Shashenka's chin. "Who are you that my ears should favor your pleas?" There's a measure of satisfaction in throwing those words back at the doomed vampire now. He leans in closer. "We. Want. Your. Final. Death."

Dmitri's gaze locks with Elizabetta's. Head held proud, eyes resolute, she nods in silent agreement—this is not the first time they've held an enemy between them. He takes one step back as she tightens her grip and repositions her other hand. Her claws dig into the flesh of Shashenka's jaw as she lifts his chin, exposing his throat.

Dmitri's voice is steady, unyielding. "Shashenka Belyakov, we hereby sentence you to death for the crimes you have committed over the last thousand years against us and many other unfortunate victims in this world."

He looks once more at Elizabetta—her eyes shine with excitement as she says, "Now, *amore.*"

With a savage thrust, the claws on Dmitri's right hand pierce Shashenka's chest over his heart at the same moment he slices the dagger across the devil vamp's throat. The cut is deep enough to wound but not decapitate. Dmitri pulls the blade free as he tears through the monster's rib cage. He watches with morbid satisfaction as Shashenka's eyes widen in terror and pain. "You deserve no mercy, but we will grant you a quick death."

Shashenka opens his mouth as if to scream, but grimaces and whimpers, "D-d-don't ... please don't."

Dmitri closes his hand around the monster's heart and rips it from his chest. He steps back but doesn't break eye contact as Shashenka gapes in horror and disbelief. With a small smile Dmitri nods to Elizabetta—it's nearly over—and she shoves Shashenka's body away from her.

Maria approaches them with a torch in one hand and a sword in the other. Her furious eyes rake over the doomed vampire on the ground before she hands the torch to Elizabetta. "*Fág an Bealach.*" The wizard's tone is firm as she lifts the sword. She takes a moment, lifting her face to the sky before she delivers the downward blow. Shashenka's head, cleaved from his body, wobbles upon the ground for a moment before it stills.

Dmitri's hand settles over Elizabetta's. *We survived ... we're free.* Together they put the torch to Shashenka's severed head and watch their former master's lifeless body fall into brittle pieces. Maria mutters an obliterate spell, and within seconds there is nothing left of the evil tyrant who ruled their realm for over ten centuries.

Into the Unknown

Elizabetta leaps into Dmitri's arms and kisses him. "We did it, *amore*. We're free!" Dmitri holds her tighter, wanting to make this moment last. Piercing howls go up around them as word spreads and their allies realize the battle is over. *It doesn't seem real.* His eyes drift from the terrace where Shashenka met his destiny to where the Druzhinas and werewolves are rounding up what is left of Belyakov's forces. Well over three thousand took part in this battle, and the mass of supernaturals gathered in the ruins is a humbling sight. Looking at the throng, it's impossible to tell how many of the vampires are captured Belyakov loyalists. Whatever maxians were aiding their enemies are either dead or seem to have escaped; the only maxians present are those who fought with them. They are massed on a terrace overlooking the main plateau.

Elizabetta seems to sense what he is thinking. "Before you were brought here, I thought our allies had abandoned us. I really don't know where they came from—I thought we'd lost before it started."

Dmitri wraps an arm around her shoulder as Matt says, "Never had a doubt. I knew we'd kick some serious vamp ass tonight."

Elizabetta slaps Matt's arm and gives him a mock indignant scowl. "Oh, please. I smelled the fear radiating off you. You were as scared as the rest of us."

"Hey now, watch it. I may resemble that remark."

"Shall we?" Dmitri motions to the crowd below.

Maria nods and leads the way, shaking her head as they walk toward the downhill path. "Well, I'll admit I was terrified, but some of the acts of bravery"—she turns back to Matt—"and chivalry I witnessed this night will stay with me forever."

When they reach the long terrace, the Druzhinas and Jacques Boucher are waiting near the northern edge for their arrival. The high warlock is quick to extend a hand and congratulate them on a well-deserved victory. Dmitri in turn thanks him for the maxians' support; they would not have won without it. *I still can't believe it.* He watches his friends and Elizabetta chatter in excitement, and he knows it will take a while before it feels real for them too.

After a few minutes of triumphant jubilation, Vladimir raises his voice to gain their attention. "We still have business to finish here before the sun rises."

He clears his throat. "Many have fallen this night—the Druzhina had one fatality, Sofia Castillo. Our allies' losses are reported at 237 werewolves, 54 vampires, and 91 maxians. Our enemies' losses were greater. We have over eight hundred enemy vampires dead or beheaded and awaiting final death. Jacques's people say that 186 rogue maxians' lives were lost. In total more than 1,600 survived the battle, and of those, 643 are Belyakov loyalists."

"There's no way we can execute that many before the sun rises." Dmitri looks over the condemned group—some are defiant and stare with hostility, while others stand hunched over in resignation. All show signs of defeat.

"We have no need to execute them all." Jacques steps forward with a small group of maxians. "We have identified less than two hundred for execution, and an almost equal number can be sent to maxian prisons across Europe. I propose we turn the remainder free—they wanted no part in this war. Now that their masters are dead or awaiting death, they are willing to integrate into new covens."

"How do we know that those we set free won't turn and regroup against us?" Dmitri wonders how the maxians came to their numbers, but there's precious little time to waste on detailed reports. Sunrise is less than two hours away.

Jacques says, "They will be cursed. All will be under a wizard's mark that will trigger an obliterate spell should they rise against you."

How is that even possible? Is it a bluff? If a single maxian can wield that level of magic, then their realm is more powerful than Dmitri has ever realized.

Elizabetta voices what he's thinking. Still awed by the return of his wife and the connection they share, he revels in the thought that no one will take that from them again—and almost misses Jacques's reply.

"It is." The high warlock bows to allow the wizard to step in front of him. "Maria?"

Her eyes go wide. "I don't know if I'm ready for that level of magic, Jacques. My captivity didn't afford me the opportunity to practice the higher forms of magic—for centuries I believed that I was merely a witch."

Jacques gives an encouraging smile. "You have it within you—your powers have always been there, and your full potential must be reached."

When the wizard looks at her friends, they simply nod their approval. Dmitri is certain that none of them can speak to these matters, but if the warlock is correct, then they can finish up here and go on their way knowing there will be no return threat. It also means that he and Elizabetta will finally start living the life they always longed for. Maria walks toward the detained group and studies them in silence, then turns back and looks at her friends. "Dmitri, Matt, will you step forward and take my hands? I can sense the magic that is needed for such a spell, but I must bind it to you and those of your kind that you wish to protect."

The wizard clasps their hands—there's an electrical zap, followed by the sensation of Maria's warmth pouring into him. Her eyes close as she intones a lengthy incantation, and Dmitri can feel the draw reverse—the coolness of his vampire essence draining from his body into hers. Through the link he also feels the pull of Matt's werewolf heat into the wizard. The Gaelic and Latin words that seem to blend into a mystical language unto itself are almost hypnotic.

Maria takes a deep breath. "It's done," she murmurs. "They cannot harm us now, or their lives are forfeit."

A loud clap of thunder booms. Dmitri looks at Maria—he's certain it's part of the spell she just cast—and tries to say something, but his words freeze in his throat. A high-pitched scream follows a sinister laugh. Dmitri spins a-round. His eyes fall on Elizabetta, and his heart constricts in absolute horror. *Guillermo!*

The sorcerer's staff pierces her belly and sticks out her back. Guillermo holds it firm with one hand as his other hand reaches for her shoulder. Before anyone can move or say a word, another roar of thunder ripples across the sky, and a blinding blast of white light forces everyone to stumble back.

"*Amore!*" Chaos erupts around them. Unable to see through the blotches of white seared across his eyeballs, Dmitri blinks rapidly to clear his vision and stumbles toward the pair, frantically pushing his way past the Druzhinas and werewolves in his blind urgency to reach her—to save her. But when he reaches the spot where Guillermo and Elizabetta stood, all he finds is a staff stuck in the ground with her blood pooling around it.

Dmitri collapses to his knees, his mind trying to reject what his eyes see. His fingers entwine in his hair, and his voice echoes through the rugged mountains surrounding Machu Picchu. "Elizabetta!"

CHAPTER 41: DMITRI

Bloodlust

The pool of blood around the sorcerer's staff is still fresh and wet. Dmitri lowers his hands and presses his palms into the cool puddle—it's the only thing that remains of Elizabetta. *How could this happen? Why wasn't anyone near enough to protect her?* They had barely celebrated Shashenka's defeat. This was supposed to be the beginning of their new life, a good, fulfilling, happy life together—a life free of demented monsters and heartache. Dmitri lifts his hands from her blood and wipes them down over his throat and onto his chest. The bloodlust inside him reaches up, wraps around her blood, and draws it into his core. Dmitri leaps to his feet and spins around, scrutinizing their captured enemies on the terrace.

"Where are they?" His voice booms across the silence that has enveloped the hundreds of supernaturals standing around him.

Vladimir steps forward. "Who?"

"Milo Kohler!" Dmitri says at the same moment Matt says, "Teresina!" But Dmitri knows there is only one vampire ultimately responsible for what happened to Elizabetta.

"We haven't accounted for individuals yet."

An anguished cry tears from Dmitri's throat as he plows into the prisoners. Several vampires flinch and shy away from him—grabbing and pushing past them, he checks each face in desperation. His friends shout, but he isn't aware of what they are saying. Bloodlust has taken control. He has but one thought—find Milo and kill him. That vampire will die, but not before he reveals where Guillermo took Elizabetta.

Dmitri is deep in the middle of the prisoners when Matt tackles him from behind. Before he can wrest free, Stephan and Kees help the mongrel pin him to the ground. The prisoners part further as the other Druzhinas and a few maxians surround him. *I have to kill ... he's dead ... let me go. Elizabetta!* His vision is clouded in red, images of Milo flashing over pictures of Elizabetta and a pool of blood on the ground. *Kill him ... mine ... kill.*

"I'm sorry to have to do this, Dmitri." Maria's soft voice intones a spell similar to the immobility spell, but he knows somehow it is different.

Rage swells through him as his mind whirls. He cannot move—he can only lie there in a frozen state. Bloodlust spikes at uncontrollable levels as two of the Druzhinas carry him away from the prisoners. His mind screams for total destruction, for not one being left alive, for the world reduced to ash.

Vladimir shouts across to the maxian council members, "Can your people get him to La Perfezione?"

Jacques grimaces. "It may be best to hold him here. We can't dump him in the middle of that estate if the locals are still fighting to take control."

"Keep him clear of the prisoners. Someone find out what's going on at La Perfezione, and let me know the moment we can move him."

No! Dmitri doesn't want to leave Machu Picchu until he extracts what he needs from Milo. Regret nips at the edges of his rage. Milo has ties to Guillermo; the despicable vampire may be the only one who can lead them to Elizabetta. *I have to get her back.*

"Maria ... please. Elizabetta ..." He can speak! Dmitri swallows hard. the pain radiating through his chest is nearly debilitating. This loss is too much to bear. If he doesn't get Elizabetta back, it will cost him his soul.

The wizard kneels next to him. "We will get her back, I promise. But until the final reports are in about the remaining Belyakov estates, we won't be able to start looking for her safely."

Through gritted teeth he says, "We don't know what Guillermo will do to her or what he wants from her. We can't afford to lose a single minute. Let me go ... at least allow me to start searching for her."

"That's your bloodlust talking, and you'll be of no use to any of us if you're out there killing everyone who crosses your path." She turns and walks away—he yells after her, but she ignores his pleas.

For what seems an eternity he's left lying on the

ground to stew in his own tormented thoughts. His need to kill, to find Elizabetta is all-consuming. When Maria finally comes back, an incensed snarl erupts from his throat, but she turns her back on him and speaks with Vladimir, Matt, and Jacques. He glares at the wizard and those standing with her.

"Will Dmitri be able to go with us to help secure the estates?" Vladimir approaches Maria but doesn't look at Dmitri either.

She shrugs. "Perhaps ... if he can control himself, but I'm going with you—to keep an eye on him. We can't afford to have him run wild in his quest to find Elizabetta." A couple of maxians step forward and lift him from the ground. They follow Maria to an area clear of prisoners and allies, and set Dmitri in a reclined position against a wall.

He hisses, "I don't need you babysitting me!"

Maria's tone matches his. "Until you get your bloodlust under control, I will shadow your every move. I will not hesitate to protect you from yourself. Once you cross that line you may never come back from it."

There is wisdom in Maria's words; some of the worst mass murders in history were committed by vampires so overcome with bloodlust that they began killing for the sake of destruction itself. A vampire on the rampage can be a dangerous and terrifying sight. Whether Dmitri wants to unleash his bloodlust or not, he must restrain it and not lose focus—or he will become the biggest risk to all of them, including Elizabetta.

He holds on to that thought as he tries to rein in the

feral urges boiling his sanity away. *Moyata svyetlina! Eliza-betta is the light that will guide me. I will not become lost to darkness.* "I'll control myself."

Maria releases the spell but doesn't seem convinced. Dmitri takes in the Druzhinas, maxians, and Matt, and his vision narrows on the werewolf standing in front of him. *I want that mutt nearby just in case there's a chance to go after Milo.* He moves alongside the mongrel, and through clenched teeth he says, "Let's finish this."

To be continued in ...

Nights of Shadow—Chaos

(Read on for a sneak peek)

Coming Spring 2016 ...

Book Three of the *Nights of Shadow* series!

CHAOS

"Where am I?" She rubs her eyes and tries to get her bearings, scanning the shadows in the dimly lit room. She's lying on a large, canopied bed with sheer white curtains draped over a dark mahogany frame. The tall ceiling and ornate molding on the walls complement the elegant furniture—they are far grander than the simple straw-tick mattress on the floor of her attic room.

"You're home." She startles at the deep, male voice, and her head whips toward the corner of the room.

"Home?" Her pulse races. *Home?*

"Yes, you're home, and you're safe now."

"Safe?" She feels stupid repeating everything he says, but none of this makes sense to her. The last memory she has is of sitting at the table with her parents for dinner.

The man walks across the room and sits on the edge of the bed. "Yes, safe ... no one can hurt you here."

"I don't understand. Where are my parents?" She looks

at the man; she has never seen him before. He's tall and slender, with a narrow, angular face and light-brown hair, and his eyes are an unnatural shade of green—so dark they almost look black. For a moment his eyes shift to a lighter bright green, then back again. A chill races over her skin. There's something about him that unnerves her. "Who are you?"

Pity and sorrow chase fear and anger across the softer lines of his face. "Your uncle will talk to you about your parents. As for me ..." His hand moves as if to take hers, but then he withdraws it to his lap. "I've been assigned to protect you ... to keep you here, to keep you safe."

Why do I need a protector? "Who are you?" The look she gives him is hard, scrutinizing. It doesn't sound as if he's lying, but what he's saying doesn't seem right either. Instinct tells her that if anything, she needs protection from him.

"Dahliorn."

She raises an eyebrow. "Dahliorn ... what?"

"Just Dahliorn."

Strange. Her eyes dart from the man to the shadows in the unfamiliar room. Then another thought creeps in, and her frantic heart drives ice through her veins. Something about being here, in this place. It reeks of evil—she can smell it.

He places a hand on hers. "Easy, Ramira. There's no reason to become alarmed."

"Where are we?"

"At your uncle's estate on Rathlin Island." He seems to realize the answer confuses her, and he adds, "Off the coast of northern Ireland."

How did I get here?

The hinges creak as the bedroom door opens, and Dahliorn scrambles to his feet, scuttling away from her bed. Ramira doesn't miss the terror that flashes in his eyes. She turns her attention to the older man in the doorway—like her father he's tall and thin, with black hair, dark eyes, and an olive complexion. *Uncle?* His teeth are clenched, and rage unlike any she's seen before flares in his eyes. "I told you not to touch her. Get out!"

Dahliorn bows his head and lowers his eyes as he scurries into the hall. Irrational fear and anger sweep through Ramira, putting her on edge. She hasn't seen her uncle since she was a small child, but she remembers her mother saying that he's very powerful and dangerous. One look at him now tells her it is true. She tries to move off the bed, but a twinge of pain in her shoulder pushes above the sharp throbbing in her head. The presence of her uncle has always triggered a headache, but this pain is unexpected.

The man walks toward her. "Lie down and relax, Ramira. You're still healing."

It's then that she looks down—a thick, blood-soaked bandage covers her upper chest below her collarbone. The dressing is saturated, and the amount of blood seeping through it terrifies her. *Am I going to die?* "What happened to me, Uncle?"

His long fingers gently pull away the bandage, giving her a glimpse of a deep, jagged wound. "I need to do another healing spell. Try to stay still."

Her uncle puts a poultice on the wound and mutters an incantation, and Ramira winces as the heat of his hand over the injury blends with the numbing effect of the poultice. "How did this happen?" she says.

He places a new bandage over the injury and pulls her bedcover up. The look in his eyes turns cold. "I don't know. Your father warned me that they were under an attack by vampires and maxians. By the time I arrived to help, your parents were dead, and you were badly injured."

Tears well in her eyes, and she swallows against the burst of grief shredding her heart. Her uncle awkwardly pulls her into a hug. "It will be all right, little one. We will have our vengeance against them someday. In time you will be the one who brings an end to the vampire realm."

The suggestion weaves through her shock and grief, and as tears flood over her cheeks a seed of hatred takes root. Through choking sobs Ramira says, "Uncle Guillermo, I will destroy them all."

Playlist for Nights of Shadow—Vendetta

The songs in this playlist fit the themes and scenes of *Nights of Shadow—Vendetta*, and some are specific to Dmitri, Elizabetta/Eliza, and Matt. They helped inspire me during the writing of *Vendetta*; hopefully they will also help you enjoy a deeper emotional connection to the story and its characters.

YouTube: http://tinyurl.com/nfeqvl3
1) "Black Roses" by Candice Night [Eliza's anthem]
2) "My Silver Lining" by First Aid Kit [Dmitri's anthem]
3) "The Sound of Silence" by Simon and Garfunkel [Dmitri's welcome to the void]
4) "Heavy On My Heart" by Anastacia [Dmitri looking for Elizabetta's ghost in the dungeon cells]
5) "Written In The Stars" by Elton John [Everything seems hopeless]
6) "At This Point In My Life" by Tracy Chapman [Eliza trying to reach Dmitri in the void]
7) "Broken" by Seether [Dmitri lost in the void, seeking Elizabetta]
8) "Something About The Way You Look Tonight" by Elton John [Eliza seeking Dmitri's love]

9) "Excess" by Tricky [Shashenka's dual torture in Venice]

10) "Witchy Woman" by the Eagles [Maria in Paris]

11) "I Found a Way" by First Aid Kit [Eliza reclaiming her mate and pledging herself to Dmitri]

12) "Peasant's Promise" by Blackmore's Night [Eliza's merging of memories]

13) "The One" by Elton John [Dmitri and Eliza's long wait is finally over]

14) "Call It Love" by Candice Night [Eliza reclaiming her life with Dmitri]

15) "All I've Ever Needed" by Paul McDonald & Nikki Reed [Dmitri's reunion with Elizabetta]

16) "Sister Rosetta" by Noisettes [Matt and Eliza beneath the juniper, laughing hysterically]

17) "Hush" by Deep Purple [Matt's Doghouse—Matt's dedication to Dmitri & Eliza]

18) "Stuck In The Middle With You" by Stealers Wheel [Dmitri's dedication to Matt]

19) Concerto Grosso in F, op. 6, no. 12 - 2 by Arcangelo Corelli [Dmitri's reunion with his violin]

20) Sonate, op 5: Capriccio detto, "Il Molza" by Giovanni Battista Vitali [Dmitri's reunion with his violin; the highs and lows of Elizabetta's catatonic state]

21) "Good as Gone" by Little Big Town [Eliza at the meeting at the maxian safe house]

22) Chaconne in G Minor by Giovanni Battista Vitali [Dmitri playing for Sally]

23) Concerto Grosso in C Minor, op. 6, no. 3 - 2 by Arcangelo Corelli [Dmitri playing for Sally]

24) "Sympathy for the Devil" by The Rolling Stones [Shashenka pre-battle at Machu Picchu]
25) "(Don't Fear) the Reaper" by Blue Öyster Cult [Battle at Machu Picchu]
26) "Kryptonite" by 3 Doors Down [Dmitri post-battle]

About the Author

Lianne Miller grew up in the mountains of southwestern Montana, about two hundred miles northwest of Bozeman. She now lives on the high plains in the northeastern part of the state, where she runs a horse ranch with her husband and an extended family member.

From riding horses to driving a semitruck and owning a small business, Lianne has worn many hats and labels, and she often claims to be a jack-of-all-trades and master of none. Now many of her days are spent writing and bringing to life the stories she began creating while raising her children. Lianne's books delve into judgment, tolerance, prejudice, and acceptance—challenges in both the human and the paranormal worlds. *Nights of Shadow—Artifice* was her debut novel, the first in this series. *Vendetta* picks up where *Artifice* left off, but there is more to come in *Chaos* and *Redemption*, books three and four of the *Nights of Shadow* story.

For news about Lianne's stories and characters or to sign up for email alerts, visit her online world:

Website: www.liannemiller.com

Blog: http://liannemiller.com/wp/

Facebook: https://www.facebook.com/MillerLianne

Twitter: https://twitter.com/_LianneMiller

YouTube Channel: http://tinyurl.com/owrvqhh

Acknowledgments

To my readers, I humbly thank you for buying this book. Please consider writing a review for *Vendetta* wherever it was purchased online. I want to hear your thoughts about Eliza, Dmitri, Matt, the Druzhinas, and Maria. Shashenka's time has come to an end, but Guillermo is the first to rise to take his place. What do you think will become of the shadow realms now? Let me know what made you laugh or cry or made you angry, but most importantly, whether you enjoyed the story.

Special thanks to my beta reader team—Mark, Elaine, Abe, Hank, Rachel, Tim, Sandy, and Ruth. Your critical and complimentary input, along with your enthusiasm and encouragement, helped make the final version of this story possible.

My heartfelt thanks goes to my family, for putting up with me when I'm in serious writing mode, and for all the times you have pushed me to follow this dream. I couldn't have done this without you.

Lastly, I want to thank my editor, Christina M. Frey of Page Two Editing, for all of her diligent and hard work. Once more you have helped me put my best work out there, and I cannot thank you enough. It has been a pleasure working with you again.

www.ingramcontent.com/pod-product-compliance
Lightning Source LLC
Chambersburg PA
CBHW070306040726
47501CB00018B/139

* 9 780996 376839 *